To Amy,
All that are lost
Shall be found!
~ Love Grandpa

THE
CHILDREN OF LYR
Book 1

DAUGHTER
OF THE
DEEP

LINA C. AMAREGO

For information contact: LCamarego@gmail.com

Book and Cover design by COVERDUNGEONRABBIT

ISBN: 978-1-7348265-2-4

Hardcover Edition: DECEMBER 2020

Daughter of the Deep

LINA C. AMAREGO

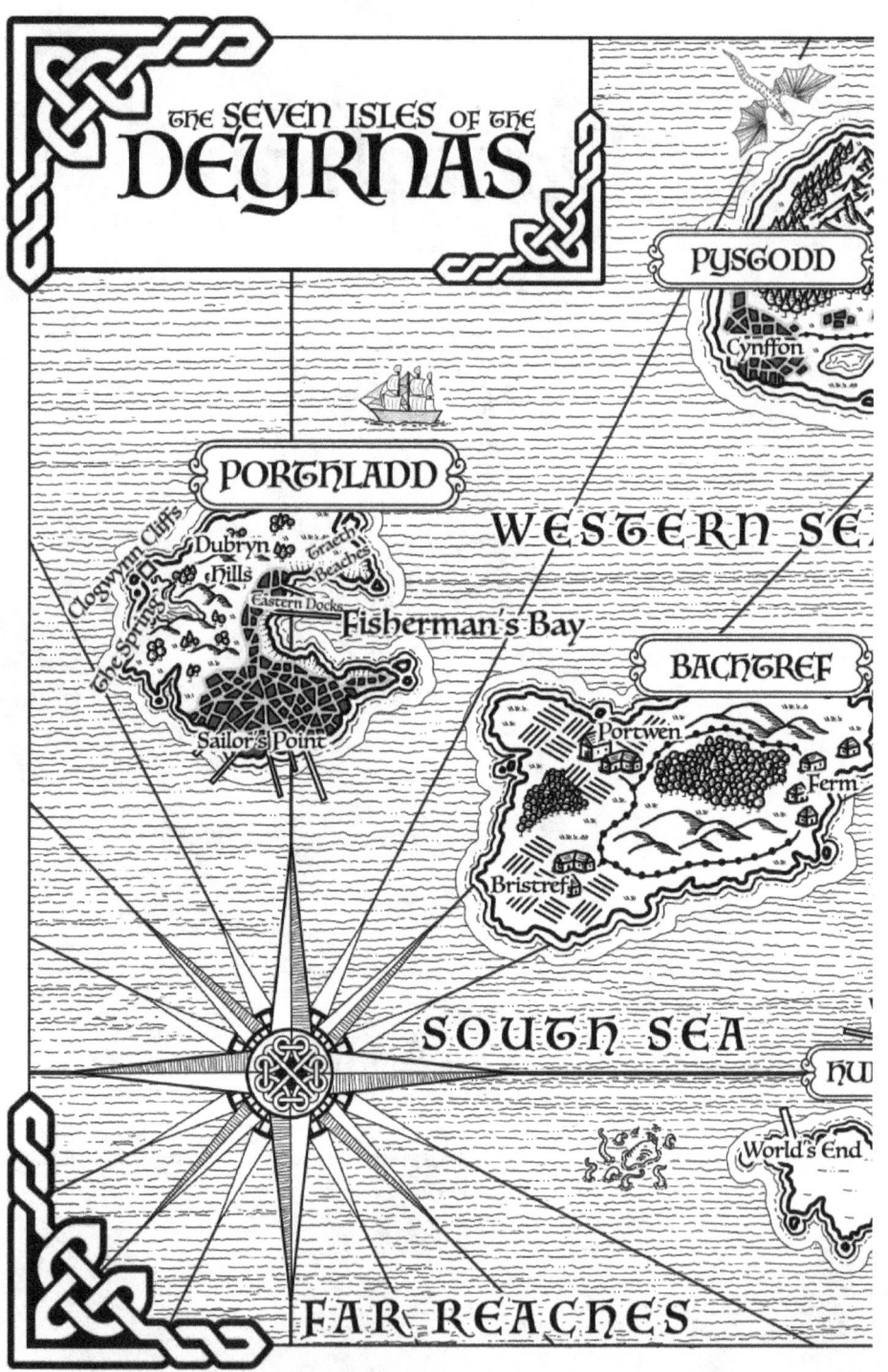

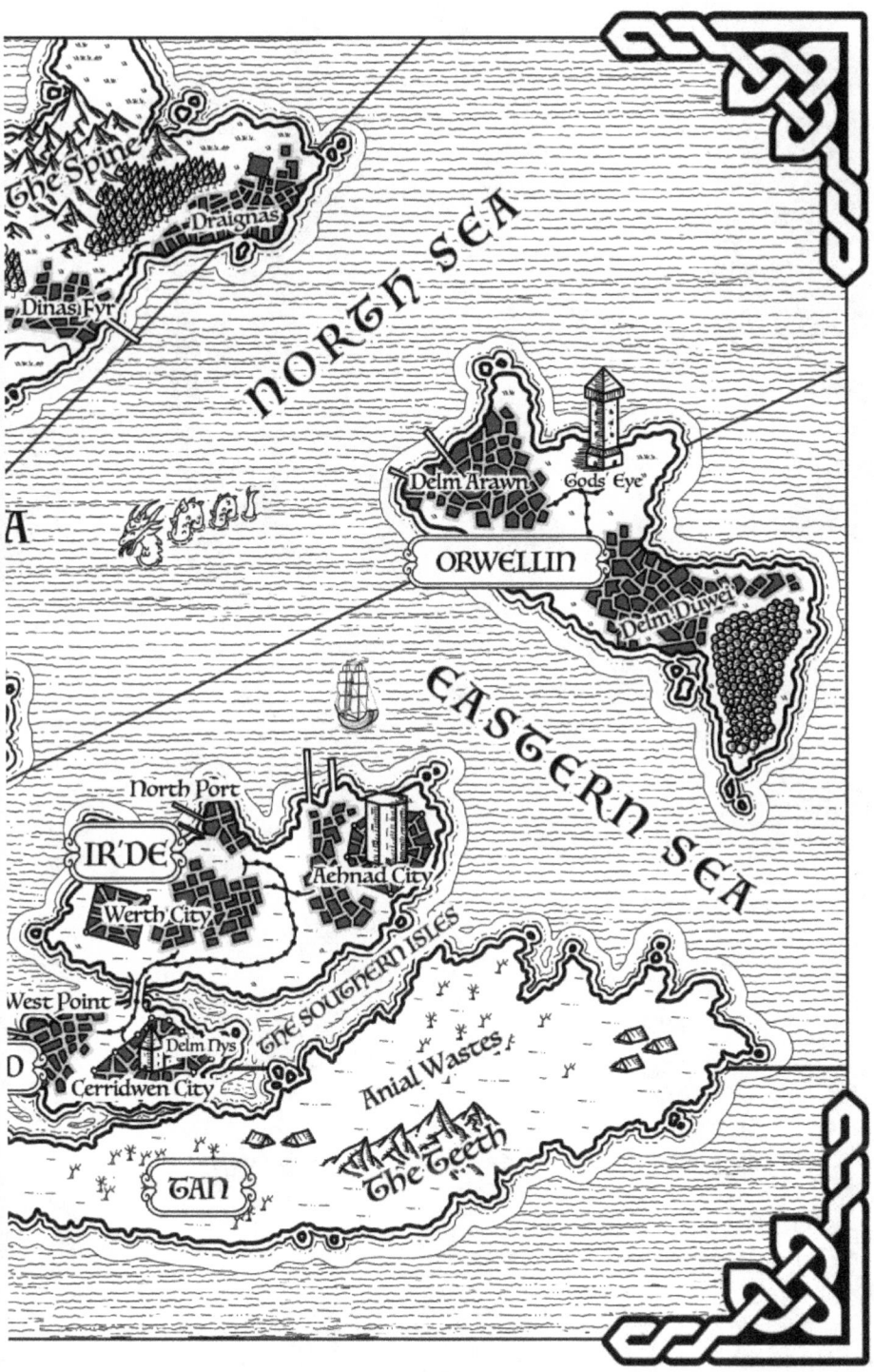

To Papa,

For teaching me that actions speak louder than words.

Here are about 125,000 words to let you know how much your actions mean to me.

I

Wars and Weddings

The sea was silent the day of my wedding. It noiselessly kissed the edges of old Esme Rhiamon's beat-up drifter, offering not even a whisper when I prayed for a sign.

It had always called to me, the sea—guiding my ship, warning me when trouble was coming. Most ships from Porthladd didn't let the womenfolk aboard, but Papa made me his heir anyway, and the sea rewarded us generously.

Yer god touched, girl. Lyr's child. I'm not going anywhere without my good luck charm.

I sighed, the nerves in my stomach jumbling up as the sun dipped lazily toward the horizon. I certainly didn't feel lucky tonight.

I used to dream of my wedding. I imagined myself standing proudly on the glistening deck of the *Ceffyl Dwr*, Papa's best cutter, wrapped in my favorite blue dress. The whole proud Branwen clan would be there as the sun set, smiles on their freckled faces while I promised myself to the man who I'd sail into the Otherworld with one day.

Now the dream mocked me as I waited on the creaking, bloodstained deck of *the Aife*, my hair matted with sweat against my brow. My men behind me slumped and sagged, still bruised and bleeding, as I prepared to bargain myself to the kin of my sworn enemy.

Yet another fight, today on the Eastern Docks. An ambush as a slew of Mathonwys tried to steal some precious—and illicit—cargo from the Southern Isles. No casualties, only a few flesh wounds. But word of the fight, so public in the bright light of dawn, had reached the Council by the noontide, and the Council's decision had been swift.

One last chance to broker peace.

The humid mist of night closed around us as the sun fully sheathed below the horizon line.

"Typical of the bloody Mathonwys to be late," I hissed under my breath, my eyes scanning the rocky shore for movement.

"Brace yourself, Keira," Uncle Aidan whispered, his graveled voice strangely comforting as he clapped a warm hand on my shoulder. "Save your sea-salt for when they're actually here." I smiled up at him, noting how grey his ginger beard had gotten as of late. He looked so much like Papa now.

I glanced again at the crew behind me. A small sea of gaunt cheeks, crestfallen shoulders, and bloodshot eyes stared back. Every face looked years older than it should, even my youngest cousin's. Tarran, only seventeen, wore the woes of a man twice his age.

There were so few of them now. The emptiness in their gazes echoed the empty spaces where the absent should have stood. I offered a prayer to Lyr, the names of those who now belonged to the Otherworld on my tongue.

Owen. Aleena. Cedric…

It had been four years since the blood feud started. Four years of sinking ships and homes burned to the ground and gruesome wounds both seen and unseen. Four years of rafts on fire and tear-stained cheeks and wives losing husbands. Daughters losing fathers.

Lyr below, what would Papa say if he could see what we've become?

I could do this for him. To honor his memory, to save what he dedicated his life to building, to restore prosperity to the family…

Even if it meant marrying—*becoming*—a Mathonwy.

"Are ya ready, girl?" Esme popped up from below deck, her wild grey curls first, and I nearly jumped out of my skin. She hoisted herself up onto the main deck effortlessly despite her age. Even though she was a member of the Council, Esme was an old sailor first. One of us. A fact she demonstrated as she crossed the deck in just a few lopsided steps and wrapped me in a crushing hug.

"As soon as the groom-to-be graces us with his presence," I chuckled into her mane of silver hair. She smelled of storm and gunpowder, as she had since I was a child, and I let her warmth soothe the waves in my gut.

"Aye, you've got yer dad's sense of humor." She pulled away to appraise me, her violet eyes shimmering with mischief. "But ye got yer mother's beauty, thank Lyr for that gift."

I raised an eyebrow. "You knew my mother?" No one knew my mother. Only that she existed, and that my Pa had loved her well.

"No, I didn't." Esme grinned wickedly, stepping closer. "But I've seen what yer Pa's people look like."

I sighed. She was right; I looked nothing like my Pa's people, the ginger and auburn curls that marked them as true Branwens, the sparkling hazel eyes that looked like sunsets. With my hair blacker than midnight and slate grey eyes, the only thing that proved I was kin were the freckles that dotted my cheeks.

"Watch it, Esme," my uncle chuckled, his eyes bright despite their exhaustion. "Sounds like yer callin' me ugly." He patted my shoulder once, as if he could read my mind.

"Hush, Aidan, ye own a mirror, ye know ye can't argue," Donnall, our second mate, jabbed from his perch on the stern. He was a bulky man, the muscle corded tightly around his forearms from years at sea, but anyone who knew him knew he had the best sense of humor on the ship. He hopped up and nudged Aidan with his elbow. "Ye better just hope ye find a blind wife."

The crew roared with hoarse laughter. For a moment, they were all whole again, all bright and sunny and strong. Aidan winked at Donnall; the joke at his expense had been well worth it, and the second mate had performed his duty admirably.

I beamed at my men, at my family, my people. Hair color be damned, I was one of them and always would be. And for them, I could do my duty too.

"Yer Pa would be proud to see ya now." Aidan's eyes lined with silver tears as he brushed a strand of hair behind my ear. I swallowed down the ball of emotion that rose to my throat.

"He can't because that damned Mathonwy boy put a knife through his neck," Weylin, the surly gunner, seethed from the group. He was a dangerous man, my eldest uncle. Rumor had it that the shining silver pistol on his hip was enchanted by the god of death himself. If Weylin had marked you, your trip to the Otherworld was guaranteed.

Esme whipped her head toward him, violet eyes flashing red. "Aye, and you've shot yer bullets through half a dozen Mathonwys." A second later, she was in Weylin's face, coming up only to the bulky man's chest, but her gaze was razor-sharp. A dark power rippled from her like the inky sea before a storm, and Weylin shrank beneath her gaze, his jaw tight. "So, unless you plan on marryin' one to make things right, I'd shut yer mouth."

There was a reason Esme's ship was one of the last floating neutral spaces. Aside from her position on the Council, she was a force to be reckoned with. No man, woman, or creature dared cross her. Not even Weylin and his fancy guns.

The sea remained silent, but the wind shifted, carrying the stinging scent of trouble with it. I turned just in time to see the imposing galleon slide through the mist.

The Ddraig. The black dragon figurehead bared its teeth at us.

Mathonwys.

The laughter of a moment before quickly dissipated as the ship glided toward us, silent as a ghost. They finally anchored portside, the metal hitting the water with a resounding splash. My men stiffened, hands flying to weapons and arms crossed against chests as they prepared for them to board.

"Madame Esme." Reese Mathonwy, the head sea-snake himself, strode across the gangway first, a grin on his scarred face. The urge to cut it off swelled in my chest, and I gripped the dagger at my waist tighter.

"Yer late." Esme put a wrinkled hand on her hip and gave him a look that could make Lyr himself shudder.

The rest of the Mathonwy men followed dutifully, all glaring and sneering as they passed, and I smirked at them in return. Thanks be to Lyr, they all looked even worse than my men. Torn, dirty clothes, their ugly mugs caked with dirt and grime and blood. Even Reese, in his expensive red Captain's coat, looked older, the wrinkles in his face only accentuating the jagged scar that covered his left eye. If it came to a proper fight, they wouldn't last ten minutes.

But my men would not survive either.

And just like that, my duty was laid before me as clearly as the stars on a cloudless night at sea.

"What a night fer a wedding, eh?" Reese boomed, his snake's smile still intact as he and his men settled into the starboard side of the boat. I sized them up while they huddled together; I didn't know which one was to be my husband, but as I looked at the scarred, mostly middle-aged faces, my sick feeling grew. Reese ran his eyes over my crew with condescension. "Such an ugly assembly of guests, though."

I scoffed under my breath as he voiced my own thoughts. Maybe I was already more Mathonwy than I knew.

"Aye shut yer mouth, boy. This is my ship and I won't be having any of yer spewin'," Esme snarled, and I swear to Lyr he flinched.

"What's the matter, Reese, scared of the sea witch?" Aidan sneered, my crew chuckling along.

"Keep talking, boy. Another word and this will quickly go from a wedding to a funeral," Esme warned. Aidan rolled his shoulders, his jaw clenched, but he didn't speak again. "Good. Now, you're all aware of why I called the families here, yes?"

Nods and grunts from both sides of the ship. Mathonwy's men still stood huddled, and my instincts prickled as I noted the strange formation.

"The Council of Porthladd has already decided," Esme continued, her voice carrying out over the silent sea. "We are tired of cleaning up yer mess, tired of the failed peace agreements. Either we fix this now, or neither family is allowed to do business anywhere near Porthladd. Full exile. So, it has been proposed that Keira Branwen marry a man of Mathonwy blood. Two bloodlines made one."

More grunting, tired and resigned, as the terms were reiterated to both families. Many may have objected, but none had the energy. The Council's chokehold was too tight, too complete, for anyone to try and fight anymore. Over the last few months, the tariff increases and permit rejections had been brutal toward both families. The Branwen coffers, once overflowing with wealth from all over the four seas, were near empty, and the winter coming promised to levy another fatal strike.

The Council knew it, too, the fight on the docks this morning only giving them the opportunity to impose their will on both families. Knew that this was the time to deliver the death blow. Knew that maybe now, we'd concede to a more permanent peace.

And we had.

So the terms were clear: betrothal or banishment. Our choice. I bit back the dread now rising to my throat. There was no going back.

"Reese Mathonwy, do ye and yer stinkin' family accept these terms?" Esme pointed a gnarled finger at him.

"We accept the terms of the Council's decision." He nodded, his eyes raking over me with a predatory gaze. Bile rose to my throat. Even in my loose trousers and my uncle's thick blue coat, I felt exposed. I prayed to Lyr it would not be him.

"And you, Captain?" Esme turned her sad eyes to Aidan.

He put his warm arm around my shoulder. "That's for Keira to decide."

All eyes turned to me.

I inhaled deeply, the scent of the salt and brine fortifying my nerves, and glanced back at my men. Tarran and Griffin, who had practically been raised as my brothers, had their whole lives ahead of them. Donnall, Griffin's father, with a family to support and loved ones already lost. Even Weylin, unfriendly and aloof as he was, deserved a chance at peace.

The sea may have abandoned me tonight, but I would not abandon my family.

"I accept the terms."

"Aye," Esme exhaled, a shimmer in her gaze, and turned to the Mathonwys. "Now, which one of ye does this poor girl have to marry?"

I held my breath and waited. Aidan squeezed me tighter to his side.

A wide smirk spread across Reese's face. "Let me introduce ye, Miss Keira."

The Mathonwy men broke their huddle, and a tall, hooded figure slipped forward. The hair on the back of my neck stood at attention. I heard the swish of metal as my men unsheathed their weapons. The figure raised his hands in defense, and with a deft flick of his wrists, lowered his hood.

My stomach lurched. "Ronan?"

"Good to see you, Keira," he murmured as he stepped forward, his blond hair shimmering in the moonlight. His cheeks were gaunter than when I had last seen him, his skin darker. But his eyes were the same sea-blue that I remembered from childhood, his smile just as haunting and wild.

And he was certainly alive, something I had tried my best to make impossible.

"Lyr's bollocks," my uncle muttered under his breath.

"I think we can put our weapons away, aye, gentlemen?" Reese raised an eyebrow at us. My men grumbled, but weapons clicked back into place. Ronan offered his wicked smile, one I knew all too well. One that I had once cherished.

"Well isn't this a surprise?" Esme raised an eyebrow, almost gleeful.

"How are you—" I stuttered, taking him in, the ghost of Ronan Mathonwy somehow standing and breathing before me. "I thought you were—"

"No, not dead." He shrugged off his cloak. His clean white shirt hugged his form, revealing the familiar, well-defined muscles in his shoulders. "Stranded on an island, thanks to you." His grin turned sinister. "But not dead. Much to your regret, I assume. You did, however, decimate my ship and my crew. So thank you for that, too."

Shame washed over me, but I shrugged it off quicker than it came. I glared at him, remembering our last face-to-face encounter.

My father's bloody corpse staining the deck of Ronan's ship, Ronan's hands the same crimson, the knife in his hand as he ripped it from my father's neck...

I shook off the memory before it consumed me, swallowing back the hot tears. I was the first mate of a proud cutter, and a Branwen at that. I would not have my men see me shaking in my boots, especially not over a stinkin' Mathonwy, dead or alive.

Even if I had loved him once. Even if I'd tried to kill him.

I painted on a smirk. "Such a shame I couldn't finish the job. Tell me, how did you manage?"

"Lyr was looking out for me." He looked out toward the ocean, something dark in his light eyes for a flicker of a moment. He quickly forced his carefully-crafted mask back into place. "But what matters now is that I'm here, and I come to find out that Keira Branwen has not only laid down her arms and stopped sinking perfectly good ships but has to marry a Mathonwy."

My throat went dry. I opened my mouth to speak, but nothing came out.

"Right, ye can catch up later." Esme hobbled in between us, breaking my trance. "Ye got a lifetime of marriage to bicker and gawk at each other. Let's get the ceremony started before I croak from old age."

"No." The word came hurrying out of my mouth faster than I could think it through. All eyes on the ship shot toward me swifter than a bullet from one of Weylin's guns.

I swallowed hard. I had to stand firm now. The gentle sway of the boat anchored me to my resolve.

"Ah," Reese goaded, stepping closer to me. His breath smelled of ale and venom. "Typical of a Branwen to go back on a deal."

I stared up at him. He would not break me.

"Keira, the Council..." My uncle's voice was weak behind me.

I held up my hand to stop him. "I did not say I wouldn't marry *any* of you bastards." I looked past Reese to the rest of his motley gang of thugs. Finally, I let my gaze rest on Ronan, sending every ounce of anger and hate his way. He would not own me. "Just not the traitor."

"Tsk, tsk, Keira, darling." Reese clicked his tongue, shaking his head. "Is that any way to talk about yer future husband?"

"She's not gonna marry the scum that killed her father!" Tarran shouted from behind me, his young voice still laced with desperate loyalty.

Shouts erupted from both sides of the ship, all of them hurling colorful insults at each other.

I kept my gaze fixed on Ronan. He stared back, daring me, his mask still plastered on. He had had the upper hand when he surprised me, but I had the advantage of surplus.

"There are other bachelors, Reese." My voice cut through the noise like the bow of a ship through water, and the boat quieted. "Rhett, Roland's son, he's of marrying age, isn't he?" I batted my lashes at him, using the weapons only a woman could wield. "Or even you. You've been out of mourning long enough."

"Keira, enough," my uncle whispered in my ear, tugging at my arm until I shook him off.

Reese chuckled, deep and dark, "What makes ye think I'd want ye?" His eyes raked over me again, and I did my best not to squirm despite the pit in my stomach. His gaze narrowed like a snake focusing in on a mouse. "Yer pretty fer a Branwen, I'm sure ye can thank yer ma for that, but even I know to sail away from sirens." He stepped back and threw his arm around Ronan, the both of them simpering. "My son here is the only one brave or stupid enough to touch ye with a ten-foot pole, Lyr bless him."

"Aye, insult her like that again." Griffin stepped in between us with his fists clenched at his sides, his height staggering next to mine. Damned idiot never knew when to walk away from a fight. "I'll paint the deck with your insides."

"I'd like to see ye try," Reese snarled. He was half a head shorter than Griffin, but snakes didn't need to be tall to be venomous.

"Enough!" Esme shouted, barging her way between the two of them, shoving hard at both of their chests. "Ye will respect each other on my ship, or ye all will be sailing to the Otherworld tonight. The terms of the deal have been set." She glared at all of us, the red of her eyes piercing in the dark of the night. "Keira Branwen can either marry Ronan Mathonwy, or both families can pack their things and find another island to haunt. I'm growing tired of this. Decide. Now. Ronan?"

Ronan had been quiet. He had always been one to calculate, to wait for the right moment to strike. Unlike his father, he did not hiss to warn his enemy. He was an adder. He'd patiently wait, lying soundlessly in the grass, until you trusted him with your weakest parts. Then he'd bite.

Now he stepped forward, ready to sink his fangs in. "I have already decided. A Mathonwy's word is his bond."

Esme rolled her eyes, then flicked them to me. "Keira?"

I would not let a few pretty words disarm me. I looked at my men again, at the tension in their muscles, their hands all twitching at their sides. They were waiting for the signal, waiting to defend my honor, no matter the cost.

I thought of their families waiting at home. Of the futures they deserved. There was no escape, no easy way out. But the choice was clear. Either my men laid down their lives tonight, or I laid down mine.

Papa had always said there was more than one way to sacrifice a life.

"A Branwen," I spat at my betrothed, "lets their actions do the talking. Esme, let's begin."

Behind me, the chorus of breaths releasing after being held for so long was all I needed to fortify my courage.

Ronan blinked twice, the only indication of his surprise. Regaining his mask, he extended his calloused hand toward me. "Shall we?"

I grabbed it tightly, digging my nails into the side. He winced. "Yes, we shall."

The ceremony itself was a blur. I was aware of the eyes at my back, Esme's voice flitting over the words, though I did not register their meaning. And I felt the heat of Ronan at my side, his stature demanding attention.

Both my men and the Mathonwys somehow managed to behave themselves, even when I secretly hoped they wouldn't.

"All right, last call." Esme cleared her throat, drawing me from my trance. "Does any member of the current assembly object to these two being wed?"

Silence. From both sides.

The ocean rippled, and the ethereal, preternatural voice whispered to me for the first and only time that night.

Finally.

"Then I pronounce ye man and wife." Esme cocked a smile, drawing a scroll from her belt. "Now ye just need to sign the contract."

"Contract?" Reese chimed in, scowling at the scroll in Esme's hand.

"Aye, a contract," she bit back. "Ye think the Council would trust a bunch of liars with a verbal agreement? I wasn't born yesterday."

"What does it say?" Ronan eyed her skeptically.

"That yer husband and wife." Esme stared him down, unyielding. "That the Mathonwy and Branwen clans are now and forever bound as kin." Her gaze intensified, the red in her eyes threatening. "And that if Mathonwy blood be spilled by Branwen hands or vice versa, the family will be banished, and the spiller must pay with their own life for their crimes against Porthladd, their kin, and Lyr himself."

"How pleasant," I scoffed as I grabbed the quill to sign, my hand shaking.

Once the paper was signed, there was no going back. One pen stroke, and any chance of me living my life for myself would come to an abrupt end.

So would the fighting.

I scratched my name hurriedly across the page. "There. It's done."

"Couldn't agree more." Ronan gingerly took the quill, penning his name elegantly to the worn page. "Mrs. Mathonwy."

2

Gauntlets and Gifts

"Keira, sit still." Auntie Vala pulled my hair with steely determination as she tried to comb the stringy mess into something presentable. I sat up straighter, compliant underneath her grip. I wished I could feel the pain, but I was numb. I was about to attend my wedding reception because I was *married*.

To Ronan Mathonwy.

To my father's killer.

The reality sat like an anchor in my gut, threatening to drag me down into the deep. The gruesome image of Ronan pulling the knife from my father's neck sat at the forefront of my mind's eye, replaying on a loop.

"You look like something that washed up on the shore, Cousin," Saeth said by way of an introduction as she entered my small dressing room in Aidan's house. Tarran's twin sister was slim, her auburn hair a little darker than her brother's, but still every bit of her a Branwen. She would've been quite pretty if her angular face didn't sport a permanent scowl.

She'd still marry better than I had. "Aye, funny, that's exactly how I feel," I scoffed.

"Saeth," Vala snapped, pointing a hairbrush at the girl like a knife, "in Lyr's name, either come help me or shut yer mouth and get yer skinny rump out of here."

Vala wasn't a sailor, but she was a warrior in her own way. Saeth rolled her eyes but dutifully grabbed a comb and began working through the week's worth of sailor's knots in my mane.

"Yer clueless uncle, letting you get married like *that*." Vala made another frustrated tug at my hair, harder this time. Hard enough to feel. "Ripped clothes, hair a raven's nest, smelling of complete arse. Embarrassing for the family if ye ask me. And in front of the Council, no less!"

"It was only Esme." I winced slightly at both the pain of the pull and the insult, sliding forward in my seat like a fussy child. "Besides, it was more of a prison sentence than a wedding."

"We all have our sentences to bear." Her tone softened as she brushed through the last knots at the bottom of my head.

I knew she spoke of the son she lost, his sentence already served. Owen had been her oldest, nearly a decade my senior, a kind boy and a fine sailor with a soft smile and a sharp mind. He had been considering marriage, a new chapter of his life about to begin, when it was all taken from him.

Another life sentence dealt by the Mathonwys.

Pins stabbed and hair pulled as Saeth and Vala finished in silence.

"Keira darling," Saeth purred when the last curl was pinned in place, "you're actually starting to look like a girl."

"Much better." Vala nodded warmly, brushing a strand of her own mousy brown curls out of her face. "Now, let's see..." She fluttered to the dusty wardrobe at the back of the sparsely furnished room.

I rarely stayed here, as I preferred to sleep under starry skies on the *Ceffyl* most nights. Sleeping on the deck wasn't always possible, but whenever the winds were warm and the skies were clear, I'd pitch my hammock between the wheel and the mast and pretend I was a tiny star in my own constellation.

It beat being trapped under this coffin-cover of a ceiling any day of the week. The lifeless space wasn't bad, with comfortable, simple furnishings, but it had never been mine. Aidan took me in as his own after Papa passed, for which I was grateful, but even here I was a fish out of water. I'd never be the proper young lady from a good family this room was designed for.

The neglect in the room showed as Vala sifted through the garments hanging in the wardrobe, sending a month's worth of dust flying. Most of the items weren't even mine, belonging to one cousin or another. Finally, Vala locked on to her target. With a flourish, she removed a midnight blue garment from its hook and tossed it to me. "Put this on, I'll help you with the laces."

It was clear I was not captaining this vessel. I unraveled the garment in my hand. The silk gown had boning and lace throughout the bodice, the skirt puffing out dramatically at the waist. The sleeves were equally inflated. It had been Cousin Finna's, designed for her twenty-first year when she was presented as a woman to the Council. But while she was five years my senior, she was also two inches shorter, so the hem would barely hit my ankles.

Aside from that, with a little wriggling and some tightening through the bust, it would, unfortunately, fit just fine.

"No," I said.

"Oh, yes." Vala smiled devilishly.

"Lyr below, I'm one of the best sailors south of Pysgodd, and you're trying to dress me up like a dolly."

Vala rolled her eyes, the expression strangely young on her careworn features. She wrenched my arms up and wrangled the dress over the slip I was wearing. "I'm trying to make you look like a blushing bride," she lectured me as the heavy material slipped over my head. "Someone the Council won't see as a threat. Not some half-wild pirate with a vendetta."

"But I am a half-wild pirate with a vendetta."

"Aye. Hence the dress." She motioned for me to turn and tugged at the corset laces.

I'd only worn a corset once before since Pa insisted I was a sailor first and a lady second, and a sailor needed a corset about as much as they needed anchored shoes. I forgot how terrible simple things like breathing became as she pulled the contraption tighter.

"Definitely designed by a man who wanted to make a woman less threatening," I gasped between breaths.

Vala tied it off and stepped back to admire her handiwork. "How do ye feel?"

"Like you just wrapped me up like a wedding gift."

Grinning, she pulled a small silver dagger from her apron. The metal glinted in the lantern light, small as a shark's tooth but just as sharp. "Aye, that's why ye tuck this under yer skirt."

Saeth's interest pricked up as I tucked the metal into the hidden pocket of the dress. "With your taste in men, Cousin, you may need it for your honeymoon."

The door behind us slammed open as I offered Saeth a vulgar gesture, and in bounced Finna, her head of wild crimson curls swishing behind her. "It's time to go, ladies, and Keira, Aidan has the carriage waiting...oh my, is that my old dress?" Her jade eyes raked over me with the candied reproach I had come to expect from her. She looked to Vala, dismissing me with a cruel smile on her full lips. "Mama, you should've had this thing pressed for poor Keira, or asked me for one of my newer things. Then again, my good dresses wouldn't fit in the bust."

Her judgement made me squirm and I hated myself for it. I was Captain apparent to this family, for Lyr's sake; I shouldn't be so easily disarmed by petty insults, especially from her. We'd been close as children. I used to follow her around like a lost puppy, but she resented me the moment Papa named me his heir. Not that she'd been sailing a day in her life, but Finna was the kind of person who could easily die from lack of attention. Still, I couldn't help the pang of jealousy as I took in my eldest cousin before me, clad in an expensive-looking violet dress that perfectly accented her generous assets.

And it wasn't just the dress. It was her, the effortless beauty of her porcelain face, the soft curves of her supple frame. Not a single callous on her hand or a snag in her hair. Prim and pampered and free of care. Free of duty. Finna would marry for love if she ever tired of having a handful of partners at once.

"Blue is your color, Keira." Saeth's compliment sounded foreign in her flat tone, sharp as ever, as she adjusted my gown for me. "And the only thing bigger than Finna's tits is her head."

I coughed up a laugh despite myself as Finna's eyes went wide. "I heard that, you little shit!"

"You were meant to," Saeth said with the cutting precision of a marksman. Finna was sour, but she was no match for Saeth's brutal bitterness. I belly-laughed as Finna poked her tongue out at her, the corset biting my sides, and said a silent prayer to Lyr for my cousins. Prissy as they were, they had distracted me long enough to make me laugh. Who knew when I'd get the chance again?

"Ye girls have filthy mouths. This is what I get fer raising ye around sailors," Vala sighed, pulling her cloak around herself and throwing mine at me. "Now let's go."

I caught it easily despite the corset, my laughter evaporating as the air was sucked from the room.

No more hiding behind pretty things and petty insults. I had run out of time, and fate waited for no one.

Finna's fox-sharp eyes caught my unease, and she offered a vulpine smile. "Let's get going, Mrs. Mathonwy."

Papa always said there were three main things a sailor had to remember above all else.

One: when you don't know where you're going, the compass does.

Two: tie your knots tightly, then tie them again.

And three: a stiff drink and a hot meal make every problem a little easier to solve.

As the Branwens, Mathonwys, and the Council alike settled into the coarse oak benches at *The Dancing Raven*, I prayed to Lyr Papa was right.

The only pub in Porthladd with a gambling license, Councilwoman Agatha Amos' little tavern was another rare neutral ground. As such, *The Raven* was no stranger to backward deals and trade meetings over cards. But a gathering of this caliber on dry land was unheard of, even for Porthladd's seediest establishment.

"Ladies and gentlemen, I'd like to propose a toast to the happy couple." Esme took her position as the master of ceremonies for the night, raised her mug of ale, and nodded to the four Councilmembers behind her. "Keira, Ronan, *Lechyd Da!*"

"*Lechyd Da*," the room responded with a disappointing lack of energy.

I watched the Council carefully from my seat, ignoring the stabbing pain in my ribs. My marriage was destined for unhappiness, but that didn't mean it couldn't be fruitful in other ways. I was finally in a position to win back the Council's favor for my family.

Ellian "The Young Lion" Llewelyn, only son of the most prominent mining and smithing family in Porthladd, sat to Esme's right. His brown curls were glossy in the candlelight, accentuated further by the deep, expensive furs he wore. With a keen business sense and a hot temper, he had earned his nickname, but to us Branwens he had always been a friend who secretly sided with us during the feud despite protests from the rest of the Council. I made a note to say hello before the night was over.

To his right, Howell Wynne, the head of the fisherman's guild, a ruffled old man who couldn't hold a conversation without mentioning cod. His face was already buried in his plate, food sticking to his salt-and pepper-beard. He wouldn't give us any trouble tonight as long as his plate stayed stacked and his mug full. I'd bet a date with Lyr that he'd leave before dessert was served.

But on the far end of the table sat Connor Yorath, lawyer and legal aid to the Council, representative of the High Council of the Deyrnas. His shiny hair was slicked to his head, emphasizing his sunken cheeks, as gaunt as a starving chicken. His fingers were long and spindly, like they had spent their lifetime holding nothing heavier than a feathered quill. Frail and sheltered, Yorath was.

He was also the most dangerous man in the room.

All permits and contracts went through him. His quill, while no direct match for the salt and steel I lived by, could end the livelihood of everyone in the tavern with one fell stroke.

He was the one who had been starving out my family for months now, decimating our shipping business just as cruelly as the Mathonwys had ruined our ships. I had to appease him tonight, too, or this union would be a wasteful one. It didn't matter if my family could sail if our people still starved. I would not let us live as smugglers and pirates any longer. We deserved legitimacy, even if I had to pry it out of Yorath's fragile hands.

On cue, he stood, his wiry frame even smaller next to Howell's mass. He clinked his glass like the high-born diplomat he was, starkly out of place in the strategic lowlight of the tavern, and cleared his throat. The room quieted again. "The Council wishes that this marriage will bring happiness to not only the couple but to their families and all Porthladd. May Lyr bless you both. Enjoy the meal, everyone."

I sighed and took a dreg of my glass, letting the warm liquid fill my constricted belly. I'd have to put on quite a show to convince Yorath this marriage could work.

If only I could convince myself first.

"Aye, cheers to you too, Mrs. Mathonwy," Ronan whispered, his breath tickling my ear as he leaned in. "You look very pretty in that dress." He smelled of rum and the sickeningly-sweet citrus fruit his family traded, the combination making me lurch. I had nearly decked Esme when she led us to the unfortunately small table "fer the happy couple."

"Ronan, you will back up, or you will find yourself a eunuch before the night is over."

He raised his hands with false apology and winked, but he scooted his chair further away. Twice.

I glanced at the long table where my family sat if only to look anywhere else. Aidan sat at the head, my usual place at his right now taken by Donnall, his place taken by Weylin, and the rest of the clan falling in behind them. At least none of them looked like they were having any fun; they all glared while they stuffed their faces, tension radiating from the back of every man and woman seated. Even young Tarran's usually sunny countenance was sullen and tired, his eyes fixed towards the Mathonwys. Only Saeth looked something other than surly, her normally pursed lips now pulled in a rare line of a smile. My guess was that it was because Weylin, her Pa, let her drink tonight.

I watched as Vala placed a gentle hand on Tarran's shoulder, breaking his trance, and they glanced at each other warmly. Vala was not his mother, but she had cared for both him and Saeth after their own Ma passed, much like Aidan had for me. No Branwen was ever left behind.

Except I was no longer a Branwen. A deep part of me ached.

I was already an outsider.

The moment was broken by Esme standing on top of her creaky chair, the contents of her mug spilling over the sides as she lifted it into the air. "Now this is a wedding, so all of ye should stop fussin' and start celebratin'!" she shouted, her cheeks already rosy from drink. "And by celebratin', I mean drinkin'!"

A few people grunted in agreement, and Griffin even let out a cheer. He never needed an excuse to drink, but having one sure made him happy.

Agatha, the owner, sat to Esme's left. She scanned the room, her hawk eyes flicking over each face with deadly precision. Her brunette coils were strapped to her head in meticulous braids, her dark skin luminous in the lantern light. She looked more like a warrior princess from the Southern Isles than the born and bred Porthladdian barkeep she was, which was probably why *The Dancing Raven* was still miraculously standing. Yet even she'd be on guard all night with the powder keg that was ready to blow her beloved tavern apart.

Her eyes stopped on Ronan and me. She looked at me like she could see straight through me—or like she was looking past me into a future I could not yet see. I shuddered under her gaze.

"Oi, everyone, drinks on the house," she declared. "My gift to the newlyweds."

A chorus of cheers erupted from both camps as I shook off the haunted feeling. Getting piss drunk for free was one idea that Mathonwys and Branwens could both agree on.

Agatha, still a businesswoman, brought out eight kegs of her cheapest ale and a few bottles of bargain-brand whiskey. Yet no one complained about the quality as the drinks flowed freely, and with it, the tension in the room slowly dissolved. Each family stuck to its respective side, breaking away only to chat with a Council member or to congratulate Ronan and me.

At least every ruddy face was now smiling, chatting, or even laughing.

Ellian somehow produced a fiddle, and before anyone could object, both clans were singing. A few of the bolder men even started a jig—still on their own sides—the merriment palpable. It was a wedding, after all, and for many, the first bit of rest and recreation in a long time.

I didn't feel like celebrating.

But Ronan did. Within minutes, he sauntered onto the dance floor without a second glance back. In another minute, he had one of the pretty blonde barmaids in his arms as he twirled her around to the music.

A sharp pang of inconvenient jealousy stabbed at the back of my mind. I reminded myself I didn't want to dance with him.

What I wanted was my pound of flesh.

Instead, I poured myself another drink.

Griffin stumbled over to me, his freckled cheeks so flushed they matched his flaming hair. He bowed at the waist, a lopsided smile on his face, and extended his hand. "How about a dance, Mrs. Mathonwy?"

"Shut your face, Griffin, that's not funny." I felt my own cheeks get hot, the pit of my stomach rolling at my new title.

Keira rutting Mathonwy.

"Oh come on, Keira!" Tarran threw his arm around Griffin, hanging onto his tall frame like the baby monkeys in Ir'de clung to their mothers. "If you don't dance with him, no one will!"

I slammed my drink down and stood. "You dance with him, then. I said no."

Tarran blinked at my tone, hurt flashing in his eyes. I never spoke to him that way. Shame washed over me, and for an instant, I wanted to take it back, to paint on a pretty mask so I'd never have to see my cousin make that face again.

But I could not laugh and dance and celebrate like I hadn't traded my future for his.

Griffin's eyes narrowed. His talent for smelling rubbish was almost as acute as his talents for drinking and starting fights. "Aye, do we have to ask your husband first?"

I glared at him, daring him to continue. He raised a cheeky eyebrow. It was exactly the reaction he wanted.

"Aye, good *cousin* Ronan," he yelled to Ronan, who now was whispering something into the barmaid's ear. He turned to us, slimy smirk intact, curiosity dancing in his eyes. Other heads followed, watching the man who was drunk enough to call over the invisible fence. Connor Yorath's gaze tracked us curiously, and I cursed my cousin's name. This was not the place for one of Griffin's games. Next to me, Tarran's face darkened, echoing the blackness that crept along my spine.

Griffin persisted, performing another mocking bow, continuing loud enough for the entire assembly to hear, "May I have a minute of your time?"

Still seated, Yorath's interest seemed to fade as he swirled the contents of his glass and looked out the window, but I knew he'd be watching closely.

"Go rot, Griffin," I growled under my breath.

Ronan stood, shrugging the barmaid off him like an old coat, and walked up to us with cockiness oozing from every inch of him. He looked at me as he addressed my cousins, "How may I be of service, gentlemen?"

Tarran took a protective step toward me, but Griffin only grinned. "See, we'd like to dance with your wife here, but she insists that we ask her dear doting husband first."

"I'm not his property," I snarled at Griffin, ignoring Ronan's unwanted attendance. "I just don't want to dance."

"Actually, fellas, I'd love to speak with Keira for a moment." Ronan took a step closer, and Tarran tensed next to me.

"You're speaking now." Tarran placed a hand on my shoulder as he puffed out his chest in a failed attempt to make his lanky frame look imposing.

"Alone." Ronan's voice was calm. He knew not to take the bait. "Please, gentlemen, humor me." He plastered on his best smile. Tarran's jaw flickered.

I looked back at Yorath, who was still watching with feigned disinterest, and rolled my eyes. "Stand down, Tarran. Give us a minute." I patted his shoulder as his eyes filled with protest, but he backed up. Griffin tipped an invisible hat and followed suit, roguishness dripping from his gaze.

I waited until I knew they couldn't hear us before I snapped, "What do you want?" My words were sharp but my smile was bright; out of the corner of my eye, I watched Agatha strike up a conversation with Yorath, and I loosed a breath. I was off the hook for now.

Ronan, taking my relief as something entirely different, extended his hand to me. "Perhaps it would be best if you and I danced together?"

"No, but thanks for wasting my time." I turned to leave.

"Come on, Mrs. Mathonwy." He came up behind me, leaning so close that his breath was hot on my neck. A miry hand found its way to my waist. "Let the Councilmembers see us. We want them to think this is going well."

My stomach lurched at his touch. "It's not going well." I stomped my foot back with lightning quickness, suddenly very glad that Vala had forced me into the pair of sharp heels.

Contact. Ronan cursed under his breath. "I deserved that, I suppose."

"You did."

"Aye," he grunted, standing upright again, the cockiness in his expression fading, "but our families seem to be getting on just fine. Agatha's gift was very generous."

"It was." I rolled my eyes flippantly, but his presence was starting to grate across my patience. Any longer and the kettle of rage I had brewing inside would start steaming and hissing. "And she told us to drink, not dance, so if you'll excuse me, this conversation is over."

Something dark and wistful flashed in his crystal-blue eyes. For a moment, he was the same open-hearted, messy-haired boy I had once loved. "You used to love to dance."

I cursed myself for my momentary weakness. The boy I loved died the same day he murdered my father.

Hatred coursed through my blue-blooded veins, stinging like a knife across my throat. "I used to love a lot of things, Ronan," my voice was just as sharp, "and you killed the most important one."

I stormed off towards my cousins without another word, hoping he had not seen the tears that sprang to my eyes.

"Come to dance, Cousin?" Griffin's tone was light, but I could see the flicker of concern hidden underneath. He nodded to me, an unspoken question: *Are you all right?*

I swallowed the ball of emotion in my throat and threw on a smile that could rival a Mathonwy's. "You're a pain in the arse, you know that?" I grabbed his hand and dragged him to the dance floor.

"That's what all the ladies say," Tarran cracked as he joined us, the sun back in his smile.

"And what do you know of ladies, Tarran Branwen?" Griffin ruffled his sunset hair, and Tarran's blush burned even redder.

"You're both hopeless," I sighed but bit my cheek to stop myself from grinning.

"Aye, that's why I fancy men too." Griffin winked. "They've got much lower standards."

Tarran's eyes went wider than tea saucers. "Lyr's bollocks."

Griffin roared with laughter and grabbed my hand again, spinning me to the rhythm of Ellian's fiddle. "Speaking of handsome men," he yelled over the music, "that husband of yours isn't bad looking, even with the stupid blond Mathonwy hair."

I clenched my fist at my side. "Hadn't noticed."

"Too bad good looks don't make up for stupidity." Griffin cracked a smile, lowering his voice. "A whole family and the only letter they can remember is *R*? Inbreds."

The laughter that sputtered from my core was genuine. I didn't know if it was the music or my cousins or the three drinks I'd already downed, but for the first time that night, I felt the warm buzz of hope in my core.

I let them take me, the fiddle and my family, as I spun around. The corset bit at my sides, making each breath laborious, but I marveled at the pain, letting it fuel my every step. My cousins tried to keep pace, our breaths all short and our faces all red. Sweat pooled at the back of my neck, but I didn't care. I danced and danced and danced, for minutes or hours or days, I didn't know. The only mark of time was Ellian's foot as he tapped along to the melody of his fiddle. And I would dance until my feet fell off or I forgot my last name, whichever came first.

My euphoria did not last long enough for either.

In our frenzy, my cousins and I had forgotten to note the unspoken divide.

"Aye, watch where you're stepping, you half-wit." A man— Rhett Mathonwy—erupted with a shove at Griffin's chest, sending him flying backward.

He landed on his feet like a cat, the mischief in his eyes just as feline. "Aye, my deepest apologies, good sir! I didn't see your clumsy feet in my way." He squared up to Rhett, who was only an inch shorter and just as wide.

If a fight broke out, Rhett might actually stand a chance against him.

"Enough, Griffin." I placed a hand on his arm.

Rhett's strong jaw flickered. "Shut your mouth, girl, the men are talking."

Ellian's fiddle stopped playing, and I knew all five sets of Councilmember eyes were boring holes in the backs of our skulls.

"I don't see any men, only two little boys having a pissing contest." My voice steadied into a lethal calm. I had to defuse this situation before the truce went completely belly up. I stared up at each of them with as much authority as I could muster. "Back up. Both of you."

Griffin didn't even look my way, his chest puffed out like a parrot. "I don't take orders from you, Keira." He took a threatening step toward Rhett.

"No, ye take 'em from me," Aidan interrupted with a thwack to the back of Griffin's head. "Now go sit down, ye idiot."

I loosed a sigh of relief.

"Aidan, this is—" Griffin moved to object, but Aidan nodded his head at the Council.

"Go. Now."

Griffin swallowed hard, realization dawning on his ruddy features. "Aye, Captain."

Rhett's gaze was full of daggers as he watched Griffin retreat. But the real enemy was far nearer.

"Is there an issue here, gentlemen?" Connor Yorath approached us, his beady eyes clouded with suspicion, his long fingers steepled in front of him as he assessed us.

"None at all, Councilman Yorath." Aidan bowed his head slightly, then clapped a hand on Rhett's shoulder. "I was just thanking young Rhett here for helping Griffin catch his balance."

Rhett shot Aidan a viper's bite of a look but nodded along.

"Ah," Yorath mused with careful calculation, "how kind of you, Mr. Mathonwy."

Rhett cleared his throat. "It was my pleasure."

"Enjoy the rest of the party, then." Connor rapped his fingers together. "Aidan, Rhett, nice chatting with you. Congratulations again, Mrs. Mathonwy."

I dug my nails into my palm and smacked on a grateful smile. "Thank you, Councilman."

He nodded his head and made to turn around. My stomach rolled at the near confrontation, but I had to seize the opportunity in front of me.

"Actually, Councilman," I called after him, and he stopped, turning back toward me. I plastered on my most innocent expression. "I was hoping to talk to you more this evening."

Aidan raised a brow but did not interrupt. The Councilman's eyes narrowed as they raked over me. Twice. "Yes, Mrs. Mathonwy?"

I swallowed my disgust and batted my eyelashes in return. I reminded myself to be a blushing bride. "Ro—*my husband* and I would love to sit with you soon and discuss some of the finer details of this new alliance. What it means for Porthladd, for our families…"

Yorath's thin lips pulled into a tight line. "I'm sure Madame Esme would be willing to go over it all with you both."

My mouth went dry, but I would not let him slip through my fingers so easily. Mustering up all my courage and battle experience, I placed a tender hand on his forearm. He felt frail beneath me, even as he tensed uncomfortably under my touch. "I'm sure; she's been very generous with her help." I raised my eyes to him, registering his stiff posture, and let my hand fall. "But I was hoping to sit with you, specifically. Your expertise, after all, is unparalleled."

He swallowed, his throat too thin to hide the motion. "Flattery does not become you, Mrs. Mathonwy." His voice was huskier now, and I fought the urge to vomit. "But send for me at the end of next week. I'll meet with you then."

Without another word, he floated back to his perch. I breathed deeply for the first time that night.

"Well, aren't you a pretty liar," Aidan chuckled under his breath.

"You taught me well, Uncle." I gave him a reproachful look. "We need him to lift those sanctions."

"Aye, that we do. We men are foolish creatures, Keira," he whispered in my ear. "All it takes to woo us is a gentle stroke of our egos. Or, too many drinks and we think we can grow gills and fight Lyr himself. Ye know Griffin didn't mean what he said, he's just drunk."

I patted my uncle's arm. "I know. I'd be angry if I didn't know he'll have the hangover from the Otherworld to deal with in the morning as punishment."

Aidan chuckled, relaxing again as the tension cleared once more. "I'd ask ye to dance, but the old leg is acting up again."

"It's all right, Uncle, I think I've had my fill for the night anyway."

"Perhaps it's time for my gift to ye, then."

I raised an eyebrow, but he only smiled and drew a small handkerchief-wrapped item from his pocket. With a glimmer in his hazel eyes, he folded it into my hand. The cloth covering fell to reveal the round bronze of a compass, the elegant words of an old engraving etched into its face.

All that are lost shall be found.

"Pa's compass?" My breath caught in my throat. "Aidan, I can't, it belongs to the captain of the *Ceffyl*…"

"Which you will one day be." He stroked my cheek. "I'm holding the position temporarily. Now, I want ye to have this. Yer *Pa* wanted ye to have this. Said his lucky compass belonged with his real good luck charm."

"Thank you, Aidan." Hot tears lined my eyes, and I wiped them before anyone could see. "For everything."

"Ah, so it's time for gifts then?" Ellian's deep voice boomed across the room, the Young Lion strutting toward us with his signature vibrato. Aidan patted my shoulder and made way.

"There are gifts? Plural?" I asked.

"It's a wedding, Keira darling." Ellian placed a gallant kiss on my hand, and with a handsome wink, slipped a small box into my palm. "Of course there are gifts."

I did not hide my blush as I looked at the tiny object in my hand. The box itself was made of decadent mahogany, but inside…

A sapphire, larger than the first knuckle of my finger, dangling from a brilliant gold chain.

I gasped at the opulence. Ellian brushed a strand of hair behind my ear as I stood speechless before him. "So you never forget what color your blood runs, Branwen."

I did not have the words to respond as the rest of the crowd gathered around us. Each family was careful to stand on the appropriate side, Rhett and Griffin's altercation still thick in the air, with the Council in the center. Ronan made his way to me, his standard smirk on his face, but his eyes narrowed darkly.

"If the Council would permit it," Ronan addressed Ellian with a hint of malice in his tone, "might my Pa present his next?"

Ellian did not bristle. "Please, go right ahead, Reese." He gestured to the old man.

Reese slithered forward, cockiness oozing from every orifice. With a flourish, he slipped a single envelope from his pocket and handed it to Ronan. "To my son and his beautiful new bride. Lyr bless ye both."

Ronan opened it with the same swagger as his father, but his jaw dropped when he read the parchment. "It's a ship."

The Mathonwys applauded with vigor, but anger rippled in my core. Of course, they would reward their best assassin with his own ship.

"Bought it fer ye yesterday. Yer now the proud Captain of the *Sarff y Mor*." Reese's brag was met with "oohs" and "ahhs" from his kin, and he turned to me with a sneer. "Keira dear, don't sink this one, aye?"

I glared right back. "No promises."

"My niece is a comedian," Aidan laughed loudly, peeping back at Connor and the Council. "What a lovely gesture, Reese."

"Aye, I suppose I might as well go next!" Esme burst through the center of the crowd, hiccupping slightly. "Since Agatha and Ellian already gave gifts, I'm sure this is an appropriate time, aye, Connor?"

Connor folded his arms over his narrow chest. "I suppose so."

Esme's violet eyes simmered with drink and darkness. Without even reaching into her dress, she produced a piece of paper and presented it to me. I blinked twice, missing the trickery. "Then here ye two go."

I read its contents once. Then again. "Lyr below, Esme. This is a deed to a house." A house of my own. Not the cabin of a ship, but a proper home. And not Aidan's or Vala's or any of the family I stayed with since Pa died.

My house.

Pa always said a good sailor needed a place to come back to.

Ronan ripped the paper from my hand to read it himself. His eyes went wide. "A house? Esme, this is—"

"It's too much," Reese piped in. "With all due respect, Madame Esme, there is plenty of room in Mathonwy Manor."

Mathonwy Manor. The den of snakes itself. I opened my mouth to protest, but Aidan beat me to it. "Keira isn't stepping foot in that place," he snarled at Reese, his usual calm completely evaporating.

"Keira can speak for herself. Er, myself, thank you." I placed a hand on my uncle's arm and gave him a reproachful look. He glanced back, and then to Connor, who had clearly taken note of the sudden aggression. He adjusted his coat as I quickly moved my focus from him, turning back to the swaying Esme. "Madame Esme, this is so kind. But it is too much."

"Well, it's already being custom-built." She shrugged. "So I can't take it back. Ye both will have to accept it."

"Then we will stay with my family until it's ready," Ronan insisted, placing a possessive hand on my shoulder.

"Not. Happening." I shrugged his repulsive grip off, Connor Yorath be damned.

Murmurs erupted from both sides. I felt the pressure in the room build once more, like a storm over the sea, the whispers carrying like a cold wind. *Hadn't these terms been agreed on before the marriage?... She took his name, and now she's got to jump ship completely?... Does she think she's too good fer us, eh?... This is a sham and a disgrace; if her father could see her now...*

The unease and mistrust of the last four years swirled and bubbled up in the tavern walls, threatening to wash the delicate peace away.

"Enough," Councilman Yorath commanded with quiet impatience, his voice cutting through the tension like an arrow. All fell silent. "If you all would listen instead of gabbing...the Council and I already have a plan for the newlyweds."

"Party is over," Esme giggled, the slur of her speech gone. "Pack yer things. I'm takin' ye to the spring."

Springs and Small Victories

Every sailor in Porthladd knew the traditions of a wedding night. I'd heard the men in my crew brag about it time and time again, shamelessly boasting about the dirty details when they thought I wasn't listening, so I knew what to prepare myself for: a trip to the spring to consummate the marriage before Lyr. One night and one day after, nothing more.

But as Ronan and I followed Esme up *Dubryn* Hill in the quiet darkness of early morning, I had no idea what to expect from the old hag and the snake. A net of fish flopped around violently in my stomach.

Esme stopped short in front of me and I almost collided with her. "Here we are!"

I paled as I took in the sight before me. The *Dubryn* Spring. Porthladd's most sacred space.

The hot spring itself was a sight to behold—not very large, barely bigger than a ship deck, but clear as a mirror. Strange white willow trees blanketed the bank, their ghostly pale branches kissing the surface of the turquoise water. On the far end, a delicate waterfall cascaded over the ash-colored rocks, the mist rising in elegant tendrils from its base, illuminated in the pre-dawn glow.

My breath caught in my chest.

It's why our people stayed after so many centuries of wandering the sea. Why exile was never an option for us. Why I'd rather marry the man I hated most than see my people barred from this land. One look at the spring and any man or woman with eyes knew it was Lyr-blessed. Some said the water brought luck, others even claimed it could heal sickness. And the Branwens had lived beside it for five generations, Lyr blessing us for it.

I didn't know if it was magic, but it certainly was breathtaking.

"Beautiful, isn't it?" Ronan's silky voice was reverent as he took it in. "Makes it all...real."

I nodded. An ease settled over me as I stared at the water; it felt as familiar as coming home and as foreign as discovering something new at the same time.

"Welp, I'm off!" Esme announced, shattering the quiet magic of the moment. "I'll come and collect ye in two weeks!"

The fish in my gut flopped again. "Two weeks? Esme, the tradition is only one night..." I protested, but her wrinkled finger on my lips silenced me.

"Ah-ah, no complaints. Ye two aren't exactly traditional, aye? I need two weeks to finish the house, so that's how long ye will be stayin' here! It's not like anyone else needs it right now. The Council doesn't have any other weddings planned fer months."

"Where are we supposed to sleep?" Ronan shoved a hand in his pocket, surveying the space with apparent displeasure.

"Yer sailors." Esme flicked him once on the forehead. "Ye can't mean to tell me a little bit of fresh air is gonna bother ye? Besides, there is a shack behind them trees. Ye can bunk in there if the weather gets rough. Yer things are already inside."

He rubbed his forehead but didn't protest further.

I squinted toward the place where she gestured. Sure enough, the outline of a building was just coming into focus in the dim light of dawn.

A very small building indeed.

"I don't know what you're playing at," I dared to snarl at Esme. The anger from the last day steamed up within me, mimicking the hot water of the spring. It made no sense why the Council would want us to stay on the holy land, to risk the wrath of Lyr himself. What were they hiding?

Esme did not balk. "Two weeks." Her eyes snapped toward me, violet pooling scarlet once more, sending a shiver down my spine. "That's final. Ye both can go into town during the day fer supplies or whatever ye may need, but ye sleep and stay here. Am I making myself clear?"

She took a step toward me, and for the first time in my life, I saw for myself what everyone was so afraid of. Esme was about my height, but in that moment, with the red of her eyes burning into me, she looked as if she could squash me under her boot without a second thought.

But I was a Branwen. And Branwens didn't back down.

I squared my feet and rolled my shoulders back. I could listen to her rules for my family's sake, but I would not be playing the Council's game. "Crystal clear."

"Good. The Council will be watching to make sure." Esme appraised me a moment longer, then cracked a smirk. "Well, congratulations, dearies, enjoy yer stay!" She patted my head, the shift in her tone disarming. Without a moment to let me recuperate, she spun on her heel and started down the hill.

"Esme, wait!" I moved to follow her, but a strong hand clasped my arm. I yanked at it, but Ronan slipped in front of me, blocking my path.

My stomach flipped again at his proximity. I shoved his chest to push him back, and he stumbled, grunting as he fell. Without hesitation, I jumped at the opportunity, hurdling over him and breaking into a run.

I was still in the damned dress, so my movements were jerky and uneven under the constraints of the pinching bodice. I was glad I had switched my heels for my boots before the climb. My feet were unsure and clumsy as I barreled down the rocky terrain.

I scanned the hill for Esme but could not find a trace of her having been there at all. *Lyr below, how far could the old woman have gotten?*

"You know it doesn't matter how long we stay here, right?" Ronan called after me, his voice dripping with honeyed condescension.

The words stopped me in my tracks.

I did not turn when his heavy footfalls approached, but I didn't run again, either. He stopped next to me and sighed, his hands in his pockets like they always were when he was thinking. "Two weeks...whether it's here, a house, or a ship...we are *married*, Keira. We said our vows. You are my *wife*. That's for this life and the Otherworld beyond. You can't run from it."

His words hit me like arrows through the chest.

He was right. I had made my choice, for my family, and I had to live with it. Branwens did not abandon their vows, no matter how bleak the consequences. I could not run back to Esme, or to my Uncle's, or even to the *Ceffyl*.

My life belonged to Ronan Mathonwy now.

"You're right." The words tasted like shite on my tongue. "I am your wife." I turned to him, purposefully meeting his eyes for the first time that night. They sparkled, brighter than the sapphire-encrusted hilt of my most treasured dagger. A younger, more naive version of myself recalled the luxury of getting lost in them. But I knew better now, and I'd had enough fool's gold to last a lifetime.

"But I am not going to make life easy for you." I kept my voice flat but firm. "You will pay for what you have done, I will make sure of it. And you will spend the rest of your life wishing I had killed you instead."

Ronan only wore his devil's smile. "If I wanted an easy life, I would've stayed on the island and married a nice, quiet girl who didn't hit as hard as you do."

I rolled my eyes and lifted my skirt as I trekked back up the hill. "I'll do more than hit you," I mumbled under my breath as my boots crunched underneath me. I refused to let his insult disarm me.

"If that's what you're into," he purred as he followed.

"Shut your mouth," I snapped, ignoring the red heat that rose to my cheeks, "and leave me alone."

Ronan shrugged but did not speak further as we crested the side of the hill to the mouth of the spring once more.

For one glorious moment, the only other sound was the trickle of the waterfall as it fed into the spring. Staring at it, I realized I had absolutely no idea what to do next.

Small victories, Keira. The memory of my father's voice tickled the back of my mind. *What do you want first, and how can you get it?*

I closed my eyes and rubbed the bridge of my nose. What I wanted was to get out of the ridiculous dress, but I had no idea how to undo the laces. Asking Ronan for help was absolutely out of the question.

Damned Esme.

I glanced over to the shack on the far side of the spring. The shoddy wooden walls were gaining definition in the rising light. She had said my things were in there, right? If I could lose Ronan for a few moments, I could cut myself out of this thing and put on something practical for the crisp chill of the morning. I folded my arms over myself as I considered my limited options.

"Never thought I'd live to see the day Keira Branwen was nervous." Ronan stepped toward the shack as if I had accidentally spoken out loud.

"I'm not nervous." I crossed my arms tighter for emphasis. "I'm chilly."

"I'd offer you my coat, but red isn't your color and it would only make you more nervous." His chuckle was laced with mischief. "Remember, I know you, Keira."

"You knew me once. You don't know me anymore. I am not the same naive little girl." I stormed toward the edge of the spring, half to reap the benefits of its heat, half to create some necessary distance.

Ronan did not pick up on the subtlety.

"You were never just a little girl." He followed, stepping close enough to the spring to kick a small pebble into it. "Little sea monster, maybe…"

"You sound like you *want* me to drown you."

"Aye, again, you mean?" He pressed closer, grace and power in every step.

"It was the storm that finally sank your ship, not my cannons." I rolled my eyes. This was ridiculous. I was an utter fool for letting this banter continue for so long. I just needed him to walk away so I could go change in peace. "And you didn't drown, or you wouldn't be here, and it would be quiet."

"Aye, it was the storm." He was close enough now that I could feel the heat of him at my back. "But you and I both know that wasn't a coincidence. Isn't that right, Mrs. Mathonwy?"

I couldn't help the shudder that ran down my spine. I convinced myself it was from the chill in the air. "You deserved it."

Silence again as we stared at the spring. I shifted in the itchy material of the dress. I needed some damned pants.

"For the love of Lyr, Ronan." I broke the quiet, no longer caring if my desperation was apparent. "Please stay over here while I go get changed."

He looked me over once and raised an eyebrow. "Aye, I will." His eyes shifted toward the shack. "But the Council...well they are expecting us to—you know—consummate things eventually."

My stomach rolled. I knew he was right, knew what the Council expected of us, of me.

Two bloodlines made one.

They wanted an heir. But I'd be damned to let them have one so easily.

"They'll be very disappointed, then." I pulled the knife Vala had given me from the pocket of my skirt and pointed it at him. "Follow me, and you'll be without your manhood."

"Lyr below, Keira, does every sentence have to end with a threat?" Ronan shot back, anger rippling across his careful facade. The feral part of me was smug with accomplishment that I'd gotten under his skin, even for a second. It was a game we played as children, one I'd always won despite his bag of snake tricks and cons. He took a sharp breath through his nose and regained his composure. "I wasn't saying I was gonna...just, we'll need an excuse, that's all. I'd never stoop low enough to take a woman when she doesn't want me."

"No." I poked again at his exposed underbelly. "You kill their fathers and force them to marry you."

Ronan sighed with frustration, running a hand through his hair. The swarthy mask he usually wore was completely gone, his expression raw. "I didn't kill him, Keira." He stared at the ground, his voice soft. "You knew how I felt about you—I could never—"

Blazing anger flashed through my core as his words ripped my softest parts. "I don't want to talk about this." I sheathed my knife and turned to head to the shack. If he followed, it would be his own funeral.

"You can't keep running away. Please, listen to me." He reached for my hand, desperation in his gaze. I jerked it out of his reach.

"Ronan." I hurled his name at him like a dagger. "You were standing over his body with his blood on your shirt. I *watched* you pull the knife from his neck."

"I found him like that, I swear! He was already dead. I pulled the knife out to try and see whose it was." He grabbed me by the shoulders, his long fingers digging in. His stare was penetrating, pleading as he continued, "Keira, I swear to Lyr, I didn't do this."

I shoved him. Hard.

I had watched him lie all our lives. Had watched him steal thousands of gold pieces from entire crowds of people with that same begging stare. He could charm a man out of his house in under a minute and swindle his last pair of shoes from his feet with a smile. It was a part of his con, the innocence, the charm, and he played it well. Too well. I had fallen for it before.

Not again.

"Get out of my face," I spat, watching my venom strike him. Hurt flashed in his eyes, but I pressed on, the anger reaching its boiling point inside me. "I do not care what you have to say. I am here for my family's sake. You mean nothing to me, and you never will. And I will spend the rest of this abysmal marriage waiting for you to rutting drop dead."

His control collapsed completely, and he twitched toward me, his face stopping only an inch from my own. "Fine. Don't believe me," he growled through gritted teeth. "Curse my name, threaten me, pray to Lyr that lightning strikes me dead right here and now. Whatever helps you sleep at night. But really think about it for one moment, Keira. What if I am telling the truth, hm? What if I didn't kill your father? Who are you going to spend all your time hating then?"

"Go," I commanded, my voice tight. "Or I'll end you. Contract be damned."

"And you say I'm the liar," he scoffed in my face and stepped back. "If you really wanted to kill me, I know I'd already be dead. Part of you knows you're wrong, and you're scared of it."

I said nothing, only stared with every ounce of hatred and anger I had spent four years saving for him.

"I didn't kill Cedric." Surprising tears lined his eyes. A new tactic for his act. "But someone else did, Keira." He turned on his heel and stalked toward the forest, the last words hanging over my head like an executioner's ax.

I kicked the nearest stone as tears streamed down my face. It had been too long since I let myself really cry. Too many years of bottling up the pain and grief my father left in his absence, mourning the life that Ronan had taken from him, and now from me. With a contract, not a sword, Ronan had killed the last part of me that was mine. And like a true snake, he had used lovely words and fake tears to try and trick me into believing it was someone else's fangs in my jugular.

The tears came now with full abandon. Sobs wracked through me, and I fell to the ground, savoring the sharp pain of the stone under my knees. I let myself cry and cry until my salty tears mixed with the sweet water of the spring at my feet. I didn't know where its thin outlet went. But I imagined the gentle current carrying my tears—each a prayer of their own—all the way to the ocean, and then to Lyr himself.

There had been many times since my father died that I longed for his calm, sturdy arms around me or the tickle of his beard against my cheek. As dawn peeked over the treetops, I realized I would give the entire world for one more moment with him. He would've known how to make this mess right.

I clutched the shallow pocket at my side where Papa's compass was now neatly tucked away under the layers of silk. Taking a shuddering breath between sobs, I pulled it out. The sunlight caught the corners of the bronze, and I had to squint to watch the little arrow spin around its axis without direction.

It had been broken since before I was born, and I assumed long before that, too. But it didn't matter. It had brought Papa luck. He even said it brought him to my mother.

I kissed the faded inscription.

All that are lost shall be found.

Unraveling the long chain, I pulled it over my neck like a necklace and dragged myself back to my feet.

I was lost, swimming in the middle of the ocean with nothing to hold on to, but I would not let myself drown. I was a Branwen, but more importantly, I was my father's daughter. I would not lose myself to anyone. Wiping my eyes, I put my tears and self-pity behind me and headed toward the shack.

Small victories. First, I would get bloody changed. Then I'd fix the shambles of my life.

As the shack came into sharper focus, I realized that was a generous word for it. It was remarkably tiny, and the roof needed serious rethatching. I pushed the rotted wooden door open and it nearly fell off its hinges. Maybe I would fix this place while I was here. If I could fix this, I could fix my own mess, too.

The inside was not much nicer. Light peered through cracks in the walls, revealing only the one room with a single straw bed in the far corner and a stove and counter in the opposite. The bed had fresh linens, but the posts looked gnarled and about ready to collapse. The single pot on the rusted stovetop did not look promising either.

Next to the door were two bags, one made of simple tan canvas, the other an opulent velvet material.

I kicked Ronan's as I grabbed the familiar canvas bag and carried it to the bed, untied the leather laces at the top, and blindly grabbed at the materials inside, tossing things haphazardly onto the linens. The pair of black cotton trousers I was looking for were of course at the very bottom. I matched them with a warm, fur-lined tunic I had gotten from Pysgodd on our last trip there.

Drawing my knife from my boot, I sawed at the bodice of the dress until I could rip it. The material was stiff, but after some persuasion, it gave, and I finally unleashed my ribs to their natural size.

I dressed quickly, glad to be in my normal clothes again, and shoved the rest of my belongings back into my sack.

A small piece of paper drifted to the floor, falling out of a garment pocket. I picked it up, squinting to read the familiar chicken-scratch in the dim light.

Keira girl,

I'd say this bag has everything ye need, but Esme didn't exactly give me much time, so I can't promise it. But I hope it's missing something important, so you'll have to come home to get it soon.

*You might be Mathonwy by law, but not by blood,
and that's what counts. Ye'll always be the pride and joy
of the Branwens. Do us proud, girl.*

-Aidan.

I read it over three more times, the tiny piece of my family enough to remind me what I had gained today.

I'd saved my family. Tomorrow, they could sail on the *Ceffyl* without the weight of extra cannons, testing her full speed in open water. Soon, we'd find a way to be together on her deck, her glorious white sails at full mast, not a care in the world as we sailed forth.

I could be happy the rest of my life knowing that alone. And I had been a selfish sea-witch to give a rat's ass what my last name was. I'd find a way to deal with my husband so my family would never have to.

"I'm a Mathonwy by law," I repeated to myself, "but not by blood."

That's what counts.

I dropped the letter and gasped as realization dawned on me.

Clever, clever man Aidan was, whether he had meant to be or not. He had delivered me my vengeance in a letter and shown me the way to fix this mess.

Last night, I was Keira Branwen. I had signed a contract that protected my family, but also bound their hands from spilling even a single drop of Mathonwy blood.

But today, by law, I was Keira Mathonwy. And there was nothing in my contract that said a Mathonwy couldn't spill Mathonwy blood.

I shoved the letter deep within the bag. I doubted Aidan had intended to spark the idea, but I didn't want him implicated either way. I'd burn it later.

My thoughts swirled with frenzied excitement. I sat on the bed, the dry straw sinking underneath me as I contemplated the downsides of committing mariticide.

The contract would stand. I had done my part and married him, and we both signed. The wording was clear...if I killed Ronan,

I would not be violating the contract. The Mathonwys couldn't retaliate against me or my family without being kicked out of Porthladd for good. They would try, of course, but it would force the Council's hand.

A Porthladd free of Mathonwys.

And if I could kill Ronan, he could kill me, too. I'd be foolish to assume he wouldn't take the opportunity once he put the pieces together, if he hadn't already.

The Council would not be happy with me, and I knew I'd still pay the price for murder. Exile would be preferable, but there were worse sentences, and I'm sure the Council wouldn't go easy. I'd probably spend the rest of my days in a dark cell, far from my family and the salt of the sea. Or at the end of a rope in the middle of the town square.

But my family would be truly safe. Even if I was clamped in irons for the rest of my life or sent packing to the Otherworld, my heart would be free. I'd be trading one prison for another, but I would be free in the ways that mattered. Ronan Mathonwy's cobra-hold on me would be broken.

My father's killer would be brought to true justice at last. No compromises or backward power grabs, only the god of the Otherworld and his judgment.

Could I really kill him?

I had killed before. Sinking ships came with casualties, and my gift had made me quite good at it. I'd used my sword to defend and wound plenty of times, so the blood would not bother me.

But I had never watched a man's life drain from his eyes as my knife slid across his throat.

The macabre image of my father's limp corpse flashed through my mind, as it had time and time again in my nightmares.

I swallowed hard. Yes. Yes, I could.

Before I could change my mind or talk myself out of it, I leaped from the bed and grabbed Vala's dagger. It was the only weapon I had, but it would be a poetic end to this bloody saga. This all started with a small dagger and a slit throat. It would end the same way.

As I pushed open the door with my dagger at my side, I heard the faint, distant whisper of a voice that had guided me all my life.

No.

The single word reverberated in the back of my skull, laced with ancient rage and wisdom. I clutched the compass still dangling from my neck.

For the first time in my life, I answered back. "Yes. This time, I'm the Captain."

I stepped through the threshold to find and kill my husband.

4

Daggers and Divorce

I found him asleep under a willow tree a few dozen paces west of the spring. He looked so young, propped up against the rough white bark, his hair falling in his eyes like the branches of the tree.

Such a lovely face for a snake.

I pushed back the white leafy curtain as quietly as possible, watching my step to avoid the foliage on the ground. His chest rose and fell in an unconcerned rhythm, unaware of the danger that lurked near. I stepped closer, quieting my own breath, and waited for a few moments to make sure he would not wake.

He had always been a heavy sleeper. When we were kids, Pa used to say he could sleep on a dingy during high tide in a thunderstorm. Pa also warned him it would get him in trouble one day.

I was about to fulfill that prophecy.

I crouched down so I was level with his face. I had loved this face; the smooth planes of his cheeks, the hard line of his jaw, the tiny bump on his sharp nose from when he broke it when we were eight. This face had been the closest thing I had to a home, once.

But he had taken my true home from me.

Now he had taken my name, too. I had crossed over the threshold of no return when I signed it to that bloody contract.

Esme had been right. The contract would bring peace at last to the island. It had sealed my fate, consigning me to live the rest of my days as Ronan Mathonwy's wife. But it also would protect my family from Mathonwy vengeance. And it had given me the gift of finally fulfilling mine.

I drew my knife. This time, I would not fail. I sucked in a steadying breath. My dagger aimed straight at Ronan's throat, I lunged.

A voice screamed inside my head, filled with an otherworldly rage.

No!

And as the air around me exploded, I was met with blackness.

I was twelve again.

I was on the Ceffyl's deck, my first silver cutlass in my hand. Sweat dripped from my brow, the hot sun beating down on the back of both our necks, scrutinizing us from its lofty perch.

Papa patted Ronan on the head and threw him a dry scrap of cloth. "Good work, boy. Go take a rest."

Ronan beamed a toothy grin. "Aye, Cedric."

"Captain Cedric to you. When yer on my ship, ye show respect, boy." Pa flicked him on the forehead, which was only as high as his shoulder. Pa turned to me and readied his dulled sword. "Keira, keep that little knife of yers in front of ye and square off."

I did as I was told and tried my best to keep my exhaustion from my expression.

Pa lunged.

I dodged his first blow, but I wasn't quick enough to parry the second. The tip of his cutlass poked at my side. I winced and cursed under my breath.

"Eyes open, Keira, you can do it!" Ronan shouted from the side, his long blond hair slicked back with sweat.

I clenched my fists. I would not let Pa's new deckhand outpace me. "Aye, I'm trying," I said through gritted teeth, and swung for Pa's chest.

He swatted away my attack with a quick parry, and with an effortless turn, stepped in and shoved my chest with the back of his elbow.

I fell straight on my bum.

"Not hard enough." He ruffled my hair. *"But better, Keira girl. We'll work again tomorrow."* He turned to walk across the deck. *"Ronan, get her some ice."*

Shame and rage flooded my cheeks when Ronan offered me a pity-dripped smile. I would not be bested. Not on my own father's ship, and certainly not in front of such a smug visitor.

I jumped up and rushed Papa, my cutlass at the ready. He spun around and grabbed my wrist, twisting in one fluid motion until I dropped my sword.

"Ye listen to me, Keira," he snarled in my face in a rare show of aggression. My breath caught in my chest. *"Ye never strike a man when his back is turned."*

He dropped my hand and shook his head, rawness in his eyes. I rubbed the tender spot on my wrist and bit my cheek, embarrassed of the hot tears pooling in my own.

Pa sighed and massaged his temple, his expression soft again. *"I'm teaching ye both to fight to protect yerself and yer kin. But I refuse to teach ye if ye lose all sense of honor."*

Ronan looked down at his folded hands, his young brow furrowed with thought. *"And what if that man has no honor, Captain Cedric? What if he tries to stab us in the back?"*

Papa walked up to me and brushed a salty tear from my cheek. His eyes crinkled at the edges as he smiled. *"I'd rather die with honor than live with the shame of being a coward and a cheat."*

My stomach sank like an anchor had dropped straight down my gullet. *"I'm sorry, Papa."* My voice caught in my throat as I struggled to keep myself from sobbing. *"I'm sorry I'm not better."*

"Better? Keira girl, yer the best there is." Pa grabbed my shoulders with firm gentleness. His sunset eyes glistened with fresh tears of their own. *"Or you will be one day, that I can promise. But being the best isn't about winning at all costs. It's about having something worth fighting fer. Ye can't take the easy way out of things."*

I nodded with a sniffle. He wrapped me in a tight hug, and I buried my face in his chest. He smelled of salt and sweat, but I breathed it in anyway. *"I'll make you proud one day, Papa. I promise,"* I whispered under my breath.

He kissed the top of my head and released me. *"Now, square off, Keira girl. We go again."*

"Aye, Captain."

"Keira, wake up, please. *Keira.*" The velvet voice pulled me back to consciousness, strong hands shaking my shoulders.

I moaned as I came to. The back of my head throbbed, and my eyes fluttered open to see Ronan looming over me.

"Oh, thank Lyr," he sighed, the worry in his brow unraveling.

I cracked him once across the jaw with a right hook. He fell over, grasping his face. My knuckles stung, but I ignored them and sat up.

The world spun.

"Lyr's bollocks, what was that for?" Ronan cried.

I moved to find my feet beneath me, but the world surged again, and I barely managed to catch myself with my hands. My palms stung as my stomach rolled. "What did you do to me?" I snarled up at Ronan.

"What did *I* do?" He clutched the red mark on his jaw, staring incredulously at me. "I didn't do anything! I was napping, then *boom*, a sound louder than a cannon. I open my eyes and see you lying down with a knife in your hand, eyes rolled in the back of your head, having some sort of fit. Then you just stopped, and I thought you had bloody died! What the hell was that about, hm?"

I blinked twice, trying to process the information, and scanned the forest floor for my knife. Only a few paces to my left...

But I was much farther from the willow than I had been a minute before. At least twenty paces farther, for sure.

Ye can't take the easy way out.

I shook off the memory, my head still foggy. My chest ached as if I was the one who had just been punched. "I—I don't—I don't know, I was trying to—" I finally stammered, trying to find the pieces.

"Trying to what, give me a heart attack?" His voice grated on every exposed nerve.

"If only." He should be dead. I should've killed him. I was going to kill him.

Yet something had stopped me...had thrown me twenty paces, sent me into a fit...

Had he done it? Did he have his own dark gift that I didn't know about? I winced as I stood up finally, my ribs sore, but at least my head didn't spin again. I watched him carefully, planting my feet beneath me before whatever power he had could knock me off them again. He simply brushed off the grass stains on his pants, seemingly unaware of what was happening.

What I was trying to do.

Never strike a man when his back is turned.

Fine. Then I'd stand against him here, both of us facing our fates. I took a deep breath, one that seeped into the tiny, hidden place where my power slept. I wasn't going to kill him in his sleep, but that didn't mean I had to fight entirely fair. Lyr had given me my gift for a reason, after all.

I waited for the lightning buzz in my chest to start, for the familiar tingling in my hands. Then, for the storm clouds to roll in, dark and ominous, as the sea in my chest roared.

I waited. And waited. Standing there in the clearing with Ronan's eyes glued to me, riddled with confusion.

Yet the buzz never came, nor did the tingles, nor the storm cloud that would signal my sure victory. I breathed deeper, trying my best to summon any scrap of my gift.

Nothing.

I huffed out a heavy sigh. I must have hit my head hard. My power only faltered when my body was too tired to sustain it any longer.

Fine. We'd do this the old-fashioned way then, Lyr be damned. I took a readying step toward my knife.

My legs had other plans as I stumbled forward.

"Ah, here, let me help." Ronan caught my forearm, his expression clouded with worry again.

I slapped him across the face, the action sending a stinging wave of pain through my scraped palm.

"Will you stop that?" he groaned, holding the side of his face again. Hurt flashed through his expression, but not from the slap. "Lyr below Keira, I'm trying to help."

"I told you not to touch me." I was in no condition to fight, especially without my gifts, but I was not going to let him have the advantage, either—not until I knew how I ended up on my back.

"What was I supposed to do before, let you lay there and die?" he asked quietly, his hands at his sides now. He did not approach, his stance soft, and I couldn't read his next move. "I suppose I should let you stumble around now like a new sailor when you're clearly not well? Despite popular belief, I do have some sense of honor, Keira."

I'd rather die with honor than live with the shame of being a coward.

I waited a moment, gauging his stance, his proximity.

He wasn't going to hurt me. "Well, I'm fine," I lied.

I couldn't win in a one-on-one fight with him, not with a tiny knife and wobbly legs. Not when I didn't know what power he was hiding. When my own hid from me. My vengeance would have to wait.

Ronan stared, either unsure of what to do next or unsure of what I was going to do. I didn't have an answer to either, but I certainly didn't like this new concerned character he played.

"You can go now," I snapped.

He shoved his hands in his pockets. Uncertainty still sat in his expression. "Not to sound childish, but I was here first."

I tensed. Did he want me to retreat then? To give him a prime opportunity to stab me in the back?

Never strike a man when his back is turned.

Not that I'd put it past a cheat like Ronan. As if I was any better.

"Fine, I'll go, then." I reached down and grabbed my knife, focusing on not falling over as I wrapped my fingers around it. The metal hilt was cool beneath my grasp and steadied me as I turned to leave.

Let him try and come for me. I braced myself for impact as I walked away.

I was met instead with Ronan clearing his throat. "Why were you…" he hesitated, and I tensed again as I waited for him to make a move. His brow knit. "Were you looking for me? Before you…"

I tried not to look like I was searching for a lie when I responded. "I was looking for a place to piss." I couldn't let him know about the loophole, not until I could fight for it.

He stepped towards me, his familiar mask of smarmy confidence creeping back onto his face. "With your knife?"

I gripped the hilt of the blade tighter. "Aye. With my knife."

He watched me, curious, but did not pursue it further. I moved to go, still strangling my knife so hard my knuckles went white.

He fell into step beside me but shoved his hands in his pockets again, a tell that he was plotting something. "Where are you going now?"

"Spring."

"To piss?" He raised an eyebrow.

"No, to get away from you," I snarled. I was tired of this cycle, the endless game of cat and mouse. Every time I parried, he'd somehow dodge. When I fled, he followed. I picked up my pace, trying to put as much distance between us as possible. My good-for-nothing legs staggered in response.

"Keira, you shouldn't swim." His eyes narrowed with false worry as he registered my weakness, which only sent another wave of fury rolling through me. "You were just unconscious...what if it happens again?"

"It won't."

"But what if—"

"Ronan, enough with the act!" I spun on my heel to face him. He stopped short only inches from me, but I did not yield. I stepped closer, breathing him in, like Papa had taught me: *Think tall, and you'll be tall.* "You listen to me. You're even more of a fool than I thought if you believe I'm buying any of this mockery for a second. I don't know how you threw me before, or what you're playing at right now, but I see you. I see what you are, Ronan. Rotten to the core. And your snake smile and well-practiced manners will not trick me into taking a bite."

Ronan's mouth flattened into a tight line. His throat bobbed once. Twice. I did not step back.

"I see," he finally spoke, defeat registering in his eyes.

Something primal in my chest roared with victory. I hadn't killed him tonight, but it seemed that I had injured a crucial part of his ego.

Think tall, and you'll be tall.

I plastered on a sickeningly-sweet smile, one I had learned from mirroring him so many years ago. "Now, be a dear, and stop following me."

"I would've followed you to the Otherworld," he muttered under his breath, hands deep in his pockets. He looked up, his face now laced with a well-honed sadness. "But I suppose you're right. I am a fool."

Without another word, he walked toward the shack. He did not look back.

And neither did I.

It was a full day before I spoke to Ronan again. Even then, the only words I spoke were "Get" and "Out" when I needed the shack to change my clothes.

I decided I wasn't going to murder him. Not while I had no clue what had stopped me. Papa always said half the trick of surviving was knowing when you were outmatched. I'd have to find some way to expose his weakness first, and then I'd make my play.

Until then, finding ways to avoid Ronan required creativity.

I knew I had not been here long enough to make the trek back into town without raising the Council's eyebrows. So I stayed, keeping myself as scarce as possible to put off seeing him. I slept on the mossy bank of the spring, still too wary to take a swim, but I was more comfortable than I thought I'd be. My sleep was deep, despite the nerves in my gut, my body finally giving in to its most basic need. I kept my knife tucked beneath me, though, ready for anyone who dared deprive me of a restful sleep.

When I woke after a few stolen hours, the majestic white willows provided ample coverage when I needed to see to my...less-majestic needs. And when my stomach growled hour later, the forest provided plenty of things to hunt.

Hunting also supplied a nice distraction from my current mess. I didn't need to think about what the Council wanted of me, or what my family needed, or what Ronan was plotting in the shack. All I had to think about was setting my traps and listening to the murmurings of the white woods.

Papa had taken me hunting in Pysgodd on my very first voyage there. The Pysgoddian evergreen forests that lined the silver mountains were some of the most beautiful in all the world. Fertile, too, despite the bitter cold. I remembered Papa teaching me how to draw a bow, how the whisper of the wood was so different from the song of the sea. How the first mighty stag fell as my arrow pierced his eye.

It was quite different hunting for rabbits in the thicket and underbrush of the *Dubryn* Forest, but I felt my father's guiding hand just the same. Finally, after a few quiet hours, I nabbed a small rabbit. Its white fur was impossible to see against the white bark of the trees, but I had set my trap well.

I skinned the poor beast and saved the pelt for Vala. She'd make lovely gloves from it, just in time for the winter cold. The stark white would pair nicely with her chestnut hair.

I knew cooking the meat on the stove in the shack would be more efficient, but I set up a small fire instead. I was more stubborn than I was hungry. It took time, but soon the rabbit was ready to eat. It was nothing like the mouthwatering version Saeth made, dipped in all sorts of spices from the Southern Isles, but it filled my belly just the same, even leaving me with extra.

I didn't bother asking if Ronan had eaten, because I didn't care if he starved.

But a small part of me wished I had someone to share my meal with. On the ship, even when rations were sparse, we all broke whatever bread we had together. Griffin would crack a filthy joke, and we'd all laugh as we drained our cups of mead, hoping it would fill the spots in our bellies that the bland gruel and biscuits missed.

Even when I had to stay on land with Vala and Saeth to learn my lessons or get fitted for clothes, the three of us would share quiet meals together. We were near silent, but never uncomfortable. Sometimes, Cousin Finna would join us and talk all about the boys—*plural*— she was courting in town. On those nights, we didn't dare to speak above a whisper or risk the wrath of Vala and her wooden spoon, but even I was pulled in by Finna's tales of conquest.

Now the silence of the forest was deafening. I only had the babble of the spring for company, and I wasn't quite sure I wanted to know what tales it was whispering.

I wondered how many years of my life would be marked by silent meals eaten alone now. How many of Griffin's jokes I'd miss. How many of Vala's quiet lectures I'd crave. How many of Finna's whispered tales I'd ache for.

My musings on solitude became secondary when the rain came. It was only a drizzle at first, but soon dark clouds rolled in, their thunder roaring.

At least it was no longer silent.

But the rain was cold, the water carried right from the Northern Sea. It soaked through to my bones, the canopy of trees no longer enough to provide shelter. I looked at the shack in the distance, its thatched roof and the swirling pillar of smoke coming from the chimney. I crossed my freezing hands across my chest and suppressed a shudder.

I wasn't that easily swayed. For Lyr's sake, I was a sailor, and a little rain didn't bother me. Instead, I found the willow with the thickest branches and huddled underneath.

After another hour of rain coming in sideways, the wind blew so fiercely it stripped entire branches off my makeshift home. I knew I'd be a fool not to seek proper shelter.

I gritted my teeth at the rain. "Lyr damn you."

A dark chuckle in the back of my mind was the only response.

Clenching my fists, I walked to the shack and opened the door without knocking. The pitiful wood of the front door moved without much force, slamming into the inside of the cabin. The shack wasn't completely waterproof, and there were little leaks in the roof, raindrops pinging into the metal of mismatched pots across the floor. But at least it was warm, the fire inviting. I slammed the door behind me again, throwing my weight against it to contend with the wind.

Ronan was sprawled across the straw bed, his long legs dangling off the end, but he woke with a start at the noise.

"Leave, now," I growled, my hand fluttering to the knife at my hip.

He rubbed his eyes and blinked in the low light of the fire, his face still veiled with sleep. When his eyes cleared, he took in my dripping wet form. "Good to see you home, Mrs. Mathonwy." He smiled crookedly and leaned back on his elbows.

"I said leave."

He frowned. "But it's pouring out."

"I'm aware, now leave." I gripped my knife tighter.

Ronan leaned forward, his hands on his knees. He winked, his eyes sparkling with mischief in the firelight. "Make me."

Slimy cad.

I pulled my knife from my hip and widened my stance "Fine, I will."

Ronan threw his head back and laughed, a cruel, dry sound. "No, you won't, because you're tired and sore and soaking wet and cold enough that your teeth are chattering. Which means you know you'd lose to my well-rested, well-fed, well-insulated self." He pushed himself up from the bed, taking two long steps toward me. He looked down, his body heat radiating off him. I bared my teeth, but he only smirked in response. "Plus, you still think I had something to do with your fit the other day, which means you think I'm dangerous."

My anger swirled in my chest, mimicking the storm outside, but I didn't let my suspicion show. I pressed the point of my knife to his chest and looked up, mustering my deadliest look. "Don't flatter yourself."

"Well by all means, if you'd prefer the position, I'm delighted to step down." He pressed closer, right into my knife. The tip of my blade created a small, red mark on his white shirt as it pierced the topmost layer of skin. He winced, but smiled through it, calling my bluff. "Either way, I'm not about to walk into the eye of the storm out there. And I know your survival instincts are louder than your stubbornness, so you won't, either. We'll just have to share, Keira girl."

Keira girl.

He was rubbing salt in an open wound, one he had ripped open in the first place. I pressed my blade further into his chest. "Do not call me that."

Ronan only grimaced wider against the pain. "Do you prefer Mrs. Mathonwy?"

The last tether that had been holding me to my wits snapped. I dropped the knife and shoved against him, hard. His eyes widened, but he did not raise his hands in defense.

"I'd prefer you keep your rutting mouth shut!" I shouted and shoved him again. He teetered back, and I banged my fist against his chest. Tears pooled in my eyes, betraying me, but I did not let up, and he did not stop me as I hit him once more; only let me rage against him, flinging both my fists and my words at him. "Does it feel good to kick me while I'm down? To torture me with your incessant teasing, because even now, I can't escape you? Because even I can't stop the rutting rain? Well, congratulations, Ronan, you've done it! You killed my father, you stole the rest of my life from me, you took my *name* for Lyr's sake, and now you have me right where you want me." I stopped hitting him, my hands red with his blood and throbbing with pain. Angry crimson welts appeared on his chest, and his bleeding had quickened. Yet he only watched me, waiting, as the tears streamed freely down my face. My voice was small and pathetic when I spoke again, my quivering underbelly fully exposed now. "So do me a favor, stop playing with your food, and show me some rutting mercy. End me now. Or if you won't, shut your foul mouth and keep it shut."

My breath came ragged and raw, and my tears flowed as readily as the rain battering the shack.

Ronan only stared, his gaze a strange mix of awe and sadness I couldn't quite comprehend.

"Yell some more," he finally said.

"What?"

"Go ahead, let it all out." He took a tentative step back, his hands still at his sides despite the blood dripping down his front. "Tell me I'm rotten and foul, call me a snake, anything. Blame me for it all. If it makes it easier, I won't even fight back, I'll keep my witty comments to myself. Anything beats the silence, Keira. I can't do a lifetime of silence."

I took a breath, waiting for the anger to come again, waiting to unleash my fury once more.

But the anger didn't come.

Nothing did.

I was empty. Whatever had snapped in me had unleashed my repressed rage, leaving me only with the space it has once taken. "You're not worth my breath," I managed to say, but it was an empty insult, and I watched as it glanced off of him.

"No, I'm not." There wasn't a tinge of sarcasm in his voice. His expression remained open, honest. "But this doesn't work if we don't talk."

"I don't want it to work," I admitted, surprising myself as the words tumbled out of me. "I want it to end."

I leaned against the bare wall, watching him stare at the floor. It was strange to be so candid with him, and I knew I was playing right into his trap, but I didn't care anymore.

The salt in my blood was gone. Any fight I had mustered up in the heat of the last few days was spent. And he kept catching me off guard, getting under my walls like no one else ever could. It was infuriating to know that my greatest enemy knew my weakest points. Yet there was something freeing about the honesty of it all. I saw Ronan for the snake and the liar he was, and he saw me for the sniveling, broken coward I was.

Maybe we were a well-suited match after all.

"No, you don't want it to work," he sighed and found a seat on the bed again. He looked as tired and hopeless as I felt, but he continued, wringing his hands as he spoke, "But you do want to make things right for your family and with the Council. That doesn't happen either if we don't talk. So let's talk, Keira. Let's make this work for our families."

My family. A glimmer of sadness echoed through the emptiness as I thought of them. I knew he was right, too. If I didn't make this marriage work at least on a surface level, my only other option to keep them safe was to kill him. And I had tried that and failed already, which meant I was running out of options.

I couldn't kill him and I couldn't avoid him forever. I couldn't even manage to stay angry for more than two days.

So I'd play. Because that was all I had left to do, or perhaps because a part of me wanted to because it was better than feeling empty. I didn't know. I didn't care.

"And what's in it for you?" I mused, donning my familiar mask. It felt shallow, but his eyes flicked up anyway. "I'm supposed to believe your good intentions and trust that you want nothing out of it?"

"My family is depending on me, too."

"I wasn't born yesterday, Ronan." I fetched my knife from where it had clattered to the floor earlier and flipped it in my hand, an action I had practiced a thousand times. It felt foreign now without my fire behind it, but I persisted. "You weren't thinking about your family when you were hiding on some island for four years. You came back to get even with me. And now you want something."

He studied me, the mischief coupled with surprise in his eyes. "You help me find your father's real killer. That's what's in it for me."

My mouth fell open, genuine shock rocking me from my sticking place. "You're taking a piss."

"I'm serious, Keira." He stood, hands in his pockets once more. The cut on his chest had stopped bleeding, and the color had returned to his face. "Help me find the prick that set me up. That's my price. Help me find your father's killer, and I'll be nice. I won't tease you, I won't bother you outside of the investigation, and I won't demand anything else of you in the meantime. You'll be free to go and spend time with your family. If the Council asks any questions, I will vouch for our healthy and happy marriage. I'll even suggest that they lift the tariffs."

A small spark of fury ignited in me again at the audacity of him. "I don't make deals with snakes," I snapped, and it almost felt genuine.

"No, you marry them." He plastered on his viper's smile, and my blood heated once more. "It's not a bad deal, Keira. We both get what we want."

Small victories, Keira. What do you want first, and how can you get it?
What did I want?

"I want more," I whispered to myself, but Ronan didn't miss a beat.

"Fine, name your terms."

I thought for a moment and then another. I wanted to turn back time to before my father died, before things had gotten so dark and complicated. I wanted my family, whole and happy and wealthy. Together. I wanted to feel like myself. Or to find myself, maybe, because I wasn't so sure who I was anymore.

And I wanted to be free of Ronan, for good this time, whether by death or some other miracle.

I couldn't have any of that. But there was something I could get if I played my cards right. "I want a divorce."

Ronan's eyebrows shot up in disbelief. "Keira, the Council—"

"I said I want a divorce." I cut him off, a new feeling swirling in my chest. It wasn't rage, or defeat, or emptiness. Determination. I was determined, and maybe even hopeful, too, as the plan formed on the tip of my tongue. As a new ending to this story emerged before my eyes. "I'll play your game. I'll let you try to lie your way out of things. I'll even smile pretty and pretend I don't feel sick every time I look at you. But at the end, whether you prove your supposed innocence or I find more evidence that you're the vile shitestain I know you are, you divorce me. You tell the Council that you want out of the deal. That it's your own fault, but you'll still uphold the peace agreement with your family. And you will. Because if you don't, I'll kill every last one of you, damn the rest of it all to the Otherworld. Deal?"

Worst case scenario, I'd find nothing, and he'd find some way to screw me over even further.

Best case scenario, I'd find something that would give me leverage. Maybe even secure my freedom and my family's safety along the way.

Ronan looked me over for a moment, calculating, a war waging in his eyes as he weighed the same stakes. Finally, he spoke, and for the first time since I'd seen him, I didn't feel like cursing his name.

"Fine." He grimaced. "You have yourself a deal."

5

Contracts and Companions

I had been genuinely in over my head twice in my short life.

The first time was when I was thirteen, Griffin sixteen. We snuck off the island in the middle of the night to see if we could sail the *Ceffyl* ourselves and nearly ran her into the shallows.

And second, when I was sixteen. Ronan and I decided to run a secret gambling den in the attic of Aidan's house during Finna's twenty-first birthday celebration with most of Porthladd, including the Council, downstairs.

Now, as I watched Ronan draft a second contract, one that detailed our new bargain, I knew I was about to add to that list.

He sat at the rickety table in the shack, leaning over the scrap of parchment he found 'just laying in his rucksack'. His sleeves were pushed up to his elbows as he dipped his quill in black ink, emphasizing the corded muscles of his forearms. I ignored how my pulse quickened. He made a show of the writing, his hand gliding over the page with deft precision. It was too precise, in fact. *Too planned.*

What in Lyr's name was I rutting doing?

When he finished, he pushed his golden hair back, a small streak of black ink marking his forehead. "Well, sign here, and so it begins, Mrs. Mathonwy." He pointed to the small line next to his name, a smile creeping across his face.

"I'm reading it first," I protested and snatched the newly-inked paper from his hands. I read it three times. At its face, unlike the last contract, it seemed devoid of any loopholes. But I didn't trust that Ronan hadn't given himself a backdoor out of this.

Yet the writing was clear. I read it aloud: "I hereby declare that in exchange for her help investigating the murder of Cedric M. Branwen, I, Ronan F. Mathonwy, will divorce Keira L. Branwen at the conclusion of the investigation and claim full responsibility for the severance. Additionally, the terms of our previous marital contract will stand even past severance, as we did technically marry and it did not specify that we had to *stay* married. The Branwen and Mathonwy clans will, therefore, remain peaceful evermore and will suffer the consequences delineated by the marriage contract if that peace should be broken. The investigation will conclude when significant evidence is found, or after one year if no evidence is found."

"Pretty good, right?"

"One month. A year is too long." I shoved the paper back in his face.

His eyebrows flew up in shock. "A month? That's not enough time to properly—"

"It just says significant evidence," I interrupted. "If we can't find any evidence in a month, there probably isn't any, and why should we drag things out longer than we need to?"

"Fine," he growled, scratching out the word *year* and writing *month* on top of it. He handed it back to me, batting his eyelashes with sarcasm. "Is it to your liking now, *your highness?*"

I scowled at him then back at the page. "Where did you learn to write like this? You always skipped out on grammar lessons when we were young."

"That's because your Auntie Vala bored me to death."

"If she heard you say that, you would be dead."

"I don't doubt it." He shrugged. "I had a lot of downtime on the island where you stranded me. Figured I'd learn to make myself useful in more ways than sailing."

I lifted an eyebrow. "I see it didn't work. What does the F stand for?"

Ronan leaned back in his chair and winked. "Fucking gorgeous. You can stop rereading it, it won't bite you."

I refused to acknowledge how the cockiness of his expression made my blood boil in more than one way. "I'm making sure it's foolproof."

"It is."

"Ronan, don't push it." I slammed the paper back down on the table, grabbed the quill from Ronan's hand and scratched my name across the paper before my sensible side could talk me out of it. "I can't believe I'm doing this."

"Get some rest, Mrs. Mathonwy," Ronan ordered as he signed the other dotted line, his name a swirling mess on the page. "The investigation starts tomorrow."

My sleep was fitful, marked by strange, semi-conscious dreams. I dreamt of the spring, but its waters ran red with blood. A man and a woman were there, both as beautiful as they were ethereal. Her hair was whiter than the caps of waves, her skin almost as pale; in perfect contrast, his hair was darker than my own, his eyes the color of storm clouds. They carried themselves with a grace not of this world, and I couldn't look away. But they were fighting, a terrible, violent fight. Their unblemished faces contorted in snarling rage as they battled in the spring, the blood staining their white clothes. I tried screaming, begging them to stop, but no sound came out, not as the man ripped the throat from the woman's neck...

Sweat matted my neck as I startled awake. I shook off the dream and tried not to consider what Pa used to say about omens. *Never wink at a raven, and always heed dreams before a journey, Keira girl.* I hoped the silly rule didn't apply to all journeys, only the ones at sea, because I definitely had a ways ahead of me.

Dawn had just broken, the light streaming in through cracks in the ceiling. The rain had stopped, and a chorus of larks sang outside.

The straw bed was more comfortable than I had imagined it would be. Ronan slept on the floor beside the stove. It was uncomfortable to be so close, but I knew that if he had wanted to kill me, he would have already.

It didn't stop me from sleeping with my knife within arm's reach. Just in case.

I gave his boot a firm kick as I passed to walk out. His only response was a strange gurgling sound as he turned over to his stomach and snored once more.

Covering my mouth was all I could do to suppress a laugh. "Heavy rutting sleeper."

I unfurled my worn blue long-coat out of my rucksack and wrapped it around myself as I walked out into the crisp morning air. The sun glinted off the white of the forest and the spring, the brightness blinding. It took my eyes a minute to adjust, but when they did, I sucked in a breath at the beauty of it all.

This place was certainly god-touched, even if it had only brought me misery.

I walked towards the spring and knelt beside it, dipping my hands into the cool water to wash my face. I watched the ripples break the glass-like surface until they filled the pond, one larger and grander than the next—and then they stopped, fading back into nothingness.

I whispered a prayer to Lyr that the ripples I created in my own life would disappear, too.

"Good morning, Mrs. Mathonwy," Ronan muttered behind me.

I almost fell into the pool as I jumped up.

"Didn't mean to scare you," he chuckled, his voice still thick and deep with sleep.

"You didn't."

"You know, it really is magic." He knelt at the side of the water, his reflection staring back at us. "The spring. My father says it speaks to people."

"Yeah," I scoffed, "and Lyr is my uncle. Reese is a liar and you know it."

"Fair." He smiled, and my stomach flipped again. "But my mother wasn't, and she swore by it."

The memory of Eleri Mathonwy's face filled my mind's eye, her kind eyes and her soft features, and I offered Ronan a sad grin. His mother had passed when we were eleven, right before he came to work for my father. Ronan's snake smile and stupid blond hair were both passed straight down from Reese. But his sea-blue eyes were his mother's, a constant reminder of the sliver of goodness she gave him. It was no wonder Reese had to ship him off to another crew. No wonder why he had become so hard and cruel in the years since.

I looked back at the spring before I let myself feel even the slightest tinge of sympathy for the snake. There was no turning back.

"She used to tell me the story." He sat back on his forearms, his weight putting dents into the supple grass, and patted the ground next to him. I rolled my eyes, but sat back, making sure to keep a few feet between us. "Lyr himself used to live here. After thousands of years of isolation at sea, with only ugly sailors for company, he took the form of a man and came ashore to find himself a woman."

"You talk too much," I sneered, surprised how natural it felt to be here with him.

"I told you, I learned a lot on the island." He winked, an easiness settling over him. "Had to keep myself from going crazy somehow. Anyway, Lyr came and fell in love with a Porthladd woman. She was beautiful, with a temper as chaotic as a storm."

The man and woman from my dream filled my head. A wave of nausea hit me and I had to look away from the spring, the image of it stained red still haunting me.

Ronan didn't seem to notice as he launched himself into the tale of Lyr and his lover. His smooth voice was as fluid and commanding as the sea itself. I was mesmerized by him, by the complex tale he wove for me—of self-sacrifice and magic spells and forbidden love. I let the words wash away everything, the contract and the feud and the mistrust, until it was just me and Ronan like it had been so many years before.

"He married the woman, spent decades with her. But after a time, he had to go back to the sea, where he belonged..." Ronan trailed off, his epic saga coming to an end. "So, he made this spring where his wife could always have a piece of him. Some say he even enchanted it so she could live forever, waiting for a time when he could return to his beloved once more."

"I wish I could believe you." My voice was tender as I tried to hold onto the last moments of peace the story created. I hugged my knees to my chest.

Strange, so strange to feel this vulnerable with anyone, especially him. Maybe it was because I was in over my head. Or maybe because I had nothing left to lose.

Ronan watched me for another second, the weight of the tale still hanging in the air. "Get dressed," he finally said, breaking the magic of the silent moment. "We'll leave as soon as you're ready."

"Where are we going?"

"Town." He stood up, looking out over the horizon. "Time to introduce Porthladd to the new Mrs. Mathonwy."

Porthladd had been my permanent residence since I was born. It was my father's home and his father's home before that, and so on and so forth for five generations of Branwens. But having spent so much of my life at sea, the main town sometimes felt as foreign as the shores of the Southern Isles.

As I walked in pace with Ronan through the cobblestone streets, I *felt* like a foreigner. Nothing had changed; not on the surface, at least. Mr. Cadwallader's Apothecary was still right across from Ms. Prichard's Bakery. The two clothier shoppes still sandwiched The Belkin Inn, and their owners were probably still arguing inside over a stiff ale.

From the moment we stepped foot into the main square, the townsfolk glared at us through wary eyes. It didn't take long for the looks to turn venomous or for the vicious whispers to start.

There goes the Branwen girl...wild, that one is. I heard she once bit a man's ear off at a dinner party when he asked for a dance... And with a Mathonwy, no less...Ronan Mathonwy... Wasn't he the boy who spent the last three years in an Ir'Desian brothel?... I wonder what they are up to now... Haven't they caused us enough trouble?

One particularly nosy woman went as far as stepping on my shoe as she passed. Her rotund face contorted with a false apology as she scuttled onward, her overflowing basket of bread in tow. It took all the self-control I could muster not to shove the bread down her throat until she choked.

I grew up here, in these streets, with these people. As I grew older, I risked my life on every voyage to secure goods for them from far-off places they could only dream of. To bring back the spices that made their dishes savory and the textiles that made their clothes soft.

Yet they looked down their noses at us. Feared us. Made it clear that we did not belong. I took a deep breath in, letting the salt-and-brine-stenched air settle me. At least the fishermen's market was close by, and just beyond that, the Western Sea. The only place I truly belonged.

"Never gets old," Ronan whispered in my ear as if he read my mind.

"Never changes either."

"Aye, hence why it's the perfect place to start our search," he snickered. "If there is any evidence, it'll still be here."

"Fair point." I assessed the storefronts that lined the streets. "We should split up, cover more ground."

Ronan jutted his bottom lip out in a childish pout. "That's not as fun."

I crossed my arms in response. "One month, Ronan. Do you really want to waste time?"

"Fine." He rolled his eyes. "We'll split up, ask people what they know. I'll take the bakery, the inn, and the apothecary. Your father frequented them, yes? Hopefully, someone will remember something that might be a clue. An argument at the bar, or perhaps someone tailing him...You take the bank, the jeweler's, and the Llewelyn's office. See if any of his business ties weren't doing well."

"Of course you're taking all the places to eat and drink. Don't get distracted."

His familiar grin snaked across his face. "I'm playing to my strengths, that's all."

I sighed, looking toward the southern district where most of the Council members held their residences. If I was going that way for the Llewelyn's, I should make another, far less pleasant visit. "Should we stop at Connor Yorath's office?"

"Hmm. Eventually, but not today." Ronan looked toward the winding south street, his lip curling with disgust. "I don't think either of us wants to answer questions about our marriage quite yet."

I knew it was irresponsible to put it off, but I didn't protest. "Meet back here at sundown?"

"Make it three," Ronan mused. "We've got another stop to make, Mrs. Mathonwy."

I rolled my eyes but hurried on my way.

The bank was first since it was the closest to the town square, but I knew it was a pointless venture. Papa's account with them was closed a long time ago, and now Aidan controlled the little that was left of the family fortune. Still, the bank was owned by the Baines family, and perhaps old Mr. Baines would have information about my father's financial activities at the time.

But as I asked the apprentice for him, I was disappointed to find out that the Baines' Bank sign on the storefront no longer meant Mr. Baines, but his son, as the former Mr. Baines was quite dead.

Perhaps that was the only way things changed in Porthladd.

I tried to keep my shoulders from slumping as I went to my next assigned task.

The jeweler proved even less helpful, refusing to see me when I asked for him. I didn't think he'd still be sore about the time Ronan and I swiped some small, semiprecious gems from him when we were kids, but he was.

His assistant, an older woman with sharp eyes and a kind smile, pitied me at least. She hinted that it had been six years since anyone from my family had even been in the shop as I left.

I rallied a thankful smile to my face, but I'm sure it looked as shallow as I felt.

I knew this entire investigation would prove useless, and I knew Ronan was just buying himself time to enact whatever plan he had up his sleeve. Despite that, I couldn't help but feel the air deflate from my sails as I followed another dead-end lead.

Finally, I walked into Llewelyn's Smithery and tried to suppress the slight glimmer of hope in my chest. The Llewelyn's had always had a close relationship with my family, and Iwan Llewelyn, the patriarch, had been a particularly close friend to Pa.

I walked through the heavy wooden door, a bell ringing to signal my arrival, and the smell of metal and coal assaulted my nostrils. "Master Llewelyn?" I called into the shop. The main workroom was in the back, but there was a small office in the front for customers. The space was outfitted with a tall desk with two oak chairs on each side and a single metalwork cabinet. But no one manned the desk, and I waited another moment before calling out again. "Master Llewelyn?"

The door to the back workroom opened with a bang, Councilman Ellian bursting through. He smiled roguishly, sweat dripping from his brow, his dark curls plastered to his forehead. His shirt sleeves were rolled up and the front buttons undone, revealing the strong planes of his bronze chest. My mouth went dry. I looked down at the floor as he walked up to me. "Master Llewelyn is my father, but I don't mind the way it sounds in your mouth."

I peeked up at him through my eyelashes. "I'm sorry to interrupt your work." Growing up on a ship full of men, I was not usually so fazed by the sight of their physique. But there was something about Ellian's presence that could make Lyr himself swoon.

"It's a welcome distraction," he chuckled and raked his moss-green eyes over me. "You look well, Keira, despite everything."

"I've seen better days." I swallowed, willing my heartbeat to slow. "But I'm glad to see a friendly face."

Ellian leaned back on the desk, and even then, he was still a head taller than me. "I'm happy to supply. What brings you here today, Ms. Keira?"

My cheeks flushed hot as I remembered my task. "Oh, nothing. I'll come back on a day when your Pa is here," I stuttered as I dismissed myself, heading back towards the door.

Ellian crossed in front of me swiftly, splaying his large hand on the knob to entrap me. "Pa doesn't come around to the shop much these days. The bugger is getting old. But I'm sure I can help you with whatever it is you need."

I took a breath. Saying it out loud to him shouldn't matter, as I had already asked the absurd line of questions twice today. But I felt small and embarrassed anyway as he waited for my response.

"It sounds silly," I finally mumbled.

"Then tell me," he laughed, "and we can joke about it together. Over a drink, perhaps?"

Maybe it was because I needed a laugh, or because I needed a drink, but I nodded. "I'd like that."

Ellian wore a bold smile that could make Lyr's knees wobble and went to the metallic cabinet. He opened the first paneled door, and after a moment of looking, pulled out an expensive bottle of whiskey and two small, copper cups. Deftly, he poured two knuckles' worth of the amber liquid in each and placed them on the table.

I watched in awe at the skill and precision of his motions. A musician by choice and a smith by trade, you couldn't deny Ellian Llewelyn was clever with his hands.

He raised an eyebrow, and I realized I'd been staring. He gestured for me to sit in the nearest chair before slumping in the farthest one. I sat, and he passed me one of the cups, proceeding to put his feet up on the desk and lean back. "Good thing I keep this on hand, eh? *Lechyd Da.*" He raised his glass before draining the contents in one gulp.

"*Lechyd Da.*" I repeated the gesture, taking a small sip of my own glass. The whiskey was unquestionably smooth going down, yet it still bit at my throat, the fire filling my belly.

"So, what is this silly thing you'd like to discuss with my father?" Ellian teased as he poured himself another knuckle's worth. He motioned to hand me the bottle, but I held up my hand in refusal. I was a sailor and had no trouble holding my liquor, but even I had qualms about getting plastered before three in the afternoon.

Plus, I needed my wits about me if I was going to make any sense of what I was about to say.

"I'm looking for information," I started, hating how stupid the words sounded. "About my father's murder."

Ellian's face darkened, his mouth forming a tight line.

"I don't think that's very silly at all. But I do think the first place to go asking about that would be your so-called husband," he growled, something primal about his rage awakening a sliver of my own.

But being angry wasn't helping me anymore. I needed answers, one way or the other, if only to squash the slimy part of myself that wanted to believe Ronan.

"I know." I kept my voice even, hiding how nervous his scowl made me. "And I agree. But Ronan is trying to prove his innocence. And if he can't…I still need answers. About the days before. About what made the Mathonwys betray him. And I know your father was doing business with both clans around that time…I was hoping he might know something. Anything."

He swirled the contents of his glass as he weighed my words. "I'll ask my father." His expression softened around the edges, and I sighed a breath of relief. He stood and walked around the desk, sitting on the edge of it now so his leg almost brushed mine. "I can't guarantee anything, but you're right. You've been mourning for too long, and now you have to live with that traitor...you're entitled to whatever answers you can get. Though I must say, I hope you don't let him distract you too much."

I looked up at him as the spark of hope in my core ignited. "Thank you, friend."

"What can I say?" He smiled the same heart-stopping smile from before. "I have a weakness for beautiful, clever women. I couldn't say no to you."

Red heat rose to my cheeks. "You flatter me too much."

"You deserve to be flattered." He shrugged and reached out to tuck a loose strand of hair behind my ear. "And more."

For a moment, I let myself wonder as the slight brush of his fingers sent shivers down my spine. I wondered what it would be like to have a man like Ellian for myself, a man as strong and as steady as the Clogwynn Cliffs. A man to depend on. A man to come back to.

"Ellian, I'm—I'm married," I said instead, not letting myself get caught in the current of *what-ifs*. At least, not for another month.

Ellian leaned back further into his hands, his eyes never leaving my face. "By law, yes, but not by love. Only one of those things matter to me."

I pulled my coat tighter around myself, feeling vulnerable under his penetrating gaze. "I should go."

"I'll call on you soon, then." He crossed to the door and opened it for me, a broad grin on his face. "If only to impart my father's wisdom, fine. But hopefully, it'll be a friendly call as well, Keira Branwen."

And there was something about hearing my name, *my name*, that sent another shiver down my spine. "Aye, that it will be."

I was glad that it was chilly out as I made my way out the door and back to the square.

"You're late." Ronan was leaning against one of the old stone water wells, his arms folded across his chest, when I returned.

"Aye, I was busy."

"Gathering information, I hope?" He raised an eyebrow and sauntered toward me, his hands deep in his pockets.

"Not exactly," I sighed, crossing my arms against the chill. "The bank changed hands and the jeweler practically threw me out."

Ronan's brow knit. "Still mad about our little jewel heist, then? Figures." He walked north, his pace heavy. I followed. "I've got nothing either. What about Llewelyn's?"

"Ellian said he'd ask his father what he knows."

Ronan stopped in his tracks. "Ellian? Where was old man Iwan?"

"Somewhere else, being old." I shrugged. "The man is sixty-three, I don't know why I expected him to still be working in the smithery in the first place."

Ronan resumed his casual pace but thrust his hands deeper into his pockets. "So you were late because you were chatting with Ellian."

"Aye, so we could get information from his father," I scoffed, hoping he didn't catch how red my cheeks got. "Don't get the wrong idea."

Ronan shrugged, his expression a lethal calm. "I'm not. I trust you."

Anger seared through me again, as hot as Ellian's forge. "No, Ronan." I grabbed his forearm roughly to halt us. "Don't get the wrong idea about why I am helping you. The contract we signed said I had to cooperate. It said nothing else. And it doesn't change the way I feel. One month, Ronan. One month and I'm no longer your wife, and you don't get an opinion about who I do or don't chat with."

Something dark flashed through Ronan's eyes, and his jaw flickered. "Yes, well. Now that you've made it crystal clear, can we please get going? We need to make it for dinner." He didn't wait for me to confirm as he continued northward, his pace doubled.

I chased after him. "You still haven't told me where we are going."

"Mathonwy Manor," he answered with his typical smirk. "There is someone I want you to meet."

6

Manors and Monsters

Aidan's townhome was by no means small, but as I took in the gaudy opulence of Mathonwy Manor, the Branwen estate might as well have been the shack. The Manor was a behemoth, its towering four stories of white stone impenetrable. At the front gates, two stone *ddraig* sat as watchful guardians, and on top of the three turrets, the red flags bearing the Mathonwy double-dragon crest reached towards the sky goddess Nef herself.

The Manor was a manifestation of the three things that Mathonwys held above all else: money, power, and dominance. I'd been here a few times as a child for dinner parties, but even now it both inspired and terrified me.

"It's homey, right?" Ronan whispered as he led me through the iron gates and up the stone path to the front doors of the snakes' den.

"And what does it have to do with our investigation?" I grumbled. "This better not be a personal call."

Ronan waved me off. "Well, feel free to investigate, as it's technically your right as a Mathonwy, but this isn't specifically for that…" His lips curled into a smile, but his eyes were still guarded. "Consider this an exercise in trust. Or forgiveness. I don't know yet."

"Neither my trust nor my forgiveness are easily won." I raised an eyebrow but did not stop him as he pushed open the door. I was glad that I'd decided to hide my knife in the sleeve of my coat.

My instincts prickled with caution as we entered the cavernous foyer, our footsteps echoing against the marble floors. Lit lanterns lined the walls, but no one greeted us. In fact, much of the interior was covered in a light film of dust—everything from the banister of the grand mahogany staircase to the gilded family portraits that lined the walls. The Manor was an empty husk, a reminder of the price of their conquests without any of the heart and fire that drove them.

"Where is everyone?" I asked before I could stop myself, my voice echoing back. *Gone, hopefully.* If searching this place for clues was my right, I would milk it for its secrets.

"Sailing." Ronan shrugged, but there was a strange sadness beneath his expression. "Or at the *Raven*. Maybe even Madame Jessa's brothel, if they're lucky."

"Anywhere but here is the prevailing attitude." A woman's voice echoed from the top of the stairs, and we both spun to look up at her. Her hair was the same golden blonde as Ronan's, aside from the few strands of silver that wove through the roots. She was beautiful, a sharp cunning in her brown eyes and secrets in her smile. And though it had been ages since I last saw her, I knew who she was.

The third of the Mathonwy siblings, youngest sister to Reese and Roland. Reina Mathonwy, the reclusive White Snake herself.

While her brothers had shouted their names across all four seas, Reina had always been more of a mystery, a local legend. When Ronan and I were younger, I remember her smiling and laughing at parties. But by the time we were eight, she had become a total shut-in. Why she stayed to herself, no one knew, and no one dared ask any of the other Mathonwys for fear of a beating.

She descended down the stairs, a living story, her hand trailing over the dusty banister.

"Reina!" Ronan shouted, beaming from ear to ear. He ran halfway up the stairs, taking them two at a time, and wrapped her up in a tight hug. I waited at the bottom of the stairs, not sure if I should say hello or run away screaming in the other direction.

"Ye look tired, boy." She stepped back, her hands on his shoulders as she took him in. Her delicate brows knit together. "Is the shack uncomfortable? When Lochlan and I stayed, it was only a night."

Lochlan? I hadn't known Reina was married.

Ronan shoved his hands in his pockets and winked at his aunt. "I'm fine, Auntie." He nodded his head towards me, and I froze in place. "This one has just been keeping me up, if you know what I mean."

Red-hot embarrassment rose in my cheeks. "Watch it."

"Ronan, ye filthy cad," Reina gasped and thwacked Ronan's shoulder. Ronan lowered his head, but I could see the smile he was trying to suppress. "Who taught ye to talk that way?" Reina shot a daggered look at him, then turned her attention my way. She flitted down the stairs and extended her hand toward me. "I'm sorry, I've been terribly rude. It's Keira, yes? Ye've grown up since the last time I saw ye. Welcome to Mathonwy Manor."

I paused, wary, but Reina grabbed my hand in both of hers and shook it. Her grip was as warm and soft as her smile, and before I knew it, I was shaking her hands back.

"It's nice to see you again," I stuttered, unsure of how to greet a myth.

"Oh, don't be silly, I'm sure this is awkward for ye." She winked and let me go, and I blinked twice, unsure if I had heard her right. She continued on, the pace of her sweet voice faster than a cutter on smooth water, "Not as bad as the wedding, perhaps, when the whole rutting clan was there. Minus me, of course, but it's been ages since you've been here, and well, circumstances as they are…"

"Auntie, you're talking too much," Ronan chuckled as he joined us at the bottom of the stairs, placing a calming hand on her shoulder.

"It's fine." I offered a tight smile, looking to Ronan for direction. Small talk was a sailor's nightmare, but a snake would know his way around it.

He nodded knowingly, and for the first time in ages, I was grateful for his presence.

"Where is the rest of the rutting lot?" he asked as he ushered his aunt through the double doors to our left and into a grand sitting room. He plopped onto a red velvet chaise on the far side, legs dangling off the edge as he leaned back. The action looked as natural to him as breathing, and I bit my lip to hold back my laughter.

"Sailing." Reina took one of the high-backed gold chairs next to him and crossed her legs as she sat. "Yer Pa wanted to make a day trip to Bachtref."

Following her lead, I took her chair's twin, sitting across from her. But I made sure to note all possible exit routes.

"Ah, well, it's probably for the best." Ronan let his head roll back, but I didn't miss the tightness in his expression.

"Lyr's ass," a young voice said behind me, and I almost fell out of my chair as I whipped around. A girl, no more than thirteen, stared at me with an open mouth, her brown eyes wide in wonder.

"Language!" Reina scolded. Ronan chuckled under his breath behind me.

I took in the girl before me, and, despite her dark hair, I immediately saw the resemblance. Her eyes the same brown as Reina's, her nose as sharp as Ronan's...and suddenly, Reina's reclusiveness made complete sense.

Reina had a daughter, and she was hiding her from the world.

Mathonwy Manor did have its secrets.

"You're Keira Branwen," the girl stammered, pointing a thin finger at me. "You're the Night-Mare of the Four Seas."

A flash of pride rippled through my chest as my old nickname hung in the air.

"Aye, but you can call me Keira. Ronan didn't tell me he had such a charming…"

"Cousin," Ronan interjected, confirming my suspicion. He stood, holding his arms open for a hug. "And where is my hello?"

"Aye, quit your whining." She rolled her honeyed eyes, but she wrapped her arms around his neck. He lifted and spun her, the giggle that rose from her enough to make any sailor smile. Ronan put her down, and she bounced back to me, beaming.

"I'm Reagan, by the way." She jutted her hand out for me to shake. "I'm twelve."

"A pleasure, Reagan." I took it and shook back, surprised at the strength of her grip. "I'm...twenty."

She leaned in and whispered, mischief in her eyes, "I heard you can sink a ship just by looking at it."

Ronan's cousin indeed.

"Reagan," Reina reprimanded again, but the edge of her voice softened.

I raised an eyebrow. "You shouldn't pay any mind to rumors."

Ronan patted her head, offering me a strange look. "Sorry, she's quite an admirer of yours."

"Is she, now? Do you sail, Reagan?"

The girl folded her arms across her chest, a dark glower shadowing her heart-shaped face. "No, Uncle Reese won't allow me on *The Ddraig*."

A forgotten part of me, the part that had raged against all the men who belittled me, that had cursed the women who sneered at me, sang with fury on her behalf. "Perhaps I'll teach you, then," I blurted out before I could stop myself.

Both Reagan's and Ronan's eyes went rounder than a full moon at midnight.

Reina, to her credit, did not balk. "How does that sound?" she exclaimed, coming over to ruffle her daughter's chestnut curls. "The best lady sailor north of the Southern Isles teaching ye!"

Reagan shot her a pointed look. "She's the best, *ever*, Ma. lady or man."

I couldn't stop myself from smiling. A kindred soul, hidden in the den of snakes.

"I like her." I nudged Ronan in the ribs, and Reagan smiled with pride.

"Will ye two be staying for dinner?" Reina eyed us knowingly, her gaze fixed on the place we had touched. I took a quick step away from him, putting the necessary distance between us once more.

"Aye, if it's not too much," Ronan answered, unaware.

Reagan jumped next to him, pulling on his sleeve excitedly. "Please stay! Ronan, you owe me a story."

"Aren't you getting a little old for stories?" he teased, flicking her nose.

"Aren't you getting a little old for stupid questions?" She swatted him away, hurling her retort with the speed and accuracy of an arrow.

Forgetting myself, forgetting where I was, who I was with, I let out a hearty laugh. Until I remembered, choking on the sound. Here I was, in the heart of my enemies' fortress, laughing and smiling like they were my people instead.

I ached for my own cousins, for Griffin's laugh, for Tarran's shy smile, even for Saeth's bitter remarks. But this tentative peace was as much for them as it was for Reagan and Reina, two more innocents living in a world of blood.

It didn't change the fact that I didn't belong here.

"I don't want to impose on your family," I declined, taking a step toward the door. "Ronan, you stay, I'll get going."

Ronan opened his mouth to protest, but before he could, my stomach betrayed me, growling louder than a Pysgoddian wolf's cry. It had been a full day since I had eaten, and my rueful stomach was having none of my noble causes.

"Sounds like part of ye disagrees." Reina smirked and sauntered to the kitchen. "Let's whip something up for ye."

I sighed, knowing resistance at this point would be futile.

Reagan clamped her hand over mine, pulling me to follow. "Besides, you can't miss Ronan telling stories; he's a natural."

I scoffed under my breath, "I'm sure he is. He's always been great at telling lies."

Reagan stopped, her eyes twinkling with delight as she turned to Ronan. "I like her."

And before I could object further, I was dragged to the kitchen by the tiny little tyrant who I was sure could steal even the god of death's cold heart.

I was a terrible cook. Always had been, despite Vala's desperate attempts at instruction. Of course, I could do the minimum to survive, especially at sea; I could clean a fish of its bones in less than a minute, and I was deadly with my knife, for people and for vegetables. But I was not a cook. I was a survivor.

Reina, on the other hand, was an artist. Her hands made quick work of things, but by the smell of the chicken roasting over the fire, quick did not mean shabby. I watched her as Ronan entertained Reagan, all of us chopping or cleaning when instructed by the artist in motion.

"What kind of story do you want tonight, little dragon?" Ronan asked as he washed his hands in the deep sink.

Reagan rolled her eyes but grinned at her nickname. "You know the one I want."

"Again?" Ronan teased as he came to stand beside me, leaning on the wooden countertop of the kitchen worktable.

"Aye, so Keira can hear it." Reagan tucked herself into a chair and rested her head on her hands, waiting for the story to begin. To my left, Reina handed me an onion to chop, and I immediately began my task despite the stinging scent of it, grateful for something to do with my hands.

"All right, where do I start…?" Ronan settled next to me, grabbing some parsley to tear as he spoke.

"There once was a girl…" Reagan coached him expectantly.

"Aye, there once was a girl, with hair the color of roasted chestnuts, who loved her Pa very much."

"You forgot her name, Ronan," Reagan interrupted impatiently, eagerness shining in her eyes.

Ronan raised an eyebrow. "Do you want me to tell the story, Reagan, or do you want to tell it?"

Reagan held her lips shut and nodded, a signal of compliance. Reina chuckled beside me as she basted fresh bread in a bath of spices.

Ronan's voice was as smooth as the tranquil water of the spring as he continued to paint his picture. "There once was a girl, with hair the color of chestnuts, who loved her Pa… Her name was Airid, and she was not only a gifted healer but a sailor as well, mighty as she was beautiful. Her Pa, Dyan, was also a healer, and he taught her all of his secrets."

Vague familiarity rippled through my mind. "I know this one…" I whispered to Reina. "But since when does Airid sail?"

"Since Ronan told the story. You'll see." She winked and handed me another onion.

I went back to my task.

Ronan was unfazed by my whispered interruption, his eyes dancing in the firelight as he leaned into his tale. "But one day, the vengeful god of the Otherworld grew jealous of her father's healing talents. He was saving too many people and denying the old god the souls he was owed. So, one fateful night, as punishment, he called on a deadly storm and wrecked Dyan's ship. He dragged him to the Otherworld himself as payment."

Reagan sat at the edge of her seat, as captivated by Ronan's magic as I was. Ronan paused dramatically, soaking up the attention like a sponge. "But the god of the Otherworld did not know that Airid also possessed the gift, even greater than her father's. So Airid stole off into the night on her ship, cutting down all those in her path—over a thousand lily-livered, good for nothing pirates, the messengers of the dark god's fury." Ronan grabbed the knife from my hand, swinging in dramatic sweeps before him. Reagan laughed brightly, clapping as Ronan danced about. "She gutted so many of the denizens of the dark that she opened the gate to the Otherworld herself with the carnage she laid in her wake."

"That is definitely not in the original," I chuckled under my breath to Reina.

"No, but it's more entertaining if ye ask me," she snickered back, watching Ronan twirl the knife like a baton. With a flourish, he sank it into the wood of the worktable and slammed his hands down in front of him.

"Then, when she reached the Otherworld, using her gifts and the herbs from her very own garden, she found her father and healed him, body and soul. And the god of the Otherworld, the fool that he was, was so distracted by all of the dark souls Airid had laid before him that he didn't even notice when she rescued her father and sailed back home."

A shudder went up my spine as I realized where I had heard this story before. Where Ronan had heard it, too.

It was forever ago, a different little girl with darker curls, a different man with a scruffier chin…

But it was impossible not to hear my father's voice in Ronan's as he approached the finale.

"And then?" Reagan asked, a shimmering tear lining her eye.

Maybe it was the onions, but I could feel the sting of fresh tears rising in my own.

"And then," Ronan's voice was reverent as he tied the last strands of his tapestry together, "they lived together and sailed together until they were old and gray and Airid's children had children. And when Airid and her father were too frail to sail and too old to heal, they journeyed back to the Otherworld together. And the god of the Otherworld, so surprised to see them, let them into his paradise without a price, because he knew he had been bested."

Reagan walked around the table, tears streaming down her pearl-white cheeks. My heart ached for the girl, the sweet sadness in her expression too old for someone her age. I wondered what corruption had put it there.

She wrapped her arms around Ronan's waist, nuzzling into his side. "The end?"

Ronan kissed the top of her head. "Aye, little dragon, the end."

"You'll tell it again after dinner, won't you?" Reagan beamed up at him through her tears.

"If my audience commands it." Ronan puffed out his chest and ruffled her hair. "After we eat, I promise."

"Like you need an excuse to hear yourself talk," I muttered, wiping my own scoundrel tears with my sleeve.

Ronan peered at me, the edge of his mouth curling up. "Are you crying, Mrs. Mathonwy?"

I thwacked his arm. "It's the onions, you daft prick."

Reagan bellowed with laughter, and for a moment, I forgot that I was an outsider at all.

We sat down around the worktable as Reina put the finishing touches on the meal, not bothering with the formality of the dining room. I ate with my hands like my crew did on the ship, and to my surprise and satisfaction, both Reina and Reagan did too, all shreds of dainty pretenses dissolving as we stuffed our bellies. And the food was heavenly, the chicken basted with both sweet citrus and savory spices, creating a dance of passion on my tongue. We ate and laughed until the lanterns had to be lit, our stomachs bloated and our hearts content.

"Keira, will you really teach me to sail?" Reagan asked as she licked her fingers.

The indulgent happiness of the moment before quickly faded. The images of Donnall's disapproving scowl and old Weylin's back turned to me filled my mind. "I don't know," I answered. Was it fair to subject this innocent girl to their animosity to prove a point? Especially considering her bloodline...I knew how my uncle's crew would respond, and it would not be kind. And even I couldn't sail the *Ceffyl* without a crew. "I'd like to, really, but my crew barely tolerates having one lady on the ship, and I was only allowed because I was kin."

Reagan's chest deflated, and it nearly broke my heart. Reina offered her a sad smile, but Reagan's brows knit together. "Aye, but we are kin now too, aren't we?"

And there was the killing blow. "Aye. I suppose we are."

Ronan placed his hand over hers, determination sparkling in his eyes. "Keira and I will take you sailing soon, I promise." I opened my mouth to protest, but he held a hand up before I could speak. "On my new ship."

I clenched my jaw, biting back the anger rising in my chest. I wanted to help Reagan, surprising as it was, but Ronan was not my keeper, and he was not about to be my Captain.

"What about your Pa?" I asked, looking for an easier out. "Does he ever take you sailing?"

I might as well have shot someone as my words ricocheted around the room. Ronan's jaw flickered and his gaze leaped to Reagan, whose sunny disposition clouded as she stared at her hands.

Reina cleared her throat, her eyes fixed on the woodwork of the table. "Lochlan, Reagan's father, never really had the chance. He passed on a few years ago when Reagan was still too young. But he would have, one day."

An anchor of guilt dropped down into my stomach. "I'm so sorry, I shouldn't have asked."

Reina patted my hand, a kind smile lighting her eyes. "Don't worry, it's no secret."

"I'm an arse," I said in lieu of an apology, and Reina chuckled.

"It's okay, he'll be back." Reagan did not look up from her hands as she spoke, but I could see the steely determination in her expression. "I'm going to sail into the Otherworld one day and bring him back, just like Airid." She looked up, a tide turning, and smiled. "But you need to teach me to sail first."

I watched Reagan with care. She was my mirror—a daughter without a father. A girl with a sailor's heart. I knew her pain as my own, and her dreams.

And I would see that she achieved them.

"Aye, it's a deal then. Ronan and I will teach you."

Surprise and awe laced Ronan's sea-blue stare. The moment passed so fast I wasn't sure if it happened, and he turned his attention back to his family. But I couldn't stop my treacherous cheeks from flushing scarlet.

Another moment passed in silence, this one comfortable.

"Auntie, this meal was lovely," Ronan finally spoke, his voice soft, "but we best be on our way soon. Keira and I will clean up, and then we'll take our leave. Before the crew gets home."

Reina sighed and leaned back in her chair, "Aye, thank ye for staying so long. Reagan, that means it's time for us to wash up and head to bed."

Reagan folded her arms across her chest. "But Ronan promised to tell me the story again."

Ronan stood to leave, planting a quick kiss on her head. "Aye, next time, little dragon."

Reagan whacked him on the arm. "That's not what you promised, you lying arse."

Ronan rubbed the tender spot, opening his mouth to refuse.

"You did promise, Ronan," I interrupted, winking at my tiny new comrade. "Why don't you go take Reagan to bed and tell her the story? I can help clean up."

Reagan jumped up and down, giggling, the sound clearing whatever darkness still lingered.

"All right, little dragon." Ronan narrowed his eyes. "First one to the top of the stairs wins!" Without a warning, he sprinted out of the kitchen faster than an eastern wind.

Reagan broke after him, her warm curls flowing behind her. "Hey, wait for me!"

Reina chuckled and began to clear the worktable, grabbing the large dish holding the chicken carcass.

"Here, let me take that for you." I reached for the heavy dish and she smiled gratefully.

"Yer a sweet girl, Keira." She turned back to the table, grabbing a spare cloth to wipe the debris from the meal. I moved to wash the dishes, needing something to do with myself. The water in the basin was tepid as I dipped my hands into it.

Reaching into the hidden part of myself, I let a single drop of my power ripple through me, warming the soapy water. It responded, bubbling up then settling, its temperature now as warm as the hot spring.

Reina and I worked in a comfortable quiet as I finished scrubbing the last of the dishes.

"That's it, it seems," she sighed, folding her cloth and placing it on the counter. Her eyes were fixed on something an ocean away. For a moment, I wondered where she went. Maybe she missed the outside world.

"Can I ask a question?" I started tentatively, folding my own hand-cloth neatly.

"Is it why I hide?" She raised an eyebrow, and all I could do was nod. "At first, it was because I got pregnant with Reagan before Lochlan and I were technically married, so my brothers insisted. Then, because I got used to it, liked it even, being away from the noise and the gossip. I was raising Reagan, and my little family was my world. I didn't need the rest of it." A sadness crept over her eyes as she paused, heaviness settling in the air around us. "Then, after…after Lochlan died, it was because I didn't know how to face it without him. I didn't want Reagan to face it either, dangerous and dark as it was."

Her words settled around us, and Reagan's dragon-toothed smile flashed in my head. I would've done everything I could to protect it, too, even if it meant caging her.

"I—I'm sorry to have upset Reagan earlier." I looked down at my hands, still pruney from the water. "I didn't know, but I do know what it feels like. To lose a father."

Reina nodded. "It's okay. It's been nearly four years now, so the wounds aren't as fresh. It's not as hard to talk about him, ye understand?"

"Aye, I do." I smiled back, leaning against the worktable.

Reina took her seat again, tracing a pattern with her finger across the oak. "Lochlan, he was a good man. Wouldn't have wanted us to remember him sadly. He was always making us laugh. So, I choose to remember the happy moments."

I sat across from her, watching her. "Can I ask how it happened?"

Her soft smile disappeared, replaced only with that same saturated sadness. "Shipwreck. An angry storm hit the ship while he was at the mast."

"That's terrible, I'm so sorry."

Reina closed her eyes, a single tear rolling down her cheek. "Aye, thank you for the apology." She opened her eyes again, the weight of her gaze heavy on my shoulders. "But I've already forgiven you."

My heart stopped. "I don't understand your meaning."

She blinked twice, her trance broken. She turned from me, hiding her face in the dim lamplight. "It's nothing, forgive me."

A knot formed in my stomach. A shipwreck, almost four years ago...

No, it couldn't be, not with the kindness she had shown me.

Consider this an exercise in trust. Or forgiveness, I don't know yet.

Maybe it wasn't my trust or forgiveness Ronan was referring to.

"Reina, what are you suggesting?" I hedged, my stomach rolling like high tide.

"I didn't mean—I didn't want to say anything, because I don't want ye feeling unwelcome." She looked back at me, new tears in her eyes. "I know yer grief, I know it like my own, and I can't say I wouldn't have done the same if I was there in yer boots that night."

My head spun. I remembered him now: Lochlan, the dark-haired scout on Ronan's ship. Ronan had hired most of his old crew, but there had been family, too, hiding right under everyone's noses...

And I remembered that night, Ronan standing over my father's body. The storm bursting forth from the dark hole inside my chest, the lightning striking the mast at my command...

A blurry form falling from the sky as my vengeance rained onto the ship deck.

My stomach lurched. "Lyr below, Reina, I..." I tried to find the words, as if there were words to make this right. "I'm sorry, I can't—"

I was a monster, as vile as the very worst of Mathonwy snakes.

"No need for sorry, Keira, it doesn't bring anyone back." She smiled, not a trace of malice or anger in her expression when she stood and grabbed my shoulders. She fortified her stare, despite the gentle tears kissing her cheeks, the intensity of a hurricane in such a slender woman. "But ye can make me a promise. Make this peace ye have started with Ronan last. Make it last so my child is the last fatherless daughter. So one day her child does not need to know the pain we have known. That you have known, too."

I swallowed the lump in my throat, refusing to let myself cry in front of her, refusing to let my own guilt mock her pain. "It doesn't change what I've done to you."

Reina let go of my shoulders and wiped the tears from her cheeks. "No, it doesn't. But ye can't change the past, Keira. Only the future. We're counting on you for that."

My heart swelled with gratitude toward the woman in front of me. I didn't deserve her kindness or her forgiveness. I had wronged her, had wronged her daughter, and it was within her right to cut me down here and now if she wanted to. "Does Reagan know? That I..."

"No." Reina shook her head. "And I won't tell her, either. She needs a role model more than she needs an enemy."

I could not reverse the tides of time. But if I could make something better for these people, for these innocent victims of my viciousness, then that would be a start. "I promise you, I will look out for her."

Ronan laughed as he burst through the kitchen doors. "Reagan is asleep, little devil didn't make it through the first four sentences..." He stopped, looking between me and Reina, at the tear-stained cheeks and sunken faces. "Is everything okay in here?"

"No, not yet," Reina mused, "but it certainly will be. I have faith in that."

"Stop talking in riddles, Auntie, it shows your age." Ronan nodded knowingly at Reina, a twinkle of mischief in his eye. She offered him a vulgar gesture, laughing now as if nothing happened.

As if I hadn't ripped a hole in her life, in her world, as if she hadn't just fed me and welcomed me despite it all.

Ronan broke my trance. "Are you ready to head back, Keira?"

I blinked. "Aye, we should go before it gets too dark." I turned to Reina, facing her with the last shreds of my dignity. "Thank you for your hospitality."

"Yer welcome here anytime." She placed a delicate hand on my arm. "Reagan is right. Yer kin now."

Negotiations and Nightmares

The trek back up the hill was agonizingly slow, the terrain still unfamiliar to both of us. It had gotten darker than expected and the moon hadn't risen to its apex yet, our only light Ronan's lantern— which made things even worse, since I was content to never speak to him again. Tricky, slimy bastard had thrown me into that house, knowing what had happened.

"You're quiet again," he mused, his breath creating mist in front of him in the cold.

I moved to the farthest edge of the lantern's pool of light. "Aye."

Ronan sighed, stopping in his tracks. "Keira, I thought we were past the silent treatment."

"You should have warned me, Ronan."

"Aye, I could've." His expression was honest. Raw. It only deepened my pain. "But you would've thought it was a desperate play at your sympathies."

"It was."

Ronan ran his free hand through his hair. "I wanted you to meet Reagan so you could see that I had reasons for this to work, too. Not to make you feel badly about what happened."

I clenched my jaw, the guilt and rage an angry storm swirling together inside me. "I didn't know Lochlan was your kin."

"Does it make a difference?" He tucked his hand in his pocket. "There were four other men on that ship that day, all dead, all with families who miss them."

"It does make a difference," I seethed, the words hot and acidic in my throat. "Because I know his name. And now I know his kin. And I have to look them in the eye and know that it's my fault, *my fault* that their world is shattered. So yes. It makes a rutting difference."

Hot tears rolled down my cheeks, my stomach knotting and unknotting in violent waves. I couldn't look at him, at his pity-dripped gaze, now that he saw me for the coward I was.

I walked onward, not caring if I tripped in the dark.

The sound of twigs crunching behind me signaled Ronan's pursuit. Finally, the light caught up as we rounded the top of the hill, revealing the spring only a few paces beyond.

"I wasn't trying to make you feel bad, I'm just saying…" He whipped around, stopping in front of me now, his gaze penetrating. "I'm saying we need to do better by them. I'm saying that if I'd known our families started killing each other for sport four years ago, I wouldn't have stayed on that island."

The tether on my rage snapped and I shoved his chest. "Aye, but you did. You left your people and my people to fight and die over your betrayal." He had started this and left me alone to deal with it. My words continued to pour out of me, a hot spring of guilt and anger. "And *where* were you? Drunk on some island under some girl, no doubt, not a care in the world for the mess you left in your wake."

Ronan's face clouded with darkness, sharp pain stinging in his eyes. He clenched his fists and shouted back, "Aye, I was stranded on an island, because you sank my ship rather than let me explain! Despite everything I did for you, everything we had together, you didn't trust me enough to even let me *try* to tell you. You sank my ship and any real evidence that could've helped us find Cedric's killer with it, might I add. And then you left me to die." Tears sprang in his eyes, but he did not move to wipe them. He opened his mouth to speak, then shut it and took a deep breath. When he continued, his voice was colder than the Pysgoddian sea. "You left me stranded and alone, mourning both Cedric and you. So, yes. I drank and hid and fucked to forget. I stayed away. Because the man who was closer to me than my own father was murdered, and the love of my life wished it were me instead."

His emotion shocked me, but my anger would not be quelled so easily. I wanted him to hurt like I did. My throat bobbed. "Until one day, by coincidence, you decided to stumble on home the moment our families were settling? Right on time, as usual, dipping out before the bloodbath and coming back to reap the bounty."

Ronan stepped closer, his jaw flickering. He was close enough that his breath felt hot on my face. "If I hadn't come home, you'd be married to my cousin, or my rutting *father*, for Lyr's sake. I wasn't about to let you sacrifice your life to a loveless marriage like that."

"Oh, as opposed to this loveless marriage?"

Ronan paused, his chest rising and falling in heavy breaths. Then he swallowed and stepped closer, a treacherous step that threatened to break me. "It doesn't have to be."

A shiver ran down my spine and my pulse quickened. I turned from him so he couldn't see the blush rise to my cheeks. "If that's why you're here, Ronan, I suggest that after this month is over you go back to whatever island girl is waiting for you."

Ronan, thank Lyr, did not come closer. When he spoke again, he had wrangled his voice into a steady calm, the last traces of aggression gone. "I'm here for you, but I'm here for my family, too. For Reina, and Reagan, and Lochlan. No more senseless death, Keira. That's what we're doing with our match."

Guilt sang through me again, chasing away the anger and replacing it with the emptiness once more. I plopped down onto the mossy ground, hanging my head in defeat. "Aye, and what a match we are. My hands are as bloody as yours now." I hugged my knees to my chest and looked up at the near-black sky. Even the stars were hiding tonight. Perhaps they were as ashamed of me as I was.

Ronan lowered himself next to me with a thoughtful sigh and stretched his long limbs in front of him, the daggers we hurled at each other still hanging over us. "Reina doesn't blame you, as I'm sure she mentioned."

I hid my face in my hands. "Reagan will, though. If she ever figures it out."

"Well, let's make things work before she does, so when it is time to tell her, she doesn't." Ronan patted my shoulder. The action was tentative, but comforting even so, despite the curses and the pain of the moment before.

Maybe we were the only two people that could comfort each other now, sinful and broken as we were.

In a moment of weakness, I leaned into him, letting my head rest on his broad shoulder. Ronan tensed beneath me but did not move to shake me off.

"Nothing we do is going to erase what we've done to each other. To our families," I mumbled, grateful for the warmth he was giving off.

"Aye," Ronan answered quietly, his voice vibrating through his chest. "But that's no excuse to roll over and give up without trying."

I laughed, the sound bitter and empty, and let my head roll off him again. "Papa used to say that."

He shifted to face me. "I'm not trying to pour salt in an open wound."

"I know." I hugged my knees tighter, another weak part of me unlocking as I talked. "You're right. I want to believe you. I really do. I wanted to be wrong then, and I want to be wrong now. But I don't know how. After what I saw, after what Aidan saw…"

The muscle in Ronan's jaw flickered again, his eyes bright with determination. "I'll prove it, somehow, someday, Keira. I promise."

I waved him off, looking back at the sky. "Don't make any more promises. We have the contract…I'll cooperate, Ronan, I will. And I'm going to take responsibility for what I did to Reina and Reagan. But that's all the promising I can handle for now."

"Small victories, then. So, what happens next?"

I smiled, grateful to hear Papa's favorite advice out loud for the first time in years, even from him. "A bath, I think. I smell."

The mischief reignited in Ronan's eyes. "Aye, you do."

I nudged his side. "Oi, like you're any better."

"Fair point." His laugh bubbled out of him. "Ladies first, then?"

I stood, brushing off the seat of my pants. "I resent that, but I'm not going to pass up the warmer, cleaner tub water."

Ronan pushed himself up, raising an eyebrow. "You're not going to dip in the spring? It's tradition."

I looked back at the spring. It was dark, the sun's warmth long gone, and the steam tendrils that covered the water during the day were stagnant. "It looks freezing."

The corner of Ronan's mouth curled up. "Not for you."

"And what makes you think that?"

Ronan looked at the ground, shoving his hands in his pockets. "You used to make your Pa tea on the ship in half the time of anyone else."

I crossed my arms around my chest, feeling exposed. "You noticed that?"

"I notice everything about you, Keira." Ronan's eyes darted toward me, then to the water. "Go, take a bath, and I won't tell anyone about your witchcraft."

"I—Thank you. not just for the bath, but for today. For bringing me to meet them." I shot him a pointed look. "Even if you should've warned me."

"It was my absolute pleasure."

Without another word, I turned to go. As I walked briskly to the shack to gather some fresh clothes, I could feel his stare following me.

I didn't know if the hot spring was actually magic, but I prayed to Lyr it was.

It was both exhilarating and vulnerable to strip down to nothing in the open. The blanket of darkness provided enough coverage for me to finally peel my dirty garments off. Drawing on my power, I waited until the gentle tendrils of steam rose from the water before lowering myself in.

I exhaled in ecstasy as I made contact. The water may not have been magical, but it was heavenly. I was glad for the privacy as I let it soothe my muscles, which had not seen rest in weeks. Walking around town today was not particularly difficult, but my body still ached, feeling the weeks of wear and little rest. If nothing else came from my sham of a marriage, at least there would be some semblance of peace, for me and my men.

I exhaled again and let myself sink underwater.

I always felt clear, looking up at the glass-like surface above me. I watched the tiny bubbles of air that escaped my nose float upward, carrying away my hardships.

Our first day of investigating had been useless. I was still married to a man I couldn't trust but couldn't hate anymore, either. My family was farther than they'd ever been. The Council was still breathing down their necks. I was a bloody murderer for Lyr's sake, and for the first time in my life, I didn't have a plan to fix any of it.

But the water didn't judge me. And the water didn't ask for an answer. The water just *was*, and it let me exist in that temporary state of nothingness, even if only for a moment.

Then the water broke its silence, the curious voice whispering the welcome into my ears.

Welcome home.

I shot back to the surface faster than a bullet out of Weylin's gun.

The dark chuckle echoed in the back of my head. *Isn't it about time we got to know each other better? You are in my spring, after all.*

"No, not in the dark, when I'm naked, thank you," I growled back at the voice, covering my exposed breasts.

I did not dare go back under, scrubbing myself with quickness and efficiency before removing myself from the water. I did not have time for chit-chatting gods.

I pulled my clean clothes on, starting with the soft blue shirt I stole from Griffin. My teeth chattered as the bitter wind slammed against my skin, and I stumbled over myself as I hastily pulled my trousers on.

The walk to the shack felt much longer on the way back than it did on the way there. I pushed the door open, the warmth of the fire hitting me and driving out the chill. "It's your turn, Ronan, I left the water warm. *Chatty*, but warm..." I called into the room as I piled my wet, heavy curls into a knot on my head.

Only to see Ronan asleep on the bed, his torso contorted at a strange angle, like he fell asleep sitting up and fell over. One foot still wore a boot, the other only a sock with a hole, exposing his littlest toe. Even in sleep, he donned his stupid half-smile, drool gathering at one side.

I rolled my eyes but didn't move to wake him.

I grabbed a spare, worn blanket at the edge of the bed. Laying my long coat on the ground, I made myself a bed in front of the fire and nuzzled up as best as I could.

And despite the guilt and rage and homesickness weighing on my soul, sleep found me.

I was on the deck of the Ceffyl, *clad in a breezy white dress that flowed around me as the wind bit at my heels. I ran to the bow and watched the waves break against it, a laugh in my heart.*

"Keira girl, it's dangerous, don't do that." My Papa's voice floated from behind me, laced with worry. But he had no need to worry, not when my true home was so close.

"It's not dangerous, Papa," I giggled. "The sea would never hurt me."

My father's brows knit together, the sky darkening behind him. "This is not the sea," he whispered. "Look closer."

Fear prickled at the back of my neck. Leaning over the bow, I looked down into the friendly water once more.

Instead, I saw blood. Deep, viscous blood, staining the sides of my precious Ceffyl. *And in it, bodies floated, eyes closed with death, limbs swollen and discolored.*

I screamed, and at the sound, the nearest body opened his bloodshot eyes. But I knew this face. "Lochlan?"

"I found you," he chuckled darkly, his brown hair matted with the dark blood. And with a quick motion, he grabbed my arm, his fingers piercing my flesh.

I screamed again, until Papa's strong arms wrapped around my waist, pulling me back to safety. I turned to see his lips pull back, revealing a row of razor-sharp teeth.

"Now it's done, Keira girl," he laughed, his shark's teeth coated in blood. "A life for a life."

He threw me overboard.

I woke with the scream that tore through my throat. I looked around, for the blood, for my father…

But they were gone. I dug my fingers into the sand around me, releasing a sigh of relief.

Sand. I was sitting in sand.

I looked up. White sand covered the ground for ten paces, until a spring—no, *the* spring—kissed the edge of it. The sound of rushing water was deafening. I turned to find a roaring waterfall pouring over a cliff face thirty paces behind me, feeding the rushing water. The trees were sparse here, but lush, their eerie white branches thick with foliage.

I was still on *Dubryn* hill, but where? And more importantly, how in Lyr's name did I get here?

I stood, brushing the sand off the seat of my pants, and inspected myself for any damage. Minus a few scrapes on my arms, I was unscathed.

A low growl behind me interrupted my assessment.

I spun on my heels, whipping toward the sound. From a tree in the distance, a pair of green eyes stared at me from the shadows. Out of habit, I reached for the knife at my hip, only to find it gone.

Another growl and the creature stepped closer, unveiling itself into the morning light. A wolf, but larger, nearly the size of a small bear.

A *blaidd*.

I was still dreaming. I *had* to be dreaming.

I pinched myself tightly. Twice.

I did not wake up. I was not asleep.

The *blaidd's* deep brown fur glistened in the morning light. As did its fangs, poking out from under its lips. But it did not bare its teeth. It only watched me, waiting. Fear turned my limbs to lead, washing over me in waves.

I scanned the sand, looking for anything that I could use as a weapon.

Nothing.

I clenched my fists, trying to breathe deeply. This was a master predator, and if it smelled my weakness, my fear…I would be its prey.

The creature took another step forward, and I stepped back instinctually. My heart thundered in my chest.

The *blaidd* blinked, registering my movements, but did not advance again.

I swallowed. I was going to have to make a run for it.

Breathing in, I let my power ripple through me. I would not be completely unarmed, in case the creature decided to attack once my back was exposed. If I could get to the water, I could get out, and then start to make sense of how I got here in the first place.

"Keira? Keira, where are you?" Ronan's voice echoed from the distance.

I tensed, the wolf snapping its head in the direction of the sound. It bared its teeth, growling deeply.

"Keira!" Ronan called again, closer this time.

The *blaidd* looked back at me, and I swear to Lyr it rolled its eyes.

Connor Yorath. The voice slithered into my head, not Lyr's but a deeper, primal voice. The animal blinked twice, then turned to leave from whence it came.

Twigs behind me snapped, and Ronan burst into the clearing. Sweet relief washed over me.

"Keira, thank Lyr," Ronan panted, resting his hands on his knees as he caught his breath. He crossed to me, grabbing my shoulders and inspecting me closer. "Are you all right?

"Get off." I swatted him away. "I'm fine."

"What are you doing out here?" Concern flickered in his expression.

I looked around, searching for the green eyes again. Wherever the *blaidd* came from, it was gone. Maybe I had imagined the whole thing, some sort of post-dream hallucination. "I— exploring, that's all."

Ronan's brows knit. "At dawn?"

I folded my arms across my chest, marching east, where I assumed the shack was. "Aye, I didn't get much sleep, since someone took the bed all night, so I went exploring." *Yes, that was right.* I hadn't slept well, and I must have sleepwalked. I had a few times as a child, back when my powers had first started swirling in my chest...

Ronan fell into step beside me, our pattern repeating. "Without your knife?"

"Aye, why do I need to take my knife?"

Ronan stuffed his hands in his pockets. "Says the girl who takes it to piss."

I slowed. He had come looking for me, was concerned on my behalf, and I was starting to believe that it wasn't an act. I didn't know how I ended up in the clearing, or what on earth my dream meant, but having someone to worry about me helped smooth the raw edges of my nerves. Rolling my eyes, I nudged him in the side. "Call it an exercise in trust. Or perhaps forgiveness. I'll leave a note next time, all right?"

Ronan kept moving, but I didn't miss the smile that pulled at the corner of his mouth. "Well, now that you're okay…Want to go sailing today?"

"What?"

"Aye, sailing," he snickered, pantomiming steering the ship. "I have a ship, and it needs sailing. And a cousin who will haunt you and me both until we take her. Plus, it's a shame for two sailors to be stuck on land. You can't tell me you don't miss it."

I peered up at him, the power in my core tingling with excitement. I imagined it, the wind in my hair, the sting of salt on my skin, the burn of rope beneath my hands…

I did miss it, almost as much as I missed my family.

We walked through a thick grove of willows, the main pool of the spring coming into view in the distance. I sighed, relieved to put the strange sand and the eyes of the *blaidd* behind me. I knew that after my morning and the night before, I would not be sleeping for days.

Relaxing, I smirked up at Ronan. "Aye, and who will help us sail this magnificent ship of yours? Reagan and I, that's your crew?"

"I'm sure I can find a few helpers. My cousin Rhett—"

I stopped walking. "No. I'm coming around to some of your kin, but even I have boundaries. Rhett killed Owen. And I know we all have blood on our hands, but Owen was good." My voice tightened over my eldest cousin's name. I knew Rhett hadn't meant to strike a killing blow that night in Bachtref. Griffin had started that fight, something Vala never really forgave her youngest son for, and Owen had interceded to protect his little brother. But it was dark, and poor Owen had never been much of a fighter. He didn't stand a chance.

It wasn't Griffin or Rhett's fault. Both families were to blame for the deaths that plagued us and the hatred spreading like scurvy. I knew I had done just as much wrong. But I would never see Owen's kind smile again or hear his sweet laugh. And while I could perhaps forgive Rhett one day, as Reina had forgiven me, I could never forget.

Ronan seemed to understand, and though he raised his hands, he did not protest. I rubbed my temple. I was dying to sail, more than I cared to admit. Even if it meant calling in some old favors. "Leave the crew to me. Besides, I have something to see to in town."

"Can I come?"

The wolf's strange, impossible message echoed through my head. *Connor Yorath.*

It was time to pay the Councilman a visit.

"No. I should see to this alone. Let's meet at the docks by noon. How many hands do you think we need to sail your new toy?"

Ronan ran his hands through his hair. Calculating. "Two more decent sailors, aside from us. One, if he's a great sailor."

A grin crossed my face. I had just the sailor in mind. "I'll make it happen."

8

Blaidds and Blackmail

For a man who presented himself so simply, Connor Yorath's office was surprisingly cluttered. Stacks and stacks of parchment, old books, journals, and other odds and ends reached toward the ceiling. They covered every visible piece of furniture save a pristine desk and two wooden chairs. It smelled of old ink and mildew, turning my stomach.

I sat straight in the wooden chair opposite the desk, waiting for Connor to make his grand entrance. Time to formulate a plan.

It was a mistake to come here without Ronan or Aidan, that I knew. But I couldn't explain why I needed to talk to Yorath. Not when my only reason was because a giant, possibly imaginary, green-eyed wolf in the forest told me to. And the *blaidd's* voice in my head had been so clear. Whether it was a warning, or a clue, or a hallucination, I did not know, but I had to find out.

I kept my hands folded in my lap like Vala taught me. It wasn't a plan, but it was a start. "Blushing bride, blushing bride," I mumbled to myself.

The door swung open, Yorath's lanky frame darkening the doorway. He brushed past me and sat in his chair, not bothering to look up as he pulled out a piece of parchment. Slowly, he reached for a pair of silver spectacles from the topmost drawer. Donning them, he scanned the contents of the parchment in front of him.

I knew this play, the feigned disinterest to try and get a rise out of me. It was one of Aidan's favorite negotiating tactics, and I had perfected it. I cleared my throat, batting my eyelashes as I did. Let him think he was in charge.

He peered over the rim of his spectacles, his voice dripping with annoyance. "And what can I do for you today, Mrs. Mathonwy?"

"Councilman Yorath," I lilted, tilting my head down as I had seen Finna do time and time again with her many conquests. "Thank you for seeing me on such short notice. It's a pleasure to see you again."

Connor looked back down at his page, waving me off like a fruit fly. "The point of your visit. Get to it."

I fought to maintain my composure. I'd have to do better. Fine.

"I couldn't stop thinking about our conversation the other night." I let my voice drop deeper and leaned forward. "At the wedding. You said you were willing to discuss my family's business."

Connor's eyes darted to me, his mouth a tight line. His gaze stopped at my chest unapologetically. "Yes, you've mentioned, but I don't know what you expect me to do."

He took the bait.

I lifted my chest further despite the wave of nausea it sent through my belly, glad that I wore my ruffled blue tunic rather than my buttoned one. "I'm sure you can think of some arrangement, Councilman, that favors us both." I offered my sweetest smile, one that would've rivaled Ronan's best. "All I ask is that the sanctions on my family's shipping and supply business be lifted. Right now, we are barely scraping by with the contracts from Pysgodd, but you know what happens there during winter. Our ships won't be able to get within a mile of the coast when the sea freezes. We need the sanctions on goods from Orwellin and the Southern Isles lifted. We can't just ferry passengers, we need to move product—"

Connor held up a hand to silence me. He stood and leaned forward over the desk, practically looking down my shirt. "Do you know how many businesses right here in Porthladd your family and this silly feud have hurt?"

The taste of sick rose up my throat, but I ignored it. "I know, a fact I'm truly sorry for, but the island depends on our business too.

We supply half the shops with the goods they need. And now with the marriage, the blood feud is—"

"The sanctions stand, Mrs. Mathonwy." Connor leaned so close his rancid breath assaulted my nostrils. I tried to hide my grimace. A slimy smile crept onto his gaunt cheeks. "There is simply nothing I can do about it without some assurance."

Typical, rutting man.

But fine. I could play interested until he signed the pardons. "What kind of assurance?" I tried to make the question sound demure, but I pouted my lips like Finna would.

Connor didn't bristle, standing straight. He locked his hands behind his back like a chancellor in high court. "Where is young Mr. Mathonwy now? Surely a husband would be concerned for the affairs of his wife and her family. It seems to me that this marriage of yours needs solidifying first."

"Ronan had his own business to attend to," I answered with confidence. The last thing I needed now was for Connor to smell the weakness in our...whatever our relationship was. "I plan on meeting him again after this. We're going sailing together and—"

"You must think me a fool!" He slammed his hand on the desk, rising with the action. I jumped, and a nearby tower of paper wobbled. "Councilwoman Rhiamon and Councilman Llewelyn might have been easily charmed by your performance at the wedding. And waltzing around town together yesterday for all Porthladd to see? Very clever, I must admit." My stomach rolled as he leaned over again, his teeth exposed like a hissing cat. "But I know very well that a contract is not enough to tame a sea witch willing to flirt for power."

"Excuse me?" I clenched my fists at my sides to keep myself from hitting him. So much for Finna's favorite tactic. But I was a lady second and a sailor first, and I had more than just tricks up my sleeve.

"Let me be frank, Mrs. Mathonwy." A thin smile tugged at the corner of his mouth. "The wording of the contract is very clear. Two bloodlines made one."

I crossed my arms over my chest. "Aye, and we're already married, in case you forgot while you were ogling my breasts."

Connor blinked twice, blush filling his white cheeks, but he did not wait to strike again. "A child, Mrs. Mathonwy. That's what the wording implies."

My heart stopped for a moment as the anchor dropped. I had walked into his trap, not the other way around.

He sauntered around the desk, and with a spindly finger, stroked my cheek. I hissed, smacking his vile hand away, but he only chuckled. "I suggest that you quit spending your time acting like a wild dog chasing after that family of yours on that sad little ship and start doing your duty as a woman."

My power rippled beneath my skin, begging to be unleashed. I stepped closer to him, and though he was taller, there was no doubt I would demolish him if it came to fists. "I am not some bitch you can breed."

"You sure bark like one," he spat but took a careful step back, watching me as he sheltered himself behind his desk once more. He offered another malice-dripped smile from his perch. "Now go on, get to it, before someone has to beat you into submission. And then perhaps we can talk about the sanctions."

The last stones of the dam holding back my uncivilized fury broke.

I had been letting other people decide for me for too long. Connor and the Council had been telling me where to eat, where to sleep, who to marry, and now when to lie on my back and take it. But I was not some soft-spoken, easily broken mare that could be mounted and ridden. Somehow, in the last few days or weeks or years, I had forgotten that. Had forgotten my wild, unbridled nature.

Taming you would be like taming the sea.

I would not forget again.

In one swift movement, I drew the knife from my sleeve and drove it into the polished wood of the desk. Connor jumped back, a small scream escaping his lips. I laughed, "If you think there is anyone on this earth who can make me submit, you are a fool. I'm no dog, Councilman. I cannot be trained to bark and rollover. No, I'm a *blaidd*." I narrowed my eyes like an animal marking its prey. Connor's face blanched, eyes widening in turn. I offered a silent *thank you* to my messenger. "My teeth are sharp, and my mind is sharper. Once I get the scent of blood, I can't be satiated until I have my enemy in my jaws. I don't know what you get out of torturing my family and insulting me. I don't know what your motive is or what you're hiding, but I will find out. And I will end it."

I pulled my knife free of the wood and turned to take my leave.

"Threatening a Councilmember will not do you any favors, Keira Branwen," Connor shouted after me, his voice shaking with fear.

I turned on my heel, staring him straight in his beady eyes. "It's Keira Mathonwy."

And because I could, I let out a wild howl before walking out the door.

I was so unbelievably stupid.

I had threatened a Councilmember. And not any Councilmember—Connor Yorath. A *High Council* member. I had put the final nail in the coffin for my family's business, and who knew what else he'd do now that I had provoked him.

I shuddered as I remembered the stench of his hot breath. He did not strike me as a forgiving man.

But Lyr below, did it feel good to watch the blood drain from his face.

Stupid, stupid, stupid.

And I knew that's what Aidan was about to tell me, too.

I stood on the cobblestone steps of the Branwen Townhouse, gathering the courage to knock. Looking up at my former residence, at the blue-green shutters and the moss growing up the side of the brown stone, I hoped they would calm the sharp edges of my nerves.

And I hoped Aidan wasn't home. The waves in my stomach crashed as I knocked on the door.

Footsteps on the other side, then the door swung open, Tarran's freckled face appearing with a grin. "Keira?"

"Oh, thank Lyr," I said honestly, glad it was him and not Aidan. Not yet, at least. I didn't have the stomach to face that conversation. I pushed past Tarran and his toothy smile, the warmth of the house too inviting to pass up. "I've been standing out here for ages. Let me in already."

The house smelled of cedar and the lavender sprigs Vala always kept fresh. I breathed it in, missing the scent more than I imagined I would.

"Griffin, Keira is home!" Tarran called down the long hallway that served as the entrance to the rest of the house. A second later, Griffin popped his head out of the cedar door at the end of the hall, his red hair loose around his face.

Another second, and he had taken the entire length of the corridor in three of his long strides and wrapped me up in a tight hug.

"Good to see you, Shrimpy," he teased, squeezing me to his white cotton shirt.

"Ow, Griffin, you're crushing me," I mumbled as I breathed him in too. Sea-salt and blackberry soap. But my stomach sank again. If Griffin was here, it meant no one was sailing today.

"Stop fussing and come sit for a while." He laughed into my hair and let me go. "We've missed you." He walked back down the hall and turned into the sitting room. I followed him, crossing my fingers that Aidan wasn't waiting around the corner.

The room was empty save for Griffin, Tarran and me.

I breathed a sigh of relief. "Where is the rest of the clan?"

Griffin slung himself onto the brown leather chair nearest to the fireplace. "Mother took Saeth and Finna shopping for new dresses or something useless like that, and senior crew aren't back home yet. It was Weylin's birthday last night."

"Which means no one will see them until well after sundown tonight," Tarran said slyly, leaning on the mantle above the fireplace. By some strange magic, he had gotten taller, the hem of his brown trousers only hitting his ankle. Maybe it was the rest of a few days on land, but he looked stronger too.

I plopped onto my favorite blue sofa, worn as it was, relief washing over me in waves. I knew Aidan being gone didn't change what I had done, but now perhaps I had time to fix it before he found out. Never thought I'd be so grateful for Weylin's birth.

"You two didn't go?" I asked, putting both of my boots on the couch—an action Vala would have roasted me alive for.

Griffin shrugged. "Weylin is boring, even after a few drinks." A grin lit up his features as he gestured toward Tarran. "And this one can't hold his liquor, so someone had to look after him."

Tarran pouted, crossing his arms. "Yes, I can, Griffin." His body may have been stronger, but he was still a boy in so many ways.

I laughed, sinking further into the sofa. "No, you can't, but that's why we like you, Tarran."

"How long can you stay?" Griffin mused, ignoring how Tarran's brow remained knotted. "Aidan will be sad he missed you."

"Not long at all," I sighed, and sat up, resting my hands on my knees. I had a purpose to accomplish, and I would not fail both of my tasks for the day. "But it was you two I needed to see, anyway. I've got a sailing proposition for you."

Tarran pricked up, and Griffin leaned forward, gripping the arms of the chair. "We're all ears."

Fish on the hook. "Today, for a day trip to Bachtref. I need a two-man crew. Or one spectacular man."

Griffin smirked, puffing his chest out. "Tarran, you can go back to bed, then."

Tarran smacked his shoulder. "Shut your mouth, Griffin. What ship?"

I took a steadying breath and kept my expression casual. "The *Sarff y Mor.*"

Both of my cousins stiffened.

"Ronan's new ship." Griffin balked.

"Technically, it was a wedding gift, so it's just as much mine."

Griffin chuckled darkly, his eyes narrowed. "Are you rutting crazy, Keira? Three days and you're already brainwashed!"

"Typical girl, Keira," Tarran sneered. "One night in the sack and you're his plaything."

I unsheathed my blade from my coat sleeve, flipping it once in my hand before pointing it at him. "Tarran Branwen, if you ever speak to me or any other woman like that again, I will remove the tongue from your skull and wear it as a necklace."

Tarran blanched, knowing exactly how well I kept my promises. "I'm sorry, that was a low blow." He ran a frustrated hand through his short auburn wisps.

Griffin sighed, watching him as he spoke, "But you know what you're saying, right? Three days ago, you would've thought you were crazy, too."

I knew this conversation was going to be difficult, mostly because he was right. Three days ago, I would've cut my own tongue out for blasphemy. But time meant nothing to the goddess of fate. I knew better than anyone that things could change faster than expected.

"It hasn't been as bad as I thought it would be." My voice was low as I tried to find the words. "And I need your help. You know I wouldn't ask if I had another option."

"No. I'm not sailing with that prick," Tarran snapped, kicking the floor where he stood.

My own frustration prickled. I moved to stand. "Fine, I guess Ronan was right then. We'll have to ask Rhett and Roland…"

"Lyr's ass you will." Griffin shot to his feet, a dark cloud over his eyes. "Tarran and I will hold you down and tie you up here before that happens."

I sauntered up to him. He had two heads over me, and I had to crane my neck to meet his gaze. "As much as I'd love to see you try, Griffin, I know you wouldn't dare. But I will make you a deal."

"This is rich," Tarran scoffed under his breath, folding his arms again.

"Oi, let's hear it," Griffin challenged, leaning into his height for effect.

I folded my arms, mimicking Tarran's surly stance. "Come with me, be a good boy, and I won't tell Aidan you lost four hundred silver pieces at the *Raven* two nights before the wedding."

Griffin leered, pride radiating through every inch of him. "Go ahead, tell him, I made it all back last night."

"Fine." I stepped around him, an animal circling my prey. "Then I'll tell Vala about Brynn."

Griffin's entire frame stiffened. He clearly remembered the saucy blonde woman from Madame Jessa's. "You wouldn't dare."

Tarran stood straighter, tensing for a fight. "Who is Brynn?"

"And don't forget Maddox and his 'chiseled jawline,' as you put it." I patted Griffin's shoulder, the action dripping with condescension. I didn't like blackmailing the man who lived as my brother, but I had to admit, I was good at it. "How much did you spend on *that* particular double feature again?"

Griffin plastered on a smile, but his left hand twitched—his tell that he was feeling the heat. "I don't need to spend a copper on love."

"Griffin, Griffin, Griffin." I walked back to the couch and eased myself into it, crossing my legs slowly. "You're forgetting one important detail."

"Am I now?" He mirrored my action, taking his leather chair again.

"This should be good." Tarran leaned on the back of the chair. He might not agree with my motives, but the boy was entertained by my methods.

"Madame Jessa keeps a guestbook full of signatures," I whispered as I delivered the killing blow. "And she still owes me for that crate of perfume I smuggled from Ir'de."

"Oi, you're ruthless," Griffin laughed. "I taught you well."

I shrugged. "I'm motivated."

Tarran stiffened, realizing the match of wills was over. And lost. "You can't bully him into coming with you."

"I can speak for myself, Tarran." Griffin waved him off. "Maybe I should go with Keira. For her protection, of course."

I gave him a wide, satisfied smile. "Aye, that's what I thought."

"Aidan isn't going to like this," Tarran barked, a desperate last attack.

My frustration bristled again. "I would remind you, Tarran, that while I may not be Captain yet, I am still the first mate of the *Ceffyl*, a position I earned through blood and sweat. That means Aidan trusts my judgment. You should try it sometime." I stood, walking toward the doorway and looked back at him. "Now, are you coming, or not?"

Tarran's throat bobbed angrily. "You can't snake-charm me into forgetting who I am, Keira."

It was a petty insult, but it still stung. I didn't let it show, crafting my mask of indifference. "Suit yourself. Griffin, let's go. We're already late."

I didn't wait for Griffin to respond as I marched out the door, grabbing my favorite dagger from the shelf as I passed. But I heard the rustle of fabric and the clanking of metal behind me as he pulled on his coat and armed himself. Then, his footsteps behind me when I walked out into the midday sun.

We were quiet as we continued, and I kept the pace brisk. An awkward silence hung between us where there never was one before.

I knew Tarran was just as confused and hurt as I was, that he hadn't lived the last three days with me to understand. But it hurt nevertheless to have his amber eyes screaming the truth of what I was.

Enemy.

Reading my mind, Griffin cleared his throat. "Don't blame the boy, Keira. He's taking your marriage pretty hard. He was only fifteen when he lost his Ma. And now he's losing you. It's a different type of loss, sure, but still...you can understand that this particular adjustment is going to be hard for him."

I slowed my pace. He was right. I was not the only Branwen to lose a parent to this silly war. And I sure as hell wasn't the only one who had to wake up every day feeling their absence. It had been two years, but Aleena's death had been particularly harrowing. I could still hear her screams as the house collapsed, the fire consuming her with it.

The Mathonwys still maintained they didn't start it, but we knew better.

But we were not blameless either. And it didn't matter who was to blame if we all ended up dead.

"Aye. It'll be hard." I stopped walking, looking up at him. "But too many innocents like Aleena have already died for us to keep at this. Something needs to change."

"I know that, Keira." He rubbed my arm with a surprising gentleness. "Just give him some time. Not everyone can change as fast as you."

"You know, you sound like Papa sometimes," I admitted, the honesty a breath of fresh air. "Wise."

The corner of his mouth twitched upward. "Quiet. I have a reputation to uphold."

Truths and Triumphs

"Took you long enough!" Ronan called from the end of the pier as we approached Sailor's Point. He wore his black trousers and bright red coat with brass buttons, a glaring contrast to the browns and greens of the docks. I rolled my eyes at the sight of him.

His eyes narrowed in turn as he took in Griffin's tall form behind me. I did not see Reagan, but I knew she was there, perhaps already on the ship.

The *Sarff y Mor* itself stood behind him, small for a cutter, but a proud pinewood craft indeed. The ship had a single mast, its white sails pristine, fastened to the bowsprit with thick rope. She was a beauty, built for speed rather than cargo, her outline as elegant and graceful as the sea serpent she was named for.

I approached Ronan and the ship, Griffin hanging back a bit, his strong arms folded across his chest like an impetuous child.

"I'm a sailor. I live by the compass, not the clock," I called back to Ronan, ignoring Griffin. A grizzled old sailor on the pier next to us shot me a dark glare, and I flipped him a vulgar gesture as I reached Ronan, lowering my voice as I spoke. "And I was busy threatening Connor Yorath's life."

Ronan's eyes widened. "You *what?*"

"Oh, and I brought Griffin." I gestured behind me for Griffin to get his surly ass in motion.

Ronan raised an eyebrow. "Busy morning, then." Griffin huffed behind me, and Ronan raked his gaze over him like a merchant appraising a disappointing haul. "This was the outstanding sailor you had in mind?"

"That's it, I'm out," Griffin growled, turning to stalk away.

I grabbed his arm to stop him, spinning him back to face me. "Griffin—"

He pointed a shaking finger at Ronan. "Another word out of his pretty-boy mouth, I punch him. Clear?"

I held my hands up to calm him. "Aye, Ronan is sorry."

"I am sorry, really." Ronan walked up behind me with a hand extended to shake. "It's more of a reflex than anything."

Griffin did not take his hand, but I watched the red clear from his eyes. "You'd do well to suppress it next time."

Ronan tucked the extended hand into his pocket, his face clear of judgment. "Aye, duly noted. Thank you for coming out here."

A small voice cut through the tension like the sharpened blade of a cutlass. "You have the prettiest hair I've ever seen."

Reagan stared directly at Griffin as she strode up the dock, a smitten blush coloring her cheeks. She wore black leather trousers and what I could only assume to be her mother's red blouse due to the way it billowed around her shoulders. It was cinched at the waist by a black knife belt detailed with hand-stitched roses.

For someone who had been hidden from the world for so many years, she sure knew how to make an entrance.

Griffin blinked twice, running a hand through his long mane. "Ah, thank you, but you're a little young for me, lass."

"I thought I told you to wait on the ship," Ronan scolded her, but Reagan waved him off.

"I'm Reagan. I'm twelve." She batted her eyelashes at Griffin. "And you're Griffin Branwen, the Swordsinger. But cousin River used to call you the fire-crotched man-whore—"

Ronan covered her mouth to cut her off before she could finish, a stunned apology in his expression. "And that's enough of that!"

Griffin's eyes went wide, then a small smile pulled at the corner of his mouth. "I like her."

"That's what I said." I shrugged at my cousin, knowing the tiny tyrant's witchcraft firsthand.

I watched as the last strands of resistance unraveled within him, his shoulders relaxing into an easy stance. He gave me a reproachful look, but it was shallow, Reagan's magic already melting away any last trace of his reservations. "Now, what is this trip for? You bound me by my bollocks and blackmailed me to come, it better be important."

"Aye, it's of the utmost importance." I looked at him seriously, but I couldn't help the smirk twitching at the corner of my lips. "We're taking her sailing."

"You're kidding, right?"

Reagan tapped the small, ornate dagger at her side. The hilt was made of gold, fashioned in the shape of a dragon's head with tiny rubies for eyes. Where she got it, I had no idea. "And you are all going to teach me how to fight."

Griffin scoffed, sticking his hands to his hips like an Orwellin statue. "I can't teach a little girl to fight."

Reagan put her fists to her own hips, mocking his stance perfectly. "I'm not little, I'm twelve. But it's okay if you're scared you'll lose…"

Griffin's jaw dropped in surprise, but he quickly regained his composure, mischief simmering in his expression. "Right, fine, I'm in. Can we get on the bloody ship, or are we going to stand here all day picking our asses?"

Ronan made a grand gesture of welcome toward the ship, hope glimmering in the blue of his eye. "Aye, deckhand Branwen. Let's sail."

Sailing again made the whole world right.

We set sail right after a delicious packed lunch from Reina's kitchen. When we were full and happy, we unleashed the *Sarff* from her cage, sailing into the high afternoon sun.

I breathed in the salt air whipping around me. It filled me to the core, awakening every last forgotten part of myself, reigniting the fire in my blood. And the work of it all—tying knots and securing the rigging and climbing the mast to track a course—it felt good.

Every callous and scrape and splinter and bead of sweat was a blessing from Lyr himself.

It wasn't the pure, primal magic of sailing the *Ceffyl*, a beast in her own right. But the sun was warm for this time of year, and the wind was steady. And the *Sarff* had a certain charm and speed that excited me, like meeting a new friend.

We were only a few leagues from the Porthladdian shore, her outline still visible in the distance, when we decided Bachtref was more trouble than it was worth. A sail around the island would do just fine.

I made my way towards the bowsprit, past where Griffin lounged on the starboard rail like a housecat. Careful not to fall, I climbed to the very tip of the ship. The white of the waves crashed against the wood, spraying me playfully.

Every single drop of saltwater that seeped into my skin remade me from the outside in. This was who I was. This person, part sailor and part sea itself, standing on the edge of a ship, staring at the edge of the world.

"This is incredible!" Reagan called from the helm where she stood, gripping the massive wheel in her small hands. Ronan stood behind her, guiding her, a stupid smile plastered on his face, his golden curls pointing in every direction.

"Aye, little dragon, it is." He beamed, adjusting her hands for a better hold. "Here, keep the helm steady, good. You feel that? That's the current tugging underneath; you have to fight it to stay course sometimes."

Reagan focused on her task, her small face scrunching up. "Like this?"

I hopped back up onto the main deck, calling up to her, "Just like that. You're doing well. The sea is on your side today."

Griffin stretched on his perch, foot dangling over the edge precariously. On a different day, I would've pushed him into the blue just for the fun of it, but I didn't want to set a bad example. I did give his boot a kick as I passed him, and he sat up, a lazy grin on his face. "The sea is always on our side when you're here."

Reagan's ears pricked up like a dog as she squinted against the midday sun. "So, it's true, you do have the gift?"

Griffin hopped up. "Aye, and we're all cursed to live with her big head."

I rolled my eyes, ignoring the urge to throw him overboard once more. Instead, I hoisted myself onto the first beam of the mast, the strain of muscle the perfect outlet for my frustration. I busied myself with the knots again, giving the sails some slack as the wind picked up.

Ronan eyed me mischievously from the deck. "Shall I tell you a story, little dragon? About the Night-Mare of the Four Seas?"

I shot him a look that could curdle milk. "Or you could shut your mouth and help me with this rigging."

Ronan frowned but stayed quiet.

Griffin, on the other hand, did not. He gracefully heaved himself up on the mast beside me, the pine beam groaning under our combined weight. "Aye, Cousin Ronan, give us a story." He winked at me as he made quick work of the knots. "Keira wouldn't deny Reagan such a treat."

"If you'd like, Griffin, you can listen overboard," I growled, bouncing on the beam so she shook slightly underneath us. Griffin had to hold on to the sail to catch his balance.

But Ronan, safe on the ship deck below, had all the permission he needed. "See, Keira wasn't always the Night-Mare of the Four Seas…" he started, leaning onto the portside railing.

"Aye, but she was always a nightmare," Griffin called loudly enough for Reagan to hear this time, and she giggled despite herself.

I leaped down from the rigging, folding my arms across my chest. "You both are pushing your luck."

"Please, Keira?" Reagan pouted from behind the helm, puppy eyes at full sail.

Ronan shrugged and nodded his head toward Reagan, whose bottom lip was now quivering for effect. I sighed, rubbing my temples, and waved him on to continue, knowing full well I'd regret it in a minute.

He smiled wickedly and grabbed the helm from Reagan, motioning for her to sit. Dutifully she did, crossing her legs in front of her. Ronan cleared his throat before beginning. "When we were little, before Keira was the cutthroat demon of the deep that she is today, she used to be afraid of swimming."

"That is not true," I grumbled.

Griffin vaulted down from the rigging and plopped himself next to Reagan. "You were, too. Until you were eight."

I opened my mouth to protest but Ronan cut me off. "Aye, she was deathly afraid. Sure, she'd go on the ship, and she knew how to kick her feet and paddle in shallow water, but she'd refuse to dip her head under."

"Said she heard voices," Griffin added for dramatic effect, winking at Reagan.

Embarrassment rose to my cheeks. I did not like this. I had wanted to show Reagan a good time, wanted Griffin to relax and feel comfortable with them both. But I hadn't imagined it would be at my expense.

There was a ghostly simpering at the back of my mind again. The same voice that had frightened me all those years ago was amused by my plight.

"Not voices, Griffin," I corrected, thinking of some colorful curses for my invisible companion. "One voice."

"Aye, if you say so." Ronan puffed out his chest, gesturing grandly to himself like a High Councilman. "But see, me, being the gentleman I was, decided to help her get over her fear."

I couldn't contain the scoff that escaped my lips. "That is not how it happened."

The memory of the story he was telling came into focus in my mind's eye: it was a Summer Solstice celebration, held at the Traeth beaches. The bonfires were higher than the masts of the ships docked, the water kissing the edges of the shoreline.

Midnight. High tide.

Reagan leaned her head into her hands, a dreamy expression across her face as she listened to Ronan's fantastical tale. "What did you do?"

Ronan leaned onto the helm, smugness radiating from his every pore. "Well, I figured if I went swimming with her, she'd feel better."

"You weren't swimming, Ronan, you were drowning. If you're going to tell the story, tell it right." I rolled my eyes with as much vague annoyance as I could muster, but the fear I felt that day rose to my throat. The way he had fallen into the water, the way the adults on the shore had continued dancing and drinking, not noticing that he was missing, not listening as I cried for help...

Reagan giggled, her eyes darting back and forth between us like we were performers from Ir'de. I kept my mask of irritation on so as not to show her the worry underneath it.

Ronan ran his hands through his hair dramatically. "No, I was pretending to drown so you'd have to come rescue me." He gripped the helm tighter, a sweet smile pulling at the corners of his mouth. "But Keira didn't hesitate, despite her fear. She jumped in right after me and saved me."

But I *had* hesitated. I froze completely, waiting for someone, *anyone* else to jump in and save him. But I couldn't.

Not until the voice spoke.

Save him. You can do it.

I had never heard the voice outside of the water before that, and never that clearly. Still my feet wouldn't move, my fear paralyzing.

If you don't, he'll die.

The voice was right. He had been under so long, and the water was so dark.

Don't be afraid. I'm right here with you.

And I jumped in, the voice guiding me when I couldn't see. A power had surged through me, one that felt like the ocean itself, moving me forward, even with Ronan's weight on my back, until we were both safe on the shore.

"If I remember correctly, she also kicked you in the shin every day for a month after that so you didn't forget what an idiot you were," Griffin laughed, the sound pulling me from my trance. I shook off the memory before it consumed me once more.

"Aye. I still have the bruises." Ronan laughed with Griffin, the sound free despite the true horror of the tale he just told. I supposed that's what made him such a good storyteller; the ability to take one of the scariest moments of a life and turn it into a laugh and a smile.

Reagan turned to me, stars in her eyes. "So you've always been the bravest person in the world."

I forced a haunted smile. "Not always. I was scared, then. So scared. And there are still things that scare me."

I thought of the *blaidd* in the woods and Connor Yorath's threats and the unanswered questions about my father's death. Even now, I still felt like that scared little girl, staring at the dark, turbulent sea, too afraid to jump in.

The voice hummed, a warm wave washing over me. *I was there with you then. I am here with you now.*

Reagan's tiny brow was knit in deep contemplation as she spoke again, "But you still jumped in. That's what really makes you brave."

Ronan raised an eyebrow. "Who knew a little dragon could have such a wise tongue?"

Reagan shrugged, devoid of the heaviness from the moment before. She raked her eyes over the three of us. "Now who is going to teach me to kick ass?"

Griffin jumped to his feet, mischief in his sunset eyes. "Depends. You want to learn the easy way," he challenged, rising to his full height in front of her, "or the hard way?"

Bastard never knew how to walk away from a fight, little girls no exception.

Ronan glanced at me, worry in his gaze, asking the silent question. *Can I trust him?*

I met his sapphire gaze and nodded, a smile pulling at my lips. His shoulders relaxed, but he still watched with a falcon's stare.

Reagan stood, brushing off her clothes, unbothered by the giant before her. "Looks like the easy way is doing a lot of talking."

A dangerous smile filled Griffin's face. "Aye, that's it, girl. You may be cute, but I can only take so much."

He reached behind his back, unsheathing the twin blades he kept there. Truth and Triumph, he called them. They were both long, nearly his arm's length, but surprisingly light, their steel remarkably thin. And sharp. But their deadliness was not just in their pointy parts. They were enchanted by the best sorcerers from Hud to obey only their master. Rumor had it they even sang to their true master when trouble was near. Griffin won them gambling in the Southern Isles and hadn't lost a sword fight since.

Reagan, however, did not balk, and only stared at them with awe, like a jewel thief at a ruby. Weighing them in his hands, Griffin flipped the one in his left hand over once and extended the handle side to Reagan, motioning for her to grab it. "Here, take this. Her name is Triumph, and she won't let you down."

Reagan took the blade from him, dwarfed by its length, her chest swelling with pride.

Griffin led Reagan to the far end of the deck and demonstrated for her how to hold the blade, correcting her stance as he went.

I joined Ronan at the helm, leaning onto it with a smile. "I've never seen him let anyone else touch that sword."

Ronan's brow knit as he watched. "Should I be worried?"

"Definitely." I smirked. "But not for Reagan."

A laugh rumbled in his chest as he watched them move, his forehead unraveling.

It was something to see, Griffin adjusting and leading her, Reagan taking it all with a smile despite the sweat beading on her brow. We watched in silence, Ronan and I, both of us sitting in the strange nostalgia of the moment.

"He reminds me of your Pa sometimes," Ronan finally whispered so only I would hear.

"I said the same thing this morning." I noted the way Griffin tucked his long hair behind his ear the same way Papa used to. The resemblance was uncanny, to an extent. "But then he opens his mouth."

"It was good of him to come."

"I didn't give him much of a choice."

"So," Ronan hedged, the laughter in his voice dissolving, "tell me what happened with Yorath. And why you didn't bring me with you."

I clenched my jaw, the anger and shame of this morning's visit rising up my throat. "It's not in our contract that you have to accompany me to everything."

Ronan's chest fell, but his expression remained neutral. "No, it's not, but it might be a good idea for next time." His gaze darkened. "Yorath is a tricky bastard."

"I don't know if he'll ever let me within twenty paces of him again, so, next time you might have to be the one to chat with him," I sighed, the admission releasing some of the tension that had been building in my core. Now the words poured out of the hole I had tapped. "I asked him about my family's sanctions. He told me I should be broken and bred, that it was all I was good for. So, I showed him my knife and heavily implied where he could shove it."

A dark cloud fell over Ronan's expression, a lethal calm settled in his gaze. "What a bloody fool," he growled, the low rumble laced with rare aggression.

I blinked at him. He was the last person on this ship to be lecturing me about foolishness. "I know. I feel terrible about it, so please don't rub it in." I hated how small my voice was, how desperate for his approval I sounded.

Ronan's eyes were fixed on the horizon, a white-knuckled grip on the helm. "Not you. Yorath." He shot me a look, the ice and malice softening slightly, revealing awe in their absence. "No one has the power to tell the sea itself to submit. He deserves every bit of your wrath."

Something unlocked within me, a key turning through my core. Funny, that the one man I was bound to by law and chains was the one to set a part of me free. "Aye," I whispered back, my eyes on the ground.

"This is nice, you know," Ronan mused, drawing me from my ponderings on irony.

"Sailing?" I watched how the wind played tricks with his hair.

He gestured at the air between us. "No, working together."

I folded my arms across my chest. I had already yielded too much to him today, whether he knew it or not, and I was not about to give up any more. "Aye. Well, we've got twenty-seven days left."

Ronan watched me for a moment, a sad sort of knowing in his eyes. I looked away. He wasn't allowed to make me feel guilty, not when I was holding up my end of our bargain.

"Aye," he finally said, defeat in his voice. Another moment of silence passed, awkwardness scenting the air. He cleared his throat, his voice now matching his favorite smarmy mask. "Reagan isn't doing too badly."

"She's a natural," I responded, my voice cold and flat. She was doing well, but indulging in her success would lead to more bonding that would only leave me even more confused about my feelings. I felt ashamed that I was behaving so badly, but a stronger part of me was childishly unwilling to do anything about it.

Tarran's words from earlier that morning rang through me. *You can't snake charm me into forgetting who I am.*

"She reminds me of you when you were younger," Ronan continued anyway, not picking up on my subtle rejection. He watched Reagan, a proud smile on his face.

"You're sentimental today," I grumbled, digging deep within myself for the strength to keep my distance.

"Aye." He directed his smile at me now, a dazzling white in the afternoon sun. "And you're radiant."

Heat rushed through me. Another part unlocked, one I wasn't even sure I still had. "Insufferable cad." I folded my arms tighter around me and pinched my arm, a punishment for my momentary weakness.

"You two want to stop flirting and come do something useful?" Griffin called from the other end of the deck, a devilish grin on his face. The bastard had a sixth sense for striking at hot iron. Reagan stood next to him, covered in sweat but echoing both his proud stance and his meddling expression.

"Aye, like showing you where you can stick that sword?" I called back, hoping those fancy blades of his were telling him exactly how much trouble he was about to be in.

"Please, Keira," Reagan responded for him, her impishness now directed toward her unlikely tutor. "Come teach this old man a lesson."

I cracked my knuckles, glad for the opportunity to put my hands to real work, and drew both my cutlass and my small dagger from their sheaths. They weren't enchanted, not even my sapphire blade, but I didn't need tricks to play this game.

Griffin preened as I neared him, both of his weapons at the ready.

We sparred for nearly half an hour, our rhythm perfectly synchronized after so many years. He blocked my every parry and I countered his every strike with perfect balance, a dance only we knew. The clink of steel hitting steel and our steady, ragged breaths provided the music, and the deck became our dancefloor. We sparred even as sweat clouded our vision because we did not need to see to know where we were.

And Lyr below, it felt so good to release it all, to let my blades and my muscles do the talking instead of my brain. I poured myself into the dance, forgetting all that had happened, all that I was except *this*: a blade, forged from steel and sweat, made to strike.

Griffin bowed out first, clearly tired from training Reagan all afternoon. While I was tired too, I was disappointed to stop. My body ached for more, for the strain and the stress and the pure exhilaration.

But reality waited.

"You really are amazing." Reagan hovered over me as I washed the sweat from the back of my neck with a bucket of cold seawater. I nearly moaned as the cool drops rolled over me, sending gooseflesh up my arms. Reagan leaned against the mast, waving her hands excitedly as she spoke. "I mean, I already knew that from Ronan's stories, but to see it in person—"

"Stories?" I stood straight again, eyeing her with suspicion.

"Aye, that's how I know what I know about people." She shrugged, but something sad sparked in her eyes. I forgot, for a moment, that she had been tucked away for so long. This girl with a sailor's heart, stuck in her stone castle with only stories to live off of. As she continued, a wickedness replaced her sadness. "Though you're his favorite to talk about, and I see why. You're a goddess with a blade."

I splashed more of the cool water over my face, hoping it would hide my blush.

"Aye, and she cheats," Griffin chuckled as he laid flat on the deck, his chest still rising and falling in heavy breaths.

"Says the man who needs magic swords." I flicked some of the water at him, and he jumped like a cat seeing its shadow. Reagan and I laughed until our sides hurt.

"Can I have a go?" Ronan called from the helm, a challenge in his stare. "It's been ages since I've sparred, and you seem to still have some fight left in you, Keira."

"No," I answered quickly. Too quickly. I cleared my throat. "Someone should stay at the helm with this wind."

"Aye, why don't I take a turn?" Griffin perked up, sauntering toward the wheel. "Aidan never lets me steer."

Traitorous rutting bastard.

"Come on, Mrs. Mathonwy." Ronan tucked his hands into his pockets and slithered toward me, the snake freed from his cage. "Let's put on a show."

I felt Reagan watching me, waiting for a response. Ronan was goading me into a fight, but I wasn't going to take the bait, not this time. "I see what you're doing, and you won't get a rise out of me."

"He's sure pissing me off," Reagan scoffed, and I shot her a glare. Clever little girl knew how to play me, too. But nothing was going to work me over this time.

Ronan made direct eye contact, his devil's smile insisting the opposite. He pulled his sword from its sheath, every part of the action saying *you brought this on yourself.* "And what *can* I get out of you, Keira girl?"

Fury sang through my blood at the cheap shot. *Fine.* If he wanted a fight, he'd get it.

Before he could open his filthy mouth again, my dagger was singing past it—straight into the wood of the mast, a hair's breadth from his ear.

Reagan gasped and covered her eyes.

Ronan did not blink, his lip twitching. "Missed me."

"No." I pulled out my cutlass again, my heartbeat hammering in my ears. "I actually prefer when you're gone."

And in an instant I was on him, bringing my sword down on his. He didn't have Griffin's size or brute strength, but he was nearly as fast as me, and after a few blows delivered in the blink of an eye, I was panting. But I didn't hold back even an ounce of my own skill. I had been waiting for this in my own way, waiting for the moment I could unleash myself on him.

Our dance was different. Dangerous, without the comfort of familiarity, but filled instead with exhilaration. We were two foxes, both too clever for the traps we set for each other, waiting for the other to slip up first. But he was panting hard too, his usually snarky expression screwed up in concentration. My victory was close enough to taste.

"Should we stop them?" I heard a concerned Reagan ask Griffin over the clanging of my blade.

"Only if you have a death wish," Griffin yawned, unbothered by the violence in front of him.

I would have to thank him for that later. I did not want to stop. Not until clear victory was mine.

"Of course you're only brave enough to face me after I'm worn down," I grunted at Ronan between blows, a smile on my face despite my exhaustion.

"Not brave," he heaved as he landed a sharp blow to my left arm. "Clever."

Bastard. No one got a shot on me.

He lunged again, and this time I stepped further in. His blade grazed my cheek, but I hooked my foot behind his and, using his momentum, flattened him. He coughed as he landed, the wind knocked out of his sails. I pressed a knee to his chest so he could not get up.

I had won. Lyr below, did it feel good to see Ronan on the flat of his back for once. "Yield," I growled, pressing down harder.

"While I don't like the circumstances," he sputtered, a stupid grin on his face, "I don't mind you on top of me."

I smacked him sharply across the face, my patience too thin for word games.

"You lost," I spat, and stood, a victor's smile across my face.

He did not look at me, but past me. When his face flooded with fear, it was not my doing.

"Reagan, look out!" he shouted, struggling to his feet.

I didn't realize what was happening until I heard the sickening crack behind me. Until it was too late. Until the beam of the first sail was already falling down, headed straight for Reagan.

IO

Sails and Sabotage

Griffin moved first as the sail fell.

Over the roar of splitting wood and fabric tearing, he dove toward Reagan faster than cannon fire. He shoved her out of the way, rolling them to the starboard side just as the huge wooden beam hit the deck, right where the little girl had been a second before.

Another loud crack as the impact split the deck boards beneath us.

My instincts screamed for me to run to Griffin, but the boards groaned underneath the combined weight of the beam, and one wrong step could cause more damage.

"Griff? Reagan?" Fear strangled my voice as I peered through the settling dust, desperate for any sign of them.

"That was too close for comfort," Griffin groaned as he stood, a deep gash on his elbow, but otherwise unscathed. He offered a hand to Reagan to help her stand. She winced once, surely a nice bruise forming on her hip, but she stood steady and brushed herself off.

Ronan choked on his sigh of relief as he ran to embrace her, hurdling over the debris without a care for the security of the ship. "Lyr below, are you okay?" He wrapped her up in a tight hug, pressing her face to him so she couldn't respond.

I mumbled a prayer to Lyr. I had been too slow to react, too involved in my own stupidity to notice the cracking in the wood. Too slow and stupid to save Reagan.

Thank Lyr for Griffin.

Careful not to aggravate the damaged floor, I moved around the debris to Griffin and patted his shoulder twice. "Well done. Now let's take care of that cut, then we can figure out how we're going to sail this thing home."

He brushed me off, his face twisted in a grin. "Don't worry about me; a little salt water and it'll be fine."

I stared up at the damaged mast, at the second sail still hanging precariously. What had caused the beam to fall, I didn't know, but Griffin and I had been fine on it earlier. Once we got Reagan safely back to shore, I'd be sure to have a closer look.

But shore first. We had precious cargo. It would be difficult to catch enough wind, but Ronan and I could row to help the *Sarff* along...

"Thank you." Ronan turned to Griffin, finally releasing his cousin from his cobra's hold, a silver tear in his eye. "For saving her. I owe you my—"

Another deafening crack cut him off, louder than the one before. I spun on my heel toward the noise.

And there it was.

Along the length of the towering pine mast, a seam, splintering from the place the beam had been hammered in. My heart thundered in my chest, my throat closing. How had I missed this?

The mast was going down. And on a cutter this small...

"Abandon ship!" The scream wrenched from Griffin's throat as he came to the same conclusion I had.

Ronan's face blanched as our gazes met. Reagan's eyes were wide with fear, tears streaming down her cheeks.

But neither of them moved.

"Go!" I screamed at Ronan, running to the starboard rail of the ship where the small dingy was lashed. "Get her to the lifeboat, now!"

Reagan blinked, but her adrenaline kicked in as she stumbled clumsily toward the rail. I started tearing at the ropes anchoring the lifeboat to the side, my fingers fumbling; Griffin made quick work of the ropes on the other side, practically ripping them apart. Another crack rang through the air, a deep chasm appearing on the mast.

Ronan didn't move. He still stood ten paces away, frozen in his spot, staring up at the mast, ghosts dancing his eyes.

"Ronan, let's go, we can't be on this when that thing goes down!" Desperation cracked my shout.

Ronan didn't even look my way.

Save him. The dark voice blared into my ears.

Stupid bastard. *"Ronan!"* I tried louder, my heart thundering. I did not have time for this.

Still no response.

I freed the final ropes from the little boat, settling it into the water with a splash. I looked back at Ronan, still frozen and lifeless in his place.

The voice shrieked through me again. *If you don't, he'll die.*

Griffin met my eyes, concern setting in now. He knew we didn't have much time. "Go grab him, I'll get the girl in the boat."

I nodded once, a *thank you* on my lips.

We moved together. Griffin barreled toward Reagan. She screamed as he threw her over his shoulders. As she realized what was happening.

"Ronan! No, let me go! Ronan!" she shrieked, her face contorted with fear and rage. She pounded at Griffin's back as he carried her over the side.

I hurtled toward Ronan, dodging the splinters of wood raining from the mast. "Ronan!" I screamed again, tackling him out of the way just as the second beam fell from the mast. It tore a new hole through the deck, the impact vibrating through us both. We hit the deck hard, debris landing on top of us, but luckily the main body of the beam landed a few paces left.

Ronan blinked, his trance broken, suddenly aware of the chaos around us. "Keira?" he stuttered, scattering back to his feet.

"Aye." I jumped back up and grabbed his arm, ready to run for the starboard side of the ship.

When the final crack ran down the mast, the whole ship moaned as the gap spread all the way down the deck.

Shit. We were not making it to that boat.

Ronan, finally aware of what was happening, must have realized it too. "Keira!" he cried again, throwing himself at me. We slammed into the railing just as the mast came down behind us, rupturing the bowsprit and the front of the hull.

Splintered debris flew toward us as water rushed onto the ship. I covered my head in my hands, but Ronan laid on top of me, shielding us both with his back. He winced and cried out as something sharp sliced the top of his shoulder.

"Are you okay?" I shouted.

"Peachy," he grimaced through clenched teeth. "Let's get off this floating coffin, shall we?"

The *Sarff* moaned again, one last defiant cry as the water rose higher. The frame tilted, the port side tipping into the water at a drastic angle. I grabbed onto the starboard railing. We had to get off this ship before she dragged us down with her. "She won't be floating much longer."

If we stood, we'd be knocked back, but if we crawled over the edge, we could hang onto something and float to the lifeboat. I prayed to Lyr that Griffin and Reagan had cleared the undertow of the ship by now, even if it meant forsaking Ronan and me.

I kicked a peg of the railing, but it wouldn't budge. I couldn't get enough leverage. Frantically, I unsheathed my dagger, sawing at the peg, hanging onto its twin as the ship bucked underneath me.

"That's useless," Ronan growled, "We have to stand and jump!" He moved to his feet, but the deck was slick. He slipped, barely catching himself before smacking his chin on the railing.

"Any other bright ideas?" I yelled at him. "Or do you want to help me with these bars?"

The voice growled in the back of my head, and a part of my core started churning like the water around us.

Of course.

I sucked in a breath, drawing on my well of power, hoping to Lyr and any other god listening that this time it would work.

I felt the familiar buzz of electricity through my fingertips. I breathed in, aligning my will to the wild surging in my chest. And when I exhaled, the water came rushing toward us.

"Hold on to me!" I screamed, grabbing the back of Ronan's coat.

And then the water carried us up and over the starboard railing.

As we rushed into the blue, the voice whispered a final warning into my ear.

Sabotage. The wood was compromised. He set you up.

I coughed and sputtered as Griffin pulled Ronan and me onto the lifeboat. Reagan quickly had us both in a tight hug, crying into Ronan's hair. "Thank Lyr you both are all right, I was so scared!"

"What in Lyr's name did you do?" I spat, shrugging Reagan off me. She looked up at me with hurt and shock, but I did not meet her gaze. I stared only at Ronan, my teeth bared.

"I'm sorry, I froze, I—" he stuttered, his whole body shaking from the cold water.

I was on him in a second, my hands digging into his throat.

I was going to end him. Contracts be bloody damned.

He choked under my grip, fear in his eyes, but he did not fight back. Cowardly prick.

Griffin pulled me off him, and I kicked so hard it nearly toppled us off the dingy. "Calm down, Keira," Griffin snarled in my ear. I stopped kicking, but I did not look away from Ronan. "What on earth has gotten into you, girl?"

"Ask him," I barked, shoving my cousin off me. "Ask him why we're even here, Griffin!"

Griffin's brow knit in confusion. "The ship sank, Keira, it's not his fault, none of us could—"

I lunged again, almost getting to Ronan before Griffin caught me and slammed me back into my seat.

"It *is* his fault, the lying prick set us up," I snarled, my power surging under my skin. "She was built to sink, Griffin. It was sabotage."

"What?" Shock and anger flashed across Ronan's face at the accusation.

Bloody liar.

"Have you gone full mad?" Griffin scoffed, grabbing my arm tightly so I couldn't jump Ronan again. "What makes you think he did it?"

"The sea speaks, Griffin. And it doesn't lie. Aren't I right, Ronan?" I sneered at the traitor.

Ronan's expression darkened, confusion and rage fighting for dominance in his gaze. "I have no clue what you're talking about, but if you think I would risk you, risk *Reagan* like that—"

"Oh please, I have seen what you are willing to sacrifice." I saw straight through his well-practiced bluff. "My father took you in as his own, and you still slit his throat in the dark of night. But this is low, even for you. How dare you put Reagan in danger like that? Have you lost all honor that you're willing to sacrifice a child?"

Ronan clenched his fists at his sides, glaring at me with an anger I'd never seen from him. "Choose your next words carefully, Keira. You're about to cross a line."

My own anger only doubled in response. "Speak another word, you damned snake, and I'll have your rutting tongue."

"That's enough, Keira," Griffin scolded me like a child, disappointment twisting his face.

I shot him a dark look. The traitor would've already had a sword through Ronan five hours ago. He had even made fun of me for being charmed by the Mathonwys. And now he was coming to their defense?

I flipped him a vulgar gesture, as childish as it was, hurt and betrayal stinging in my eyes. Tarran had been right all along.

"Did the sea say it was Ronan who sabotaged us?" Reagan asked me with steel in her stare, a challenge in itself.

"I don't answer to you." My voice was cold, my fury transforming from burning fire to icy hatred. I knew she did not deserve the acidity in my tone, knew that she was just another innocent charmed to believe this man's blue-eyed lies. I hated myself, both for trusting him in the first place and for my non-answer now. If it wasn't so bloody cold, I'd swim back to Porthladd if it meant getting space from him.

"Did the sea say it was me?" Ronan pushed again, a glimmer of hope in his eye. "Because if it did, by all means, run me through right now."

The words pounded through my ears once more, their truth evident but their wording vague.

Sabotage. The wood was compromised. He set you up.

I watched Ronan, his stare expectant. Bloody viper, snapping at any chance to talk his way out of things.

"Not exactly." I crossed my arms, leering at them both. "It said the wood was compromised, and *he* set us up. And I don't care if it was Reese or Rhett or which one of your snake cousins commissioned the wood, this bastard knew." I pointed a steady finger at Ronan, the ice in my veins fortifying me. "I'm sure of it."

"I'm not," Griffin spoke again, quiet. My head snapped toward him faster than a lightning strike, and he raised his hands in defense, continuing with caution. "I'm not saying it wasn't sabotage, or that a Mathonwy wasn't behind it, but…Ronan had no way of controlling when or who was on the ship when it went down. No way of assuring who got hurt…hell, he's the one bleeding right now…"

I looked at the angry red pooling at Ronan's shoulder, the bruise forming over his left eye. At the scratches on Reagan's cheeks.

There was truth in Griffin's words, odious as they were. Had Griffin not pushed Reagan out of the way, or if I hadn't saved Ronan…they'd be in far worse shape than they were now. And even if Ronan had planned the shipwreck, even if he was willing to sacrifice Reagan, chancing his life in the process was a steep risk. One a self-preserving snake like him wouldn't dare take. Not someone who preferred daggers in the back under the cloak of darkness.

"We've all been played, Keira." Ronan's voice was a lethal quiet as he stared at me. "I swear on my mother's grave, I didn't know."

Truth. The voice sang clearly through me, so loud in my ears, I shook.

"What?" I answered out loud, astonished and angered. "No, you said—"

He speaks truth. The sea commanded once more with its ancient authority, the weight of it bearing down on me like an anchor.

"Fine. But if you don't feel like being specific, in the future, shut the fuck up," I growled at the sea before looking back at my companions, all of whom were staring at me like I had six heads. I rubbed my temples, letting the motion soothe the waves turning in my core. "I believe you."

A collective sigh went through us. Griffin released my arm, patting my shoulder instead.

"And?" Reagan folded her arms across her chest, tears still in her eyes.

I sighed, a wave of shame washing over me. What a rutting monster I was. "And I'm sorry." I suppressed the urge to look away from her, the cowardly part of me shriveling in shame. I met her gaze instead, doing my best to keep my voice from quivering. "For what I said. See, I told you I'm not really brave. I hope you can forgive me."

She held my gaze for another moment, deciding. Calculating. Finally, she offered a soft smile. "Teach me the disarming move you used on Ronan earlier and we're even."

I was surprised at the relief that washed over me, at the way my frozen heart warmed just a little. "Aye, with pleasure."

Gathering my courage, I made eye contact with Ronan, his sapphire stare penetrating. His expression was guarded, but the anger had dissolved around the edges.

I nodded once at him, the closest thing to a sorry I could manage. "How's your shoulder?"

He nodded in return. "I've had worse."

I looked again at the blood still oozing into his shirt. He was being brave, by the looks of it. "I'll see to it when we find a way back to land."

Griffin pulled the oars from their holsters, ready for the long row back to shore. He dipped one into the water and handed me the other. "We better move then, before it's dark."

"Aye." I nodded, thrusting my own into the brisk blue. Without any hesitation, Griffin and I started the back-breaking work of rowing, the familiar pull of the water daunting.

"Can that asshole voice in your head do anything to make this quicker?" Griffin chuckled through metered breaths.

Reagan's brow furrowed. "The more important question now is if Ronan didn't do it, who did? Does the sea want to throw us a hint?"

I waited for the voice to speak again.

Silence.

Fuck you, meddling bastard. I thought to myself, hoping the prick would hear it. I was starting to think my gift was more of a curse.

My power rippled through me, anger fueling it anew. I exhaled, willing the water to move us forward as I rowed. "I don't know who did it, and the sea isn't being very forthcoming anymore. But I'd love to have a few words with whoever the bastard is when we find him."

A dark cloud fell over Ronan's face, echoing the darkness in my heart. "It looks like our investigation just got more complex."

Stitches and Stories

By the time we made it back to shore and said our goodbyes to Griffin, it was already dark. And by the time we made it back up the hill after returning Reagan to a furious Reina, the moon was high in the night sky.

Ronan had to lean on me for the last leg of the trip. He'd hit his leg pretty hard when he slipped in the wreckage, and the bleeding from his shoulder made him dizzy. Blood already stained through the makeshift stanch Reagan had made on the trip back.

But as we crawled up to the spring, a wave of relief washed over me. Every muscle in my body ached, his weight on my shoulders only adding to it, but salvation was near. "I never thought I'd be glad to see this place."

"Aye." Ronan winced, his face alarmingly pale. "Home sweet home."

"Do you think you can get yourself to the spring?" I asked, and he nodded. "I'll find us something to eat, and then we'll look at that wound of yours."

He removed his arm from my shoulder and shot me a skeptical look. "In the dark?"

"I'll bring a lantern. I need the spring water."

"Aye, Captain Keira." Ronan saluted me, a hand over his heart, and hobbled toward the water.

I moved quickly to the shack despite my protesting muscles. The room was dark, forcing me to fumble through it for the lantern and flint. As soon as I had light, I rummaged through my sack. Aidan had sense enough to pack me a needle and thread, presumably in case I needed to mend my limited clothing supply. Tonight I had another type of stitching in mind.

Next I grabbed the small, cloth-wrapped loaf of bread from Vala. It would be stale by now, but nothing beat her berry bread, old or not. I had hoped to save it for when I needed a taste of my family, but Ronan and I needed sustenance more than sentimentality, and the few blocks of cheese left from Reina's pack wouldn't quite cut it.

I rummaged through Ronan's bag next, looking for the last necessary ingredient for our night. *Red shirt, red coat, red underpants*— Lyr below, did this man need some color variety in his wardrobe— and finally, the little silver flask I knew he never went anywhere without. I hoped it contained something strong.

Gathering my things, I headed back outside to Ronan.

He slumped by the edge of the spring, his head lolling to the side. I ran to kneel next to him.

"Ronan?" I tapped his face, my heart racing. His blue eyes fluttered open, half-aware.

"Princess Keira." He gave me a lopsided smile. "You came to rescue me."

"Hush up." I rolled my eyes, unwrapping the bread and breaking off a piece for him. "Here, eat this first."

He nodded, his eyes focusing again, some semblance of clarity returning to his expression. Too exhausted to be anything but compliant, he took a bite. "Where did we get this?"

I took a small bite for myself, the familiar taste smoothing out the rough waves in my stomach. "My uncle packed it for me the other day. I was saving it, but we'll both need our strength."

"Thanks for sharing, then." Ronan took another bite, eyes bright. "This isn't bad."

I wrapped the rest up. Later—we'd eat later. "Vala will be pleased to hear it. Now, drink this." I handed him the flask, the silver glowing in the lanternlight.

Ronan raised a wary eyebrow. "That's not water."

"No, it's not. A fact you'll appreciate once I start stitching that cut of yours."

I shook it at him, and he took it, unscrewing the tiny silver top with slow fingers. He raised it to me before taking a long swig. "Aye, *Lechyd Da.*" He handed it back, and I took a swig myself to calm my nerves. Whiskey. It burned my throat as it went down, not as smooth as Ellian's.

"*Lechyd Da.*" I poured another swig's worth over my needle to disinfect it. It took me a minute to thread the needle, my face screwed up in concentration; Ronan chuckled to himself as he watched. Finally, I got the damned thing through the hole. "Okay, now shirt off before we burn out of oil."

A devious expression filled his face, a hint of the sparkle returning to his eyes. "If you wanted me to strip, Keira, all you had to do was ask."

"One more comment and I'll forget to be gentle." I pointed the needle at him like a cutlass, but I couldn't help the way my lips twitched upward. Even when he was bleeding out, the bastard found a way to crack a joke.

Gingerly, Ronan removed his shirt, wincing as the fabric brushed his shoulder.

My mouth went slightly dry as I watched him. Even in the lanternlight, the smooth planes of his chest were visible, every muscle cut from marble. He had always been fit, and I had seen him shirtless more times than I could count. But there was something different about him, something new. The island had done him well.

And on his chest, right over his heart, black ink. At the center, sharp lines that intersected, surrounded by intricate, symmetrical swirls forming a knot.

Ronan eyed me, beaming with male pride. "Impressed?"

"No." I hoped my traitorous cheeks didn't show the heat that rose to them. I focused on the tattoo, on the delicate linework. "What's this?"

"Protection charm." He touched it, tracing the ink with his finger. I froze. "Got it on the island. Keeps those who'd harm me from doing so when I'm not aware."

A phantom pain lingered in the back of my head, and my jaw dropped. The first day at the spring, when I had tried to attack him…

It was a silly protection charm, simple and oddly specific, but effective. I laughed, a harsh, shallow sound. Ronan furrowed his brow in embarrassment. "What's so funny?"

"Nothing," I scoffed, rubbing the back of my head at the memory of the pain. There was still a fading bruise. "Just...let me see that shoulder."

Ronan complied, shifting so his broad shoulder was right in front of me. I swallowed once, adjusting to his proximity, grateful for something to focus on. To his credit, Ronan didn't wince as I cleaned the wound, pouring some of the whiskey over it. The gash was deep, but I couldn't see any bone or fragments of wood. It was a clean cut.

I inhaled, concentrating, and began my work. He only let out a small yelp when the needle pierced his flesh, then clenched his jaw as I made the second stitch.

A pang of a different pain shot through my heart. He had been brave enough to hold in his cries this entire time, though it had to hurt. And to think I had accused him of planning it, had called him a liar...

I made my next stitch as delicately as I could.

"So, this island..." I began, partly to distract him, partly because I needed to distract myself. "How did the locals know how to do this?" I gestured to the tattoo with my chin, keeping my eyes steady on my work.

Ronan paused, watching my hands as I knit his skin back together. "They were a strange mix of people. Lots of personalities, some shy, some...well..." he hedged as if deciding how much information to give me. "But knowledgeable. In so many ways."

I shot him a look, annoyed at his vagueness. "Have I been there? I've never seen markings like this."

Ronan grinned but kept his response short. "No, I don't think many people have."

I made another stitch and Ronan winced. I shot him a teasing look. "For someone who loves to tell stories, you seem reluctant to tell your own." I stopped stitching to wash the wound again, pouring the water over it carefully. It buzzed in my hand, eager to greet me, and I grinned despite myself when it coated my palm like an old glove. Ronan watched, his expression soft and open. My voice came out quieter than I expected. "You were gone for nearly four years. On an island none of the sailors in Porthladd have ever seen or heard of. Miraculously still alive, yet you've said nothing on how."

Ronan stared at his hands, laughing to himself. "I don't think you'd believe me if I did."

"I don't believe anything you say." I shrugged, beginning my stitching anew. "So, what's stopping you now?"

Ronan stared up at the sky. Underneath my fingers, I felt his pulse quicken. "Have you ever heard of the *Hiraeth*?"

My eyes went wide. "The Isle of Lost Things?" Again, with the stories. "Ronan, that's just a legend."

There was a solemn truth in his eyes as he looked back. "The inhabitants wouldn't take too kindly if they heard that."

I stopped stitching. "*Hiraeth*. How in Lyr's name—"

"In Lyr's name, quite literally," Ronan scoffed. I stayed quiet, unwilling to shatter the truth of the moment. He continued softly, his voice catching in his throat, "After the ship sank, I was lost, in every sense of the word. But instead of letting me die with my ship and my crew, Lyr took me to the isle. It's not all rainbows and waterfalls like the stories say. It's beautiful, yes, but it's dark and dangerous, too. Full of things that many of us would prefer *stayed* lost. I was alone for three days, injured and hopeless, trying to avoid the horrors lurking in the shadows...and that's when the women of the Annwyn, the ones who live there...they took me in, nursed me back to health. And they let me stay, gave me work...they became my people. *Hiraeth* became my home."

He tilted his head back at the stars again, if only to keep his silver tears from falling.

I didn't know if the story was true, or if the island existed at all, but Ronan had found a home. And he gave it up to come back to a place full of hate and violence.

"Why'd you come back?" The way looking at him made me feel was unbearable, so I looked at my hands instead. "Why sacrifice it all?"

"Danura—the head of the Annwyn clan—had a vision. A message from Lyr." His voice was warm as it caressed her name, like remembering a dear friend. A pang of jealousy stabbed at me, and I clenched my fists. Almost in response, his expression darkened. "It said there had been a blood feud, and in order to end it, you were going to marry my cousin Rhett, so—"

"So you came back," I finished for him, "to save Rhett."

"No. Frankly, Rhett can rot," he snorted, raising an eyebrow. But his face fell quickly, the laughter evaporating. "But I didn't come right away. I was still—well, I thought that you'd be better off without me, and that since no one had come looking for me…I didn't see the point. Dangerous and primal as it was, I was happy there. I had people who cared for me, who wanted me." There was real hurt in his expression, a brave vulnerability I'd never seen in him.

I didn't know what to make of the man before me, the snake turned sparrow. "But?"

The storyteller in him took the reins, his lips pulling upward. "But Lyr spoke to me himself. Told me it was my destiny to come back, to take Rhett's place. And that I owed him a price. A life."

A knot formed in my stomach, Ronan's bloody hands and my father's body flashing through my mind.

I had almost forgotten.

"A life?" My voice was low, my buried anger rumbling in the depths once more.

Ronan did not notice my shift in mood. "Mine, for saving me. Apparently, he doesn't do work for free. So, he made me a deal. Either I pay my life debt the old-fashioned way, or I go back to Porthladd, marry you, and find out who killed Cedric. More than one way to sacrifice a life, he said."

My heart stopped at the mention of my father's name. At the casual use of his favorite lesson. My anger dissipated as quickly as it came.

I knew very well what I had sacrificed for this union. I had never thought that Ronan might have given something up as well.

"That's a nice story," I managed, the heaviness of his honesty settling over me. I picked up the stitching once more, desperate for something else to think about.

"Aye. If only it were just a story," Ronan laughed through the pain as I finished the last two stitches.

I admired my handiwork. It wasn't perfect, but it was even, and he'd heal. I cupped more water in my hands to clean it off. The water buzzed again, whispering to me, nearly giggling as I moved to pour it over the wound. I breathed in, letting my gift giggle back. Slowly, I poured it over the line of crimson on Ronan's shoulder. It responded with a faint glowing as the water calmed the angry red, the mark looking days old in a matter of seconds.

Ronan's eyes went wide. "How are you doing that?"

"Hmm?" I blinked, concentrating on the last drops of water before I looked up at him to respond. "Oh, it's part of my gift. Though I can't always do it. I'm surprised I can now, actually, since usually when I call on my gifts like I did today, I'd be passed out on the ground by now. But the spring...it makes things easier." The words bubbled out of me like the water slipping through my fingers.

Maybe the spring *was* magic.

"Passed out?" Ronan's brow knit as he stared at his scar, wonder and confusion in his eyes.

I pursed my lips as I tried to find the words to explain. I had never told anyone this much about my power. Papa had me keep quiet about it outside of the family, as people would use it as an excuse to fear or hate me. And even amongst my family, there was still an uncomfortableness whenever I brought it up. Another reminder of how I was *other*.

But Ronan just stared, expectant and curious, not a single trace of fear in his eyes. I bit my cheek before I continued. "The ocean, it's vast. Bottomless. No matter how much of its energy you sap, it never runs out. It always replenishes itself. But me, well, I'm human. I'm limited. And sometimes it feels like trying to catch the whole ocean in my palms. But I can't hold on too long without it slipping through my fingers...and once it's gone, I take longer to recover."

Ronan's face lit up in awe as he rubbed his finger over his fading wound. "Amazing."

I couldn't help but smile. Perhaps my gift was more than just destruction after all.

"Anyway, that should do it." I cleared my throat, censuring myself before Ronan could untie the last of my knots. "But you'll have to be careful not to rip the stitches."

"Aye, Mrs. Mathonwy, I'll be careful." He grinned, pulling his shirt back over his head. "Thank you for stitching me back up."

I shrugged, thankful to be less...distracted. "You got hurt saving me. Now we're even."

Something glimmered in his eyes, enhanced by the lanternlight. "You saved me too, though. When I was—when I froze."

I waved him off, gathering my supplies again. "Yes, but I've tried to kill you twice as many times, so it doesn't count."

Ronan stopped my hand just as I was about to clean off my needle in the spring. I shuddered at his touch. His expression was intense as I met his gaze. "And I'm—I'm sorry. For everything I've put you through."

I pulled my hand away, shutting the doors he was trying to open inside me. There were things no amount of truth-telling and healing could change. I steeled my expression. "We should get some rest. Tomorrow, we'll figure out who really should be sorry."

"I won't argue there." Ronan stood, offering me a hand. I took it, and he hoisted me up despite his own fatigue.

I gathered my things, walking toward the shack at a brisker pace than I needed to, Ronan stumbling behind.

It took me a moment to start the fire, Ronan slicing off one of the last pieces of cheese as the warmth finally filled the room. He handed me a morsel, and I popped it in my mouth, savoring its smoothness. It was a comfortable silence as we prepared for sleep, our strange partnership at its finest.

Ronan spoke first, grabbing the spare blanket off the straw bed. "I'll take the floor tonight, you get the bed."

I snatched it from him, rolling my eyes. "No, you're injured. You get the bed."

Ronan grabbed the edge of the blanket before I could lay it on the ground, a mischievous look in his eye. "But you rowed us four leagues to shore."

I mustered my best scowl, ripping the blanket back. "Ronan, bed. I'm not arguing with you."

"Fine, fine." He shoved his hands in his pockets and ambled backward to sit on the bed, his eyes never leaving me. "Goodnight, Keira."

I turned my back to him, feeling his gaze still on me as I made my makeshift bed on the floor. I blew out the lanterns, hoping that darkness would hide my blush.

What in Lyr's name was happening to me? Blushing like a little girl. Over Ronan, of all people. Sure, he'd always been attractive, but I knew better than to fall for a pretty face with a serpent's tongue.

Then again, I knew nothing. Ronan had been telling the truth today after the shipwreck. And as crazy as his story was tonight, there was truth to it, too. If he was telling the truth about being sent to find my father's killer, about his innocence...it changed everything.

Except for the fact that my father was gone, killed by someone on that ship.

And someone was trying to kill me now.

My mind raced over the day, over the slew of problems ahead of me, vast as the sea itself. I'd almost died today, and I didn't know who wanted me dead. Aside from Connor Yorath, who, if he didn't hate me before, certainly did now. And the rutting *blaidd* stalking me.

I flipped over, trying to find a muscle that wasn't sore. My body was desperate for sleep, my limbs heavy and stiff at the same time, aching to be coddled, but the wooden floor might as well have been jagged rocks.

I laid on my back, staring up at the ceiling. I hated not being able to see the stars. Stars always made things seem smaller. Manageable.

I shut my eyes instead and waited for sleep to come.

It did not.

I sighed and sat up, looking to where Ronan's dark form was curled up on the bed. He looked comfortable, his breaths rising and falling steadily. He needed it, too, after what he had been through today. Another shipwreck. Another unanswered question.

Small victories, Keira. What do you want first, and how can you get it?

My body needed sleep more than I needed answers right now. I knew I would regret this later, but I was hoping to be wrong.

Grabbing my blanket, I stood up and walked to the bed. "Move over." I nudged Ronan a little less than gently.

"Hmm?" he murmured, not even opening his eyes.

Heavy rutting sleeper.

"I said move over." I shoved him again, harder than the first time. He woke with a start, surprise on his face. I shooed him to the far side of the mattress, and he shifted slightly. I sat on the edge of the bed and pointed a finger at him. "If you touch me, or comment, or make this any more uncomfortable, I'll stab you."

He grinned, realization dawning on his face, but he crossed his hand over his heart. "Aye, no roaming hands or pointed comments, I promise." He laid back down, still giving me ample space despite his long limbs, and patted the space beside him. "Just get some rest."

I was a bloody fool.

I laid down quickly and shifted, my back to him. Even with space between us, the heat from his body drifted toward me. The mattress was comfortable, but I was not.

The voice in my head chuckled. *Sleep, Keira girl. You'll need it for what's ahead.*

I sighed, focusing instead on how my body sank into the straw mattress, how soft it was even with two of us weighing it down.

"Goodnight," I whispered to my companion, sleep nearer than I thought it would be.

"Goodnight, Mrs. Mathonwy."

And sleep took me in its arms.

12

Snakes and Sanctions

I woke up warm, the scent of citrus and sweat coaxing me to consciousness. My eyes fluttered open, taking in my surroundings. My head was on Ronan's chest, his uninjured arm wrapped around my shoulder.

I nearly fell off the bed as I came to, kicking him when I scurried to the edge.

Rutting bastard didn't move. Stupid heavy sleeper.

I hustled to grab my things, pulling my boots on first. I had things I needed to do, the most important one being getting some space from Ronan and his ridiculous citrus smell. Preferably before he woke up.

"Where are you going?" Ronan yawned, stretching as he sat up. His golden curls stuck up in every direction, but he looked well-rested, the color returned to his cheeks.

Lyr's bollocks.

"Town," I answered sharply, focusing on my boot laces. "I need proper healing supplies so your shoulder doesn't get infected. And we need more than a stale loaf of bread and a few cubes of cheese."

"Great, I'll come with you." Ronan swung his legs over the edge of the bed, reaching for his own boots by the fire.

"No, you're going to rest. I'm not taking chances." I halted him with a hand on his arm, ignoring how my fingertips tingled at the feel of his sun-worn skin. "Besides, we don't know who the target of the shipwreck was. If it's you and people see you limping with your arm wrapped up, you'll look weak. We don't want word getting back to whoever tried to hit you that you're still recovering."

Ronan frowned, leaning back on his hands. In truth, he was the picture of good health, but if he came, I might not be. "So, what am I supposed to do? Sit here like an invalid waiting for my nursemaid?"

"Aye, exactly that." I patted his knee and stood, grabbing my blue coat and wrapping it around me. It smelled like fish and armpit. "I won't be long." Mostly because I needed a rutting bath.

Ronan did not protest further, to my relief, his hands hanging in his lap. "Can you at least check on Reagan for me, then? Reina will give you more food; it'll be killing two birds with one stone."

I stopped, my hand twitching toward the dagger at my hip. "You want me to walk into Mathonwy Manor *alone* and pick up groceries?" A Branwen, alone in the den of snakes…if I ran into Rhett, or worse, Reese…

Anger murmured in my gut, my power rumbling in response.

Ronan raised an eyebrow. "Aye, exactly that. But the crew should be out today, especially if Reese has heard by now what happened to my ship. They'll be scouring the wreckage or roughing up whatever poor cad they bought it from."

I scoffed, venom in my voice. "Or cursing Lyr that their little scheme didn't go according to plan."

Ronan folded his arms across his broad chest, looking at me like I was a misbehaving toddler. "I know you think they're good for it, but I don't see why they would want me dead."

I shrugged. "Necessary casualty to kill me, I suppose."

Ronan bristled slightly, the insult striking an exposed nerve; then he sighed once, censuring the tension in his jaw. When he spoke again, it was cold, calculating. "Aye, but it doesn't add up. Reese needs this alliance to work just as much as you and I do, Keira. He's a prick and a liar, but he isn't stupid. Without us, the war continues, and Reese has too much to lose now."

I pulled my smelly coat closer around me. I didn't need to fight with him now. "We'll see about that. I just don't believe that he wouldn't know, either." I moved to the door, effectively ending the conversation. "Go rest. I'll be back by tonight."

And I did not look back as I walked out into the crisp morning.

If Mathonwy Manor was intimidating before, it was paralyzing now. The waves in my gut crashed against my every nerve, alternating between nausea and unadulterated rage. But before I could decide whether to knock, the front door wrenched open, and a small face peered up at me with guarded eyes.

"Good morning, little dragon." My voice was warm, but I couldn't hide the shame that still sat on my shoulders. I'd made my peace with Ronan the night before, stitching up the wounds I'd caused—both seen and unseen. But Ronan was not the only victim of my wrath.

Reagan stared, eyes full of decisions, marking if I was friend or foe. After a moment, a smile beamed where her doubt had rested, the sun peeking out from behind the clouds. "Keira!" She wrapped me in a vice-grip hug, nearly knocking me off the top step.

Friend, then. Forgiven. Even when I didn't deserve it.

I hugged her back with all my strength. "How are you feeling?"

Reagan pulled back and dragged me into the house, the marble echoing underfoot. Her eyes lit up, the last edges of her hurt fading in the foyer's soft light. "I've never been better!"

I patted her curls. "I'm sorry yesterday had to be your first experience sailing. I promise it's not always that scary."

A smirk flashed across her face, the expression so much like Ronan's. "Aye, but hopefully it's always that exciting."

I chuckled, headed toward the staircase. I didn't hear anyone else moving about, so perhaps by some strange miracle, the sailors were already gone for the day. The knots in my stomach slowly unraveled. "Is your Ma home?"

Reagan hesitated, her chest falling. "Aye, she's in the sitting room, but I don't think you'll want to see her right now."

"Still mad?" I whispered like a thief to their accomplice, trying to cheer her up. I deserved Reina's anger, and I'd take it head-on if needed.

Reagan still frowned, looking down at the ground. "Not exactly, just—"

I waved it off. It was sweet for her to worry, but I knew Reina would come around eventually. "I'll pop in quick, say sorry again."

I took long strides toward the sitting room and pushed open the door.

"Wait, you—" Reagan called after me, but she was interrupted by the impact when I slammed directly into Reese Mathonwy.

I stumbled back, regaining my composure faster than a cat falling off a windowsill. "Reese."

He grinned, the expression dripping with malice. "If it isn't the newest Mrs. Mathonwy." He leaned on the doorframe, blocking my entrance to the sitting room. "How goes it, Keira?"

I picked at my nails. "I'd be better if you weren't here."

Reina's head popped over his shoulder, an apology in her eyes. "Reagan, why don't you go play upstairs," she called around Reese, her voice stern.

Reagan pouted, the dark god burning in her eyes. "And miss the fun part?"

"Reagan, *now*."

She huffed up the stairs, stomping her feet as she went.

Reese's eyes didn't leave me, his gruesome scar crinkling as he narrowed them. "So, yer letting yourself in now? My, my, guess ye really are kin."

I lifted my chin. "Just stopping by to check on Reagan. Making sure she wasn't too shaken after your plan almost killed her."

Anger flashed through his eyes, my attack striking true. "My plan? Girlie, only one of us has a reputation for sinking ships, and it's not me." He stood to his full height, snarling, "Perhaps I should be asking ye just how that brand-new ship went down. I spent a pretty penny on it, ye know."

He'd have to do a lot worse to intimidate me when my white-hot hatred burned through my veins. "Aye, I'm sure sabotage costs quite a bit."

"Enough, both of ye." Reina looped under her brother's arm, putting herself between us, a hand on Reese's chest. "Reese, if yer going, I suggest ye get going."

Reese glared at her, clearly unused to being reprimanded in his own home. But he quickly redirected his rage toward me, pointing a gnarled finger in my face. "Ye watch yerself, girl. Anything happens to my boy, I'm coming for ye first."

Something snapped inside me, a primal, territorial wrath singing through my core. "Clever spin, Reese, that was almost convincing," I snarled, my lips curling back from my teeth like a rabid dog. "Ronan might buy the concerned father act, but I don't. And when I prove it was you who sank that ship, it won't be me you'll answer to."

Reese ignited in response, shoving Reina out of the way as he grabbed the collar of my coat. "Ye've got some nerve, coming into my house, accusing me of harming my own kin...yer trying my patience."

I grabbed his wrist, digging my nails into the flesh until he dropped his hold. I painted a smile on my face. "But I thought I *was* kin now."

Reina smacked his arm and pointed at the door. "Go, ye bloody cad. Now." Reese shot her a dark glare, but he stalked off, slamming the door behind him as he left. She pinched the bridge of her nose. "Sorry about my arse of a brother. Ronan's okay?"

"I'd say sorry for my own bad behavior, but I'd be lying," I admitted, and her face softened. "Ronan's fine. I stitched him up last night. I need to stop at the apothecary for some salve and the market for some food, but he'll be okay."

She loosed a sigh of relief, ushering me through the sitting room into the kitchen. "Yer not going to the market for food, I'll pack ye something right now." She didn't hesitate to busy herself, throwing all sorts of goods into a wicker basket.

"Thank you. I'll repay your kindness someday, I promise." I took a seat at the worktable; helping would just impede her system.

Reina tossed a few apples into the basket and shot me a look, brandishing the bright red fruit at me. "Aye, ye can start by not nearly drowning my daughter next time ye take her sailing."

I tilted my head. "Next time?"

Reina shook her head, putting the finishing touches—some leftover roasted chicken, two whole loaves of orange bread, and a mouthwatering pastry for desert—in the basket. "If ye think a near-death experience is enough to scare that girl out of the water, ye don't know her like I do."

Strange pride swelled through my chest—the little girl inside me relishing in her new equal. "You're probably right there."

Reina handed me the basket, which was heavier than I expected, and put her hands on her hips. "I couldn't stop 'again' from happening no matter how hard I tried. So, I'd appreciate it if ye could keep a better eye out next time."

I nodded. "Yes, ma'am. Thank you for the food."

Reina took a seat, watching me with knowing eyes. "Reese didn't do it, ye know. He'd throw himself off Clogwynn Cliffs before he hurt Ronan. Ye didn't see him after last time, after he thought Ronan..." She trailed off, the dark memory bringing silver tears to her eyes. "Anyway, I know my brother has done his share of despicable things in his life, and I know he hasn't been much of a father to Ronan, but even he has lines he wouldn't cross."

I headed toward the door, the weight of her words hanging in the air. "That's what everyone keeps saying." I managed a wry smile. "I'll send Ronan your love."

I walked slowly through the main town despite the heavy basket in my arms, savoring the chance to think to myself. As usual, wary eyes followed me, watching me like a wild animal.

Maybe I was, with the way I had been acting.

Mr. Cadwallader, the apothecary, didn't give me too much trouble when I picked up the salve for Ronan's wound—though he did charge me twice the price, almost depleting my meager stash of silver. I walked out of the shop counting my last twelve coins, almost missing my uncle as he brushed past my shoulder.

I turned, dropping my coins as I did, and grabbed his arm. "Aidan?"

He turned around in shock, but his expression melted into a smile. "Ah, Keira girl!" He embraced me tightly, his whiskers scratching my cheek. "What a sight for sore eyes."

"Cousin Keira, what a pleasure," a voice called from behind us.

Dread ran down my spine. I let go of Aidan to take her in. "Finna, you look..."

Words failed. She wore a deep purple dress that accentuated her robust form and a fox-fur wrap that matched her luscious red curls. Attached to her arm was none other than Ellian Llewelyn, dressed in his own expressive wolf furs.

My heart sank. The two looked like a couple from a storybook.

"Mm, thank you," Finna simpered, though I didn't compliment her.

Ellian removed his arm from Finna's despite the way her lips turned downward and grabbed my hand. He kissed it once, desire thick in his green eyes. "Good afternoon, Mrs. Mathonwy."

I grinned despite myself, even more so when Finna's eyes widened in disbelief. "Ellian. What brings you here?"

"I was just telling your Uncle here the good news." He dropped my hand slowly, something reluctant in the action. "About the sanctions and tariffs."

"What?" My stomach sank.

Yorath and the sanctions. Lyr below, what had I done?

I looked to Aidan, waiting for my reckoning; but he beamed at me, clapping Ellian on the shoulder. "Ellian tells me you paid a visit to Councilman Yorath yesterday. And last night they passed your request at the Council meeting. Unanimous vote." He winked, joy radiating from him. "Good work, Keira girl."

"I—I don't—" The information settled over me, my heart thundering in my ears.

Finna shot me a glare, then quickly replaced it with a smile and rested a delicate porcelain hand on Ellian's bicep, batting her eyelashes. "Well, it's been so nice of you to come out and tell us yourself, Councilman."

"The effort was worth it to stumble into my favorite Branwen." Ellian patted her hand but made eye contact with me. "Connor said your argument was very convincing." A knowing grin tugged at the side of his full mouth. "Your shipping and carrying license is now fully restored. The world is your oyster, Keira."

I blinked at him, my head swirling.

The tariffs were lifted and my family could sail free again. Tears welled in my eyes, threatening to spill over. "I don't know what you did, but thank you."

"I did nothing. I'm only the messenger." Ellian tucked a strand of hair behind my ear, and I froze, heat rushing my cheeks. My eyes darted to Aidan, knowing how inappropriate the gesture was, but he didn't seem fazed. Ellian cleared his throat, a hint in his eyes. "Well, I'd best be off, but I hope to see you soon. We still have the business we discussed in my office the other day to attend to."

The investigation. He had information.

I nodded. "Aye, I look forward to it."

Ellian waved goodbye to the others. "Aidan. Finna."

Finna's fox eyes flitted between us, brimming with suspicion. "Don't be a stranger, Councilman. You should stop by Branwen Townhouse soon. I'll make you a nice meal as a thank you." Her voice was husky as she tucked a pristine curl behind her ear. "Now that we're all such good friends."

Ellian gave a tight-lipped nod. "Aye, I'll be in touch." He flashed me a sensual grin. "Goodbye, Keira."

He sauntered away without another word, Finna staring after him like a child whose toy was taken.

Aidan turned to me, patting my arm, his brow knit with worry as he appraised me. "It's good to see ye in such good health. But I'm worried about ye, girl. Griffin told me what happened on the ship yesterday. Has Ronan been good to ye?"

Finna pursed her lips, raking her eyes over me with a scowl. "Judging by the state of her hair, I'd say he's been more than good to her."

I cocked my head to the side, the insult pouring salt into an open sore. I waved her off. "Why don't you go throw yourself at Ellian some more and let the grownups talk?"

Finna looked at me like she had swallowed a dagger dipped in dog piss.

Aidan pressed his lips tightly together to suppress a smile and cleared his throat. "Finna, why don't ye go on ahead? I'll catch up in a minute."

"Good to see you, Cousin." She grimaced before stomping off in the direction of the townhouse.

"Likewise."

Aidan focused back on me, his wrinkles spreading at his eyes as they narrowed. "Are ye okay? Ye can tell me honestly."

I exhaled deeply for the first time in days. "Aye, Ronan's harmless enough, I think." The words rushed out of me, the familiarity of Aidan's presence breaking open my walls. "But I'm more worried about what happened on the ship. Someone is out to get us, and I've never been more confused about who I can trust and—"

Aidan grabbed my shoulders gently, silencing the tidal wave. "Well, ye can trust me. And the family. We are here for ye, no matter what yer last name is, or how grumpy yer cousin can get when she's hungry." A smile tugged at his lips. "Ye've done so much for us, it's time we help ye out a little. I'll look into the matter of the ship. We'll find whoever has been botherin' ye, and we'll take it to the Council."

I pulled him into a tight hug, breathing in his scent. "I missed you so much."

"I missed ye, too," he murmured into my hair, then pulled back, patting my cheek, "but I know ye'll be okay. Yer pa used to say yer the fiercest thing on two legs. Nothing can bring ye down."

Aidan looked so much like Papa now, the grey in his beard and the wisdom in his eyes. With a few soft words, he had melted my troubles in the way only a Branwen man could. My heart felt full enough to burst. "Can I ask you a favor?"

"Of course."

I looked at the ground, finding the words. "Can you check on the status of the house? The shack hasn't been bad, but...well, it's not very roomy."

The scent and heat of Ronan's chest flashed through my mind.

Aidan's brow furrowed, his mouth twisting up the way it did when he was troubled about something. "Aye. I'll reason with ye straight girl, it's been difficult to get the families to agree on this house. Madame Esme is taking care of it, but it may take some time. But I'll see to it that it gets done as quickly as possible." This time, his grin didn't reach his eyes.

"Thank you." My voice came quietly, tears lining my eyes. I had missed this so much—Aidan, my family…

Feeling like I wasn't alone.

Aidan nodded in the direction Finna had gone, a playful grin tugging at his lips. "I'd better be on my way before Finna bites my head off."

"Don't let me stop you." I hugged him once before he walked away.

"Stay brave, Keira girl," he called over his shoulder.

I watched his form fade into the distance, the warmth and ease he brought fading away with him. My heart sank.

I hadn't been brave, not in the least bit. I had been childish, and cruel, and scared…so scared of it all.

But I would be brave. For my family, for their future, I could.

✦I3

Baths and Bargains

I ran back to the spring despite my protesting muscles, my joy too much to contain. Somehow, I had not consigned my family to poverty. Somehow, I had escaped Connor Yorath's wrath, at least for now. Somehow, the rest of my worries seemed far away, like I was looking at them from a star's eye view.

All my worries save how bad I smelled.

Small victories.

Lyr below, did I need a bath. I went to the shack first, setting down the heavy basket of goodies Reina had given me and grabbing some fresh clothes. Ronan was not there, but I hadn't seen him as I passed the spring, so perhaps he'd gone to town after all, the cad. I walked toward the spring, stripping my coat as I went. I'd need to soak that rutting thing, too.

I clumsily pulled my shirt over my head as I walked, not willing to wait. The material snagged on my matted hair and I struggled to yank it free.

A throat cleared.

I froze.

I was not alone.

"Do you need a hand?" Ronan asked, smarminess thick in his voice.

"No, I'm fine." I pulled the shirt back down to cover myself, prepared to give him a piece of my mind—only to see him, stark naked, bathing in the spring. He must have been under water the first time I passed. I blushed and averted my eyes. The water skewed certain parts, but I was not about to wait for a clearer picture.

"Ah, I'm sorry." Ronan's voice was higher than normal, embarrassed splashing signaling his movement. "Give me a moment, I'll get out—I just hopped in for a soak."

"No, stay, I'll wait 'til later," I insisted, stumbling toward the shack.

A deep purr from Ronan. "You could join me."

I spun on my heel, shooting him a dagger-sharp look. "You're pushing your luck, Mathonwy."

"No, wait—" He covered himself, heat rising in his cheeks. "I didn't mean it like that. I won't look, I swear. But that water is warm, and I'm sure you need it as much as I do after yesterday. It's a large spring…"

He was right. The main pool was almost as large as the *Sarff's* deck, which left plenty of room to not see anything…and the tendrils of steam rising from the turquoise surface were both a beckoning finger and a thin blanket of coverage. But thinking of being on the same *island* as a naked Ronan sent the fish in my gut flopping again.

I eyed him, wary. "If this is a trick, Ronan, I'm not interested."

He softened, sinking further into the steam. "Keira, my mother used to bathe me, you, Griffin, and River in the same tub when we made a mess of ourselves at parties. Until we were six. Think of it like that."

I raised an eyebrow, sticking my hands to my hips. "Aye, but I guarantee a lot of things have changed since six." I wiggled a finger in the general direction of his nether regions.

To his credit, he did not balk. Instead, mischief tugged at the edge of his lip. "Aye, true. But you were nearly sixteen when you used to go skinny dipping on nights you knew I was on lookout."

My jaw dropped, my arms flying across my chest even though I was no longer exposed. "That's—"

He held a hand up in resignation, the other still covering himself. "I'm not teasing you, and I won't look. I'm just saying you have no excuse not to come have a hot bath." His tone was earnest, but something else glimmered in his eye. "Plus, you smell bad."

"I do not," I lied through my teeth, blush rushing up my cheeks.

"Yes, you do, my eyes were burning this morning when you were snuggled up to me." He gave me a teasing look, but there was kindness hidden in it. "Come, have a bath, for both of our sakes."

The warmth coming from the water sang to me, my own scent stinging my nose. I sighed, pinching the bridge of it. Lyr below, I was a rutting fool. "Fine. Turn around."

"Aye, Captain Keira." He grinned, turning around slowly. I waited a moment to make sure he would not peek, watching him carefully; he leaned against the far bank, the lean musculature of his back straining slightly. The line of him was undeniably elegant in the water, and heat rose up from my core again...but not the kind that reached my cheeks.

"Can I turn around yet?" Ronan whined as he pivoted half an inch over his shoulder. I shook off my trance.

"No, stay." I kicked a small stone into the pool, the ripples lapping against him.

Laughter rumbled through his chest. "Aye, Captain Keira, I'll stay."

"Stop calling me that," I snapped. Hesitant, making sure he was not looking, I stripped. "You know I wasn't skinny dipping for you," I sneered, flinging my boots off, then my pants. "I like the feeling of just me and the ocean, and—"

"I know, I know, but a man can dream." False impatience coated his tone. "Can I turn around already?"

I pulled off the last of my garments save for the small white bands of fabric that covered my breasts and bottom. Carefully, I lowered myself into the warm water; I had to bite back the moan that rose to my throat as it soothed my every ache.

I crossed my arms, watching Ronan from the other side of the pool. "Aye, you can turn around, but keep your eyes high or I cut them from you."

Ronan turned, slowly, and waded closer. To his credit, his eyes did not falter from mine, did not dare peek below the surface. "You know, you don't have to threaten me to respect you. I already do."

He was still five or six paces away, but it was too close. I swallowed hard, shrugging to conceal my discomfort. "It's a reflex."

Ronan tilted his head, a bad idea twinkling in his eye. Then he smacked the water, sending it splashing towards me. He was still far enough that I didn't get the full brunt of it, only the last droplets, but I shot him a reproachful look anyway.

"What was that for?"

"Sorry." He shrugged, mimicking my action and tone. "Reflex."

My power bubbled underneath my skin, the challenge playing to my more primal parts. "Oh, now you'll pay." I dared to move closer, my feet scraping along the rocky bottom of the spring, my own hands ready to splash.

A satisfied grin crossed his face as I approached. "Keira, you've never beaten me in a splash-off before and you won't now."

My control over my power snapped, the beast inside chomping at the bit. A dark laugh rippled from my core. "That's only because I let you win."

Unleashing my gift, the buzzing in my hands like lightning, I sent a wave of water hurtling at him.

He turned his face just in time to save himself from a mouthful of water and whipped back around as the water settled, his shoulders shaking with laughter. Ronan held his hands in the air in surrender, beaming. "Whoa, all right, I yield. Take it easy."

I moved my hands to the ready splashing position again, narrowing my eyes. "I don't do easy. I have a reputation to uphold."

Ronan cocked his head. "Not with me, you don't. You don't have to be anything with me you don't want to be."

"Except your wife." The words tumbled out before I could think.

Ronan stiffened, his jaw clenching. He waded further from me, sinking deeper into the water. When he laughed to himself, the sound was shallow. "Aye, well, even that won't be for long, since I can't say rutting *no* to you."

The laughter in my core died, the shift in his tone throwing me off my center. "You drafted the divorce contract, Ronan. And you *love* saying no to me, you always have."

"What? Lyr below, Keira, you must've hit your head during the wreck." Some of the playfulness returned to his eyes, but he did not back away from the subject. Instead, he pushed further, my discomfort only growing as he added, "I used to follow you around like a dog, begging for even a glimmer of your attention. You called, and I'd follow."

My voice was smaller than I wanted it to be. "That's not true, you always—"

"Oh, I always teased you about it." Ronan rolled his eyes, a sharp edge to the humor in his tone. "But you were in charge. Captain Keira, even then. Remember when we were ten and you convinced me to steal from the jeweler so we could buy our own ship and sail away together?"

The memory swam clearly into my mind's eye, the shimmering emeralds we stole, the way Ronan begged me to run away with him. "I didn't convince you, that one was your idea!"

Ronan held up a finger to silence me, wading closer once more. "It was my idea to whisk you away on a ship and marry you, it was *your* idea to steal to pay our way."

I sank deeper into the water. "Fine, so I problem-solved for your plan. But it wasn't always like that."

"Name one time." He settled into the near bank, smugness radiating from him.

A new memory filled my mind of the same satisfied grin on his much younger face. "When we were fourteen. At your cousin River's eighteenth."

Ronan's eyes shot to mine, shock wreathing his features. "That's different."

"How?" I looked down as the emotion of the memory consumed me. The scent of citrus and lilacs, the music of the band and the laughter, the feel of his warm hand in mine, my nerves bubbling within me like the sips of champagne we snuck. "It was your idea to dance, your idea to sneak off to the turrets with a bottle of gin..." I met his gaze, the warmth of the water making me brave. "And your idea to steal my first kiss."

Ronan waded closer, his eyes heavy-lidded. "Aye, it was my idea, one I don't regret in the least. But I did ask you first. And if I recall correctly, you said yes."

Heat rushed my cheeks and filled my belly. I raised a brow but remained still. "Aye, something I sorely regretted when you almost bit my lip off."

He chuckled, the mischief in his eyes restored. "What can I say, I had no idea what I was doing back then. And I got better that summer, thank you very much."

I was the one who waded closer this time, consumed by a boldness I had not felt in years. "Only because I taught you," I challenged, my heart beating louder than cannon fire. He was close enough to reach out and touch now.

His eyes asked questions I couldn't answer; he was so near, I could see the pretty ring of grey in the center of his irises, muted by the sapphire but not extinguished.

My throat went dry as he spoke again, his voice husky, "Well, I've learned a few things on my own since, if you'd like me to show you."

Another door unlocked inside me, heat pooling deep in my core.

A part of me wanted him. A part of me always had. And he was right in front of me, waiting to be claimed, inviting me to take what I wanted.

Or maybe I just wanted to pretend, even for a minute, that it wasn't him. That it wasn't me. Not Mr. and Mrs. Ronan Mathonwy…just two strangers swimming on a starlit night. Two people without a history, people with desires and needs that met each other's, no strings attached. No expectations, no family quarrels to consider. I was a twenty-year-old woman, for Lyr's sake, a lass in her physical prime, and it had been ages since I'd been kissed. And maybe, even with all that had passed between us, it wasn't so bad to want something for me.

Ronan must have sensed my walls coming down as his hand brushed the side of mine in the water, his invitation still heavy in the air between us. His touch sent a wave of tingles up my arm and down my spine, the power in my core purring in response.

My lips parted slightly as I moved closer to Ronan.

Not Ronan, I reminded myself. Just a man with wants, whose lips were now only a breath from mine, whose glorious ocean eyes burned with surprise and anticipation.

My voice was barely louder than a whisper when I finally responded, "So show me."

I closed the distance before I could remember myself.

His lips were soft against mine, tentative at first as if he couldn't believe this was happening. But after a moment, they pressed back, eager and hungry. His mouth opened slightly, the movement fluid and commanding. I yielded to him, and we were moving together, our lips meeting and parting in a dangerous synchronicity. The tension I had been holding dissolved, and, in that moment, all I knew were his lips, his wicked tongue tracing circles over mine, his teeth scraping ever so gently across my bottom lip. My hands wound their way around his neck, pulling him closer, wanting *more*. Then, his wide hands at my sides, moving me through the velvet water toward the bank until my back was against its rocky surface. His hands trailed further down, exploring the curve of my hip, something daring in the gesture, daring me to open, to yield...

I went rigid in the water.

My hand moved to his chest, *Ronan's* chest, right where his protection charm covered his heart. I pushed slightly, if only to preserve the protection over mine.

We were not strangers. As much as the part of me that longed for affection screamed for more inside my head, the reasonable part of me knew better. Knew that this did not end well for either of us.

Ronan yielded to my silent request. Our lips broke apart, his hands dropping from my sides. For a second, I felt cold without his heat, but I shook off the feeling.

Ronan's eyes were still clouded with desire, but he waited quietly for an explanation, his expression searching.

"Ronan, I'm not—" My voice broke. "I'm not there yet."

The heat of the moment dissolved as quickly as it came, and I pressed myself further into the rocky edge of the spring, grounding myself to reality. Ronan nodded knowingly, not a single trace of anger or dissatisfaction in his gaze. "Yet?" He floated backward to give me space, a primal smile lighting up his face. "Yet. I can handle yet."

I sighed, the raw edges of my nerves smoothing over as we melted back into our comfortable roles. I splashed him lightly. "Insufferable cad."

His eyebrows shot up in pleasant surprise. "And you didn't threaten me just then! My, my, you really are in a good mood."

"Aye, I am in a good mood, if you must know." I leaned back onto the nearest bank. The water worked its magic, unraveling my knotted muscles as I sank deeper, the strange intensity of the moment before vanishing with my aches. "It's hard not to be."

"Yes, well…" He settled onto the opposite bank, stretching his arms behind his head with a smirk. "Kissing me tends to have that effect on women."

"Oi, you're pushing it," I scoffed, but even his crude comments couldn't take away my smile. The stars were finally peeking out above the white treetops; I wondered what they thought as they watched us, exposed and vulnerable as we were. I glanced back at Ronan and caught his expectant gaze. Lowering yet another wall, I sighed, "My family's shipping license was restored. Sanctions are cleared. Tariffs are lifted."

Genuine excitement spread across his face. "Lyr below, Keira, that's incredible, how—"

"I don't know." I beamed back at him. "I think I scared Yorath, or maybe Ellian pulled some strings—"

Ronan's face fell, shattering the excited frenzy. "You saw Ellian?"

I folded my arms across myself underwater, suddenly feeling the exposure, as if I wasn't pressed up to him just moments before. "Aye, he told me and my uncle about the Council's decision."

His brow knit tighter. "You know, you should be careful around him." His eyes flicked back up to me, darkness roiling in them, his voice a lethal low when he continued, "I was doing some thinking…the nails and the iron from the ship were probably from him. And he's always been on your family's side, and the way he looks at you…well, he'd have reason to want me out of the way."

Annoyance prickled at the back of my neck. "First of all, Ellian is a friend, a good one. I trust him, and I don't think he'd ever put his business on the line for whatever petty jealousy you think he has." My voice came out sharper than I expected. I paused, regaining my control. "And second, the sea said the *wood* was compromised, not the ironworks. Trust me, after a lifetime of vague whisperings, if the sea is being that specific, it's for a reason."

Ronan looked down, a quiver in his voice. "What makes you believe him so easily when you wouldn't believe your own name if it came out of my mouth?"

"Ronan—"

"It's fine, Keira." He turned in one fast movement, waving me off before I could speak. Shamelessly, he lifted himself out of the water, grabbed his coat, and covered himself in one swift motion. He glanced back over his shoulder, and I didn't miss the blackness lingering in his eyes. "Enjoy your bath."

Without another word, he stalked off into the night.

"Ronan, wait," I called after him, but he did not turn around.

I sighed, sinking under the water, guilt weighing like an anchor in my gut. For every wall of mine he knocked down, I had another one in place. But Ronan, despite the deceit and the cleverness he wore as a mask, had always been one to wear his heart on his sleeve. I had once again stomped all over it.

What was worse, I wasn't so sure he deserved it anymore. At the very least, he had been honest with me since the ship, and maybe even before that. He had let me into his world, into his family, and had asked very little in return. I had conceded nothing to him but my name and a kiss.

Lyr below, a few days ago I would've drowned myself before ever admitting Ronan Mathonwy deserved better. But he did. He deserved things I could not give him. A partner who trusted him. A woman who loved him.

I sank further into the water, hoping whatever magic it held was enough to wash away my guilt and confusion.

A dark rumble itched at the back of my mind. *Make it right, girl.*

I shot back up to the surface, anger boiling in my core. "I'm not in the mood for a lecture, thank you."

At once I raised myself from the water, donning my clean clothes as fast as I could. Staring at the shack, I sucked in a breath. *Make it right.* I could try.

I raised my chin and walked straight to the shack, banging open the door. "Ronan, please talk to me, I—"

The wind left my sails. Ronan lay face-down on the far side of the straw bed, his back rising and falling in even waves.

He could sleep through anything, hurricane or heartache.

Careful not to wake him, I crawled onto the bed, settling beside him in the soft hay. I didn't know how to be what he wanted me to be. And I didn't know how to be what *I* wanted, either, because I didn't know what that was.

But I could try to make it something close to right.

"Goodnight, Mr. Mathonwy," I whispered before shutting my eyes.

I hoped to open them to something better tomorrow.

I woke to a cold bed and a note next to my pillow. A small part of me fell—the same stupid part that had kissed him and crawled into this bed the night before. The part that bathed and batted my eyelashes at him.

He had every right to be angry at me, and a larger part of me did its best to convince me I didn't care. I snatched up the note, unfolding it with frustrated fingers. The words flowed over the page in elegant strokes, his trademark swagger somehow infused in the ink:

Good morning, Mrs. Mathonwy,

You looked so peaceful as you were drooling on the pillow this morning, I couldn't bear to wake you. I went into town. Don't miss me too much. I'm tired of being cooped up like an invalid, and you never replenished my whiskey.

If you would be so kind, I'd love it if you would join me at the Raven for dinner this evening. And before you say no, I have a surprise you won't want to miss. Wear something nice.

Your darling husband,

Ronan Francis Mathonwy

Covering my mouth to hold back the laughter that rose to my throat, a small spark ignited within me. "Francis, of all names.

Insufferable cad." I read the letter again, admiring the way he swooped his *y*'s…

I threw the letter down like it was boiling hot. Had I lost my rutting mind?

I *had* lost sight of myself, letting him past my defenses one by one, letting him awaken dormant parts of me. Even if he was telling the truth about everything, even if I was wrong…

There were certain courses I couldn't see to the end.

I pulled on fresh clothes and donned my still-damp coat. Hastily, I braided back my hair, wishing my fingers were as deft as Vala's or Saeth's.

Grabbing my knife, I stormed out the door. I needed to hunt something.

As expected, running around through the woods did not solve anything. But it numbed the symptoms, my task concrete, simple: find some meat, catch it. Don't think about kissing Ronan.

After an hour of setting traps, I caught two rabbits. I had wandered pretty far into the *Dubryn* Forest by then, where the spring turned into a stream and the grass underfoot became sandy. To where I had woken up only two days before.

It seemed like a lifetime ago, or perhaps a different person's life entirely.

Cleaning my knife and tying my conquests to my belt, I moved to go. I was here to find a meal, not to become the *blaidd's*.

I turned when I heard movement in the trees behind me.

Crouching down, my legs aching underneath me, I hid behind the nearest tree, trying to quiet my breath while I strained to listen.

Another few crunches of leaves, then a voice. A very human voice.

"I told ye already, this is bigger than yer little crush. It's bigger than all of us, ye oversized fleabag." The voice, a woman's, whispered intensely to an unidentified partner.

A deep growl answered.

I stiffened. Lyr below, was she talking to a *blaidd*?

Slowly, I moved my hand to my knife, gripping the hilt tightly as I waited. The voice came closer, laced with a viciousness that matched the *blaidd's*. "Growl at me like that again and I'll turn ye into a coat."

Recognition sang through me; I'd know that gravelly voice anywhere. Knife in hand, I stepped out from behind the tree, my suspicion confirmed when her wild grey curls came into view. "Esme."

Startled, she flipped to face me, expression wild. She blinked as recognition settled in, a controlled smile creeping up her wrinkled face. "Ah, Keira girl, you look well."

I eyed her suspiciously, my knife still tight in my hand. "What are you doing? And who were you talking to?"

She glanced over her shoulder, offering a vague wave of her hands. "Ah, just talking to myself. And I was on my way to come check on ye!"

I pointed my knife east, opposite to where she had been going. "The shack is in the other direction."

Esme's smile turned into a grimace. "Aye, but you weren't in the shack, were ye? No."

"Did you need me for something?" I kept my voice even, but the tension in the air was suffocating. I had always trusted Esme implicitly. Never questioned her quirks and oddities, only accepted them as fact. But as she eyed me like a trapped animal, waiting for a way out, I wondered if my judgment was as skewed as Ronan seemed to think it was.

"I came to talk to ye about the house, actually." She tilted her head, her shoulders relaxing like she'd decided I wasn't a threat. "There have been some complications. It may take longer than I expected."

I sheathed my knife again, though I did not take my eyes off her. "What kind of complications?"

"Animals is all. Critters got in and trashed the place a bit." She waved it off, but the red of her eyes flashed for a moment. "It may be an extra week until we clean it up enough to get working again."

My stomach sank. Another week at the spring, away from town. Away from my family, away from the sea. Another week of confusing interactions in close quarters with Ronan. "Can Ronan and I help you clean it up?"

A grin splayed across her face. "No, then it wouldn't be a surprise!"

"Esme, I can't stay here a third week." I hated how desperate I sounded, but I needed to get back to my life. Perhaps then, surrounded by normalcy, I could figure out what I wanted to do with the rest of it.

Esme hobbled closer, grabbing my shoulders in her surprisingly tight grip. She offered a soft smile that reached her violet eyes. "Keira, ye can do anything. Now go wash up, I hear ye have a date tonight, and yer covered in mud. Brush your hair a bit." She patted my cheek, and turning on her heel, slinked off into the forest again.

"How did you—Esme, where are you going?" I followed after her, somehow struggling to keep up with her long strides.

"Back to town!" she called over her shoulder, picking up her already-quick pace. Lyr below, what did this woman eat?

"That's it?" I yelled, my voice raw as I tried to catch up with her. But she kept dodging between trees, the white willow branches hiding her from sight.

"Aye, that's it," she giggled, her voice far away. "Have a nice night, Keira!"

And like a ghost, she fully disappeared behind a tree, the remnants of her laughter echoing through the white wood.

14

Ravens and Revelations

Esme's visit made me too uneasy to sit at the shack any longer. I jumped at every sound, imagining the *blaidd* around every corner waiting to sink its teeth into me.

The questions rattling around in my head did nothing to soothe my nerves. Who was Esme talking to? And what in Lyr's name was she talking about?

Then there were the darker questions, the ones that sent the hair on the back of my neck straight up. Who had trashed the house? And who had sabotaged the ship?

Sitting and waiting for answers would do me no good. Perhaps a visit with Aidan would. At the very least, he'd want to know about the house. Perhaps he'd even have answers.

It was already well into the afternoon, which meant I didn't have much time to waste if I was going to visit Aidan and make it to the *Raven* in time for whatever ridiculous surprise Ronan had planned. But that didn't stop me from donning my favorite sky-blue tunic, the one with black ravens embroidered along the high, silky collar. It hugged what little curves I had, wrapping around me and buttoning at the sides, hitting just past my hips. Vala had made it for my eighteenth birthday, one I didn't get to celebrate with a fancy party and a gown like everyone else in Porthladd. Instead, I spent that Samhain on the *Ceffyl*, freezing in the waters of Pysgodd, smuggling venison back home for the harvest feast. But Vala hadn't forgotten and had the beautiful garment ready for me when I returned.

I felt foolish wearing it now, my hair a crow's nest, my boots caked in mud, my blue coat with tears in it; but Ronan had instructed me to wear something nice, and for reasons I could not fully explain, I did.

Without further hesitation, I made my way to Aidan's, tugging at my hair to make it presentable as I went. The walk into town went quickly, my bath and two nights of real rest restoring my legs beneath me. Despite my confusion and worry, knowing I'd be greeting my family with our future restored put wind in my sails.

But the townhouse was dark as I approached, the only lights coming from the back windows of the kitchen. I knocked twice, but no answer. I pushed open the front door, the wood creaking louder than I expected. The hall lanterns were still lit, signaling life inside, but no one came to greet me.

"Hello? Anyone home?" I called into the empty hallway. No one responded, but I heard shuffling from the kitchen beyond the hall.

I rolled my eyes. If this was Griffin playing a trick, I wanted none of it.

"That's enough, Griff," I grumbled as I walked into the old kitchen, which still smelled of chicken and stew from lunch. Aidan must have splurged.

But Griffin was not in the kitchen.

"Ah, Cousin Keira, what a wonderful surprise," Finna simpered, leaning against the far counter. At the table next to her, old Weylin sat with Saeth, a dark glare on his wrinkled face. Saeth, to my surprise, was the only one not sporting a scowl. She only stared down at her bowl of stew, her red locks in a tight braid that accentuated her sharp grin.

The rest of the chairs were empty and looked like they had been for some time. No plates or discarded food in front of them.

"Finna, a pleasure as always. Saeth, Weylin," I responded tightly, taking in the strangely-bare surroundings. Of all my family, these three were the least fond of me and often made it quite clear. But I was not here for them. "Where is Aidan? I need to talk to him."

"Making demands already," Weylin grumbled, shoving another large bite of the chicken into his mouth. He chewed with his whole face. "Can't ye see we're eatin'?"

"Yes, I can see that quite clearly, thank you for talking with food in your mouth." I tilted my head, annoyance prickling at the back of my neck. I didn't have time for this. "But I asked where Aidan was."

Weylin clenched his fists, snarling at me like an old grizzly, "Piss off, I don't answer t'ye. Go back to yer bastard husband."

When Finna snorted with laughter, anger flashed through me. I grabbed the hilt of my knife out of reflex but stopped myself just short of drawing. Forcing a sigh, I rolled my shoulders back. I was not here to fight, I was here to talk with Aidan.

Saeth's eyes flicked to her father, embarrassment flushing her cheeks. Sometimes I forgot how much she resembled her late mother, with her pretty doe eyes and silken auburn hair. Poor Aleena, Lyr carry her. How such a sweet creature had married this man, I had no idea. Perhaps she was better off in the grave.

Saeth looked back down at her bowl again. "Aidan's on the ship, with the rest of the crew."

Weylin shot her a furious look for speaking out of turn, and an anchor dropped through my gut. "What?" My head spun, confusion taking hold. "Without me?"

Saeth offered a small nod, refusing to meet my eyes.

A ball of emotion rose to my throat.

My crew had left me behind.

Finna giggled and pushed herself off the counter, sauntering to me until she was right in my face. "Aye, Cousin, it seems they didn't need you. Now that you whored yourself out to the Council and the shipping bans are lifted, your purpose was served. They set out for the Southern Isles last night."

The insult stung an exposed wound, igniting my temper. "And what have you done to help this family, Finna?" I snarled, hot tears in my eyes. "I may be the Council's whore, but at least I got something in return. What have you got from your men aside from a case of the scratches and a better view of the ceiling?"

Weylin slammed his fist on the table. "Oi, ye watch yer mouth! Filthy Mathonwys teach ye that?"

Heat flared through me again, but I bit it back. I would not start a fight here, no matter how many petty insults they threw at me. Weylin was an ungrateful, hateful person, but he was still my kin. My blood. *My crew.* And I would not forget that, even if he had.

I turned to Saeth, controlling my breathing as best as I could. "When will the crew be back?"

"What does it matter to you?" Finna rolled her eyes, bored of my presence. "I heard you went sailing the other day with Ronan. What do you need the *Ceffyl* for now that you have a new captain?"

The way she scrunched up her face sent my blood boiling. I barely swallowed the vile, venomous words that I wanted to hurl at her. She was a spoiled, prissy bitch who had wasted her youth on men who discarded her like table scraps. But she was also a sister, still mourning Owen's death, and a woman trying to find a place in a world that did not favor her kind. I knew Finna wasn't who I was really cross at. The real betrayers were the people who left me behind today like the rest of the extras.

My crew. And they were a sea away.

"Saeth." I looked at her, desperation rising in my throat. "When are they back?"

Weylin watched her, his eyes daring her to try it. But there was salt in her stare when she looked up at me. "Three days at most. Tarran said they were only going to Tan."

"Tan?" My head spun again. That was in the Southern Isles, where the warrior tribes lived. Tannians were the fiercest soldiers and mercenaries in the entire Deyrnas, but theirs was a desert island filled with sand and sun. I tried to piece it together out loud. "The shipping bans are lifted and they go to the one place in the Deyrnas without any marketable goods?"

Weylin chuckled dryly, enjoying my distress while he grabbed another drumstick from the plate.

I caught it before he could shove it in his wrinkled mouth. "What do you know, old man?"

He stood, huffing angrily. He was old, but still tough enough to get a few good shots in if it came to fists. I stood my ground as he snarled in my face, "I know that without Aidan here, ye don't tell me what to do. And that ye should run home to yer rutting husband before things turn ugly."

"Yes, run along Keira," Finna mimicked him like the squawking parrot she was.

I spun to face her, my best Mathonwy snake smile plastered across my face. "You know what, I will. Ronan Mathonwy might be a liar and a killer, but he's a gentleman. We owe each other nothing, but he still at least speaks to me with respect."

Finna pursed her lips but seemed devoid of another witty response as she folded her arms across her chest. I looked back at Weylin, pointing the drumstick in his face like a dagger. My voice was a lethal steady, but my power raged and swirled through my core. "Meanwhile, the only reason you still have this rutting food in front of you is because I have sacrificed everything I have to keep this family safe. Without me, and without Ronan *rutting* Mathonwy marrying me, you'd all be dead or starving by now. And you can't even manage a polite hello." I slammed the chicken back on the table and wiped my hand on Weylin's shirt. His face went red, a vein in his forehead threatening to burst. He opened his mouth to speak, but I cut him off, turning to Saeth before he could. "Saeth, send someone to inform me when the crew is back."

Saeth had to bite her lip to keep from laughing, but she nodded, a glimmer in her eye. "Aye, Keira, I will."

I didn't stay for the colorful collection of curses Weylin threw at me. Instead, I pointed myself in the direction of the *Raven* and did not look back.

"Another one, Agatha, if you would." I waved my now-empty glass in the barkeep's general direction.

It had been an hour since I pulled up a seat at the almost-vacant bar and ordered my first round of whiskey. The other patrons kept their distance, leaving me to drown my sorrows on my own.

Four drinks later, Ronan still wasn't here.

"Whoa, slow down there, sailor." Agatha leaned on the other side of the bar, a warning in her dark eyes. "Ye haven't had yer dinner yet."

I leaned in, running my finger over the rim of the glass. "Well, my husband is late, my family is insufferable, my crew is gone, and I almost died twice this week." I nudged the glass towards her, a shallow smile tugging at my lips. "So, tell me, what else should I do?"

She crossed her arms and raised an eyebrow. "Ye can stop acting sorry fer yerself and stick yer chin out like the proud young woman I know ye are."

I blinked twice. "Excuse me?"

"Ye heard me." She grabbed my glass and poured water in it, sliding it back to me. Her stone face did not soften as she continued, tapping the bar with a stern finger. "Women like us never got anywhere by whining about things. We've gotta fight fer what we want. Ye think I came into this bar—into a *Council position* for Lyr's sake—'cos I complained about it? No. I worked my arse off and told the men who called me crazy to get lost. I made it happen fer myself."

I took a reluctant swig of water. I knew she was right. If Papa were here, he'd say something similar. I swirled the contents of my glass sullenly anyway. "I can't exactly tell my family and my husband to get lost. Trust me, I've tried."

Agatha smiled, her white teeth bright against the ebony of her skin. "Then change their minds. Yer a clever spitfire of a girl. Ye'll think of something."

Her kindness unlocked another hidden part of me. I pinched the bridge of my nose to stop the hot tears in my eyes from falling. "I'm just so lost. I thought I was doing the right thing, but my family hates me for it. And I thought Ronan was the enemy, but he's...well, it's different." Maybe it was the drinks I already downed that made something warm sing through my core just thinking of him. But then the thought of his face sent another wave of confusion through me, the memory of his lips on mine more than I could handle right now. "Where do I start to make sense of it?"

Agatha appraised me, her lips pursing into a tight line. After a moment, she rolled her eyes, huffing as she held up a finger for me to wait. "Hold on."

"Um, all right." I watched her dip beneath the oak bar and pull out a small, black wooden box. She set it gingerly on the bar and opened it with her long, careful fingers, pulling out a set of ornately decorated cards. She placed them in front of me, giving me a wary side-eye.

"Now, I don't do this fer everyone, but yer a good customer and I can't bear to hear ye moaning any longer. So shuffle."

I looked down at the cards, at the black tops and the golden eyes on the back of each that seemed to stare up at me. They had to be from Hud, the most mysterious and mystical of the Southern Isles. I'd never been, as they were not fond of outsiders, but word of their magick arts had penetrated the entire Deyrnas.

I knew Agatha's parents were from the south, but I didn't know she practiced the old ways. "What—"

"Just do as yer told."

Hesitantly, I grabbed the cards and shuffled them. They were warm in my hand, and my power reacted, curious tendrils rising from my core.

"Hand 'em back to me."

I followed her orders, happy to be rid of the strange tug of the cards. Agatha took them and flipped over the top one, setting it before me. Her mouth scrunched up as she evaluated it.

I inspected the card myself, the artwork both beautiful and uninviting: a man holding a golden chalice, his crimson hair flowing behind him, a crown of seashells atop his head. He rode through cresting waves on a real *ceffyl*, the sea-horse's eyes made of sapphires. On the man's shoulder sat a black raven, so similar to the one embroidered on my collar.

"What does it mean?" I asked, re aching out to stroke the card with my fingertip. It seemed so familiar, though I had never seen anything like it.

Agatha looked up, sadness swimming in her dark eyes. "King of Cups," she explained, her voice low so the other customers wouldn't hear. "A man of the water, generous and selfless, keeps a level head. Full of love, but he trusts too freely."

I stared at the man in the card again, his kind eyes staring back at me. I swallowed the ball of emotion that rose to my throat and nodded. "Aye, I've got an idea of who that could be."

Agatha flipped over another card.

I gulped at the sight. "That one doesn't look too nice."

A man, falling from a white marble turret. Angry red flames reached towards him, waiting to consume him.

"No, it isn't." Agatha pursed her lips again. "The Tower. Means betrayal." Her eyes were dark with warning. "Someone closest to ye."

The dark gift in my core growled in response. "Figures," I scoffed at it, but I could not shake the chill that ran through me. Agatha tilted her head, gaze full of knowing. She did not hesitate to turn over the final card.

I gasped when I looked down at it.

The dark god Arawn himself stared back at me from his bone-made throne. His mighty, blood-crusted sword gleamed in front of him, his white hounds snarling and nipping at his feet.

Agatha's face was ashen as she spoke, a quiver in her stone voice, "Death. Or Transformation, I'm not sure. What was can no longer be, not in the same way. A sacrifice."

I knew this story and was no longer interested in its retelling. I flipped the card back on its face and cleared my throat. "Welp, it's all spot-on, if you ask me." I straightened up and downed the rest of my water, wishing it was something stronger. I laughed, the sound hollow. "Only, one problem. This isn't the future, it's the past."

Agatha's dark gaze did not lighten at my laughter, her stare going directly through me. "I'm not so sure, girl."

The tavern door banged open and I almost fell off the barstool as I snapped around. Agatha hurriedly shoved the cards back in their box.

Ellian's shoulders shook with silent laughter as he regarded me from the doorway. "Ah, Keira, just the lady I was looking for."

"Ellian," I said, breathless. My cheeks were hot from both the embarrassment and the drinks. Agatha's strange magic still hung in the air.

In four long strides, Ellian crossed the length of the tavern and slid into the seat beside me. He smelled of coal dust and liquor, a strange but delightful combination. He nodded towards Agatha. "How are you tonight, Councilwoman?"

Agatha's face went cold, her voice sharp. "I'm just fine."

Ellian ignored the iciness in her voice, turning back to face me instead. His green eyes glimmered in the lanternlight as he leaned in. "Now, tell me, what's a pretty girl like you doing drinking alone in a bar?"

"I'm waiting for my husband." I gave him a reproachful look, but the heat in my core ignited despite myself. I pointed to my now-empty glass. "And trying to forget."

Ellian would not be discouraged, his smile bold. "Well, that won't do." He grabbed the empty glass, our hands brushing, and held it up towards Agatha, his jeweled eyes never leaving mine. "Agatha, two shots of your finest whiskey, please."

"Aye." Agatha's gaze flicked between the two of us, a disapproving scowl distorting the smooth planes of her face. "Behave yerself, boy."

Ellian tilted his head and gave her his best puppy-dog eyes. "Don't I always?"

Agatha did not soften. She grunted and grabbed the glass, turning to make us drinks. Her expert hands worked quickly, and she shoved the drinks in our direction before stalking off to the other end of the bar.

I eyed Ellian suspiciously. Agatha was rarely so unfriendly to paying customers, especially those with Ellian's expensive taste, but I did not press. I took a swig of my whiskey. "You said you were looking for me?"

"Aye." Ellian grinned, leaning in close enough where I could feel his sweet breath on my face. He lowered his voice and added, "I spoke to my father the other night, and I have some news for you about your inquiry."

My pulse quickened as hope and dread fought for dominance in my chest. I smacked his arm. "Spit it out, then!"

Ellian laughed again, the sound rich and full, "Aye, hold your horses, girl, how many of those have you had?" He pointed to my refilled glass, an eyebrow playfully raised.

I grinned despite myself, the whiskey and his laugh melting my hardened exterior. "None of your business; now tell me what you know."

Ellian swirled and sipped his drink, enjoying taking his time. Finally, he spoke, his gaze distant, "Listen, I'm not Mr. Mathonwy's biggest fan, but I don't think he did it."

An anchor plunged through me. "What?"

"My father, he's getting old, so his memory isn't what it used to be, but he sounded sure." Wistfulness littered Ellian's gaze as he whispered, forcing me to lean closer to hear him. "The reason both families were doing business with him then...they were forming a coalition, Keira. Your father and Reese, they had a whole plan to monopolize the shipping industry. Not just in Porthladd, but across the Deyrnas."

My head spun. Papa and Reese Mathonwy, going into business together? Their relationship before the feud had been friendly, and we often did business with one another, but Reese was always driving up prices and Papa would never start a business with someone that dishonest. "That changes nothing. So, Ronan killed him so their family could take all the credit and the profits. That sounds more like it."

Ellian grinned, but it didn't reach his eyes. "That's what I thought, but no. See, my Pa was still a Councilmember then, and he saw the contract they proposed to Connor. They stood to make a lot of money, Keira. More than Lyr himself." Ellian paused and took another deep sip of his whiskey. His jaw flickered, and when he spoke again, a lethal edge laced his voice. "Reese is a snake, but you know he can't say no to a profit like that. He had no motive. And the contract was clear. It was in both their names, so in the event either of them passed or broke their word, sole proprietor was the Council. Not the families."

His words and the whiskey swirled in my stomach, a wave of nausea hitting me. If he was right, it changed everything. If Ronan and the Mathonwys were innocent...then I started this war. With the wrong family.

I swallowed hard, looking to Ellian to tell me he was kidding, to tell me he was wrong. When he didn't, I said, "Ronan might have acted on his own. I saw him pull the knife out of Papa's neck. Aidan saw him sharpening the same knife earlier that day..."

Ellian shook his head. "I know you saw what you saw, but maybe there is another explanation. I don't have many nice things to say about your husband, and there is a very significant portion of me that wishes you'd hate him and forget him forever." Ellian cracked a flirtatious smile that only hastened the whirlwind in my chest. "But if he did do it, his reasoning would've been worth risking his family's entire fortune and future. That doesn't strike me as very likely."

I took another swig of whiskey. It burned going down, but I relished the sensation. I hoped it would ground me in my body as I tried to pull my head out of the hurricane of thought that swirled around me.

Ronan wasn't lying. Ronan hadn't killed my father. The blood feud was my fault.

No, not mine. My father's killer, whoever they may be, was responsible for all of this. They were the ones who wanted my father dead and this deal dead with him. They were the ones who framed the Mathonwys to ensure our mistrust.

My power rippled through me, violent and tumultuous as a storm.

I looked back to Ellian, my voice a deadly calm. "If, somehow, you're right, and he didn't do it…"

Ellian shrugged, polishing off his drink. "Then who? I don't know. My father didn't say anything about enemies, only that the Council took its time with the deal." His face darkened considerably as he continued, his voice a low growl, "Connor thought they weren't getting enough of the cut. But Cedric died before it could be put through."

"Connor," I seethed, slamming my glass on the bar. "Do you think—?"

"No, not directly." Ellian waved off the idea before I could do anything stupid with it. "He is afraid of his own shadow, he couldn't kill anyone. I'm sure you of all people know that, young wolf." A grin tugged at his lips, the darkness fading.

"True. But I don't trust him."

"Oh, you shouldn't. If he had anything to do with it, it was indirect. He doesn't get his hands dirty." He wiggled his fingers and sucked in his cheeks to mimic Connor's wraith-like expression. I couldn't help the laugh that bubbled from my throat. Ellian laughed with me, our shoulders shaking, and for a moment it all seemed manageable. Papa's death, Ronan's innocence, the shipwreck…

The shipwreck.

My laughter cut off abruptly, another wave of hope wracking its way through my core. "Can I ask another question? About Council business."

Ellian eyed me, leaning in closer. "Aye, you can ask, but I may not be able to answer."

"The ship Reese bought Ronan…it sank. Someone toyed with the wood." The words sputtered out of me as fast as my whiskey-slow mouth would move. "Would anyone on the Council know the vendor?"

Shock flashed across Ellian's face as he registered the news, but he quickly recovered, smoothing his face back into its confident mask. "Connor might if it was on the permit."

I narrowed my eyes and held my drink up, a toast to the slimy Councilmember with all the answers I still needed. "All roads lead to Connor." I downed the rest of my drink, the whiskey burning through me.

Ellian chuckled as he watched me, his green-eyed stare heavy. "I'll see what he knows. I doubt he'll be very forthcoming with you right now."

"Aye, thank you, Ellian." I reached out and placed my hand on his forearm, the whiskey emboldening me. The warmth of his skin beneath mine sent a shudder down my spine. "For everything."

"No need to thank me." He ran his free hand through his dark curls, the action slathered in honeyed smugness. "Just have another drink with me."

The whiskey was already making my cheeks warm. "I think I've already had too many. And Ronan should be here soon."

Ronan, who I was married to. Who was probably innocent. Who I owed the biggest apology of my life to. Who I *kissed* last night.

"I'm sure he wouldn't mind two friends having a drink, especially since I just cleared his name for him." Ellian reached past me to grab my glass. His arm brushed mine again, leaving a trail of gooseflesh in its wake. "And we are celebrating."

I gulped, my mouth suddenly dry. "What are we celebrating?"

"Friendship, shipwrecks," he mused, mischief in his gaze, "whatever answer gets you have another drink."

I rolled my eyes, but I conceded. "Fine, just one more."

Ellian beamed, holding the glasses high to catch Agatha's attention. "Agatha, darling, another?"

Agatha sauntered over, her arms crossed tightly across her chest. "Ye sure, Keira?" She shot Ellian a dirty look.

"Aye, Agatha, I'm not whining." I gave her an apologetic smile. "I'm celebrating."

Her stone gaze softened a little as she grabbed the glasses without any further protest.

"That's the spirit," Ellian teased as she handed them back to him, now full of amber liquid. He pushed one toward me, his eyes wandering over my frame. "You look lovely tonight."

"Do you say that to every woman you talk to?" I scoffed, taking a dangerous sip of my glass. "My cousin Finna wished you would."

Ellian waved her name from the air like smoke. "Your cousin is a lovely girl, but she lacks your magnetism."

I sipped my glass again, heat rising to my cheeks. "You always have an answer."

"Only when I know I'm right." He winked, then reached out, tucking another strand of hair behind my ear. His fingers lingered, their calloused tips brushing my hot cheek. He watched me reverently when he spoke, his voice husky. "You, Keira Branwen, are one of a kind. A gift from the gods. I'd be a fool not to tell you that much."

Sweet heat filled my lowest parts, and I bit my lip. Lyr below, did this man have a way of turning a phrase.

I pulled away from his touch. Thinking of him like this was yet another complication in my already-twisted situation. There was Ronan to think about. Ronan who was innocent. Ronan whose warm lips had claimed my own only yesterday...

I shuddered at the thought.

"My name is Keira Mathonwy now," I reminded Ellian gently, unable to muster any more certainty in my tone. "I'm married. To Ronan."

Lyr below, I was a fool. I finished my drink in another sip, needing something to do with my Lyr-forsaken mouth.

Ellian chuckled, clearly aware of my reaction and pleased with himself for it. "But not for long, right?" He winked again, a twinkle in his eye. I froze as his words struck me. He continued with velvet excitement, "Ronan submitted that contract of yours to the Council today to be authorized. Clever, I must say, the divorce terms. I for one will be voting for its *immediate* approval."

The contract. Our secret.

My heart sank to my gut. "Ronan submitted it?"

Ellian's brow furrowed in confusion. "Aye, he didn't tell you?"

Ronan had submitted our divorce contract. Just when I thought...when I thought I wanted...

I have a surprise you won't want to miss.

Rutting snake.

"No, no he didn't," I growled, slamming down my empty glass.

Ellian tilted his head, placing a soothing hand over mine. "Is it not what you want? I assumed the divorce was your idea."

It was my idea. I knew that. But something had changed between us after the shipwreck, and though I was not letting down the last of my walls... I thought there had been another shift last night with our kiss. An understanding. A *yet*.

But Ronan was playing pretend, as he did best. He took matters into his own hands to show me just how little he cared.

Well, two could play that game.

"Yes, it was my idea." I smiled at Ellian, but it did not meet my eyes. I leaned closer to him, my leg brushing against his beneath us, and he stiffened in his seat. "Typical Ronan, trying to take credit."

"Typical." His eyes were heavy-lidded with desire. "Well, if it makes you more comfortable, I'll wait for it to be approved before I woo you." A smile crept along his face as he leaned in further, close enough to whisper in my ear. "But I consider this me throwing my name into the mix."

And as he pulled away, he sealed his promise with a warm kiss on my cheek...

Just as the door to the tavern opened once more, and Ronan's crestfallen eyes met mine.

15

Masks and Miscommunications

"Keira?" Ronan's voice broke over my name. His jaw was set hard, but genuine hurt brimmed in his sapphire eyes.

My head spun, certainly not because of the whiskey.

Ronan, who was innocent. Who I had tried to kill not once, but twice, for a crime he couldn't have committed.

Ronan, my husband, whose expression was blank as he took in the scene in front of him. Whose sharp eyes noticed Ellian's intimate proximity, the empty glasses on the bar.

Ronan, who had finally had enough of me. Who had sealed our separation the second he submitted our contract for approval.

I didn't know whether I wanted to slap him or kiss him.

I did neither, opening and shutting my mouth like a fish on a ship deck.

"Ronan," I finally stuttered after a long pause. My heart thundered in my chest, the two sides of myself warring within me for purchase. "I—"

Ellian looped a casual arm around me, and my entire body tensed with the action. His booming voice cut me off before my mouth could form the next word. My stomach rolled as he leered at my husband, the action territorial. "Ah, Mr. Mathonwy, so glad you could finally join us."

I watched Ronan, my mouth dry and my head cloudy. His face hardened as he tried to cover the rawness he'd let slip. "Really, Keira? *Him?*"

The word was intended to stab, and it found its target between my ribs.

Ellian chuckled darkly. "I was only trying to keep your charming wife company," he answered, speaking about me as if I weren't there. Rage and confusion boiled in my chest as he pulled me tighter to his side, his eyes still locked with Ronan's in some staring contest. "A girl like her, all alone...you should take better care of her, Ronan."

My confusion replaced itself with disgust. I shrugged his heavy arm off me. "I don't need taking care of, thank you." I knew the game he was trying to play with Ronan, but I was not about to be the trophy.

Ronan only scoffed, shoving his hands in his pockets. His usual mask of indifference crawled over his face, sealing away the last bits of openness. My stomach sank as he stared at me, his eyes cold and distant, devoid of the warmth I'd somehow grown fond of. "Well, have fun with her, then. But be careful, she'll try to drown you as soon as you trust her."

My rage bubbled over. "You're one to talk about trust, *Ronan*," I spat his name at him like venom.

Ronan, who was named innocent of one betrayal, only to strike with another.

Gazes turned toward us; the other patrons sensed the tension in the air shifting, their curiosity brimming.

But I didn't care. Let them stare. "Why didn't you tell me you were taking the contract to Council?"

A brief glimmer of confusion flickered in his mask, but it faded as quickly as it came, replaced with his snake's smile. "Shouldn't you be thanking me?" The corner of his mouth turned up in a cruel twist. "Now there is nothing stopping you from snogging this prick in some dark corner."

Ronan, who could disarm me with a single smile and a pretty phrase.

The last of my anger fizzled out, leaving only the hurt.

Ellian's anger had not dissipated. He stood to his full height, a growl in his voice as he squared up to Ronan. "Watch your tongue, lover boy, my patience is wearing thin."

Ellian had two inches on Ronan, but Ronan's smile only grew wider, his voice a lethal calm. "Then you should watch where you stick yours."

The insult was intended for us both, slashing through my core with brutal efficiency. I swallowed down the emotion rising to my throat.

Ronan, who might have loved me.

"Haven't you idiots had enough?" I found a voice again, but it didn't quite sound like mine anymore. I clenched my fists at my sides, every ounce of energy focused on hiding the hurt from my expression.

Ronan's gaze flicked to me, his eyes still steeled over as the tension in his shoulders released. "You're right. I've had enough." He backed away, not in defeat, but in sheer apathy as he regarded us both. "Have a nice night, Councilman."

He turned on his heel and made for the door with haste.

I moved to follow him. "Ronan, wait—"

Ellian's long fingers wrapped around my arm at the crux of my elbow. The grip was gentle but still strong enough to hold me to my spot. His expression simmered as he stepped closer. "Let him go, Keira darling, we'll have fun on our own."

I paused for a second, the warmth of his long fingers halting me. My first instinct was to chase after Ronan, to give him a piece of my mind or stop him or—whatever.

But was that what I wanted?

Ellian watched me, his emerald eyes liquid and luxurious, expecting an answer.

I could stay, could let myself get lost in his gaze, in how easy being with him could be. No Council edicts or contract loopholes or people trying to kill me. Just the comfortable life of a Councilman's wife, for me and my family. He'd wait, if I asked him to, for the divorce to go through. For me to sort my feelings for Ronan out. For me to finally give up the endless cycle of fighting and running so I could settle down.

You've whored yourself out to the Council...

Finna's hurtful words in Aidan's house seemed like a lifetime ago, but they rushed through my head now, battling away the idea.

I was no one's whore.

I pushed his hand off my arm, affording him some gentleness. "I'm not your darling, Ellian."

I didn't settle. I was a fighter. And I still had a bone to pick with my husband.

Shock and hurt spread across Ellian's dark features. He had every right to be confused; Ronan was right. I had flirted with him, and I didn't stop him from flirting right back. I had crossed lines, ones I had denied even existed. And I couldn't help but feel guilty as I turned and walked out the door, not waiting for a response. I did not wait to see how deeply my words had struck. I had bigger problems to deal with than Ellian's bruised ego.

I caught up to Ronan a few paces up the cobblestone street outside the *Raven*. The street was empty, most people already holed up in their homes or drinking in the tavern behind us, and Ronan's stride was quick with his anger. My own boiled underneath my skin. I tried my best to keep the quiver out of my voice as I called after him, "Where do you think you're going? You think you can just run away?"

Ronan did not turn to look at me, refusing to slow his pace. He only called over his shoulder, "You do it all the time, figured I'd give it a try."

I stopped my pursuit, the hurricane in my chest threatening to steal the last of my breath from me. "Fine!" I screamed, my voice raw and desperate. "Piss off back to your island, see if I care."

Ronan offered a vulgar gesture as he stalked further down the street. "I will!"

"Good!"

"Great!"

"You know what? No." I ran after him, letting go of any pride I had. "No, you're not getting off that easy." I grabbed his arm and pulled him to a halt. His expression was blank save a glimmer of annoyance. I swallowed back the tears yearning to spill over. Instead, I let the anger simmering in my gut do the talking. "You're a right ass, and you deserve to hear why."

He scoffed in my face, cruelty covering the hurt in his eyes. "Please, Keira, you haven't shut up about it since I came back. I've heard enough. You want me to be the bad guy? Fine. I'll be the bad guy. I'll take all the insults and the blame. I'll piss off and stop ruining your happiness as the future Mrs. Llewelyn." He shrugged my hand off him, the disgust in his gaze matching his tone. "Just leave me alone."

He didn't wait as he stormed off, his last words hanging in the air like an anchor ready to fall and drag me down with it.

But I was not finished. I did not settle.

"Mr. Llewelyn," I spat Ellian's name at him with all the venom I could muster, "was only in the bar tonight to clear your rutting name."

Ronan stopped moving. "What?"

I clenched my hands, nails digging into my palms. I would not cry, not now. "You heard me. He had just finished telling me about the contract between our fathers. How you couldn't have killed my father without forsaking your own. How innocent you were. And just as I was thinking of all the things I wanted to say to you, the things I had to apologize for, he also informed me that you submitted the divorce contract. Without me." My voice broke, as fragile and weak as I felt. "How could you?"

Ronan's calm mask shattered. "How could I? Keira, the contract was your bloody idea, you've been practically begging me to submit it all week!" He shouted, his face red. I froze, the fire so foreign on his face it startled me. But he pressed on, whatever leash he had on his temper fraying completely. "How in Lyr's name was I supposed to know you changed your mind?"

I let the question hang in the air for a moment. Part of me knew he was right. Knew that I had pushed him too far, had been too stubborn, had waited too long to fix things…

A part of me didn't care.

A part of me cared too much.

"What about last night?" I finally spoke, my voice small. "I thought the kiss meant something to you. I told you, I'm not ready yet, but I was trying! I was learning to open up, to trust you, to—" I halted.

To what—to love you?

The words caught me off guard as they flitted through my head, but I couldn't say them. Maybe not to anyone. I cleared my throat and continued, my voice stronger now, my walls fortifying me as they rebuilt themselves brick by bloody brick. "But now how can I, when as soon as I let my rutting guard down, you go behind my back to the Council and call it quits?"

The rage melted from Ronan's frame, his shoulders slack again. He ran a frustrated hand through his hair, the moonlight turning the blond curls white. "Lyr's ass, Keira, I wasn't calling it quits." His voice was calmer, but not cold, and my walls were on the brink of shattering once more. "I submitted the papers because I thought that's what you wanted, what you deserved. You deserve to be married on your own rutting terms, and you deserve to find a way to keep your family safe at the same time. But I was not giving up on us. I was trying to give us a chance to start over and try for something real this time."

Something real.

The words rattled through me. He had wanted to give us a chance, wanted to give me space.

Another piece of me cracked. His expression was open, maybe even hopeful, and I knew he meant what he was saying.

Something real.

But something else sat like a stone in my stomach. Though I had never admitted it out loud, I thought it was already real. It was real to me.

I wished I could have said it sooner, but my time had run out. He had already decided for me, giving up for the both of us just as I was about to give in.

"And you decided that all on your own, without just asking me what I want, what I think I deserve?" My voice was harsher than I intended it, the hurt seeping through the jagged cracks.

The openness in Ronan's face disappeared, replaced with the cold cruelty of his mask again. "And you didn't wait to hear my side of the story before cozying up to another man in front of half the town."

The insult caught me off guard, slicing deep. "I was not—"

"Do not lie to me, Keira," Ronan growled, feral and furious. He stepped toward me, the towering heat of him enveloping me. "I deserve more respect than that. He may have initiated things, but I saw the way you looked at him…like he was the last piece of meat and you were starving. I may have interrupted things before you could pounce, but you would've mounted him right there if I hadn't walked in."

My control disintegrated, and I slapped him across the face.

The stinging in my palm mirrored the stinging tears in my eyes. I expected the disrespect from my family; I didn't expect it from him. It hurt more than I'd ever admit out loud. Another brick added to my wall. "How dare you speak to me like I'm one of Madame Jessa's whores and then demand my respect in the same sentence!"

Ronan blinked, holding his face where I struck him. "Keira…I didn't mean it like that, but what do you want me to say?" His face was pained, not just from the slap. "You know how crazy Ellian makes me—how crazy you make me!"

"You think you're the only one who feels crazy?" A hoarse laugh escaped my throat. He always knew which blows to land to send me over the edge. "You make me doubt everything I know, everything I am, my choices, my *family*. You make me feel absolutely out of control, and I am scared witless of it. *You* scare me." The admission came out of my mouth before I could think, but there was no hiding the truth in it.

Ronan stared for a moment, not even a flicker of emotion in his face as he realized the same.

"I'm sorry to be such a bother, then." He shoved his hands in his pockets, reverting back into the man he once was. With a sneer, he shrugged his shoulders. "I guess I'll be out of your hair soon enough."

"Ugh, that's not how I meant it." I pulled at my hair, wishing I could smack some sense into this boy. Maybe I hadn't hit him hard enough the first time. "Why are you being like this?"

"Being like what?"

"I don't know, like my cousin Finna after one of her flings ends things with her!" I shouted. Ronan's eyebrows flew up in surprise, but it only exacerbated my frustration. I poked his chest as I continued, my words acerbic, "Your mood shifts like the tide and you twist everything I say and I just...ugh, why must you make it so difficult? Why do things between us have to be so ridiculously complicated?" The poke became a shove as my anger flurried within me, beating at his chest. "Why, why did it have to be like this for us? Why can't I just forget about you, and you forget about me, and we both can be happy?"

He grabbed my wrist to halt me, his grip firm but not painful. The calluses of his hands brushed against my skin and I stopped struggling. His voice was low, but not soft, his gaze barreling down into my soul. "Because I rutting love you, Keira."

My heart stopped. A moment passed, then another. Ronan's chest rose and fell in heavy breaths, but his eyes were clear, his expression honest.

I swallowed hard before speaking, my hand going slack under his grip "You—what?"

Ronan released my wrist from the cage of his long fingers, but he did not step back. I could feel his sweet breath on my face, the citrus and shiplap scent intoxicating. He tucked a strand of hair behind my ear. When he spoke again, his voice was soft. "Aye. I love you, Keira Branwen. As I have since we were ten years old. And I'll probably love you forever, no matter how many times you try to divorce or kill me. And that gets complicated." He let his hand linger, the tips of his fingers trailing down the side of my neck.

Lightning followed the path his touch carved. The world spun underneath me, shifting like the sea before a storm, and it took all I had not to fall over.

Ronan Mathonwy loved me.

I searched his expression for the lie, for the tell of his deception, but I found none. Only the smooth planes of his face, the off-center ridge of his angular nose, and the bright blue eyes, expectant and waiting.

He was waiting for me to speak. To tell him I loved him too, to jump into his strong arms, to feel him around me, to sail off into the sunset and put our past behind us for good...

"You shouldn't."

I hated myself as I said it, hated the way Ronan's face scrunched up in confusion. "What?"

And I hated what I was about to do. I steeled myself, praying to Lyr and any other god listening that the traitorous tears pooling in my eyes wouldn't fall.

I brushed Ronan's hand off where it had settled on my shoulder. "You shouldn't love me."

Ronan eyed me warily but smiled, a wide, toothy grin, so different from his usual half-cocked smirk. "Trust me, I've tried not to. It's not something I can control. But I do love you." He took my hand, tracing small circles into my palm, his voice reverent. "With every rotten part of me."

My breath caught in my chest. I wanted to tell him he wasn't rotten. That he was good and innocent and that everything I had said to him in anger meant nothing now. That I was the truly rotten one. That I didn't deserve any happiness after the things I had done, but I wanted it. So badly, I wanted it with him.

I didn't want much in my life. A good ship, a safe place for my family, enough money and food to get by. But I never wanted anything for me and *just* for me.

Until now. I wanted Ronan. I wanted to grab him and tell him I loved him back. I wanted the life we might have had together if my Papa hadn't been killed. If I hadn't killed Lochlan, and if Owen and Aleena and Reid and Rodger hadn't died, too.

But that life was not possible. There was no undoing our past, even if it wasn't Ronan's fault or mine. Our families would never see eye to eye. We could be married for twenty years, with a whole litter of mutts of our own, and the families would never accept it. Accept *them*. My conversation with Weylin and Finna tonight made that clear enough.

Ronan submitted the contract because I deserved to be married on my own terms. But he deserved more, too. And I knew it made me a rutting hypocrite to decide for him, but he deserved a happy life with a wife his family could love and cherish. Someone who hadn't killed his kin, who hadn't spent years cursing his name to Arawn himself.

Something real.

He deserved something real.

Papa always said there was more than one way to sacrifice a life. Even the lives we wished we had.

I cemented the last of my walls, the one I kept around my heart. I looked up at him, open and innocent and good.

"You don't deserve me," I growled, the hate in my voice not meant for him but for myself.

Ronan's crystalline gaze clouded with confusion. His hands flew to his pockets again. "I thought you said something changed."

I swallowed hard. *Lyr below, do not let me cry.* "Not enough."

"Right." I watched as Ronan's wall got its final brick. "Goodbye, then, Keira."

He didn't look back as he walked off into the night, and I didn't follow him this time.

I waited until he was fully out of sight before I fell to my knees and let the sobs overtake me.

16

Fortresses and Fool's Gold

Ronan did not come back to the spring that night, nor for four nights after.

Having slept on a ship deck in a hammock for most of my life, I never knew how empty a bed could feel.

How empty *I* could feel.

I played our fight over and over again in my head, a constant, echoing loop of what I had done wrong.

But this was what I wanted. This was for the best. I had wanted him to be mad at me, to hate me, even. I had taken away his right to choose a path for himself. Even worse, I had taken the broken parts of him, the parts he *trusted* me with, and shattered them further. Perhaps beyond repair.

I tried to fill my time with menial tasks. Hunting when I could, cleaning my clothes, fixing the shack. I stopped in town despite the sideways glances and stiff conversations to buy building materials. I hoped no one noticed that in every shop, I was glancing over my shoulder for him.

He was never there.

After spending far more than I wanted to on nails and hammers and paint, I began the task of forgetting myself in my work.

Fixing the shack was almost fulfilling. Every broad swing of my hammer felt almost as good as swinging a sword. Every mended floorboard was like repairing a ship deck. Papa had taught me the basics of handiwork since the entire crew had to pitch in on ship repairs. The shack was no ship, but the principle of "hammer and nail" was the same. I enjoyed feeling anything other than useless.

With every scrape and bruise and splinter, I reminded myself of all the pretty revenges I was owed.

To my crew for abandoning me, I wished rough seas that would make them all hurl.

To Ellian Llewelyn and his bedroom eyes, a case of the scratches that lasted a whole month.

To whoever trashed the new house, a shard of glass in their shoe.

To the person who sank Ronan's ship, a splinter in their eye.

To Connor Yorath and his seedy decrees, a quill through his writing hand.

To my father's killer, a knife wound straight across the throat.

And to myself, for all the wrong I had done and had yet to do, the worst that the dark god could imagine for me.

Papa once said revenge was a ring and everyone in it loses. Maybe he was right. Maybe my revenge wouldn't fill the hole in my heart.

Maybe it would. Maybe I had nothing left to lose.

By morning on the fourth day, the shack was complete. Working day and night, only stopping for supplies, food, and a few hours of stolen sleep had numbed my hurt, but it left nothing to be savored. Not a single squeaky hinge to grease or rickety plank to fortify. No more leaks or holes to patch.

No more distractions.

I sighed, admiring my handiwork, the only proof that I was capable of fixing things as much as I destroyed them. The shack almost looked homey now, the wood freshly stained and painted, fragrant smoke swirling from the small chimney. Perhaps I'd ask Vala for some of her lavender beds to decorate the windows, add some much-needed color to the place. Even though my marriage might have ended here, perhaps it would bring the next couple some happiness.

A familiar cough behind me snapped me from my trance.

Esme stifled a laugh when I jumped, a glimmer in the violet of her eye as she regarded the shack. "Ye did a lovely job, girl."

"Lyr below, Esme, do you ever just say hello?" I clutched my chest to make sure my heart was still beating. Gathering my breath, I ran my hands down my front, smoothing out my coat and my ruffled calm.

Esme ignored my quip, still staring fondly at the cozy exterior. "I've been meaning to give this old thing some attention. I've been a bad landlady."

Surprise arched my brow. "This is yours?"

"Ehh, technically I sold it to the Council a few decades ago, but I'm still the one to look after it." She shrugged, nonchalant as ever, but I could see the way pride squared her shoulders. "Still feels like mine. Lots of memories, ye know?"

The scent of citrus-soaked skin and the feel of parchment between my fingers filled my mind before I could stop myself, a fresh pain stinging my eyes. "Aye, I know."

Esme's sharp gaze missed nothing. "Ye know, when I told ye to go see him the other day, I was hopin' ye'd patch things up like ye did this shack...not tear it all down."

I sucked in a sharp breath. She might as well have punched me.

I had spent enough time punishing myself for my behavior over the last four days, but hearing it from her only ignited my rage. "Frankly, Esme, you weren't making much sense at all the other day." My words were gentle, but my tone was venomous. "You can save your lectures for your woodland creatures."

She brushed my braid behind my shoulder, a gentle smile unrecognizable on her usually harsh features. "I'm not tryin' to blame ye. No need to get prickly with me, girly." With a wink, she turned back to the shack. "Ye remind me of my husband that way."

The heat in the pit of my stomach cooled. "You were married?"

"Aye, once upon a time."

I stared at her now, watching the shadow of a lovesick expression fill her features. I'd known Esme my whole life, and she never failed to surprise me with her antics, like she had the other day in the woods. Strange was normal for Esme.

But to imagine her, young and *married*, was beyond the usual abnormal. A foreign loneliness for a time and a place I'd never been flickered in my core. My tone was softer as I spoke to my friend again. "I had no idea. When did he...what happened?"

"He was a man of the sea, and to the sea he went." She shifted her gaze toward the spring, caught in some memory too intimate to share. I let myself imagine the man brave or stupid enough to wed the sea witch. As if reading my mind, a wicked smile lit her face. "But heavens, did he have a temper like a storm. Stubborn as a mule, he was. Couldn't tell him nothing he didn't want to hear."

My cheeks reddened as I realized exactly which qualities I shared with the man.

Esme didn't falter, continuing her tale, "There were days we fought like cats and dogs. Sometimes, it felt like when we weren't fighting, he was doin' something to cause the next fight. Anyone who knew us knew we weren't meant to be together."

"So why stay?" I asked, not sure I wanted to know the answer. Thick emotion coated my throat. "Why stay if all you did was hurt each other?"

Esme studied me for a moment, her expression unreadable. "Because we loved each other more than we loved anything else. More than I loved myself, more than he loved his people...and that kind of love is something even a god couldn't stop."

A moment passed in silence as the weight of her words blanketed the fall air around us.

"I'm sorry for your loss, then." I stuffed my hands in my pockets, swallowing back my tears.

I expected to see misty tears in Esme's eyes, too, but instead, she wore a smile that radiated pure joy. "I'm not. Loving is losing, sometimes. It's better to have loved and lost than to not have loved at all." A gnarled elbow nudged my side. "Tell me, Keira, would ye trade all the happy memories of yer father if ye knew it was going to end like it did?"

It would've been less of a shock if she threw ice water in my face.

Papa's words echoed through my brain. *All that are lost shall be found.*

My compass suddenly sat heavy around my neck, a reminder of just how far I'd strayed from Papa's teachings. He had never been one to run from a fight. Even when he knew he'd lose, even when his chances were slim and the stakes were dire, Papa stayed.

What a disgrace to his name I was. Strange and confusing as Esme might be, she was right. I had chosen the easy way out. By sacrificing my own feelings, I had forfeited the fight before it even started. Before I could give Ronan the chance to hurt me.

My excuses slipped away like lines in the sand. I lifted my chin, a sad imitation of my father's confident stance. No more running. "Never."

Esme squeezed my arm, her hand warm despite the morning chill. "Ye did a lovely job with the shack, girl. Now go fix yer mess. We're rooting for ye."

Without another word, she turned to go, slipping into one shadow or another.

This time, I did not follow her. My guilt and rage were stones in my shoes, too heavy to carry.

I was never a saint. I was as stubborn as the tide and as cold as a winter storm, and there wasn't much I could do to change who I was. But if my Papa could see me now, see the rotten coward I'd become...

I needed to talk to Ronan. About what happened. About what still needed to happen. I had been an imbecile, but I wasn't running anymore. And I didn't care if he hated me, as long as he *talked* to me.

We still had a contract, after all.

After bathing twice for good measure, making sure every bit of grime and sweat was washed off me, I made the trek into town. All the way to Mathonwy Manor.

The colossal house was even less inviting when I wasn't actually invited, but I had nothing left to lose. So, I knocked. And I held my breath as I waited for an answer.

A blonde head popped out from behind the door as it swung open, but not the blond I wanted to see.

She eyed me with suspicion, so guarded compared to when last I saw her. "Keira."

I swallowed hard, my nerves corded in my stomach. "Reina, I need to see him, please."

Her thin lips pulled into a tight line. "He doesn't want to see ye." Her voice was laden with pity. "Please leave."

I caught the door and wedged myself between it and the frame before she could shut me out. I did not come all this way to run for cover with my tail between my legs. "But I'm a Mathonwy now, right?" She raised an eyebrow, but her gaze softened as I continued, desperation in every word, "Aren't I allowed in the house either way? If I could talk to him, just for a minute…"

She held up a gentle hand to stop me. Her eyes were kind, but not soft, her ethereal grace unyielding. "Keira, I'm not one to stand in anyone's way, but I will stand in yers if you're here to hurt him more."

"And I'm not one to chase after a man, yet here *I* am." There was an edge to my voice as I lodged myself further into the doorway. Reina had shown me nothing but kindness, but I wasn't above throwing my weight around, even with her. I kept my eyes fixed on her, hoping she'd see the steel behind them. "I need to talk to him."

Reina sighed, rolling her chestnut eyes at my half-hearted attempt at intimidation. "At ease, sailor. I don't think this is one ye can fix with that bull-headed persistence of yers." She placed a gentle hand on my shoulder, and I melted under her touch, my resolve wavering. Her eyes crinkled as she offered a sad smile. "He's not ready to talk. But he will come around."

I took a step back, the wind leaving my sails as my emotion balled in my throat. "What am I supposed to do, then?"

She shook her head, searching for a solution. I knew she did not have one. "If he says he needs time and space, ye should give it to him."

I let out a breath, and with the exhale, the last of my determination. "Fine. Will you tell him I was here, please?"

I hated how small my voice sounded, but pride was not what I needed for this moment. I needed…I needed him to know I cared. His words from our first night in the shack whispered through me. "And tell him that…that he can hate me, if he wants. He can yell at me and curse my name and call me a snake. Anything but the silence."

"Of course, deary."

A small glimmer of hope flickered through me. "And remind him we still have the other side of the contract for two and a half weeks. He'd better start helping me investigate." Reina's brow knit in confusion, but I waved it off. "He'll understand."

I didn't wait for a response as I marched down the steps.

I meandered around town aimlessly after leaving Reina, the sun still high in the sky. The brine-and- salt smell of the fish markets was the closest thing I could get to sailing. I breathed it in, letting it soothe the raw edges of my nerves.

Going home to Branwen Townhouse wasn't an option, as the crew was still gone and I had no intention of ever speaking to Finna or Weylin again. The spring was too empty to face alone, especially without the work of the shack to distract me. A part of me wanted to start canvassing shop owners again, to keep up the investigation even if Ronan had abandoned it.

No, not abandoned. I had been the one to force him away. Which meant I needed answers more than ever. Not to prove his innocence—I was already sure of that. If I was honest with myself, I had started to believe it well before Ellian produced evidence. Perhaps if I couldn't make one wrong right, I could make some progress with another.

But without him, my attempts felt shallow. Without his jabs and snarky remarks, his optimism...it felt *wrong*. After a few half-hearted questions to some of the local fishermen, my investigation led me to a shrimp stall on the east side of the market, as did my grumbling stomach. Freshly caught and grilled, it was dipped in a sweet orange sauce that only made me miss Ronan and his citrus-scented laugh even more.

It quelled my hunger but did nothing to fill the emptiness in my core.

I journeyed through town for a few more hours, my feet carrying me forward without direction. The sun hung low in the sky, casting its golden rays across the buildings and streets. The whole town glowed in its wake. I let it warm my face as I walked through, hoping it could warm the coldest part of my heart, too.

I didn't know how I found my way into Madame Neirida's
Odds-and-Ends shop at the edge of town until I was standing in
front of it. The forbidden fruit was a beacon as the sun caught its
glittering facade. Papa never did business here, since according to
him, Madame Neirida was a siren in maiden's clothing. But perhaps
her eclectic—and mostly illicit—shop, and the secrets it held, would
help me unravel some of my own.

I pushed through the door and the scent of dust and
debauchery assaulted my nostrils. A bell signaled my arrival, but no
one was behind the cluttered counter.

It took me a moment to get my bearings, my senses
overwhelmed. Every wall and rack was covered—strange trinkets
and baubles piled upon stacks of fabric and chests of all shapes and
sizes. It all sparkled in the sunlight that poured through the window,
like I was stuck inside a fairy's treasure hole.

Fool's gold, most of it.

On one table, I spotted a pair of candlesticks I could've
sworn used to be in *The Dancing Raven*. I moved to inspect them
closer, and sure enough, the black raven insignia was engraved at
the bottom of the silver. My pockets were large enough to hide
them, and Agatha would be pleased to see them returned. I didn't
think it counted as stealing if they were stolen in the first place.

As I went to grab the first, a head popped up from behind
the counter.

I dropped my hand faster than an anchor in the shallows.
Agatha's candlesticks would have to wait.

"Can I help you, deary?" The woman asked with a raised
eyebrow. Her hair was almost as dark as mine, but with deep purple
streaks through it that accented the lovely olive tone of her skin. She
folded her arms across her supple chest, the black bodice of her dress
darker than any fabric I'd ever seen.

Madame Neirida, in the flesh.

"Just looking." I offered a smile, doing my best not to look
guilty. I turned to another wall, one with hanging coats and cloaks of
all shapes and sizes. I started thumbing through them, doing my best
to seem invested.

Neirida did not say anything further, but I could feel her
stare boring holes into my head.

I kept flipping through the coats aimlessly until one caught my eye. Maroon velvet, so deep it was almost plum. The fabric was thick and warm, deep gold embroidery lining the collar and sleeves. Long cut, it would come to a man's thighs or a woman's knees. On its face, golden buttons with compasses carved into them. It was gaudy and expensive-looking, but there was a flamboyant charm to it. It would take an impressive sailor to wear this coat and not be drowned by it. I examined it further, the material soft beneath my fingertips. On the breast pocket, there was a design: a gold-embroidered crest of strong lines intersecting and melting into elegant swirls.

I ran a finger over the pocket design, the marking so eerily similar to Ronan's tattoo. Like the whole thing had been made for him. Something dark and wistful gripped my heart, and my throat bobbed as I turned to Neirida. "How much for this?"

"Twenty gold pieces," Neirida mused. I tried not to balk at the price. Expensive as it looked, then. She walked out from behind the counter, a cleverness in her gaze that reminded me of Papa's warning about her. I could see in the swish of her walk how men would be fooled by her siren's dance. "But for you, deary, it's only fifteen."

"Ah, no thank you, then." I removed my hand from the fabric, tearing my eyes away as I nodded to Neirida.

"I'm willing to barter." She stuck out one hip, leaning on the nearest table of nonsense. "If you don't have the coin, perhaps something else of equal value."

I moved toward the door, chuckling darkly. "Thank you, but I'm afraid I have nothing of value."

Neirida stepped into my path, blocking me from the door. Her eyes narrowed toward my chest. "How about that compass around your neck? Looks like it could be worth something."

Papa's compass.

"It's broken," I answered too quickly, my hand flying to where it sat on my chest, the metal cold beneath my fingers.

Neirida did not give. She reached out, tapping the chain with an intrusive finger. "Still made of brass. I could melt it down, make it into a prettier trinket."

I stepped back out of her reach, bumping into a table of baubles. "I'm sorry, I can't." My voice was firm, a glimmer of my normal strength finally returning.

"Ah, too bad, then." She stepped back, relinquishing some space between us. A knowing smile crawled across her face. "The coat would look so splendid on him, wouldn't it? Bring out his blue eyes."

"Wha—"

The door behind her opened, silencing me before I could finish my question. A familiar head of brunette curls passed through, her jaw dropping as she locked eyes with me. "Keira love, is that you?"

"Vala? What are you doing here?" I pushed past Neirida, who moved out of my way this time, retaking her perch behind her counter. Ignoring her, I wrapped my aunt in a tight hug. Her arms enveloped me, her lavender-and-fresh-bread scent nearly bringing tears to my eyes.

After a long moment, she whispered into my hair, "Don't tell yer uncle, but I've been sellin' some of Finna's old things here, trying to bring in some extra money. Hopefully, I can stop when the crew comes home. This place gives me the shivers."

I pulled away to take her in, praying my eyes would not betray me with a stray tear. "Your secret is safe with me."

She nodded gratefully, then pursed her lips to one side as she got a better look at me. "Oh, look at yer face, what on earth have ye been doing in that shack? Are you getting any sleep?" She pinched my cheek and I groaned as she continued her assessment, but a warm tinge of my former fire bloomed under my skin. "The bags under yer eyes could carry a weeks' worth of groceries."

"It's been a long few days." I swatted her hand off my face, but the action had no power behind it.

The door opened again, another familiar scowl walking through. "Hello, Saeth."

In typical Saeth fashion, she scrunched her nose as she looked me over. I must've looked like a shipwreck, but she threw on a fake, thin smile anyway. "You look well, Cousin."

"You're a terrible liar," I chuckled, something warm filling my core for the first time in days.

"True," she stated in her signature to-the-point way, dropping her grin. Saeth did not judge, only assessed. "But the intention of being kind was there."

My heart swelled with a strange sense of kinship toward my youngest cousin. I had always mistaken her candor for bitterness, but now I saw how she cared, in her own, very *Saeth* way.

"Kind doesn't suit you, Cousin. And I mean that as a compliment." Crossing the two feet between us, I hugged her tightly, her bony frame severe in my arms. She stiffened under my grip, but after a moment, her right hand patted my back, and I let her go. Her eyes were wide with disbelief, but the slight smirk that returned to her face was genuine this time.

Vala clicked her tongue again, patting down a stray curl from my braid. "Oh, my poor Keira, I know it's been rough on ye since the incident the other night. I heard about it and I just feel awful I wasn't there."

I shrugged noncommittally, pretending that the reminder of my behavior the other night didn't send a wave of nausea through me. I didn't want to think about how badly I'd messed things up with Ronan, not when I was finally feeling something other than completely empty. I smiled, but I knew it didn't reach my eyes. "Don't be silly, why would you have been at the *Raven*?"

Vala stopped her fussing, eyes narrowing. "I meant at the house when my idiot brother-in-law and that rotten daughter of mine were bullying ye." She folded her arms with a stern look. "Why, what happened at the *Raven*?"

Lyr's bollocks. She was talking about the fight at the house. So news of my fight with Ronan hadn't reached town yet. I sighed with relief, my smile less forced now. "Nothing, I—nevermind, just a joke. I'm fine, Auntie, I promise." I turned to Saeth, changing the subject. "Is the crew back yet?"

Saeth shook her head. "Not yet. Should be tonight or tomorrow morning. I'll send for you, don't worry."

"Thank you." I patted her arm, and to her credit, she didn't flinch at the physical contact this time. Mischief swam in the green of her eye.

"It's my pleasure after seeing you make Pa and Finna squirm."

Strange creature, Saeth was, but I realized that in my absence, I had grown quite fond of her. I gave her a wink, our mischievous hearts finally seeing eye to eye.

"Enough, or ye'll be squirming next." Vala narrowed her eyes at Saeth, but the threat was empty, and I swore her lip twitched upward as she turned to me. "And ye better take care of yerself. I worry about ye. We all do, even the ones who have the worst ways of showing it. And if ye really want to bring the husband fer dinner, just give me a nod, and I'll prepare something special for ye both." She placed a gentle hand on my shoulder, giving me a reassuring squeeze. "Some of us see what ye've done for the family, and none of us should be looking that gift horse in the mouth."

As the emotions swirled and collided in my chest, I couldn't decide what to feel first. My gratitude toward Vala's kindness was genuine and brimming at the forefront. But it was tinged with sadness, knowing that Ronan wouldn't be coming to dinner anytime soon. That was my fault, not Weylin's or Finna's or anyone else's.

"Thank you, Vala." I did my best to hide the quiver in my voice, the lie in my words. "I'll see about dinner someday soon. But I best be off."

Vala nodded, a soft smile crinkling her eyes. "Take care, Keira girl." She didn't press further as she and Saeth both stepped out of my path to the door.

"Excuse me, Miss." Neirida sashayed toward me, the deep velvet coat already draped across her arm. She held it out to me expectantly. "Don't forget your coat."

"I told you, I can't pay," I snapped. I was tired of her games. Papa was definitely right about this one.

She did not so much as blink at the sharpness of my tone. "Consider it a gift, then." She shoved the coat into my arms with surprising force. "On the house this time. Courtesy of a new friend."

"I couldn't—"

She held up a hand before I could finish my protest, her eyes filled with iron determination. "I insist, Madame Keira. Fate wills it so."

I looked at the coat in my hand, felt the smoothness under my fingers. And though I knew it was stupid with every bone in my body, I tucked it underneath my arm as I walked out the door. "Aye. Thank you."

17

Councils and Conditions

I made my way back to the spring in a daze as the sun dipped toward the horizon. It was growing colder, the fall equinox only a few weeks out. Most years, I spent the holiday in Bachtref with the entire Branwen clan. We'd gorge ourselves on the seven breads and spiced wine that made the harvest holiday famous. It was the one time a year Auntie Vala boarded the *Ceffyl*, and it was always a sight to behold as she clutched the rail, her face greener than the Bachtref fields we sailed to.

The memory was as warm and bright as Vala herself. She was a gift I had taken for granted, a fact solidified by her behavior this afternoon. She'd put aside her grief, her role as the mother of a slain son, and invited Ronan to dinner. Just as Reina had chosen to forgive me for Lochlan's death, then again today for hurting Ronan.

If these women, the innocent bystanders who bore the most hurt, could find it in their hearts to forgive, then what was stopping the rest of us?

If Ronan managed to speak to me again, maybe I'd invite him to Bachtref this year. Maybe getting out of Porthladd for a bit was exactly what we needed. And if any of my family members took issue with it, I'd find a way to forgive them, too.

As I rounded the hill to the shack, I clutched the coat closer to myself for warmth and a comfort that wasn't entirely physical. I didn't know if I'd ever get the chance to give it to Ronan, and I knew taking a gift from Madame Neirida was more trouble than it was worth. But it made me feel closer to him somehow. Like there was still a chance

The distinct noise of footsteps on new floorboards made my stomach flip.

I threw open the door before I could second-guess myself. "Ronan?"

"Good afternoon, Mrs. Mathonwy."

My heart sank to my stomach as I took in the man before me. Connor Yorath sat on the edge of the bed with legs crossed, clad in an austere black coat and tails ensemble. The collar was high on his neck, the rigid formality of it eerie against the homeliness of the shack. He folded his hands in his lap as his predatory gaze took me in.

I dug my fingers into the fabric of the coat to keep from wrapping them around his rutting throat. "Connor. What are you doing here?"

"Addressing me casually won't help your case, Keira. I don't need a reason to be here. If you haven't forgotten, this is the Council's property you've been haunting." He picked an invisible speck of dust off his sleeve and flicked it at me. His beady eyes flitted around the shack with clear displeasure. "Though I see you've added your own personal touches. Dare I even ask if you applied for proper permits from the builder's guild?"

I took a step toward him and set the coat on the countertop. I wanted my hands free, after all. "The spring belongs to Porthladd, not the Council."

"Is there a difference?" He shrugged, but his eyes hovered over the dagger at my side for a long second. "But I do, in fact, have a purpose to my visit."

"Lucky me." I pulled the chair out from the table and swung it around, straddling it. Papa always said the person who stood first in a negotiation only stood to lose. I wasn't about to play nice, but I wouldn't play scared either. My smile was venomous as I continued, "Come to ruin another trade deal? Or perhaps sink a ship?"

Connor met my venom with his own, the saccharine smile garish on his gaunt features. "I have no idea what you're on about, Mrs. Mathonwy, but I'm sorry if you're having a rough time."

"If you're sorry, Lyr is my uncle," I scoffed, flipping him a vulgar gesture meant to disarm him. This was a sailor's shack now, not the court of the Council. His pretty manners would not serve him here.

Connor's face scrunched up as he seemed to grasp my meaning. "Abrasive as ever, I see. No wonder Mr. Mathonwy has thrown in the towel so quickly." He adjusted his sleeves with a grimace. "Which brings me to my point. The Council has approved your divorce papers. In a little over two weeks' time, you will no longer be a married woman."

His words both struck an open wound and shocked me. Two weeks and Ronan could leave me behind without a second thought. No legal obligation tying us together.

I swallowed down my fear. Later. I'd process the loss later. Now, Connor's odious presence demanded my attention, and I could show no sign of weakness. I did my best to hide my ruffled feathers, plastering on my best Mathonwy mask. "And the second half of the deal still stands?" I picked at my nails to feign disinterest like I had seen Ronan do so many times. But my blood boiled underneath my skin, anger crashing into my nerves. I hated that I needed Yorath, even a little, to keep the families safe. And if he had created another loophole, I would have to end him right here and now. I pressed on, censuring my voice into a false calm, "Our families are still held accountable to the peace agreement?"

Connor nodded once, his expression devoid of emotion. "Of course. The Council's only goal has been peace."

I watched him another moment, waiting for him to show his hand. There had to be a "but" to this, some sort of back door he wasn't revealing. But he kept his expression infuriatingly blank. I sighed, leaning back in the chair. "Fine. Thank you. If that's all, you should go before it gets dark."

Connor only uncrossed his leg, settling further onto the bed. I'd have to set it on fire later if only to erase that stomach-churning image. He sneered at my expression of disgust. "We do, of course, have a condition. To ensure both families hold up that particular side of the bargain."

And there was the other shoe.

I stiffened in my seat, clenching the back of the chair so hard my knuckles turned white. I tried to keep my expression neutral. "There's the *but* I was waiting for. Fine, how much?"

Connor chuckled to himself, the soft sound grating on every nerve I had. "You must have gotten quite close to that husband of yours. Using bribery as a tactic?" He stood, crossing to where I sat, and placed his spidery fingers on the back of the chair. He seemed almost imposing as he leaned over me. Slowly, he dragged a single finger down the side of my cheek, his voice dipping into a growl. "No, Ms. Keira, this condition is not monetary."

I swallowed down the taste of sick that rose to my throat at his touch, but the fight was not lost. Connor had stood first. Which meant his power over the situation was not as complete as he'd like it to be.

Which meant it was my turn.

Quick as a bullet, I grabbed his littlest finger and yanked it back from the chair as I stood. Connor's eyes went wide and he cried out in pain, doubling over as I used the grip to tilt his arm behind him with an easy spin. I leaned over him and growled in his ear, his little finger now my personal rudder, "Spit it out before I decide you don't need all ten fingers."

"Let go," he spat back, but I simply applied more pressure. He screamed again, his breath ragged. "*Please.*"

I dropped his finger and kicked the back of his knee. He fell forward, catching himself with his hands, and I crouched down next to him, relishing the way his eyes hurled daggers at me. "Start talking sense."

"Mark me, you'll regret that," Connor seethed as he staggered to his feet, using the chair to lift himself up. He adjusted the collar of his ridiculously formal suit with a smirk that failed to hide the fear in his eyes. "The Council agrees that the best way to keep you in line is to keep you both close. Therefore, Ronan and his family will be working for Mr. Llewelyn. And you will be working for me. Consider it community service."

My head spun. I had disarmed Connor easily, but he had pulled the rug out from under me. Did Ellian know about this? Or worse, did he *want* this? My fury sang through my core at the possibility of either truth.

I crossed my arms in front of me, knowing Connor would not let another physical attack go uncountered. But I pressed on, my voice razor-sharp, "What do you and Ellian, a lawyer and a blacksmith, want with a bunch of sailors?"

"I don't know what Mr. Llewelyn intends to do with his new charges." Connor rubbed the knuckle of his littlest finger, hatred in his eyes, and wet his lips swiftly. "But I can imagine a few ways you could be of use, Ms. Keira."

My gut fell to the floor. I scoffed, laughing his advance off to keep from hurling. "And you expect me to believe the other Council members agreed to this malarkey?"

"They signed the agreement, including my amendment to it." Something dark glimmered in his beady eye. He leaned in again, dangerously close, his hot breath heating my cheeks. "It's not my fault if none of them bothered with the fine print."

Something feral roared deep inside me. Connor's pen had always been dangerous, but I thought that somehow I had evaded its wrath when the sanctions were lifted. That somehow, I had scared him into submission when we last met.

I had only poked the sleeping beast, turning its rage to me alone.

If it was about my family before, about controlling our money and our power, it had become personal when I threatened him. I was the sole target now. Connor wanted me under his fragile fingers, a puppet master pulling my strings.

I growled back, my own inner beast rising to the challenge. I was no one's puppet. "You're a pitiful bastard. First, extorting my father and Reese four years ago, then signing off on crooked ship-building codes, and now this? And why, because you want more money? Power? *Sex?*" I laughed, the sound wild and harsh. "I wouldn't touch you even if you threatened to kill me. You *disgust* me."

Connor blinked at my insult, opening his mouth to respond, but I held a finger to his grotesque lips. When I spoke again, my voice was smooth as glass and just as sharp-edged. "You might think your title is enough to get you whatever you want, but I know you had a grimy hand in all the tragedy that's fallen on my family. I will stop at *nothing* until you pay for it. If you think your fucking pinky hurts now, you are wholly unprepared for the *world* of hurt I will bring you."

Connor shoved my hand from his mouth, something unbridled in his expression. Something *excited*. "You would do well to remember that, soon, I will also be your employer. It would behoove you to speak kindly to me, and to watch where you stick that pretty little finger of yours." He brushed past me and walked briskly towards the door. Straightening his sleeves, he looked back, his thin lips peeling back over a toothy grin. "Have a nice day, Mrs. Mathonwy. Enjoy that title while you still can."

"Careful, Connor darling," I called out as he pushed open the door in a desperate attempt at the last word. He froze in his place, his back rigid with tension. I thumbed the dagger at my side. "There are *blaidd* in these woods."

He closed the door behind him without turning back.

I hurled my dagger at the door, sticking it right where Connor's head had been a moment before.

And just like that, the shack I had worked so hard to fix had another hole in the wall.

Nothing I built was meant to last.

18

Coats and Compromises

I spent the next hour and a half alternating between using the walls for target practice and packing my things. At some point, thunder and rain rolled in, and I was glad for the noise that muted my cries of fury and frustration. I had fucked myself and my family over in a spectacularly *Keira* way, like I had every day since my father died.

Every chance I had to save my family, I failed, putting my own anger and pain before what mattered. Every chance I had to make things right with Ronan, I ripped to shreds, dragging him into a fight that was never his and breaking his heart in the process. Now the full weight of the Council was pressing down on my shoulders because I couldn't keep my pride in check for more than three minutes with one of the most powerful men in the Deyrnas.

So, I did the only two things I was good at: I threw my knife, and I prepared to run. Maybe the only thing that could help my family now was having me out of their gods-damned way.

It was full night when the door slammed open behind me while I picked my knife from the opposite wall. I sighed, resigned to whatever cruel fate Connor had designed for me.

"I thought I told you to fuck off." The words felt empty as I turned around to face him.

Ronan stared at me with guarded eyes, his blond hair dripping in his face. He wore his famous red coat over a white tunic, the rain-soaked fabric clinging to him. "Aye, I'm just here to get my things."

"Ronan." My dagger clattered to the floor as I took a staggering step towards him

He came back.

"Who else would it be?" He crossed his arms across his chest, the action accentuating his corded muscles. "Another lover?"

I shook my head, words catching in my throat. "Councilman Yorath was here—"

Ronan's eyes narrowed as he took an instinctive step toward me. "What did he—" He stopped himself, the wall behind his eyes shifting back in place. "Nevermind, I don't care."

He moved to the bed and grabbed his velvet pack from underneath it. Without hesitation, he tore through the contents, offering not a single glance in my direction.

But he had come back.

He came back, like he did when he found out about the Council, as he had been doing our entire lives.

"Ronan." His name was both a challenge and a prayer on my lips.

His stormy eyes flicked up at me for a breath of a second before he returned to his task. His voice was strained as he spoke. "Would you mind stepping out while I pack? It'll be easier that way."

He was back, but he hadn't forgiven me. Not yet.

Yet. I could handle *yet.* "I tried to visit you. Did Reina tell you?"

"She did." A quick response accented by the thud of another item tossed into his bag. With a sigh, he pulled the drawstring tight and effortlessly threw the bag over his shoulder.

"I wanted to explain." I sidestepped in front of him before he could make it to the door. My heart hammered loud enough to rival the thunder outside, but my voice was quiet. Pleading. "Please, don't go."

He finally met my gaze, his stare icy and piercing, devoid of any hint of mercy or forgiveness. "You're in my way."

"Please, Ronan." I rooted myself to where I stood—anything to stop my knees from shaking. I took a steadying breath and bit my lip, my own stare unyielding. "A wise man once said this doesn't work if we don't talk. I'm sorry I hurt you, I truly am. But there are still things we have to talk about."

I watched my words—*his words*—register, a layer of ice melting as they did. He didn't move or speak for a moment while he calculated. Neither did I, even though every instinct in my body screamed to throw myself into his arms or run in the opposite direction.

His voice was small when he said at last, "What if I don't want it to work?"

I bit back the fear that rose to my throat. "Then that's your choice. You have every right to walk out and I can't stop you. Can't blame you either. But I—I want you to stay." My voice cracked over the last words, leaving me exposed as I stood before him. All my cards were on the table, and it was his hand. I was his for the taking. Or for the leaving, I supposed.

He waited another agonizing moment. "Why?"

"Why what?"

"Why do you want me to stay?" His chest rose and fell in slow breaths, but his eyes held no more malice. Only a distance I couldn't name.

"Because," I started and stopped, the nerves I had been holding down now tangling with my tongue. "Because you didn't deserve the things I said to you the other night, and now I know you're innocent. But our families should know about the deal… and Connor has complicated things further, and we still need to find Papa's real killer…"

"You're right, I am innocent," Ronan mercifully interrupted my rambling, but his eyes still asked questions I couldn't answer, "as I have said from day one. But we can deal with the Council, our families, even still search for Cedric's killer if I go back home. I gave my word to Lyr himself that I'd figure it out. I'm not turning back now. And I think we'd work even better, actually, if we aren't constantly distracted by each other."

A part of me felt relieved. He wasn't abandoning me completely. He never had. We still needed each other, tethered together by a fate we couldn't ignore.

But that didn't mean he *wanted* me, either. And a part of me—a much larger part than I had ever expected—deflated with disappointment as the logic of his words struck me.

"I think we work better together," I admitted, both to him and myself, "when we aren't fighting or trying to kill each other."

"Maybe." He shrugged, breaking eye contact, and shifted the weight of the pack on his shoulder—readying to leave. "But that's not enough to stay, Keira."

"Then stay because I want you to." I blurted out before I could think, shifting between him and the door once more. A whirlpool of emotions swirled in my chest, desperate and tumultuous. "Stay because you love me, and I—"

I cut myself off.

Stay because I love you. I almost said it, almost laid it all bare in a way I hadn't for anyone before.

"You what?" Ronan pried, frustration rippling from him as his fingers balled into fists at his sides.

I was running out of time, out of things to say to convince him. But I couldn't bring myself to say *that.* Maybe not to anyone. Not when the words were a curse, when loving someone meant running the risk of losing them.

The last time I uttered those words, they'd been the last thing I'd said to him.

Goodnight, Keira girl. I love ye to the stars and back.

I love you too, Papa.

I shook away the chill that ran up my spine. No, I'd promised myself I'd never say that again, no matter how badly I wanted to. But maybe I could show him.

"I—" I floundered for the words, "I have a gift for you."

"Stay because I love you and you have a gift for me," Ronan laughed dryly, hurt creeping along his features. "Keira, I'm not interested in trinkets. I'm not Finna."

"No, it's not like that." I waved my hands furiously in front of him, all tact and grace gone. "Trust me, for one second, please. And…and close your eyes."

"More games." He raised an eyebrow and sighed, pinching the bridge of his nose. "Fine, Keira, but if this is a trick…"

"Just close your eyes," I commanded with all the authority I could muster. I waited until he begrudgingly squished his lids shut before I stumbled to where the coat lay on the counter.

Lyr below, what was I doing?

I fumbled with my buttons, my fingers frantic as I refused to answer that question for myself.

I didn't bother to check if he had peeked as I slipped off the white band around my chest and pulled the coat over my shoulders in its place. I turned back to face him, ignoring how smooth the fabric was over my bare skin, and how rough the waves in my gut were.

Sure enough, his eyes remained closed, his brow pulled tightly together. A gentleman in snake's clothing.

I sucked in a breath of courage and knit my arms across my chest. "Open them," I ordered before I came to my senses and changed my mind.

His sapphire eyes fluttered open, then raked over me. His lips formed a hard line. "You bought yourself a new coat."

My breath was high in my chest as I spoke. "No, it's for you."

He crossed his arms. "Then why are you wearing it?"

I swallowed my fear as I unfolded my arms so the coat fell open, revealing my bare chest beneath it. Finna had told me stories as a girl about the art of seduction, but my mind went fully blank as I stood naked before him. But I did not break eye contact, did not let myself run and hide, exposed and vulnerable as I was. I lowered my voice as I spoke, both an invitation and a question, "So you have to take it off me."

Ronan went still, his only movement the bob of his throat. "Keira, I—"

I cut him off before he could finish rejecting me, taking a brave step forward. "I don't know if I can say what you want me to say. Or if I even know how to say it at all. Not because of you, but because of me. Of who I am." I paused, and Ronan's expression softened. The small victory rang through me before I continued, letting the storm in my chest tumble from my lips, "I'm bad at words. I know that. But I'm good at letting my actions speak for me. And even if our families hate us and the Council tries to screw us over every chance they get, I want you. Stupid and selfish as it is, I want you. And I want to show you I'm willing to make things work."

I took another step forward, placing a tentative hand on his broad chest. The heat of him warmed my fingertips, the nervous knot of rope in my core untangling slightly. His eyes widened, never leaving mine, not even daring a peek below my throat.

Gingerly, he reached out, wrapping his long fingers around the velvet lapels of the coat. But the corners of his full lips pulled downward, and he tugged the edges of the coat together to cover me once more before taking a step back. "Love and sex are not the same thing, Keira."

I hadn't expected anything from him, but the rejection stung.

Finna once said the difference between lying with a man and loving him was in how much of yourself you were willing to give. It required very little to give a man your body. Loving him required giving a piece of your soul.

I realized I'd give my life for Ronan.

Emotion was thick in my throat and my eyes faltered to the ground, unable to handle the intensity of his gaze as embarrassment filled my belly. "For me, they are the same. With you, at least. But if you don't want me, I understand."

A deep chuckle helped brush away the heat that rose to my cheeks. I looked back up at him, a tiny sliver of his true face peeking through the cracks in his mask. "Keira, it's not that I don't want you like that, I just..." He chose his words carefully, the familiar kindness I had grown fond of brimming in his eyes. "I don't want you to feel like you have convince me or try to prove anything."

New heat rose in my core, excitement and reckless abandon pulsing through my veins. Part of him still wanted me. Still loved me, maybe.

The last civilized part of me made way for my instincts. I was a gods-damned sailor, a warrior, and I would fight for what I wanted. I would fight for us.

I grabbed his face, his blond stubble coarse against my calloused palms as I stared him straight in his sea-blue eyes. "I've got nothing to prove. I want you, Ronan Mathonwy. Lyr below, for the first time in my life I want something badly enough that I'm not going to give it up for anyone."

He blinked back his shock, voice quivering, "Rotten as I am?"

My stomach twisted at the words, at the broken parts he exposed. Parts *I* had broken with my own cruelty and rottenness. I stroked his cheek, the warmth underneath my fingertips the closest thing I'd ever felt to a home. "Aye, Ronan Mathonwy. As cruel and rotten and wicked as we can be, we deserve each other."

I didn't hesitate as I pressed my lips to his.

The kiss was different from the last—no more pretending we were strangers, no more hiding from the truth. Instead, I savored the smooth planes of his citrusy lips, the gentle firmness as he finally started kissing me back. My hands snaked their way around his neck, pulling him closer.

My Ronan. My *husband*.

His hands slid to my shoulders, gently brushing the coat away from them, his fingertips sending shivers up my spine. For a moment, his lips left mine as he looked at me, at the trail of gooseflesh along my arms, at my peaked breasts. My throat went dry.

A whisper escaped his throat. "You're so beautiful."

The words undid me.

I was ravenous as I tore his coat off him. Clumsy, not with uncertainty, but sheer hunger as I undid the buttons of his soaked shirt. Ronan echoed my desire, his mouth finding mine as he slid the damned thing over his head before I could finish.

There would be time for buttons and slow exploration later. Now, there was no time, only him against me, pressing me up against the cabin wall. Only my legs wrapped tightly around his waist as his hands roamed my backside. Only his wicked mouth moving to my neck, my collarbone…

A moan rose from my throat as he made his way to my breast, his tongue flicking over its peak, sweet heat pooling at my center.

He chuckled against me, arrogant as ever. But he was mine and I was his. Every rotten part. And I wanted all of it.

Ronan's tongue stopped its exploration, and he paused to look at me. A cocky half-smile tugged at his glorious mouth. "You know, there are things we need to talk abou—"

"Later." The word was barely a growl as I enveloped his mouth with mine again, lacing my fingers through his rain-knotted curls.

In one swift motion, he carried me to the straw bed. *Our bed.* He laid me down, his mouth never leaving mine, pressing into me in all the right places. My hand traveled to the space where we met, to where the impressive length of him was still concealed by his black leathers. I managed to free the tie with one hand, a lifetime of undoing sailor's knots finally coming in handy as he slipped free.

I placed my palm against his bare skin, savoring the silken hardness of him. His answering groan was enough to send the beast in my chest roaring with victory. I bit at his lip as I wriggled out of my own trousers, the thin fabric far too thick of a barrier.

He paused, rigid against me as he pulled away. His eyes searched mine. "Are you sure?"

I rocked my hips against him as an answer, a wry smile on my face as he twitched against me. "I've never been more sure of anything in my life."

A free hand stroked my hair out of my face as I nuzzled my cheek into his palm. "I want to make sure, I—"

"Ronan." My hand covered his. "Make love to me."

"Aye, Captain. He exhaled with relief and leaned to kiss me.

I pressed a finger to his lips. "No. Say my name."

"Keira." The word was both a prayer and a groan, a desperate plea for relief from the rising heat at our centers.

I placed my hands at either side of his face, his heavy-lidded eyes boring into mine. "My last name," I corrected, my breathing labored, "call me by my last name, Mr. Mathonwy."

His answering smile was bright enough to light up the night sky. "I love you, Keira Mathonwy."

And we consummated our love until the sun rose.

✧ 19

Kisses and Keys

We woke the next morning still entwined, our fingers interlaced across his chest. And though we had less than a wink of sleep, and I was sore in ways I didn't think possible, it took us all of three minutes before we were on each other again. He moved against me like a wave meeting the shoreline, until release crashed over the both of us, hotter and brighter than a thousand stars.

The tide had somehow shifted between us during the night, our bond made whole. It didn't matter that I was a Branwen and he a Mathonwy, or that we had done terrible, awful things to each other. Like lines in the sand, it was all washed away, the last four years vanishing with the high tide.

Papa used to say fate was a mistress that always had an answer and never needed a reason.

Watching the early sun peek through the window and caress the side of Ronan's face, I had no reasons. But for the first time in my life, I had an answer. For the first time, I truly belonged to something. To someone. And he belonged to me.

"Can I ask you a personal question?" I asked after some time, my fingers tracing the outline of his tattoo.

His chuckle was deep as he pressed a kiss into my hair. "After last night, Keira dear, nothing is personal. Ask away."

I shifted so I could tilt my chin up to look at him. "Before me, how many women?"

Ronan propped himself up on his elbow, casting a suspicious look at me. I raised an eyebrow, and he sighed, rolling his eyes. "One."

"Was it like that?" I kissed the sensitive spot on the side of his neck and he shuddered, setting the beast in my chest roaring with primordial victory. "With her?"

Ronan's pointer finger hooked underneath my chin, bringing me to face him once more. He flashed a dazzling smile, pride radiating through every inch of him. "Not even close."

I frowned, and when he saw the questions still brimming in my expression, he continued, sadness creeping into the corners of his smile. "I met Siobhan during a very lonely period of time on the island. She was kind in her own way and helped bring me back to life, so to speak. She's a very dear friend. But the...physical aspect...it was never more than a convenient way to keep the numbness at bay. It was better than feeling nothing at all."

My chest ached for him, for the sorrow he had borne, for the life he had given up to be here. With me. And though there was a significant part of me that wanted to flay this other woman and fry her like a fish, I was grateful for her, too. For what she had given him when I had forsaken him.

I kissed his cheek, both giving and asking for forgiveness. "I am so sorry for what you had to go through because of me."

"Not because of you." He laid back down, pulling me tightly into the crook of his shoulder. "I could've fought to come home too. My exile was self-inflicted."

I nuzzled into him, content to never leave his side or this bed again. "You're not rotten, you know that, right?"

"What?" he chortled, the sound sending vibrations through his chest and into mine.

"The other night, and today. You called yourself rotten and wicked. But you're not." I admired the smooth plane of his chest, felt the strong heartbeat beneath that kept the time for both of us. I looked up at him to tease him, but my words were sincere. "A cocky bastard, sure. But I see *you*. I see the good. And I'm sorry it took me so long to admit it."

Another casual kiss against my forehead, but I could hear the tightness in his voice as he responded, "It's all right, Mrs. Mathonwy, I'll forgive you if you give me another kiss."

He cupped my cheek, leading my mouth home to his once more. The kiss was quiet, but the fire that had consumed us both multiple times last night was just beneath the surface, threatening to ignite us once more.

I groaned against his mouth. "As much as I want to, we have business to attend to."

"Can't we deal with it later?" His voice rumbled deep in his chest, primal and hungry, while his hand made lazy strokes against my thigh, the promise of more stirring the heat in my core. "Pretend it doesn't exist for a little while longer?"

In truth, I wanted to forget about it all. Pretend that we were the only two beings left on earth, two stars in our own constellation. But the anchors of reality still sat heavy in my gut, and the longer I waited to deal with them, the deeper they'd sink. There were more questions that still needed answers.

I stayed Ronan's hand before it could travel any further and undo me. "Our divorce contract was approved."

He went still, his hand falling from my side. The strong muscles in his jaw clenched twice before he spoke again. "Ah. Well, that does complicate things."

I sighed and sat up, untangling myself from him to clear my head for what needed to be said. I covered myself with the thin sheet, gripping it tightly, my knuckles white against its cream hue as I delivered the bad news. "It gets worse. Connor Yorath slipped in a condition. For the terms of peace to stand, I have to work for him, and you have to work for Ell..." I hesitated to finish his name, the night at the *Raven* still too fresh for either of us to handle. "Mr. Llewelyn," I finished, the words burning my throat as I spat them out.

Ronan shot up faster than cannon fire, rage apparent in every rigid muscle of his stone-cut frame. "What? Esme and Agatha signed off on this?"

"My assumption is they didn't read the details. Esme has been..." I struggled for the right word for her madness, "acting strange lately."

"Stranger than usual?" He grumbled as he pulled his trousers on with frustrated haste.

I unknotted my fingers from the sheet, grabbing the nearest shirt—*Ronan's shirt*—from the floor, and pulling it over my head. It smelled like rain and citrus, but now was not the time to indulge in it, or it would be off and on the floor again before he could say my name.

I sighed, thoughts of Esme and giant wolves extinguishing the last of my desire and turning it to ash in my mouth. "She was here the other day, and she told me not only has our homecoming been delayed thanks to some petty vandals... but I'm pretty sure I heard her talking to a *blaidd* in the woods."

Ronan stood, pacing across the floor. His hands tucked in his pockets as he tried to piece together what I was saying. "A *blaidd*? In Porthladd? Keira, you aren't making any sense."

Hearing it said aloud, I realized how preposterous it sounded. I steadied my gaze, the power in my core singing the truth of the absurdity. "I know what I saw and what I heard. I trust Esme, but she is definitely hiding something. I think to try and protect me, but I don't know why."

Ronan paused his pacing, running a hand through his bedhead. He padded over to the bed and plopped onto it with a sigh, lowering his messy blond head into my lap. "I believe you. We'll talk to her when we go to the Council to try and get that contract nullified."

I brushed a stray strand of hair out of his eyes. I couldn't help but smile, the rage and fear secondary to the marvel of what I felt for him. My Ronan. *My husband.* "Thank you. But we'll need more proof than my word and your vote of confidence. We'll need a copy of the amended contract."

Donning his favorite smirk, he stared up at the ceiling, a bad idea forming in the corner of his eye. "I don't think the rest of the Council will be too pleased that Connor tried to fool them. I don't care if he's a High Councilman. He's still accountable."

"We'll see to that," I promised both him and myself. The memory of Connor's black eyes peering down at me floated in my mind's eye, and I shuddered.

Papa always said the best way to defeat fear was to make it afraid of you instead. When I was done with him, Connor Yorath would piss himself at the very mention of my name.

Ronan's eyes darted around the room like he could see the tapestry of a plan in front of him, his voice just as excited. "We should talk to our families, see if we can get any of them to agree to join us. Strength in numbers. And it would be a good show that we still mean peace. Reina would come, maybe my Pa and Uncle Roland if they thought it was an opportunity to stick it to the Council. Perhaps your uncle could join us, he's been pretty amicable."

My stomach dropped faster than a stone in a still pond. In the cacophony of the last few days, between all that happened with Connor and Ronan, I had forgotten about my crew. About their betrayal.

Another question without an answer.

"My uncle and the crew are still out to sea," I muttered under my breath in a thinly veiled attempt to hide my shame.

Ronan sat up, concern laced in his azure stare. "Without you? Where?"

"Tan." The word was acid on my tongue.

Clouds darkened Ronan's expression. "What in Lyr's name are they doing in that wasteland?"

I met his stare, my own storm in my chest crackling. "No clue, but Saeth said they should be back today. I intend to find out."

Ronan placed a gentle hand on my knee, dissipating the storm with a single touch. "I'm so sorry, Keira."

"What for?"

He tucked a strand of my hair behind my ear, his fingers lingering at my neck. "You've been dealing with this all on your own because I was off licking my wounds and feeling sorry for myself."

"Would you prefer I lick them for you?" I waggled my eyebrows at him, satisfied when he choked on a cough. Laughing, I covered his hand with mine and gave it a gentle squeeze. My crew had abandoned me, but Ronan had not. And if it was us against the world for the rest of time, I liked our odds. "We both were wrong, me more than anyone. And I could've found a way to tell you sooner." I laced my fingers through his, and his smile made my heart flutter. "But from here on out, no more secrets or hidden agendas, okay?"

"Aye, Captain Mathonwy." He winked and leaned in, sealing this contract with a kiss instead of a quill.

"So, in the spirit of honesty," I said when our lips parted, the plan finally forming in my mind's eye. *An answer to a question.* "How do you feel about helping me plan a robbery?"

With new light in his eyes, his signature snake's smirk slithered across his face. "What are we stealing?"

It was near midnight when we approached Connor Yorath's brick-laid office in the center of town. It was mid-week, so most people had trickled back to their homes hours ago to ready themselves for work at dawn. Ronan and I had to be sure we wouldn't be seen, so we waited for even the drunks and bums to stumble to the south side of town, where they'd resume their revelry at the *Raven* or Madame Jessa's.

"Are you ready?" Ronan whispered as we slithered through the alleyway behind the building. The alley was rarely used, only for deliveries and more...*private* clients of Connor and the other law clerks. But Finna used to fool around with one of Connor's squires, a tawny-haired boy named Ewan Jamison. In passing, she had mentioned that the alley was the perfect place for discretion, and that Ewan had kept a key to the backdoor for her right on top of the door frame.

I stood on my tiptoes, feeling blindly for the key and praying that young Mr. Jamison was stupid enough to have left it after my cousin left *him*. My fingers brushed against something small and metallic.

The key.

I grabbed it and held it up between Ronan and me, the old copper glinting in the moonlight, and smiled triumphantly. "Just like Finna said. Now I'm ready."

Ronan's brow knit with concern. "No, I mean, are you sure you're ready to do this?" He looked over his shoulder again, keeping his voice low. "If we get caught, he'll hang us."

He was right. This plan was barely-thought-out and risky.

But arrogance already coursed through my veins, the kind that made people jump from cliffs or double a bet on a bluff. What I was doing was just as stupid, but I would be lying to say I didn't enjoy the rush of it, and it made me bold.

I had a bone to pick with Connor—one that was worth the risk.

I placed a hand on Ronan's shoulder. "Then let's not get caught."

Eyes rolled, but I knew Ronan well enough to know the same current ran through his blood. "How many times am I going to let you talk me into something stupid before I learn?"

I snorted as I turned the key in the lock and pushed open the door. "Be quiet and stay alert."

Ronan leaned back into the doorframe, cool as a cat while he assumed his lookout duties. "Aye, Captain. Be careful."

"Careful is my middle name." I smacked a quick kiss on his cheek before walking into the storage room.

"Lyr help us both," Ronan chuckled before I was out of earshot.

I turned left into the room, nearly nicking my shins on a crate of spare inkwells. The room was full, teeming with papers and crates of a similar nature, the disorganization echoing what I had seen in his main office. Careful not to smack my shin again, I felt my way through the room to the nearest lantern along the wall. Striking the flint, I lit the wick and grabbed the lantern from its perch.

I took a moment to get my bearings in the light. On the far side of the room, there was a door, the back entrance to Connor's office. I climbed over piles of paper, crossing the room in a few steps. Sucking in a hopeful breath, I wiggled the brass knob.

With a satisfying click, the door opened. Clearly, this entrance was so rarely used, he didn't feel the need to lock it. The small victory roared with pride in my chest as I took in the cluttered space. Another, less-victorious part of me fell when I realized how long it would take to find a single document in this maze of papers.

I moved first to the desk, where there were only a few organized piles of parchment. The deal was signed yesterday, so there was a good chance it remained in these stacks. Or at least I hoped so, as I peered at the enormous mountains of dusty, untouched papers that littered the room.

After half an hour of sorting through the desk, the oil of the lantern burning lower and lower, there was still no sign of the damned thing. Only day to day shipping contracts and building codes or household grievances to be brought to court. Discouraged, I plopped down into Connor's high-backed chair with a sigh.

A knock at the door sent me scurrying for cover, just as Ronan peeked his head around the corner. "Any luck?"

I shot him a look that could fry a fish. "You're supposed to be the lookout. But no, not yet. Just a bunch of lawyer stuff." I picked up the topmost paper, a permit for a man named Sean Quinton for an exotic pet store, and threw it across the room. "This is pointless. There's nothing here, he must have the papers we're looking for with him."

Ronan's arms circled my waist as he placed a kiss on my forehead. "Let's keep looking. There has to be something." His eyes scanned the room, a smirk on his face as they landed on the mahogany desk. "Have you checked the drawer?"

I smiled back, another answer to another question. "No, but it looks like a good place to hide a contract." I crossed and bent before the first drawer, shimmying the handle, but I was met with resistance. I looked back up at Ronan. "Still remember how to pick locks?"

He crouched beside me, producing a pin from the inside of his coat sleeve. Mischief shimmered in his eyes. "Like I could forget. I'm a Mathonwy." With deft fingers and a few prods with the pin, he had the lock open in less than a minute. He beamed with pride. "That should do it."

"Insufferable cad." I rolled my eyes, fighting my own grin as I opened the drawer and peered inside.

The contents were disappointingly normal. A pair of spectacles, a spare quill, and handkerchief. No papers or contracts to be seen.

"Another dead end," Ronan grumbled, running a hand through his hair.

But at the edge of the drawer, a small crack in the polished wood caught my eye.

"Maybe not." I pressed at the opening. Sure enough, it shifted under the pressure, sliding back to reveal a hidden piece of folded parchment.

I grabbed it with hungry fingers, pulling it from the sheath. The paper was old, frayed around the edges, so definitely not our contract, but whatever was worth hiding so carefully was worth a look.

I unfurled it across Connor's desk, my breath catching as I took it in.

It was a map, the sharp lines of the seven islands of Deyrnas carved into its face in the familiar patterns I had memorized. Angry red exes littered the four seas. And in scratchy, feverish letters, one word repeated itself over and over again.

Hiraeth.

"Lyr below, what in the Deyrnas?" Ronan cursed under his breath.

I traced the map with my fingers, marking the distance between every x. Every failed attempt to find what Connor clearly wanted desperately. I looked back at Ronan, my thoughts swirling in a chaotic whirlpool. "He's looking for *Hiraeth*. Why?"

"I don't know, and I'm guessing he doesn't want anyone to." Ronan's eyes widened as he studied the map. "But Keira, *look*."

I followed to where his finger pointed—to a name scrawled in the corner of the map:

Cedric Branwen???? Traveler.

Seeing my father's name brought tears to my eyes and searing rage to my core.

Connor Yorath was looking for *Hiraeth*. And somehow, Papa had been involved, had perhaps even seen the island himself. Had known its secrets.

Maybe even died to keep them.

A muted shuffle outside pulled me from my acidic thoughts. "Did you hear that?" I whispered to Ronan, my senses on high alert.

He shrugged. "I don't hear anything."

I whacked his arm, my ears straining for any further sign we were no longer alone. "This is why you were supposed to be the lookout."

Another crash sounded, this time much closer. The storage room. "Did you hear it that time?" I hissed, ducking behind Connor's desk and pulling him with me. My heart thundered in my chest, every muscle in my body coiling, ready to run.

One heartbeat, then another.

Crash. This time followed by a deep growl. My stomach dropped through the floor.

"That's our cue to leave," Ronan whispered, grabbing my hand and dragging me the way we came.

I tugged him back in the other direction. "No, front door, the sound came from the storeroom."

He nodded silently, fear wide in his eyes. I crossed the floor in three steps, cursing to Lyr as the floorboards creaked underneath me.

I froze, every muscle rigid, the noise deafening in the quiet of the night. Ronan and I made eye contact. His mouth moved without a sound, perfectly forming the single word.

Run.

My body did not hesitate to obey. I barreled through the front door with abandon onto the moonlit street, Ronan hot on my heels.

And I swear to Lyr, a howl echoed in the night behind us.

20

Loyalties and Lies

Ronan and I ran until our legs were lead and our breath was fire in our lungs. We took backroads, looping through the residential areas of town, hoping to throw anyone who pursued us off our trail.

No footsteps followed, only the impending sense of doom and the echo of the *blaidd's* ethereal howl. We stopped behind a quaint row of townhouses, our hands on our knees as we sucked in ragged breaths.

"We should be safe," Ronan panted, sliding against the wall in exhaustion.

I grabbed his arm with the last of my strength, pulling him back to standing. "Not until we're back at the spring. If anyone sees us out, they can place us at the scene, and we can't have that."

"Place you at the scene of what?" A voice called down the lane, and I jumped to attention, drawing my dagger. Every muscle tensed for impact as I squinted into the darkness.

"Wha—"

"Don't worry, it's just me." Griffin's arms were crossed as he stepped into the pool of light from the nearest lamppost, a smug grin plastered across his freckled face. "You should've seen the looks on your faces."

The sight of my cousin should have loosed a breath of relief, but tension still coiled in my core.

Griffin, my best friend, my brother in both arms and in spirit, had gone with the crew. Had left me behind without even a word or a warning.

I watched him approach as a wolf would a rabbit. Sometimes, in all our familiarity, I forgot how imposing he looked. His twin swords stuck up from his back, the corded muscle of him accentuated by his sheer height. He'd ripped the sleeves off his Branwen-blue coat months ago as a scare tactic. At the time, I told him he was ridiculous, but now I saw his point.

Ronan squared up next to me, his expression mirroring mine as he tried to decide if Griffin was foe or friend.

I lowered my dagger but narrowed my eyes. "You're back. How did you find—" Another, smaller figure slipped out of the shadows, another head of ginger hair haloed in the light. I pinched the bridge of my nose. Of course. "Saeth."

She pulled her ground-length cloak tighter around her, her fox eyes pleading. "I'm sorry, Keira, I went to the spring to tell you they were back, but you weren't there. I thought something was wrong."

I opened my mouth to speak, but Griffin held up a hand, aggression dissolving from his stance. "Don't worry, she came to me first. Aidan doesn't know. And we had a little help." He tapped the hilt of the sword behind his left shoulder. *Truth.* "It seems like you've been causing some trouble, Cousin."

I watched them again, no hint of malice or misdirection in their gazes. Nothing but the familiar faces of my family.

They'd come to help, the worry in Saeth's furtive glance proof enough.

Friends, then. The knot in my stomach unraveled, a wave of relief coursing through me. Griffin was trouble incarnate, the god of mischief made man, but I could trust him. I always could. Yet I'd be lying if I said him leaving without me didn't sting.

I pursed my lips. "I could say the same for you. How was Tan?"

"Honestly?" He winked playfully and pushed my shoulder, disarming me in the way only he knew how. "Awful. If I never have to see that desert again in my life, I'd die happy. I know you should've been there, but Lyr below, be glad you weren't."

"What were you even doing there?" Ronan stepped forward, his hands tucked into his pockets, the mask slipping back into place. "Besides sneaking around behind Keira's back."

It was his armor, I realized, one he'd grown accustomed to donning whenever the enemy was in striking distance. One he didn't need, not anymore.

I placed a gentle hand on his shoulder and felt the tension release underneath my fingertips. Griffin's eyes darted to the spot where we touched, noting the affection in the action. His gaze met mine again, and he raised a curious brow, asking a question in our unspoken language. *Jumped ship, then?*

I shot him an unfriendly look in return. *Start explaining.*

He sighed, conceding first in our battle of wills. "We don't know. Aidan said it was to establish a new passenger deal, but we know that's bullshit. It's been… different since you left."

My lips formed a hard line. The only passengers available in Tan were the warrior clans who inhabited the island. Wherever Aidan was planning on ferrying them, I knew trouble would follow in their wake. I shuddered at the thought.

Different, indeed.

"Different how?" Ronan asked for me, his tone softer now. I offered a grateful nod.

Saeth's brow knit, augmenting the sharpness of her already razor-edged features. "Aidan seems a little lost, and Pa is always in his ear...you know how poisonous that old arse can be. So, I hope whatever trouble you were getting into tonight is going to help us fix things at home, too."

Her words thickened the air around us, the truth and weight of them apparent. My head spun as I tried to form a map between the fragmented pieces. My crew was in trouble or maybe *was* the trouble. Connor was hunting something, and sooner or later would be hunting us, too.

But perhaps there was a way to fix both problems with one solution.

"I don't know yet," I said, only the outline of a plan in my head. "It's a long story."

Ronan's voice anchored me back to the present moment. "We should head back to the spring. If anyone else sees us..."

"We'll escort you." Griffin insisted.

I opened my mouth to protest. "You don't have to——"

It was Saeth's hand this time that rose to silence me. "I know you both have this hero complex you're working through, but let us help, okay? You two lovebirds aren't the only ones capable of doing something useful."

I looked at Ronan, who simply shrugged, knowing he was outmatched by Saeth's needlepoint tongue. "Right, then. Don't slow us down."

Griffin grabbed Ronan's flask, taking his third long swig of it. He slammed it back onto the shack's small table, the action reverberating through the room. We'd been sitting like this for an hour, both Saeth and Griffin captive as we filled them in on the events of the last week. They'd been quiet, only offering appropriate gasps and murmured curses as Ronan wove his tale. I plied Griffin with the liquor he needed to swallow such a story.

Griffin now twirled an accusatory finger at Ronan, who sat opposite him at the table, leaning back in his chair comfortably. "Let me get this straight. You're not a murderer?"

"Aye." Ronan shrugged and took the flask for himself, draining the last of it as the first rays of morning sun streamed through the window.

Confused, Griffin looked to where I leaned against the door, my arms crossed in amusement at the scene before me. He folded his arms across his broad chest as well, his brow knitting as he sorted through the web of information we'd presented. "And our families have been killing each other for four years for no good reason, and the proof was hidden by the Council."

I nodded in confirmation, and Griffin's expression darkened.

Saeth sat on the edge of the straw bed, knees pulled to her chest, her long blue skirt bunched up around her. Her voice was flat as she spoke, her eyes dagger-sharp. "And Connor Yorath is somehow behind it all and may have had Uncle Cedric killed for it."

"That about sums it up," Ronan chuckled dryly, the whiskey's effect taking hold.

I had to fight the smile that threatened to show. Insufferable cad.

Griffin slammed his fist against the table and stood, shattering the false sense of calm. "Why can't we skewer the bastard now, then? Keira, your Pa, Aleena, my *brother*…" His throat bobbed and he blinked, regaining his composure. "It's all this scum-bucket's fault. Their blood is on his hands."

My heart ached at the sound of their names, *my family*—at the reminder of what had been lost.

Not lost. *Taken.*

Griffin continued his tirade, "I don't care who Connor paid to do it, that scrawny prick reeks of guilt. I've got a good sense for it." He gripped the hilt of *Truth* again, drawing the long sword and extending his lethal arm.

I held up my hands, approaching him like one would a rabid animal. "That's what we think, but if we act without proof, he'll retaliate. He's not above going over the Council's head to the High Council."

Griffin's jaw tightened, but he sheathed his sword without another word, plopping back into his seat with a heavy *hmph*.

"What about the map?" Saeth twirled the tip of her copper braid around her finger, lost deep in thought.

"A stolen map with doodles and Cedric's name is hardly proof of conspiracy and murder. All it proves is we were the ones that broke in," Ronan sighed, frowning with one eye into the now empty flask, "even if it does confirm our suspicions."

"What can we do?" Griffin's growl echoed the one in my chest.

"We find it first," Saeth answered, something dark simmering in her gaze.

Ronan leaned forward on the table. "Find what?"

A grin sinister enough to rival a Mathonwy's adorned her thin face. "Whatever Connor was looking for in *Hiraeth*."

An idea formed in my head, the last piece of the map I had been trying to put together.

I had underestimated my youngest cousin. Saeth saw everything. She saw and she *planned*, with fire in her eyes and ice on her tongue. I shuddered at the thought of what she might have been had it been her training on the ship all her life instead of me.

Griffin scoffed, waving her off as so many of us had before. "No one knows where *Hiraeth* is, Saeth. That's the point."

"That's not exactly true." I pushed off the wall, making eye contact with the clever girl. "Right, Ronan?"

Ronan leaned back in his chair, realization dawning over him. "And I think I know what Connor was looking for."

"What?" Griffin shook his head, still four steps behind us.

But Ronan was not waiting for him to catch up, his pace hurried with excitement. "I wasn't the only thing from my ship that washed up on the shore. What if Connor has reason to believe there's evidence there? Something that can tie him to the murder?"

Saeth's brow furrowed, a knot in her net. "It would be gone by now, washed away or ruined."

Ronan did not falter from his line of thought. "Again, not exactly. *Hiraeth* is a strange place...time doesn't affect things the same way."

Griffin threw his hands up in exasperation, and I nearly spat a laugh at him. "Is everyone here mad? How would you even know something like that?"

"He's been there, you idiot." Saeth stood, smoothing her skirt, her posture tall with triumph. She winked at Ronan, the movement so quick I almost missed it. "I thought you still looked young for your age."

Ronan rested his hands behind his head, crossing his boots on the table with pronounced arrogance. "Keira dear, we're going to need a ship."

Standing outside of Branwen Townhouse had never felt *wrong* before, but I was an outsider now. My crew was no longer mine, this house was no longer home, and I was no longer a Branwen. Not in name or in heart.

Even donning my blue coat that morning had felt like a betrayal. I didn't deserve to wear our colors when I was here to swindle the *Ceffyl* from under my uncle's nose. After Papa died, Aidan had taken me in, clothed me and fed me, had given me a purpose and a position in the crew. Even if he'd left me behind, even if he'd been changed by desperation and ambition, he was still family. Still the head of the Branwen clan.

I just didn't know who or what *I* was anymore.

"Can you do this?" Ronan whispered from where he crouched underneath the windowsill, Vala's lavender plants concealing him. "We can find another way."

"She's got this." Griffin stretched like a housecat beside me, a confident smile smoothing the edges of my nerves.

"Aidan would give her the deed to the house if she asked. Perks of being the favorite." Saeth rolled her eyes at Ronan as she leaned against the door, a twinge of jealousy in her voice.

I smoothed my coat against me, pulling on the mask of who I used to be. Keira Branwen. First mate and favorite daughter. Sailor and stalwart loyalist. "You're not the only skilled liar, Ronan."

Ronan crept closer so I could see the anchoring blue of his eyes. "True, but Reese wouldn't hesitate to give me the *Ddraig* if I asked."

I offered my best reassuring smile, one that hid the deep well of uncertainty that pooled in my gut. "It's too big. We wouldn't have the crew."

Ronan nodded with a sigh, seeing through my facade in the way only he knew how, but he retreated anyway. "I'll be waiting in the *Raven*."

I watched him disappear around the corner of the house before I let the final layer of my disguise slide into place. For him, and for Papa, I could lie and cheat and pretend. Could betray my family and myself.

I gave Griffin a single nod, and he opened the door, ushering Saeth and me in with a mocking twirl of his hand.

Saeth slipped through the door and up the stairs without a second look back. She had to hurry to her bed without a sound before her Pa noticed she'd been out all night.

As I walked into the main foyer, the familiar smell of fried fish and nutmeg assaulted my nose and shook my resolve. It was a Branwen tradition: fresh fried fish and Vala's famous nut bread for breakfast the morning after the crew came home. The whole clan would get up early to claim a bite before it was gone. Some, still aching and unwashed from the voyage before, were willing to trade extra rest or care for a taste of the delicacy.

I breathed it in, memories of sunlit mornings and sea-scented smiles filling my mind. I reminded myself I should've been here this morning, woken by Griffin's grin or Tarran's sleepy smile. Instead, I was left behind.

My resolve became stone again as I walked into the kitchen to see my uncle bent over an almost-clean plate, a satisfied rosiness on his wrinkled face. Captain ate last, as a thank-you to the crew for their work. The rest of the table was littered with empty plates, only the echo of merriment left behind.

Aidan's eyes locked on mine, surprise and delight lighting his amber irises. "Keira girl? Oh, it's so good to see ye."

I smiled brightly, not having to fake the genuine warmth that spread through my core. I crossed the kitchen in three bouncing steps, pressing a quick kiss to the old man's cheek. "Good morning, Uncle. Fish and bread?"

Griffin slumped into a nearby chair, patting his abdomen expectantly. "Is there any left?"

"None for boys who spent the night gods-know where." Aidan shot him a reproachful look, but I saw the smile that threatened to pull at his mouth. I relaxed into the chair next to him—the right-hand girl back in her rightful place.

Aidan's expression softened. "Ye look well, Keira. Vala told me about the unpleasantness with Weylin, and I promise ye, I've already spoken to him about it."

"No worries, Uncle." I placed a hand on his, my heart aching. It felt so natural to be here, to be this person. A part of me wished it were still real. I continued my deception, though it felt like a truth on my tongue, "Families fight. It's water under the bridge. I'm just glad to see you home in one piece. Tan? What were you thinking?"

Aidan leaned back in his chair, his brow furrowing. "Aye, Tan. Donnall has a friend there, an old drinking buddy who said one of the Tannian warrior clans was looking for contracts with sailors for passage. Ye know how the Southern Isles are—most of them would rather just float off and leave the rest of the Deyrnas behind. Keep all their spices and textiles and magick to themselves. Seems the Tannians are looking to expand, branch out into private security and such. It's lonely at the bottom of the world."

A dark wind swirled in my chest. The venture was harmless enough, but I could see the danger of it lurking just beneath the surface, even if he couldn't. I did my best to school my features, remembering my mask. "Aye, I'm sure. Did we get a contract?"

"No, actually, and it's my fault for not bringing ye, isn't that right, Griff?" He winked at my cousin. Griffin did his best impression of his own nonchalant shrug, but his eyes caught mine, a secret warning in them. Aidan didn't notice the stolen glance, and continued his tale, picking at the last scrap of bread on his plate. "The leader of this particular band of fighters was a lady, and she didn't trust a ship full of only men. When I told them about ye, they didn't believe ye existed. Last time I sail without my good luck charm, I'll tell ye that!" He gave my arm a warm squeeze, a familiar kindness filling his eyes.

He might as well have squeezed my heart. My throat bobbed, my steadiness wavering. This man had given everything for me, for this family, and I was repaying him by lying through my teeth and betraying him. "You sound like Papa."

There was a twinkle in his honeyed eye, only furthering the resemblance to my father—as if fate was mocking me with it. "Aye, I feel just as old as him these days, if that's what yer saying."

I stayed quiet, knowing another word would be my undoing. If only Papa could see me now: a snake in sheep's clothing.

Heavy footfalls sounded down the staircase, saving me from my thoughts. "I thought I heard you, Keira." Tarran's smile was wide as he bounded through the doorway, sunny as ever.

Sunny indeed, since his skin almost matched his flaming red hair.

Griffin doubled over, laughter erupting from him. "Lyr's left arse cheek, look at that sunburn!"

I stood and crossed to my lobster of a cousin, my own smile entirely real. "I'd hug you, Tarran, but it would hurt too badly."

"That's all right, I'd probably deserve it." He shrugged, pulling me into a tight bear-hug anyway. I hugged him back, the smell of Vala's burn ointment searing my nose-hairs, but I didn't care. Tarran whispered into my hair as he pulled me tighter, "I'm sorry for what my Pa said to you, and for what I said, too. It doesn't change how I feel about Ronan, but none of this is your fault or your choice."

"Apology accepted," I said, and meant it, as I pulled back. "Not that I could stay mad at you if I tried."

Relief washed over his features. "I missed you."

"I missed you too, Tarran."

"That's a good lad." Aidan's chair creaked as he pushed back from the table, a hand on his full stomach. "Now, why don't ye and Griffin go run to the market and see if Vala needs a hand? Poor Donnall has been with her all morning, and I have a feelin' she'll need even more help carrying things. I swear, that woman can spend my money like it's her job."

Griffin groaned in his seat, but Tarran answered dutifully, pride inflating his chest. "Aye, Captain."

I laughed as they left, Tarran leading and Griffin shuffling behind.

"See ya later, Keira," Griffin called over his shoulder, but I heard the unspoken message. *Stay strong.*

I returned the pointed look. "Don't have too much fun without me." *I'll fill you in later.*

After the front door closed behind them, Aidan and I made our way into the sitting room. Aidan lowered himself into his favorite brown armchair first and sighed, his sharp gaze shifting to look at me. "So, Keira girl, what actually brings ye home? I can't imagine it's just to say hello, as much as I'd love that."

A smile crept over my own face. This was the Aidan I knew—kind and generous but never dull. At one time, he was the sharpest man I knew, the cleverest Captain on the four seas. How this time apart had changed him, I had no idea, but he was still Aidan. Or at least, in part.

"You see right through everything, don't you?" I answered, remembering what he'd once said about ego. *We men are foolish creatures, Keira. All it takes to woo us is a gentle stroke.* I plopped onto the blue couch, leaning back like it was the most natural thing I'd ever done as I prepared for the lie. "I do have a favor to ask, but it's a big one, so feel free to say no."

Aidan steepled his fingers, readying for the negotiation. It was a game we'd play often, the game of deals and trades, needs and supplies. "Why don't ye ask it first, then I'll give my answer."

"I need the *Ceffyl*, only for a day," I asked point-blank, unwavering. Aidan himself had taught me that the best way to ask for something was to pretend it was already yours. But I continued, softer this time because Aidan needed to think he was still in charge if I was going to play this right without getting caught. "It's been awful being cooped up in that shack, and I need to sail. After the incident on Ronan's ship, I only trust our girl."

It wasn't entirely untrue. I did trust the *Ceffyl* more than any other ship in the world, and Lyr knew how desperate I was to sail.

When we were thirteen, and Ronan was teaching me how to pickpocket, he said the best lies are always the ones that were based in truth. I watched Aidan carefully, hoping to Lyr that Ronan was right.

Aidan nodded, but I noted the sympathy in his gaze as he took in my proposal. "I'll consider it. How far is the trip?"

"Just around the island, she'll be docked again by sundown the same day." The lie tasted like acid on my tongue, but I clung to my mask for dear life. First mate and favorite daughter. "I don't want the Council getting nervous. They just approved my divorce contract, so I'll be on my best behavior."

At this, Aidan sat forward, captivated by the information. "They approved it? No conditions?"

I let his question hang in the air for a moment. This was the real test, the real lie. If Aidan knew what we knew about Connor, he might try and stop us to save the contract. He'd sacrificed so much to broker the deal between the families, there was a chance he'd be against such a brazen trip. There was an even greater chance he'd be appalled at the bolder accusations we were about to make.

It was a chance we were unwilling to take, no matter how badly I wanted to blurt the whole thing out to my uncle and beg for his help.

"Only a slight one. I have to work for Connor Yorath for a while so they can be sure." The words flowed out of me, sounding just as unpracticed and hopeful as I wanted them to.

Aidan nodded again, still so lost in thought that the lie had gone undetected. "Good, Connor will take care of ye. Weaselly as he is, he's good on his word."

My heart stopped. I knew my uncle wouldn't approve of me derailing the contract and stealing his ship to go to a magical, mysterious island. But I expected some resistance to the idea of a Branwen working for anyone other than another Branwen.

Perhaps Weylin had changed him after all.

Aidan spoke again before I could challenge the idea, a smile clearing the pensiveness from his expression. "Seems like ye need a celebration. Ye can take the ship, but I don't think I can spare any of the senior crew. Donnall, Weylin, and I have business here. But ye can take the boys if they'll go, and I'll give ye some money to hire a few extra hands to help ye sail her."

Triumph roared through me at the victory. The *Ceffyl* was ours, even if she had been won with lies and traps.

I'd rather die with honor than live with the shame of being a coward.

Shame fought for purchase in my chest, the celebration inside ending.

I crossed the room and wrapped my arms around my uncle in a hug. If only it were enough to forgive my betrayal. Only snakes killed with a kiss, and I was now the very worst of them.

"Thank you, Uncle," I said when I wished I could be saying sorry.

✧ ✦ 21

Corsets and Councilmen

Ronan and I were at the docks by sunrise, too anxious to sleep or wait at the shack. So, we gathered the last of our belongings from the tiny room, knowing we weren't coming back. With a prayer of thanks to the spring, we moved forward in the hazy darkness of the early morning. Neither of us dared a single glance back at the white willows or the shack that had become home.

We sat on one of the eight wooden crates of supplies, Ronan's arm around my shoulders, our muscles rigid with impatience. We'd prepared as best we could. Now all we could do was wait. Reina donated what she could spare—a few baskets of clothes, medical supplies, and a stolen crate of oranges—but it wasn't enough. It had cost a pretty penny for the rest, but we had no idea how long we would be gone or when we could next make port. I used the money from Aidan to hire extra sailors on the haul instead, the need for food slightly outweighing the need for manpower.

We still needed a crew, and as the sun continued its ascent into the morning sky, the anchor in my gut grew heavier.

They were late. And we were running out of precious time.

"Do you think they'll show?" Ronan breathed against my hair, his citrus scent fresh and comforting. He'd worn the coat I bought him. The sight of it had my pulse quickening. I leaned into him, into the steady beat of his heart. As long as he was by my side, I had a purpose. As long as his heart beat, I had a home.

I swallowed hard, schooling the basket of fish in my gut into submission. "Griffin will make it happen, even if he has to lie to Tarran to get him here. What about on your end?"

It had been a big decision to invite Ronan's family to join us. I still didn't trust Reese as far as I could throw him, but Ronan did, and I trusted *him* with my life. I knew a mixed crew would bring out the worst in all of us, some wounds too deep to overlook. As it were, we were slim on options and men.

Papa used to say being the Captain meant making the hard choices. Reese hadn't killed my father, hadn't started this war. My kin were as much at fault as any Mathonwy. More importantly, Papa had a vision of peace, one that included both families. The contract he devised was a fair one, and, had it seen completion, it would've been his legacy. Together, we would have dominated the four seas, our influence unstoppable and our bounty plentiful.

Despite all the wrong and the hurt that happened between us, perhaps that dream was still possible. It was my duty to see it come true.

Ronan stood, unwrapping his arm from around me. I shuddered at the sudden chill and tried not to pout as he stuffed his hands in his pockets, worry thick on his brow. "Pa won't come. He was furious when I mentioned it. He still doesn't trust you, but he's an old fool. Roland might. He's a good man and a fine sailor, plus he's always been a betting man, the best in the family. He can sniff out a good hand when it's in front of him."

I ran the numbers in my head, the anchor in my stomach only sinking deeper. "That makes four, maybe five people to sail the *Ceffyl Dwr*. To an island no one knows exactly how to get to. Perfect."

Ronan's eyes flicked to mine, desperation brimming in their azure rings. "Can we do it?"

I looked back at him, letting the smooth planes of his face settle the waves in my mind.

We couldn't, not really. We were on a fool's errand with limited supplies and fewer men, sailing a ship far too big and fast for the numbers we had, chasing answers that hid somewhere east of the sun and west of the moon.

But I was Keira rutting Mathonwy. I was the best gods-damned sailor in the Deyrnas. I was Cedric Branwen's daughter, the greatest Captain the Seven Isles had ever seen. Like him, I was born of the sea and the stars, raised to defy those who told me I couldn't.

And the man standing before me was my equal in every way, my partner, *my husband*.

We couldn't. But we would, or we'd die trying.

I cleared my throat of doubt before speaking again. "A full crew is eight sailors, but we've sailed her with as few as five before. Griffin and I tried to sail her alone once and we almost did it. So, we'll make do with what we have." I stood and crossed to him, grabbing his calloused hand in mine. "You and I can do anything."

The wrinkles in his forehead dissolved as he placed a warm kiss on my forehead.

"I heard my name before that disgusting display of public affection." Griffin shattered the intimacy of the moment with a sly grin as he approached, a canvas sack in his arms and his swords on his back. "You'd better be saying good things."

"You wish." I offered a vulgar gesture but winked at him anyway, relief unknotting the tension in my shoulders. But it didn't last long as I noted the absence of another body. "Where's Tarran?"

Griffin's grin fell. "Not coming. I'm sorry, Keira. He was going to, but Weylin found him sneaking around and put his foot down. You know the boy can't say no to his Pa." He set his pack down on one of the crates with a heavy thud and an apologetic half-smile.

"Damn Weylin." I clenched my fists, fingernails digging into my palms, and inhaled sharply through my nose, offering a silent prayer to Lyr for his aid. The sea-god had been silent for days, and I didn't want to think about what that meant. I hoped he was still listening as I turned to Ronan. "We're counting on your side now."

"The *Ceffyl Dwr*, sailed by a handful of Mathonwys." Griffin shook his head in disbelief, plopping down on the nearest crate. "One or more of the gods has a sick sense of humor."

Almost on cue, two tall figures approached the end of the dock, both clad in scarlet red long-coats.

Mathonwys. Roland and Rhett.

I swallowed hard, fighting the reflex that automatically sent my right hand to the dagger at my hip. Griffin did not move from his position, but I could sense how he stilled, a cat ready to pounce. I placed a hand on his shoulder, a signal to stand down. These men were my kin now, the only two willing to join us, and the only shot we had at finding Papa's real killer. At realizing Papa's vision.

I rolled back my shoulders, willing away the tension that rested there.

Roland strode forward first, a wide smile on his leathered face. Rhett stayed at the end of the dock, arms crossed with a scowl. Roland seemed not to notice, clasping Ronan's forearm in a firm greeting.

Ronan's answering smile was enough to peel back another layer of my uncertainty. "Uncle Roland!"

"Good to see ye, boy," Roland answered, his voice like ground rocks. He was Reese's younger brother, closer to Aidan's age than Papa's. Rumor had it he smoked a full pipe a day, and it had visibly aged him. Yet his sun-beaten, smoke-soaked face remained youthful, his smile boyish and his eyes full of kindness. I'd never spoken to him, even as a child, but we had grown familiar in other ways. It was a marvel how much a face could change when it wasn't at the sharp end of my sword.

I nodded gently, and he returned it easily as if we hadn't spent the last four years doing exactly that.

"Captain Keira Mathonwy," he croaked in his frog's voice. "That's got quite a ring to it. It's a pleasure to sail with ye."

I opened my mouth to speak and shut it again, no words right for such a strange occasion.

"Thank you for coming, Uncle," Ronan interjected for me, sensing my discomfort, "but I can't say I'm not surprised. Pa seemed adamant."

Roland chuckled, the sound grating but light in its intent. "Aye, but yer Auntie Reina has a way with words, and I know who the real boss is." He winked and gestured over his shoulder at his son, who still pouted at the end of the dock. "Ye have room for another?"

Griffin's back went ramrod straight, the hair on his neck standing at attention. Ronan didn't notice as he chuckled along with his uncle and waved his cousin over. "Rhett, why don't you join us?"

Rhett made his way down the dock like a sullen child. "I'm not here by choice." The pout on his face was so out of place on a man of his massive size. He was almost Griffin's height, and just as broad, but one sharp look from Roland had him obedient.

I studied at the pair, two sides of the same strange coin. Roland, the old man with a boy's spirit. Rhett, the youngest and strongest among us, with the hardened heart of an elderly hermit.

Griffin sensed that Rhett's leash had been tightened, the smile carving into his freckled face with glee. He stood to his full height, stepping directly into Rhett's circle of space. "Aw, did daddy dearest threaten to put you in time out?"

I went still as I watched the two dogs sniff each other.

Rhett bared his teeth, his wide hand flying to the broadsword hanging from his side. "Another comment and I'll take away your manhood."

Griffin's hand went to a...different sword...with a gesture vulgar enough to make me blush. "Fancy a grab?"

Rhett's eyes went wide with rage, and Ronan bit his lip to hold back a chuckle.

I sighed at them, stepping into the small space between Rhett and Griffin. I placed a firm hand on Griff's shoulder. Rutting *boys*. "Do not start, Griffin."

His hands went up in surrender, but he did not wipe off his shit-eating grin. "Aye, aye, Captain."

Rhett exhaled sharply through his nose and stalked off, bumping into Griffin's shoulder as he growled to no one in particular, "I'll be on the ship."

I pinched the bridge of my nose. Ronan and I had been raving lunatics to invite family. A sore part of me wished I'd saved some coin for a few hired hands instead of this mismatched pack of feral boys who would surely drive me to an early grave.

This was going to be a long rutting trip.

"Don't mind the boy, he'll warm up." Roland patted my shoulder, the gesture startlingly casual. He extended a hand toward Griffin before I could say anything else on the matter. "Reina told me what ye did to save young Reagan. Far as I see it, we Mathonwys owe ye a life debt. I'm proud to sail with ye."

The sincerity in his voice cut through the tension like a clean arrow, direct and straight. Griffin eyed him before taking his hand in a firm shake, his own expression settling with uncharacteristic shyness. "Aye, well, the girl grows on you like ivy. I'm proud to know her and call her kin."

My heart swelled at the sight before me. Our families still had hurdles to overcome, but perhaps they weren't as insurmountable as they once were. Perhaps they weren't so far out of reach, but only a handshake and a *thank you* away.

Perhaps, if I could be even half the captain my father once was, we'd not only make it out of this alive but be something close to content.

"We are glad to have you." I gripped Roland's shoulder, swallowing the instinct to avoid any further contact, and nodded my head at the ship where Rhett still sulked. "Both of you. Lyr knows we need the help."

Knowing dripped from the look Roland shot his nephew. "Are ye going to tell us where we're actually going before we get on, or will ye wait until we're too far out to jump ship?"

Ronan stared at me as he addressed his uncle, reverence in his gaze. "Definitely the latter."

Griffin stretched and cracked his knuckles, the Swordsinger donning his role like an old glove. "Good, so this will be fun."

I nudged my cousin with my elbow, hoping his confidence was contagious. "Well, seems like this is it." I cleared my throat and turned toward the ship, my hands on my hips, as Papa used to. Maybe one day I wouldn't feel so small in my Captain's coat. "Everyone, grab something. Let's get going while the tide is in our favor."

The drumbeat of heeled footsteps down the dock's planks halted me in my spot. "Wait, Keira, wait!"

I spun around as one of my cousins barreled toward me, her unbound red hair a wall of flame behind her. She ran wildly, awkward as she tried to remember how, carrying her skirts around her.

Griffin dropped the crate he was lifting. "Saeth?"

"I'm coming with you," she huffed between sharp breaths, a hand on her corseted side. She was dressed for market day in town, wearing a sky-blue day dress with an embroidered corset. Pretty, but impractical for the sea and the *Ceffyl*. Yet the look in her eyes was all steel.

A part of me sang with kindred recognition of her loyalty, at the bravery she showed by even coming today. Tarran, a sailor by blood *and* experience, hadn't dared defy their Pa. But Saeth came.

Saeth came in a Lyr-damned corset and heels.

"Saeth, you don't sail on a good day," I reasoned with her, hating the words as they came out of my mouth. Even if they were true. "And this isn't a trip where I can guarantee good days."

Saeth stood straighter, schooling her breath into a measured tempo once more. "I said I'm coming," she stated with all the grace of a high-born Lady and all the salt of a sea-born sailor. "I refuse to sit and wait for someone else to fix things for me. I'm bored of listening to Vala and Finna gossip about clothes all day. I'm tired of listening to my Pa go on and on about the damned Mathonwy traitors. And I'm sick of waiting for something to rutting happen in my life. So, I'm coming, and you can teach me what I need to know along the way."

The power in my core rippled at her words, at the sheer will behind them.

Papa once said it was a Branwen's birthright to sail the *Ceffyl*. What kind of Captain would I be to deny her that right? Especially when we needed sailors more desperately than fish needed water. When we needed sharp minds and willing hearts even more.

I looked around at the meager crew. We could count our numbers on one hand. Five experienced sailors would be enough to sail, but there would be little rest. If anyone fell ill or injured, we were doomed. An extra set of hands, even inexperienced ones, could make all the difference on our fool's journey.

My eyes found Ronan, who nodded, his eyes reflecting the truth back to me.

I extended my hand toward my cousin. "Fine. Welcome aboard, deckhand Branwen."

She grabbed it with surprising strength and shook it once, our bargain sealed. "Aye, Captain Keira."

"Keira, she can't," Griffin whined, but I held up a hand to silence him.

"Yes, she can, and you're going to teach her." I suppressed the desire to laugh at his expression, his mouth still hanging open. I signaled to the crew, my own sense of pride reinvigorated by Saeth's courage. "Let's move out."

Saeth stuck her tongue out, but her eyes lit up like stars. Without hesitation, she grabbed a sack of supplies and hauled it over her shoulder before staggering clumsily up the gangway to the deck. With a shrug in my direction, Griffin followed suit, lifting the heaviest crate with a grunt and a grin. In a second, Roland grabbed the other side with a nod to Griffin, the two moving in a comfortable synchronicity as they loaded the ship.

It was hard to swallow back the wave of gratitude that rose to my throat as I watched my cousins, old and new.

Within fifteen minutes, we had the ship loaded and the sail hoisted, the mid-morning air alive with the faint scent of hope. Griffin and Roland were busy securing the rigging while Saeth changed into something more suitable below deck. Rhett had mumbled something about checking out the quarters before stalking off below, but we were as near ready as we'd ever be. All that was left was to lift the anchor and shove off. We didn't have a heading, but we had a crew and purpose. That was enough, perhaps, to defy all obstacles.

Or so we thought—until one strode right up the gangway in expensive leather boots.

"Good morning, Mrs. Mathonwy," Ellian crooned as he invited himself aboard, emerald eyes squinting against the sun. He wore an embroidered green tunic and a finely-made leather long-coat, making him appear both wealthy and dangerous. He carried no weapon, but the way the fabric hugged him reminded me that he didn't need any. A lifetime as a blacksmith forged him into something as sharp as any sword he'd ever crafted.

My stomach knotted tighter than the mooring ropes that still held us to the dock. Everyone aboard halted, our breaths held, as he leaned casually against the railing like he owned it. Ronan stiffened next to me, every muscle tense with apprehension.

In the wake of the last few days, with all the plotting and planning, I had forgotten about the man I'd left behind in Agatha's bar. The man who was once a friend, who had cleared my husband of guilt without asking anything in return.

The man I might have offended beyond repair.

The man who was also a Councilman, who had approved Connor's shady condition, whether he knew or not. Who had more than one thing to potentially gain from stopping me today.

I cleared my throat as I tried to assess if it was my friend or the Councilman that stood before me today. "Ellian. What are you—?"

"Quite a crew you've got here." He pushed off the railing, taking long, deliberate strides across the deck to me. "Where are you headed?"

"None of your gods-damned business." Ronan was between us in one swift motion, his voice a lethal calm. His hands remained in his pockets, his stance casual, but anyone could hear the threat behind his words. "Now get off her ship."

I slid my hand in his and squeezed before he decided to act on that threat. Whether Ellian was here as a friend or foe, punching him across the jaw would only delay our departure. We needed to move before any other Councilmembers caught wind of our escape.

After a moment, I felt Ronan relax beneath my fingertips, and I let out a small sigh of relief. I smiled brightly at Ellian, hoping to stir any friendly feelings that might still exist under the wreckage. "Just a day trip, that's all."

Ellian blinked but did not return the smile. Instead, he looked past me, at the stacked crates and oversized sacks tied to the deck. "Quite a haul for a quick sail." His eyes flicked back to me, filled with curiosity and edged with something darker. "If I were a betting man, I'd say you are going much, much farther than that. Does your Uncle know? The rest of the Council sure doesn't."

A stone dropped in my stomach. A small piece of me was relieved that the Council did not know yet, but Ellian sniffing us out on their behalf was not much better. If I didn't deal with him immediately, we would be screwed.

I felt the eyes of my crew at my back, heard the subtle shifts of hands wrapping around hilts, of hearts ready to come to my defense. They were my family, all of them, even Rhett pouting belowdecks. The promise they carried by even being here, the purpose that had brought us together despite the odds, was worth fighting for.

No man, friend or foe, Councilman or not, would stand in our way.

I did not want to fight him, but I would do whatever necessary to see this thing through.

I pushed past my husband to square up to Ellian, my Mathonwy smile plastered across my face and my Branwen hand at the dagger on my hip. "Ellian Llewelyn, I'm going to say this once." I kept my expression open as I craned my head back to meet his gaze. "I am sorry for the other night and how I treated you. You are a very, very dear friend, but nothing more, and I shouldn't have let you believe otherwise. If you'll accept, I'd love to continue that friendship... but if you don't get off my ship right now, I'll throw you overboard myself."

Ellian's throat bobbed as he weighed my words. After a moment, a soft smile finally broke across his face. "I'm hurt, Keira, that you think so little of me. I'm not here to stand in your way."

I let out the breath I forgot I'd been holding. "Good. Then please step aside. We have to be going." I moved to step around him to show him the way, but he held an arm out in my path.

"I said I'm not here to stand in your way. I didn't say I was leaving."

I narrowed my eyes, my patience growing thin. "What?"

He shrugged and sauntered to the nearest crate. With a cocky flourish, he sat like he belonged there, one leg dangling in front of him, the other tucked underneath. "I'm coming with you. So, do I sign in, or do we just get moving?"

"Oh, piss off," Griffin moaned.

"Listen, yer Councilman-li-ness, I know yer all high and mighty. But there are six of us and one of ye," Roland croaked from his perch in the rigging. "Do the math."

Ronan did not move from his spot behind me, but his voice sliced through the air with deadly precision. "Translation: Get off the rutting ship. Now."

I shot Ronan a warning glare over my shoulder. The dam holding back his rage was about to burst, and I couldn't blame him. If anyone had a reason to dislike Ellian Llewelyn, it was my husband. My priorities were clear.

I adjusted my Captain's coat and turned back to where the Councilman perched. "Ellian, you can't come."

He tilted his head like a confused dog. "Why not?"

"You're not a sailor." *And my husband is about to wring your neck.*

Ellian leaned back on his forearms, basking in the midmorning sun with a triumphant smile on his face. "Ah, but I'm able-bodied, wouldn't you say, and I'm a quick study. Plus, if I can't come, I'll have to tell your Uncle and Connor what you're doing and that you broke into his office the other day."

The words were a slap across the face despite their casual delivery. Rage flashed through me, and before I knew it, I had drawn my dagger. I knew without looking that Ronan and Griffin had done the same.

I was on Ellian in two long strides, the point at his throat as I spat, "You wouldn't dare."

Ellian sat up and threw his hands in the air, his suave demeanor falling as he stared down the tip of my knife. He swallowed twice before talking, a bead of sweat forming on his brow. "Look, I know I'm not doing a great job of convincing you right now, but I'm really not trying to get you into any trouble. I'm trying to help you out of it." Gauging my willingness to stab him, he placed a hesitant finger on the tip of my dagger and lowered it. My rage settling, I let him. He continued, his words rushed and stripped of their former boldness, "Consider my attendance as protection from the Council. Because Connor will find out you've gone, and he will know it was you who broke into his office, if he hasn't guessed already. You'll need a damned good excuse, and someone who the Council doesn't see as a liar and a thief to deliver it. Let me help you if only to apologize for crossing the line the other night."

I let his words sink in for a moment, my knuckles still white around the hilt of my dagger. What he said made sense but trusting anyone on the Council right now was a risky move. There were too many moving parts for me to connect the pieces. "What about the contract?"

His brows knit together in genuine confusion. "What?"

"Connor's horseshit amendment to our divorce contract. I work for you, Keira works for him," Ronan answered for me, his sword still ready in his hand. He waved it in Ellian's face as he illustrated his point. "You're talking a big game for someone who seems to be stirring up an awful lot of trouble."

Ellian's eyes went wide as he crossed a hand over his chest. "I swear on my mother's grave I knew nothing about that, Keira." He stood, his expression pleading as he spoke in hushed tones, "But if Connor is making moves like that, he's getting anxious about something. And if he thinks I'm either too stupid to notice or that he can trust me, you're going to need my help even more than I thought you did."

I scanned his face for any sign of deception, but I was only met with genuine concern.

I took a deep breath, reaching into the place where my power slept, hoping for some sort of guidance from Lyr or whatever god was listening.

There was none. Only evidence of me, and the weight that rested on my shoulders as captain.

There was a significant chance he was lying. That this was part of Connor's trap, and if I let him stay, he'd try to derail our search or try to murder us all while we were sleeping. But his argument was convincing, and his eyes were clear. I had learned the hard way with Ronan that it's better to give a person the chance to prove themselves before making a judgment.

I flipped my dagger once and sheathed it. "Fine."

"Not happening. Keira…" Ronan protested, raising his sword again, but I stepped in front of him.

"He's right, Ronan." I lowered his sword with one hand and placed the other on his chest, tracing the space where I knew his tattoo hid. "If we don't find what we need and we come back empty-handed, Connor will end us, if he isn't already writing up our arrest warrants. We need some insurance, if not for us, then for our crew and our families. Moving product for the Llewelyns is exactly the cover we'll need. We can call it an early start to the contract terms."

Ronan's jaw tightened, hurt brimming in his eyes. "After everything, you still stand up for him."

"No, Ronan, I'm standing up for us. Nothing has changed." I kept my voice low so only he could hear, my hand caressing his cheek. "Plus, if he's on the ship with us, we can keep an eye on him. Make sure he doesn't tell anyone anything."

Ronan hesitated a moment longer, then pressed a kiss into my palm. "Fine. Lyr below, woman, you're lucky I love you."

"I'm the luckiest." I reached up on my tiptoes to kiss him on the cheek before addressing the crew. "Let's get ready to move, we're wasting daylight," I bellowed, as I had heard my father do a thousand times before. Somehow, in my core, I knew he would've made the same decision. I shot our newest member a look, my confidence not at all feigned for the first time that day. "Ellian, you too. If you're going to be here, you're going to work."

"Aye, aye, Captain." He nodded with a sly smile. "I've always wanted to say that."

22

Lightning and Lost Things

The first few hours of sailing felt like coming home. I stood behind the *Ceffyl's* familiar wheel with the sun on my skin and the wind in my hair. With a near full crew at my side, I was invincible, holding my destiny in my hands, my fate etched into the smooth oak handles.

The feeling was contagious, the taste of hope thick in the air. Griffin and Roland had struck up a game of cards; so far, Griffin had only lost one bag of silver to the sly old fox. Ronan perched himself on a crate, one eye on a book, the other on Ellian, who was locked in a serious discussion about market pricing with Saeth. They both had been more helpful than I could've anticipated. Ellian could've passed for a seasoned sailor with how quickly he found his balance, plus he had made it his personal mission to check every metal fastening aboard for faults.

Saeth took longer to adapt. Green around the gills at first, she found her sealegs after an hour and set herself to mending the few tears in the sail faster than they ripped. Even Rhett seemed something next to cheerful, his arms still crossed but his scowl melting as he sunbathed on the bow. The sea was calm, the wind steady, and the sky clear. Nothing could go wrong.

But by sunset, the strong southern wind we'd been riding changed. By midnight, it had died down altogether, and with it, the hope that we could outrun the world of trouble at our backs.

I tried focusing on the place where my power slept, sending a distress call to the storm in my chest. Nothing responded; only stagnant silence where there was once a howling hurricane.

By sunrise the next morning, we were dead in the water.

There were thankfully enough of us to row her. Ellian and Griffin were already shifting the massive oars into their slots while Roland showed Saeth how to tie them in place. But without a proper heading, it was tricky. It was one thing to correct a course, it was another thing altogether to wing one.

"Do we have our heading yet, Captain?" Griffin called impatiently as he left Ellian to slide the last oar into its hold.

I wanted to scold him for his tone, but I couldn't help the nervousness sloshing in my own gut. "Ronan, our heading?"

Ronan shut the book he was reading with a smack. "It's not that simple."

"Like hitting a moving target blindfolded, so you've said." Griffin rolled his eyes and stomped up to the gallery like a petulant child. "Which makes no sense. Does that book have anything we can go on?"

Ronan's hands slid into his pockets, his face a perfect mask of confidence, but I heard the uncertain edge in his voice. "No, it does not. I was reading for pleasure."

"Since you're no help anywhere else right now?" Griffin muttered loud enough for both Ronan and me to hear.

Ronan's facade cracked as he snapped in retort, "Since you and Rhett have all the brutish business covered, I thought it would be best if at least one of the men on this ship could read. Don't worry, I can teach you if you'd like."

Griffin threw his hands up in mock surrender. "Lyr below, someone is touchy. Has your lunar cycle started, Cousin Ronan?"

I slammed my hand on the wheel. "If you two boys are done bickering like old wives at the market, there is work to do. Griffin, go help Ellian and Rhett secure the sails."

"Aye, Captain," Griffin grumbled, sticking his tongue out at Ronan as he passed.

Ronan's shoulders fell as his mask did. He slid off the crate, his limbs heavy, and coiled his arms around my waist. "Sorry, Mrs. Mathonwy, I can't help but feel a little useless right now. I don't need a reminder from Griffin."

"You're not useless." I stroked his cheek, relieved when some of the clouds cleared from his sky-colored eyes. I hoped I was doing a proper job of hiding the doubt in mine. "But a heading would be nice. We have to start somewhere. It's been a full day. Aidan will know we lied, the Council will know we're gone, and who knows what's coming after us."

"Like I said yesterday, when I came back, it was only a day's sail due north." The uncertain lines of his forehead creased further. "I'm sure we are close, but *Hireath* knows how to hide. It's how they survive. We just have to keep pushing south and circling the area until it decides to show itself."

I stood on my tiptoes to kiss Ronan's cheek, and a small hint of a smile tugged at the corner of his mouth. "We'll find it, Mr. Mathonwy." I said a quick prayer to Lyr that I wasn't lying through my teeth.

Griffin cleared his throat, drawing our attention. "Oh, my most heavenly Captain, the sail has been adequately secured." He jumped down to the deck with a bow and a riotous grin, gesturing to the topmost beam where Ellian and Rhett had indeed tied the final sail into place. "Can we please, oh pretty please, have a heading now?"

I shot him a vulgar gesture, the tension both on the ship and in my gut too thick for games.

Rhett also had enough. "Will you shut up?" He punched the mast, shaking the rope ladder so hard he nearly knocked Ellian from his foothold. "Some of us are trying to work, and we don't need your incessant barking making this cock-up of a trip even worse."

"Calm down, boy," Roland chuckled as he tied the last oar into place. He winked at Saeth, who suppressed a smirk as she copied the old man's technique.

Rhett only bristled further, an animal being baited.

"Yes, listen to daddy, Rhett," Griffin cooed, but there was a sharpness to his teasing, a wicked smile spreading across his face. "There's no need for hostility."

"Griffin, enough," I warned him, watching as Rhett's expression went from irritated to enraged.

He climbed down from the sail with minimal effort, a predator stalking his prey. Jumping from the lowest beam, he landed on his feet, his eyes shooting daggers at Griffin. "Another word, Branwen, and I'm tossing you overboard with the rest of the chum."

"Rhett," I tried to interject, but I was too late.

Griffin's grin went feral. "I'd be happy to toss around with you, Blondie."

Rhett's fist connected to his face with a smack and chaos erupted.

Griffin lunged, his teeth bared, and the two became a whirlwind of fists and kicks as they rolled around on the deck.

"Stop it!" I yelled, stomping down the stairs, my own frustration boiling in my veins. I brushed past Roland, who simply crossed his arms and looked on with amusement.

"Enough, Rhett!" Ellian moved to tear him off Griffin, but a kick to the abdomen sent him flying.

The dam that held back my rage broke. In a tidal wave of fury, my power awakened in my chest, clawing its way out of my throat. "For Lyr's sake, I said *stop!*"

With a clap of thunder, a gust of wind tore the two apart and sent them soaring into the starboard railing. Saeth, who had stepped out of the way just in time, tilted her head towards me. "Nice."

Griffin rubbed the back of his neck, but he threw a dislodged piece of wood at Rhett, who had already made it to his feet again and was ready for another round.

In two steps, I was between them, shoving Rhett back on his arse. "Lyr below, haven't you two had enough fighting? When will you idiots get it?" Another clap of thunder emphasized my point. The wind picked up around us, so I kept my voice low as I growled at them, "We've been played. All of us. Toyed with by a slimy arse of a man who wanted us to be so consumed with killing each other that no one would stand in his way while he took what he wanted. And this behavior? The petty insults and fighting? You two are letting him win."

Griffin shot me a defiant glare, his sunset eyes turning red. "Connor didn't kill Owen and Aleena."

I stood over my cousin as lightning lit the sky. "No, you did, Griffin." Griffin blinked as my words stung him. I turned my gaze to Rhett, who lowered his eyes in shame. "We all bloody did. We all killed Owen, and Aleena, and Lochlan, and Reid. Because we all let

Connor turn us into his puppets. And now he's trying to control us even further."

They fell silent as I spoke, all shifting in discomfort as I looked at each of them. I swallowed back the tears that rose to my throat. "We all have a choice here. No one said it would be easy, but we can put the past behind us. We can find this gods-forsaken island and do something right for a change. We can stop Connor, avenge our families, and make him pay his toll. We can free Porthladd from his insidious chokehold and maybe, just maybe, build something good. Something we can live in and love without spilling any more blood.

"Or, we can keep fighting and killing each other until there is nothing left." I drew two of my daggers and flipped them over in my hands, presenting them handle-side to Griffin and Rhett. "Your choice, boys."

Griffin stared for a long time before he nodded. "Aye, Captain."

I turned my attention to Rhett, waiting. He frowned, but his eyes held a faint glimmer of respect. "You can't make me like this prick but I'll play nice."

"Good." I sheathed my daggers with a flourish, the storm in my chest dissipating as I exhaled. "Ellian, Roland, take them to the brig."

Ellian pricked up like a dog at dinner time. "Oh, me?"

Roland uncrossed his arms. "Aye, Captain Keira, it would be my pleasure."

Griffin stood to protest. "What, Keira, we just said—"

I held my hand up to silence him. "I heard you both, and I'm glad you chose that way." I waved to Ellian, who grabbed the back of Griffin's arm right on cue. "But a few hours bonding belowdecks will serve you both well. The rest of us might actually get some work done in peace and quiet."

"Oh, thank Lyr." Saeth smirked, immediately unfastening the oars. I winked at her as I climbed the mast to lower the sails again.

Griffin tried to tug away, but Ellian held firm, and my cousin pouted in my direction. "But what about the rowing?"

I smiled as I freed the first set of knots. "Didn't you notice? Wind picked up."

"Let's go, lads." Roland grabbed a scowl-clad Rhett as he led Ellian into the cabin. "We'll be back up in a moment to help ye, Captain Keira."

As they descended below, I said another prayer of thanks to Lyr for the help, dramatic as his timing was. The familiar dark chuckle responded in my head, more distant than I remembered, but there.

You needed a push.

My responding scoff was coated in sarcasm, but underneath it, relief washed over me. Perhaps we weren't entirely on our own.

I released the first sail as my husband joined me in the rigging.

"Are you sure they won't kill each other down there?" The worry had cleared from his face as the god-sent wind played with his hair.

"No, but hopefully you and I can actually think now."

"Aye, Mrs. Mathonwy, I'm not complaining." Ronan straddled the main beam and leaned back, taking a deep breath in. "Peace and quiet, nothing but the salt air and a breeze."

The cabin door banged open, making both of us jump.

Ellian stormed through. "Captain, we have an issue."

"Or not," Ronan mumbled.

"What is it, Ellian?" I slid down from the beam, ignoring the familiar burn of the rope in my palms.

With a sigh, Ellian stepped out of the way as Roland marched up the cabin stairs, his fingers wrapped around a much smaller arm.

An anchor fell into my gut as dirty cheeks and chestnut eyes smiled up at me. Somehow, in all the confusion and tension, we had missed the little stowaway hiding gods-know-where.

"What on earth are you doing here?" I snapped.

"Reagan!" Ronan leaped from the rigging, running to grab her shoulders as if to confirm she was indeed real. He patted her down for injuries, but she swatted him away. "How did you—?"

Reagan batted her eyelashes and jut out her bottom lip in a practiced pout. "I heard you talking to Uncle Reese and I didn't want to miss out again, so I snuck on the ship and hid in the bottom room no one was using." She shrugged, proud of her misadventures, and flashed a smile at me. "I want to help."

I pinched the bridge of my nose. "Reina is going to kill me."

"Reagan, this is dangerous, you shouldn't be here." Ronan's tone was stern and unfeeling, but I could see the sheer horror in his eyes as he kneeled before his cousin. I placed a soothing hand on his shoulder, but he shrugged me off. I tried not to let it sting.

"But I *am* here. I'm *supposed* to be here. I can feel it." Reagan puffed out her tiny chest. Something forgotten in mine swelled in response. She looked to me again for alliance, sensing my wavering resolve. "And I can fight! I've been practicing, Keira, I promise—"

"No." Ronan silenced her and stood, not bothering to wait for my order. He brushed past me and marched up to the gallery. "We are turning around immediately to take you home. Reina is already going to roast me alive and serve me up for dinner."

"Ronan—" I followed after him.

His hands were already on the wheel, his gaze forward. "I said no."

I stuck an arm out in front of him, drawing his attention back to me. "Ronan, we can't turn around. Connor—"

"Fuck Connor, Keira!" he bellowed, fear turning his expression wild. "It is too dangerous for a little girl on this ship!"

I swallowed back the anger that rose to my throat, knowing it wasn't really me he was furious with. Fear brought out the worst in everyone, me more than anyone perhaps, and he had been patient for far longer than I deserved.

But I had an entire crew to make decisions for now. And if we turned around, any chance at a future where Reagan could truly be safe was lost.

I kept my voice low and steady. "It wasn't too dangerous for me, and I was a little girl, too." I placed my hand over his, grabbing the wheel, forcing him to look at me. "This is my ship, Ronan. *My ship*. I'm the Captain. I decide the crew, and I decide the heading."

"And she's *my* cousin!" he hissed.

"Mine too!" I spat back, and he blinked twice. "I'm your wife, remember? Your kin are my kin. We'll keep her safe, Ronan, I promise. But we can't afford to lose our chance here."

Ronan's nostrils flared, hurt and confusion brimming in his eyes. "There are worse things to lose, Keira."

Reagan had made her way up the stairs, her expression pleading. She tugged on Ronan's coat sleeve. "I'm not a baby anymore, Ronan. I know I have a lot to learn and that I should have told you, but please. I can't live on stories anymore."

"Keira." Ronan's throat bobbed angrily. "I can't."

I stroked the back of his hand with my thumb. "I swear to Lyr, we aren't losing anything on this trip, Ronan."

"Sometimes you have to lose something to find it again," Reagan mumbled with a small laugh.

I paused, the hairs on the back of my neck standing at full sail. "What?" I shifted my attention to the little girl, an idea rippling in the back of my mind.

Ronan raised his voice again. "Keira, this is not over—"

"No, hush." I held a hand up, the pieces in my mind swirling together as the wind picked up its pace. "What did you just say, Reagan?"

Embarrassment flushed her freckled cheeks. "I don't know, you reminded me of it...it's something Mama says sometimes when she's confused." She shrugged, mimicking Reina's smooth cadence as she repeated herself. "'Sometimes you have to lose something to find it again.'"

I scrambled for my compass, pulling it out from where it rested against my chest. Opening it, I watched the delicate needle spin as it always did, pointing nowhere in particular.

But perhaps nowhere in particular was exactly where we needed to go. The answer had been in my possession the entire time, hiding in plain sight. I ran my finger over the familiar etching, only the second half of Papa's favorite saying.

Somethings, Keira girl, ye have to lose something to find it again. But all who are lost shall be found.

"Ronan, we have our heading."

Chords and Constellations

It took us another three days to get properly lost.

We let Saeth, Reagan, and Ellian take turns navigating, hoping their inexperience would translate to dumb luck. Only Rhett protested, and for good reason, since it was a terrible plan by all standards, but our options were limited.

We moved at night after the sun had set and our only guides were the stars. Even those we tried to ignore, my power providing us with ample cloud cover whenever I could conjure them. If anyone caught wind of which way we were going, we'd make as many counterclockwise circles as it took for us to be unsure again.

But it was a dangerous game, not knowing. We prayed to any god listening that we were heading in the right direction. Not knowing where *we* were meant we couldn't predict where *anyone else* was, either. For all we knew, we were sailing straight into unfriendly waters.

Our best friend was distraction, and predictably, Griffin was the first to embrace it. By the afternoon of our third day at sea, he had lost six bags of silver to Roland but won back a few gold pieces when Rhett and Ellian decided to join the game. The four of them each drank their weight's worth in ale—enough to forget where they were or who they were with.

As much as losing myself in a drink and a round of cards sounded like a happy way to pass the time, the nerves twisting my stomach made me lurch at the thought of it. To make matters worse, while Ronan had given in to keeping Reagan aboard, he wasn't happy with it; or, by extension, with me. He'd been cold and distant, reading in corners, his blond hair always in his face as he hunched over a book. Our conversations were not curt, but they were short, our only real interaction when he finally shuffled into my cabin late every night, passing out as soon as his head hit the pillow with little more than a mumbled "goodnight".

As much as it pained me, I gave him his space, but it didn't help the growing hole in my chest.

So, I trained, showing the girls all the tricks of the trade save navigation. Reagan and Saeth watched and learned with hungry eyes and eager hearts. They'd tie and re-tie knots until they had them down perfectly, or until their fingers bled, whichever came first. At sunrise and sunset each day, I taught them to fight, and even as their limbs shook and sweat drenched them, they devoured each lesson with twin smiles.

"Good work, Saeth," I said after another tough session at sunset on the third day. I sheathed my blade and threw her a scrap of cloth. "You still lack power, and your stance is wide, but you're quick."

A wicked grin carved her face as she caught the cloth with new ease. "Aye, Captain." Wiping her forehead, she motioned to Reagan, who jumped up from the deck for another round. Leaving them to spar, I stretched my stiff limbs and sat back on a nearby crate. My muscles ached, but I relished the pain. It had been so long since I used my body regularly that I had gone soft.

I couldn't be soft anymore, not with so many depending on me. I wiped the sweat pooling at the back of my neck, staring at the open ocean before us. "Anyone have a clue where we are?"

"Not in the slightest," Ronan mumbled, flipping the worn page of yet another book. It was his sixth in three days.

I pushed off the crate and sauntered to where he sat on a step, one knee pulled up to his chest. Perhaps adrenaline had made me bold, the hour of fighting reinvigorating the warrior in me. Like fruit from a tree, I plucked the book from his hands. He reached for it instinctively, but I held it above his head, my best Mathonwy smile stretching across my face. "Still sore at me for letting her stay?"

He shot me an annoyed glare, but the corner of his lips twitched despite himself. "I'm not sore, I'm…" he sighed and looked to where Reagan still play-fought, his brows furrowed. "I'm worried. That girl is the last piece of either of our families that is truly good. If something happened to her…"

Still feeling bold, I shifted to sit on the stair across from him, leaning on his bent knee. "That's why we won't let anything happen."

"I know." He pushed a strand of my damp, matted hair out of my face and kissed my forehead. "But I'm allowed to worry for the people I love."

The clatter of Reagan's dull sword made me jump. I turned to scold her for not being careful, only to see her head craned back to face the sky, the rising moon illuminating her round cheeks. My heart melted as she looked up with wonder.

"The stars are different here," she exclaimed.

Ronan exhaled beside me, warmth finally spreading to his eyes. "Aye, Reagan, you see different stars depending on where you are. That's how sailors can use them to navigate. And to tell stories." He lowered his voice, slipping into his favorite role. Tucking one arm around my waist, he pointed to a constellation I'd never seen before. "Those stars there, see? They look like a princess, don't you think?"

Reagan's eyes followed where he pointed as she tried to draw it out for herself. Griffin stumbled over from the cabin, his face red even in the flickering lanternlight, hiccupping as he spoke, "Stargazing, are we?"

Saeth offered him a pointed look as she finally lowered herself onto the deck to rest. "Better than losing yet again to Roland."

"The old arse cheats," Griffin groaned.

"Griffin, do you see the princess?" Reagan skipped over to him, pointing out the constellation in the sky, her eyes rounder than the moon itself.

Griffin swayed as he tilted back to look at it, his own smile lopsided. "Looks more like a fish to me."

"Maybe she's both." Ronan winked as his other arm encircled me, pulling me closer to him. Mischief twinkled in his eyes, brighter than the stars. "You've heard of sirens, haven't you, little dragon? I've got a story if you'd like to hear it."

"Honestly?" Reagan raised an eyebrow. "I'd rather listen to Ellian play his fiddle again."

Ronan deflated. "Really, now?" He hid his disappointment with a forced grin, and my heart ached. I kissed the back of his hand, my own smile genuine.

"Did I hear my name?" Ellian emerged from belowdecks, his long arms draped around a drunk Roland and sour-faced Rhett. Letting go of his two crutches, Ellian lowered himself in a bow and almost fell forward, Roland catching his arm just in time. "What do you say, Captain, will you have a song or two from your humble minstrel?"

A laugh sputtered from my chest. "Of course, go ahead."

Reagan jumped up and clapped, pulling a slightly green Ellian toward his violin case.

The clouds in Ronan's eyes were almost enough to extinguish my laughter. I patted his knee with my free hand, snuggling up closer to him. "Don't be jealous, Mr. Mathonwy."

"Bastard invites himself on board and now he's stealing my best audience?" he laughed, but it was a shallow sound. "Of course I'm going to be jealous."

"Aye, but you have something arguably better than he does." Something ignited in my core, spurred to life by the laughter and his closeness. I pressed a quick kiss to his neck and shifted so I was fully on his lap. "I could think of a few things that are easier to do when Reagan is...distracted."

"Oh?" His voice was velvet dipped in honey, his eyes now focused solely on my lips. "And what would those be?"

Heat rose through me, primal and possessive, as the rest of the ship disappeared. It had been almost a whole week since our moment in the shack, the memory of his body against mine still taunting me. I stroked his collarbone as it peeked out of his linen shirt. "Let's go belowdecks for a while, and I'll show you."

A chuckle rumbled through his chest and he licked his full lips, only furthering my desire. "Patience, Keira girl. When I bed you again..." His voice was dangerously low as he nipped my ear. I bit back a groan, entangling my fingers in his shirt. "I want to do it where no one can hear you moan my name."

"You two are disgusting." Saeth's dagger-sharp tone split me from my trance, and I shot her a look that could bleach a raven. Her answering eyeroll was unfazed as she nodded toward the small circle the crew formed around Ellian. "Come over and sing with us before I puke."

Ronan stroked my hair but scooted away from me, the night air cooling us both. He winked and slid off the step, leaving me with only the absence of him. "Let's go have some fun, Mrs. Mathonwy."

I frowned, but he was right. There would be time for *that* when we were finally home. Entire days of it, perhaps, if I had my way. He held out a hand, and I let him lead me to the circle of our collective, mismatched family. I plopped down next to Griffin, Ronan flanking my other side, making sure to sit far enough to avoid the unspoken temptation we both knew awaited us the moment we were alone.

Rhett, who was sandwiched between Reagan and Roland, sat directly opposite me and narrowed his eyes. "You both have gone soft."

I opened my mouth to retort, but Griffin beat me to it, spreading his legs and wiggling in Rhett's direction. "I can show you something hard if you'd like."

Rhett's jaw dropped as Roland smacked his hand across Reagan's eyes.

"Griffin!" I snapped.

"I was serious about that one." His speech was slurred, but his eyes were bright. He leaned in to whisper to me, his breath like hot arse and whiskey. "You're not the only one with a thing for blonds."

Rhett choked on a cough and stood from the circle. "I'm going to bed."

"Just give a shout if you'd like me to join you!" Griffin waggled his eyebrows as Rhett stalked off into the cabin.

I smacked my cousin across the back of the head. "When I told you two to get along, that is not what I meant."

"What can I say, I'm irresistible." A girlish giggle escaped his throat as he rubbed the sore spot already forming on his head. Part of me was itching to give him another one as he continued, winking at me, "Don't worry, we won't rock the ship too much."

I looked to Ronan for solace, who only shrugged and wrapped a heavy arm around my shoulder. I snuggled closer to his side, happy to be near him and further from Griffin and his antics.

"Lyr below. Councilman, ye know anything an old sailor can croak to?" Roland cleared his throat and shook his head. "Perhaps something loud enough to drown out drunken idiots?"

"Please," I groaned, and Roland gave a grateful smile.

"Aye, Captain Keira." Ellian brandished his fiddle from its case like a sword from its sheath. He was a sailor now, but he was still Ellian, stuffed to the gills with suavity and pomp. By whatever strange fate had brought us all together, he was one of us now, every cocky inch of him.

I watched his deft fingers fly over the strings with ease. The melody was bright, the strings bouncing against the mahogany like dancers in a jig. It filled the space, each note dragging us into the dance, feet tapping and heads bobbing. Roland started humming, the sound like steel against rock, but I swayed to it anyway. Griffin was the first to recognize the tune, belting his favorite verse out as loud as he could.

"Oh little lady Lainey,
her waist so slim and dainty,
would dance when it was rainy
And drink when there was sun."

Picking it up, the rest of us joined, so out of key that it was hard to even hear Ellian's expert playing. Ronan's smooth tenor was the only thing mooring us to the tune, his voice thankfully carrying over the rest of us croaking fools. Reagan watched on, giggling at the absurd words, clapping to the beat.

My chest swelled, the memory of another little girl singing her first shanty on this ship calling a tear to my eye. I sang louder, filled with a pride I couldn't name and a joy I couldn't replace.

"Her husband was a sailor,
Who sailed from Ir'de to Baylor,
So, Lainey screwed the tailor,
Whenever he'd away."

"You have the voice of a siren, Keira." Griffin nudged my side as the verse died down. He flipped his red hair and batted his eyelashes, the motion so eerily similar to Finna I nearly choked on a laugh.

"Aye," Saeth snorted, leaning back in the most unladylike position I'd ever seen her in, "makes me want to drown myself."

I took off my boot and tossed it at her. She ducked as it whizzed by her head. It nearly hit Ellian instead, violin shrieking as he tumbled out of the way, his normal grace nowhere to be seen.

"Another word, Saeth, and you'll be sleeping in the brig," I couldn't help but chuckle, my threat empty, "or in Griffin's room."

Saeth's only response was to pinch her lips together as she suppressed her own laughter, my message received.

Reagan scooted closer to her, linking an arm through hers like sisters at a dress shop. Saeth stiffened for a second but melted as Reagan beamed up at her. "So, does this mean we are all friends now?"

Saeth's smile held no trace of her signature sharpness. "Silly little dragon, we're *kin* now."

"Except Ellian," Griffin hiccupped, swirling a finger at the Councilman. "He's sort of like the pet."

Ellian pointed the bow of his fiddle at Griffin like a dagger and poked him in the shoulder. "Yet you're the one with fleas."

We were lost in our laughter and song for another hour until the moon was high and bright. Something had shifted with the salt-scented wind, breathing new peace into us all until our sides were sore and our hearts were full.

Ellian's chords turned from major to minor, the jigs and shanties bleeding into soft, melancholy lullabies. Ronan knew the words to each one, his humming sweetening the air around us.

"Oh, mother moon,
Rising from below,
Our protector and our light.
Will you keep us safe,
Safe from the dark,
Our watcher in the night?"

I sighed against my husband's side as he sang, each word repairing a part of my waxing soul. Eyes grew heavy as the moon watched us this night, blanketing us in her warm glow, and we knew it was time to retire.

Roland offered to take the watch. Griffin peeled off first, half-crawling to the cabins, too drunk to stand. Saeth followed, carrying a semi-conscious Reagan, both of them heavy with sleep. Ronan and I made our way to my cabin not long after, falling into the plush pile of blankets and pillows with twin sighs. The second our bodies hit the bed, any residual desire from earlier was replaced by exhaustion. We barely had enough energy to pull off our boots and coats, nevermind any other physical activity.

Within minutes, Ronan was out like a candle in a rainstorm, his breathing slow and steady. His head rested in the crook of my shoulder, his arm draped across my abdomen. I brushed the blond waves out of his eyes, but they were tightly shut. My body ached to join him in the dream realm, my limbs sinking into the softness of the mattress, but my mind raced.

Tonight, something had changed. With a song and the stars, our mismatched band of misfits had become a real crew. We had a united purpose, the wounds of the past secondary to the promise of tomorrow.

But with everything we gained, we risked losing so much more.

I stared up at the familiar wooden ceiling. When I was little, and the weather was too rough to sleep above deck, I would pretend the knots in the wood were stars—my own little constellations.

I hadn't had the heart to take the Captain's quarters across the hall, insisting Reagan and Saeth share it, making some excuse about comfort. Maybe it was because I was afraid I couldn't fill Papa's boots. Or perhaps it was the guilt that still bit at my heels for lying to Aidan, the most recent occupant. Or maybe, with all that was changing, I needed the familiarity of the one space that had been mine.

But now, even the soft, cotton blankets in my favorite shade of blue from Ir'de couldn't bring me comfort. Ronan soon snored lightly, his once-soothing touch now suffocating as he wrapped himself further around me.

I needed the sky, not some sad imitation of it.

Careful not to wake him, I slithered out from under his arm. He grunted once, but his eyes did not so much as flutter. I covered him in a blanket, his face so young in sleep. Pulling my discarded coat back on, I pressed a quiet kiss to his forehead.

Heavy rutting sleeper.

Floorboards creaked as I made my way up to the deck, but the ship was otherwise quiet, the only other sound the sea slapping against the hull.

I inhaled deeply as the night air caressed my skin, soothing the waves in my gut. "Roland, I'll take the next watch."

The old man rubbed tired eyes as he climbed down from the crow's nest of the foremast. "Aye, Captain, I'll get some rest."

I clapped him on the shoulder as he walked past, grateful for his compliance. As much as I had grown fond of his company, I needed my space.

Once he was safely belowdecks, I dragged my hammock from the equipment hatch. The thick canvas fabric, made from an old sail, was damp, but I didn't mind as I fastened it between the mizzenmast and the wheel. Once properly secured, the ropes pulled tightly, I eased myself onto it and tucked a hand behind my head. The sides of the hammock cocooned me until all I could see were stars. Thousands of them freckled the deep purple sky, the night clear and open.

Wherever we were, the sky really was *different*. I'd been avoiding looking at it for fear I'd regain my sense of direction, but I was truly lost for the first time in a long time. Even if I didn't know their names, the foreign constellations still understood my worried heart.

I counted near four hundred before boots across the deck shattered my momentary peace. I straightened at the sound, pressing up on my forearms.

"Mind if I join you?" Ronan's hair was sideways with sleep, the smooth planes of his chest visible, the dark lines of his tattoo peeking out. He hadn't bothered buttoning his shirt back up.

My chest ached at the sight of him. *My Ronan.*

I sat up further, the hammock swinging gently with my movement. "Sorry, did I wake you?"

"I'm the heaviest sleeper north of Tan." He pushed my hair behind my ear, cupping my face in his wide hands. His lips brushed my forehead in a whisper of a kiss. "I woke up to take a piss, and I missed my wife. Everything okay, Mrs. Mathonwy?"

I leaned into him, relishing in his sea-salt-and-citrus smell. "I couldn't sleep, and I always feel better under an open sky than below-deck."

Gentle hands stroked the back of my head. "Well, scoot over, Captain Keira."

After some swaying and adjusting, he settled beside me in the hammock. I rested my head on his chest, his heartbeat and the sound of waves matching their pace. I don't know when this became the most natural thing in the world, his arm around me, my hand over his heart, our legs comfortably tangled together. I would never stop being grateful for this man; my sheep in snake's clothing, my compass and my heading.

"Am I crazy for this?" I mumbled against him.

Ronan quirked an eyebrow. "For sleeping in a hammock?"

I shifted to face him better, my head propped up on my hand. "No, for this trip. I'm risking the lives of half the people I love, abandoning the other half, just so I can maybe find a way to link Connor to Papa's murder. But what if there's nothing? Or what if we do find something, and Connor just has us killed before we can say anything?"

He was quiet for a moment, staring up at the newly-acquainted stars. "Do you remember my first trip on this ship?"

A memory of a surly ten-year-old stroked a far corner of my mind. "Vaguely." My head swirled like Pysgoddian storm clouds. "We sailed to Pysgodd for a final haul before the waters froze over."

A deep chuckle reverberated through his chest. "Aye. And do you remember how useless I was because I was so damned cold?"

The image sharpened into a fur-clad, semi-soaked Ronan, pulling a grin out of me. "It wasn't your fault. You were used to the Southern Sea."

He shrugged, his eyes still distant. "Fair, but I never wanted to be a sailor. I didn't even like trips with *my* Pa, but it was the family business, and I was the oldest male. I had no choice in my destiny. It was set before I even had a name." His throat bobbed with a rawness that ripped me open, vulnerability laced in every syllable. "When Mama was alive, I used to make up excuses to stay with her instead, to take care of her. But after she passed and Reese told me I was coming to learn from Cedric, I was miserable. There was no more escaping."

I had heard Ronan tell a hundred stories in my life, but this was not one of the grand fantasies he was used to telling. Yet somehow, it was also the bravest I've ever seen him. No mask, no characters, only Ronan. My Ronan. "I'm sorry, I didn't know any of that."

A smile finally reached his eyes. "But that all changed on that first trip."

"Why?"

His hand found the side of my face, his thumb stroking my cheek, every callous more luxurious than the finest silks from Ir'de. The moonlight shimmered in his eyes, my favorite blue now lined with silver. "Because even though I was freezing my arse off and I was homesick, even though I cried myself to sleep every night for a week, I got to see you every day doing the thing you loved most."

A scoff escaped my lips. "What? Ronan, that's—"

His toothy smile halted my speech, the sight so rare and beautiful. And he was smiling *at me* that way, like it was somehow my doing.

His voice was a raft on smooth water, buoyant and gliding. "You made sailing look like the greatest thing in the universe. The way you *smiled*. Even in the bitter cold, even with blisters on your hands and cuts on your face and bruises everywhere, you came alive. I wanted to follow you, through whatever dark and wet and cold we faced. Because even if I was a useless, crying mess, I knew *you* could handle it, and you could make it all better." He paused to brush his lips against my cheek. "So yes, Keira Branwen-Mathonwy, you are crazy for doing this. It's impossible and improbable and we might all die. But... there is still a slight chance that something good can come from this. And if anyone can pull it off and bring justice for your father, maybe make a better life for the rest of us in the meantime, it's you. I'm following you wherever you go. That's my destiny."

Tears caught in my throat as I stared at my husband, unable to voice the gratitude that swelled through me. "I— Thank you, Ronan. But you're the one who makes it better, at least for me."

His arms encircled me, holding me like I was something fragile. "Then I'm finally serving my purpose."

"Will you tell me another story?" I nestled further into his embrace. "Maybe I'll get some rest."

"Of course. Any in mind?"

"Dealer's choice."

One hand pointed to the sky as the other traced circles over the skin of my shoulder. "See that constellation there? The one with the hunter's bow?"

I followed his direction to a small cluster of stars just above the horizon. "Aye, I think so."

He exhaled once, and spoke low, his voice my own personal lullaby. "That's Gwynn, the hunter god. He used to be one of Arawn's greatest hunters."

I flicked the tip of his nose. "Don't say his name, it's bad luck."

I couldn't see his eyes, but I could hear them rolling as he spoke. "Fine, Mrs. Mathonwy. Anyway, Gwynn was the leader of one of *his* packs of hounds, until one day he ran away from his duties in search of love."

I closed my eyes, letting the warmth of him next to me and the melody of his voice do its work. "I've never heard this one."

Ronan stroked my hair, continuing absentmindedly as the threat of sleep tugged at my consciousness. "It was one of my favorites on the island. Nelle and Marina, two of the island women, used to tell it—" He shot up suddenly like a bullet out of a gun, nearly toppling us both from the hammock. "Oh, I'm so rutting dense!"

I rubbed the sleep out of the corner of my eye, but Ronan was already twisting out of the hammock. "Ronan, what—?"

Without waiting for me to catch up, he bounded across the deck to where the old spyglass rested on the bow. "Keira, we have to be close. If I can see that constellation...."

Realization smacked me hard across the face. I scurried to where he stood, jerking the spyglass from his hands and pressing it to my eye.

In the moonlight, peeking through hazy clouds, a sliver of land emerged from the deep, biting into the horizon.

I lowered the spyglass, Ronan's incredulous expression matching mine. The word was a prayer on my lips. "*Hiraeth?*"

He nodded once, and hope flooded my gut with warmth. "Aye, Keira girl. *Hiraeth.*"

24

Horses and Hidden Treasures

We cast anchor half a league offshore, worried about what lurked in the shallows and beyond. Up close, the island was just as mysterious as it was from afar. Mist shrouded the beaches, only a few delicate palms daring to show themselves.

I swallowed my fear as we lowered the scouting boats to half, our crew armed and ready for whatever hid behind the haze. My eyes locked on Ronan, the first light of dawn finally brightening our faces. "You're sure it's safe to disembark?"

He nodded once, a distance in his expression I had no name for. "Aye, it's safe enough, but someone should stay back with the ship." When he finally met my gaze, there was steel in it. "And Reagan."

Reagan stomped her foot on the deck. She'd been the first ready when we sounded the call, a red velvet long-coat around her shoulders and her ornate dragon dagger strapped to her hip within minutes. "Ronan, I have to go, I—"

Ronan's look was icy enough to silence a full-grown polar bear. "No. You will remain on this ship, or so help me Lyr, you'll be punished for a year. And when Reina's done with you, I'll punish you again."

Her returning glare could set a barge on fire, the familial resemblance clear as dawn. "Fine."

"I'll stay." Roland ruffled his niece's hair, offering me a wink that quieted my gut full of writhing fish. "Let the young folks do the searchin' and scavengin'."

Ronan kissed his cousin on the forehead and signaled the rest of us to the boats. "Let's get moving. We don't want to get stuck here at night."

"Why not?" Griffin yawned as he adjusted his tunic and climbed over the rail, the swords on his back crooked. He'd been the hardest to wake.

Ronan dropped over the railing and into the lifeboat with far more grace, every muscle tense with readiness. "The island is safe, yes, but it's wild. Certain...*species* more than others." He offered a hand to help me over. "And guess when they come out."

"Fair point," I answered, and though I didn't need it, I took his hand as I found my footing.

Rhett climbed in next, taking a surprising seat next to Griffin. I narrowed my eyes at my cousin, who only shrugged in response.

Saeth followed without a moment of hesitation. She wore a pair of my old leather trousers and a deep blue coat that hugged her tightly, and for the first time in her life, she looked as sharp as she truly was. Ellian was at her back, looking far less sure and far greener, either last night's liquor or this morning's task in his throat. But I was grateful to him, and the expert sword at his hip, all the same.

Once settled, Ronan and I took to rowing. No one spoke, the task ahead settling heavy over our tongues and hearts. With my back to the nearing shore, I watched my beloved ship grow smaller—her deep cedar wood, the graceful *ceffyl* carved into her bow, its sapphire eyes gleaming in the rising light. She was precious, as was her cargo.

A scared part of me recalled an old sailors' warning Aidan used to quote: *Ships that find Hiraeth never find home.*

As we landed on the sandy shore, I offered a silent prayer to Lyr. *If you're listening, please let us survive this.*

Nothing responded.

I sighed as I took in the island. The sand was so clean it neared pink, smooth white rocks peppering its surface. The mist still hugged the treeline, but the deepest shades of green were visible, vines tangled together in intricate knots.

She was both beautiful and deadly.

I looked to my crew, their faces pale as they secured the boat to a nearby tree. I signaled quietly, begging my voice not to quiver when I spoke. "Let's move in teams of two, we'll cover more land that way. We meet back here at sunset, hands full or not."

Ronan nodded, his face unreadable. "Stick to the coast as much as you can. We're looking for a shipwreck, so that's the most natural starting place. Not to mention it's easy to get lost inland." He kept his tone even as he fumbled in the pocket of his coat for some scraps of paper. He handed one to each of us, the page lined with handwritten shapes and obscure markings. "I drew some maps, but I can't promise that things haven't changed since I've been gone."

I folded mine carefully and stuck it in my breast pocket, right next to Pa's compass. When my fingers brushed against the cool brass, a calm washed over me, Papa's spirit fortifying my own. "Rhett, you'll be with Ronan, Griffin, you're with Saeth, and Ellian, you're with me."

Griffin cocked his head to the side, color coming back to his face. "Actually, Captain, if you don't mind, Blondie and I have a score to settle, so we figured we'd make this little excursion a competition."

I pitched an eyebrow. "Rhett?"

The burly blond rolled his eyes, arms folded across his black tunic. "His idea, but yes."

I considered the pair for a moment, weighing the odds of losing one or both of them if I let them wander into the jungle alone. They were staggeringly high, but my cousin's expression was steadfast, his mind already made up. The odds of changing his stubborn head were even slimmer.

"Fine," I conceded, turning instead to the other hardheaded redhead. Her eyes still were without fear, bright and ready. At least I could trust one of them. "Saeth, go with Ellian." I faced my friend, my protective instincts prickling. "If anything happens to her, you're dead, are we clear?"

He grinned, but it didn't reach his eyes. He nudged my cousin playfully, covering his doubt like a champion. "Psh, this little she-wolf will be fine; it's me that I'm worried about."

I looked at each of their faces once more, memorizing every detail. Griffin's constellation of freckles, Saeth's sharp chin, Ellian's lopsided grin, even Rhett's full-lipped pout. I had asked them all here, to the edge of the world, and they had come. Some more reluctantly than others, but they still continued to follow—for me or for Papa or for truth, I didn't know.

Now they were about to hunt for a needle in a haystack of unknowns, unblinking in the face of danger. It was not a gift I could ever hope to repay, their loyalty and goodness. But Lyr be damned, I'd protect them all until my dying breath.

"No one gets left behind today," I choked around the ball of emotion rising to my throat. "That's an order."

Finally, I looked to Ronan, my truest of companions.

"If anyone finds anything, or if you're in trouble, send up a single flare and we'll find you." Ronan patted the flare gun at his side, one that matched five the others carried. His eyes found mine, softening ever so slightly. "Let's move out, we are wasting daylight."

Hiraeth was like nothing I'd ever seen before, but something about it sang to my very core.

As we hacked our way through the thicket of the jungle, my eyes could not drink in enough of it. We didn't stray too far from the shoreline, still hearing the waves lapping against it. But even in our shallow excursion, there was so much newness. Flowers in colors I'd never seen before dotted every tree, their petals full and untouched. Vines climbed the trunks in patterns so intricate, they looked painted, somehow both wild and ordered. Sunlight poured through the treetops despite their thick greenery, bathing everything in pools of gold. Birdsongs I'd never heard wove intricate melodies through the air, a symphony to search by.

And the *smells*. Sweeter than any pastry I'd ever tasted, more fragrant than the best spice stalls in Ir'de. There were so many I couldn't tell where one stopped and the next started.

A gentle breeze licked the back of my neck, playing with the few strands of hair that escaped my braid. I called to where Ronan searched a few paces ahead, "I thought it would be hotter, but the weather is actually quite nice."

"Aye, nice enough to lose yourself. Stay alert."

I watched the sculpted muscles in his back move through his sweat-soaked shirt. He'd taken off his bright red coat an hour before, tying it around his waist. I admired the shape and color of him, so beautiful and bright, like he belonged to the island and its wonders. I supposed he had, once. "Is it everything you remember?"

This halted him, and he turned. His eyes sparkled brighter than any of the flowers we'd passed, but they held that same sadness I could not name. "It's like nothing has changed at all."

He pressed on without another word.

Curiosity tugged at the back of my mind as I breathed in the sun sweet air. "Where do the people stay during the day?"

Ronan's laugh was dry. "You wouldn't believe me if I told you."

I sped up and caught his arm, spinning him to face me. His eyes were guarded, sending a twang of hurt through my heart. "After everything, Ronan, you really think that?" I folded my arms across my chest. "I thought we said no more secrets."

His gaze softened, my Ronan peeking through the cracks of his mask. "Aye, but that's not my secret to tell." He offered a smile that I believed and tucked an unruly strand of hair behind my ear. "Let's just keep looking, Mrs. Mathonwy. It's easy to get lost, and a day here could mean a week or a year out there. Trust me."

My heart ached for more, but I bit my tongue. "Aye, let's keep moving." I led the charge this time, and he let me, falling behind in an easy pace.

We walked another two hundred paces or so, the foliage growing denser as we moved. But the longer we walked and the higher the sun rose, the more worried I became. I thought of my cousins, roaming this same unfamiliar terrain. We had seen nothing to scare us yet, but my heart shuddered at the thought that they might have. And still, aside from some inspiration if I ever decided to take up painting, we had gained nothing useful from our journey.

I cursed myself for being so enamored. This was a mission with lives at stake, not some tropical holiday.

"See anything yet?" I called behind me, hoping he could make anything out of the maze of color and distractions.

"No, but it's here." His voice was quiet, but it still cut through the air clear as a bell. "I can feel it."

I cursed, almost tripping over a particularly stubborn vine. The sun inched ever higher, the waves crashing nearby louder now, signaling noontide. "It could've washed away by now." Frustration bubbled within me, the birdsong grating against my nerves. "Lyr below, we are complete idiots. We should never have come."

"No, we aren't idiots—" Ronan started and stopped, then his voice dropped to a lethal growl. "Keira, stop moving."

My head whipped around. "What the—"

I stopped speaking as I saw his face, the color gone from his cheeks, every muscle rigid. I followed his fear-filled stare twenty paces to our right, to a small pond in the midst of the thicket.

To where a *ceffyl dwr* watched us.

He stood eerily still in the pool, gazing at us with ancient, sunken eyes. Blue, inky skin pulled tight over a muscled frame. Water dripped from his seaweed-colored mane, mist rolling off of him. Lowering his head, he took a step toward us, a webbed fin peeking out of the water.

A part of me screamed to run, to get away. But another, deeper part of me was transfixed by him, a ship called to his shore.

Ronan's survival instincts leaped into action before mine did. He tugged at my sleeve, his voice urgent. "Keira, we have to run, don't look in its eyes."

But the *ceffyl* already held my eyes with his. I swatted my husband away. "No, Ronan."

He stepped in front of me, shaking my shoulders, half-dragging me from my spot. "Keira, it's a trick. He'll drown you, please, let's go!"

I pushed Ronan back this time, the power in my chest swirling, begging me to stay.

No, not to stay. *Follow.* The voice was not Lyr's, but another's, softer than the sunken god's, but just as warm. The *ceffyl* turned, gliding through the water in the direction from which it came. Deeper into *Hiraeth.*

"We're supposed to follow."

Ronan grabbed my arm, his voice pleading. "Keira…"

We are the same. Duweni.

The voice slithered into my head again, another wave of warmth washing over me. Of sameness.

I looked at my husband, my hand on his face to calm the worry. "He's safe. I feel it."

The *ceffyl* looked over his shoulder, patiently waiting for us to accompany him.

Duweni. Gods-born.

I nodded to my new friend, then to Ronan again. I stroked his cheek with my thumb. "I think Lyr sent him to help us."

Ronan's eyes searched mine, likely for signs of enchantment or insanity, but my instincts sang with the truth. I kept my expression open. After he had decided I wasn't hypnotized or crazy, he loosed a sigh. "Right, because that makes sense here." He pinched the bridge of his nose, staring after the *ceffyl*, who neighed impatiently. Ronan shrugged, trudging after him. "Fine, let's follow the notoriously murderous water horse."

25

Shipwrecks and Shallows

We followed the *ceffyl* for another six hundred paces, weaving through the densest parts of the island, where flowers bloomed larger than my head and vines the size of pythons wrapped around trees. His pace was slow, and he'd huff every ten minutes or so, as if to remind us that it was our fault when we tripped over ourselves. Ronan kept a wary eye on his back and his hand at his sword.

Somehow, the deeper we went, the surer I became, the storm inside quickening with excitement. All my fear and doubt dissolved, and for the first time since Papa died, I was truly sure that I was exactly where I was meant to be.

The *ceffyl* halted on the edge of a clearing, where a tiny inlet carved into the shoreline like a jagged tooth. I inhaled a sharp breath as I took in the sight before me. Where the water lapped the land, the broken hull of a ship and its scattered remains littered the beach.

Triumph sang through my every inch. I whipped my head to Ronan, whose eyes scanned the wreckage in disbelief. "Would you look at that? Not bad for a murderous water horse if you ask me," I teased, too giddy to contain myself. Ronan opened his mouth to retort, but I held up a hand, turning to the *ceffyl*. Before I could think, I threw my arms around its thick, slimy neck, wrapping it in a tight hug. To its credit, the animal did not flinch. "Thank you, friend."

He playfully nipped the back of my braid and let out what I assumed to be an amused neigh.

I let go, patting his mane, my gratefulness immeasurable. "How do I repay you?"

The voice slithered into my head again, this time tinged with sadness. *We are the same, Ariannad. Duweni. You will pay us all back in time.*

I froze at the name. Though I'd never heard it before, a familiarity rang through me. I opened my mouth to ask another question, but with one last knowing look, the *ceffyl* turned to go, trotting off into the treeline without another word.

"My wife talks to horses," Ronan mumbled, his hands deep in his pockets. "Wonderful."

I shot him a stony look, but I felt my lips twitch. Filled with renewed courage, I swaggered toward the wreckage, my boots denting the damp sand. "He led us to your ship, didn't he?"

Ronan did not follow, his feet rooted to his place. A frown tugged at the corner of his mouth. "Keira, this...this isn't my ship."

My head swiveled back around, scanning the wreckage again. She was about the right size, but the wood was old and rotted. I could still tell by the shape of what remained of her bow she'd been built for passengers, not cargo.

Too old. And decidedly not Ronan's.

My heart sank as my triumph scattered in the wind. I bit back the tears rising to my throat.

Of course it wasn't that easy. Nothing ever was.

I turned to go, anger rising through my core. I'd been so foolish to drag my rutting family out to this flower-scented shithole. I had no plan and no real evidence, only a gut feeling and an impulse, my only guide a mythical fucking horse.

I had wanted so desperately to believe there was an answer, I had tried to make one. This was nothing more than a mirage, sand where there should have been substance.

I stomped back the way we came, letting the tears fall freely. It was time to stop playing pretend and go home.

Ronan held out a hand to stop me before I reached the trees. He squinted at the ship against the sun. "Wait, Keira, look."

He pointed toward the back half of the hull, to where the faint imprint of faded letters decorated the wood. I swallowed, reading the barely-legible word twice.

Deithwyr.

Traveler.

A stone dropped through my gullet as the word rang through the back of my mind. I read it again, remembering the last place I'd seen it scratched in feverish handwriting.

We'd thought it was a warning, or a question, perhaps. Not a ship's name.

Maybe I really was as stupid as I was sailor, but my heart sang at the hope of an answer. "Ronan, I think...I think this was Papa's." I stumbled back toward the wreckage, my limbs commanding themselves as I took it in.

"*The Traveler.*" Ronan followed me, digging through some of the debris, turning over a half-rotted crate. A threadbare blue coat tumbled out, a familiar family crest embroidered into the front of it: a *ceffyl dwr*. My heart stopped as Ronan picked it up, shaking out the dust and sand. "So, he came here. But why lead us here and not to my ship?"

The *ceffyl* had brought us here for a reason. Just not the one we were expecting.

I let my fingers graze every piece of debris, every missing piece of my father's story. Another overturned chest spilled as I lifted it, dozens of worn parchments floating out. I lowered myself into the sun-soaked sand, combing through each paper delicately, my fingers shaking. More shipping contracts than I could count, most of them dated over twenty years ago. Permits from all over the Deyrnas, signed and sealed by some of the greatest Councilors the Seven Isles have ever known. Status letters in my grandfather Argus's hand, the chicken scratch that used to sign my birthday letters bringing silver tears to my eyes.

I picked up another letter, this one in my father's handwriting. My eyes soaked in every word. It was a rather dull progress report addressed to Argus, detailing a particularly disappointing haul from the Pysgoddian fur markets. But my father's voice sang through it, his optimism and cunning clear even in the worst of times.

As I held the letter to my chest, another, smaller piece of paper fluttered to the ground. I picked it up and my heart swelled a thousand sizes. It was a rendering of Pa and the crew, probably drawn by a Huddian artist, the likenesses near-perfect.

"Look at this." I held it up to Ronan, gently caressing the center of the picture where Papa stood tall in the same blue coat Ronan had found. His beard hadn't even come in yet, only a thin red mustache that barely covered his upper lip. By the look of it, he was only a few years older than I was now. "He was so young."

Ronan pointed to the two small boys next to Papa. "Are those your uncles?"

I reluctantly tore my eyes from Papa to look where he pointed, studying the boys further. One sported a mop of dark red curls and freckles, with a wide smile missing two front teeth. The other had the same ginger hair as my father next to him, a stony look on his young face. "Aye, Aidan and Donnall." My finger traced over Aidan's face, over the cunning in his eye even though he couldn't have been more than twelve. He looked so smart, dressed in blue finery, his first dagger proud at his hip, but his limbs were still so gangly and frail. A pang of homesickness washed through me. "Look how scrawny Aidan was."

Ronan chuckled, settling beside me in the sand. He nodded to another figure in the background of the photo, the spitting image of Tarran. "Look how pissed off Weylin looks in the back."

I looked at his face, *at Tarran's face,* and for the first time in a very long time, I felt a tinge of sympathy for my eldest uncle. "Weylin was the oldest of the boys, but Grandpa still chose Papa to succeed him. Weylin knew it was the right choice, but he was grouchy about it. Or so the story goes," I explained quietly, tucking the picture into my coat pocket. If I held it any longer, the tears would start flowing so heavily I wouldn't be able to see it anyway. I couldn't bear to part with this gift, even if it brought us no closer to our goal.

Perhaps that was the reason the *ceffyl* had led us here. Here, to where my father's forgotten legacy was strewn across a lost beach.

There was so much I didn't know about him. He had been a boy before he was a man, a simple deckhand before a captain, a lover before a father. Lyr below, he'd been to *Hiraeth* and back and never breathed a word of it to me, or perhaps to anyone.

It wasn't the only secret he'd kept from me.

I had accepted the fact that I didn't know my mother long ago. Without even the slightest idea of who she was, there was nothing to miss, but she wasn't my only parent veiled in mystery.

Maybe finding out how Papa died didn't actually solve the problem. Perhaps my real goal was to learn more about how he lived.

Perhaps I'd know for sure after I brought Papa's killer to justice.

Ronan cleared his throat, bringing me back to the island. "There isn't much else here." He picked up another dislodged piece of shiplap, examining it closer. "This wreck has to be at least twenty years old. Even the island doesn't have enough magic to preserve it for that long." He tossed the useless piece of wood back into the sand.

I nodded, part of me still a thousand miles and a quarter of a century away. "Aye, but I'm still glad we found it." My throat bobbed, but I swallowed back the scoundrel tears that had been threatening to spill over for the last half hour. "It's almost as good as finding Papa again."

Ronan pulled me to him and wrapped his long arms around me. I let an errant tear slide down my face as he pressed me to his coat and mumbled into my damp hair, "Almost as good as finding his killer?"

His words were a flint against a wick, reigniting the anger that had died down in my heart.

Today had been a gift. This glimpse into Papa's past was a reminder of where he came from, the same salt and steel and sea I was born to inherit.

But someone had stolen his future. My future with him. I was owed a debt no amount of nostalgia could settle.

I pulled away, venom dripping from my fangs. "No, not as good as that. We still have another shipwreck to find."

Ronan matched my steel with his, determination settling on his brow. "Aye, and fast. We don't have much light left."

Just as the fire started in my core, a red flare lit the sky, setting the horizon ablaze.

Ronan snapped around, a dark look clouding his expression. "Let's hope that's an answer to our prayers, not trouble."

We ran due north as fast as our feet could carry us toward the flare, the smoke signal still swirling high above the treetops.

I did not pause to note the flowers or the smells, the cacophony of distractions whizzing by me as I wove through them. I did not falter when I tripped, or when branches and thorns scratched at my limbs. I just kept moving, wishing that I was running toward an answer, too afraid of the alternative.

Every other unsure footstep, I mouthed a prayer to Lyr, the thought of how many things could've possibly gone wrong running through my head. *Let this be a good signal. Let them be all right.*

The sight of a tall redhead standing straight as we burst through another beachy clearing was enough to ease my frantic pulse.

"Griffin!" I threw myself at my cousin and wrapped him in a vise-grip of a hug. I breathed him in, never imagining I'd be grateful for the scent of his sweat. I loosened my grip, holding him at arm's length to appraise him. "Griffin, are you all right?"

He was the picture of good health, the mischief in his eyes brighter than ever. "More than all right, I won."

"You cheated," Rhett grumbled behind him, drawing my eyes from my cousin to what actually stood behind him.

My mouth went drier than the inside of a stone. "You found it."

This time, the wreck was unmistakable, even if the parts were so scattered it barely resembled a ship anymore. Deep red paint covered the wood, still as fresh as the day I sank the damned thing. The distinctive dragonhead, once attached to the bow, snarled up at us from her place in the sand, proclaiming her master for all the Deyrnas to see.

Ddraig y Mab. Dragon's Son. Ronan's first ship.

The ship Papa died on. The ship that would sink his killer, too.

My eyes flicked to my cousin, his cocky smile still plastered on his face. He tapped the hilt of one of his swords. "Truth here has a keen eye."

I gripped Griffin's shoulder if only to steady myself as the world swayed beneath me. "Griffin, I never thought I'd say it, but you're a genius."

Ronan stumbled toward the wreck, looking as pale as I felt.

Last time he saw this ship, he lost everything. Now, it held the key to everything he had to gain. I moved to him, his pain my own, his joy and hope mine, too. I slipped my hand into his, squeezing it tightly.

He broke from his trance to address his cousin. "Have you had a look around? Anything of use?"

I held my breath as I waited for an answer. Rhett glanced back to Griffin, who nodded once. I blinked twice at the action, the strange partnership that had somehow formed between them, but that was a question for another island. Rhett jerked his head toward the wreckage, signaling us to follow. "It's...better if we show you."

They led us through and over fallen sails and jagged stakes. I followed, my legs somehow working beneath me, even though the rest of me felt like I'd been in Pysgoddian waters for a month. Frozen.

Griffin stopped in front of the remains of the foremast, her red wood in pristine condition. And in front of her, laid down on a scrap of cloth, an obsidian-hilted dagger with a sapphire eye.

"We found it embedded in the mast." Griffin pointed, but did not dare touch it. "When the main beam split, she must have fallen just the right way…"

Rhett's voice was dangerously low as he crossed his arms in front of him, shaking his head in awed disbelief. "I don't understand how, but it still has bloodstains."

I stared at the dagger, at the dried, brown blood that sure as rain still coated the steel.

Papa's blood.

I swallowed back the bile that rose to my throat. The sapphire called to me, begging me to remember it, like I'd known it before. But every part of me was numb, my ears ringing like someone had fired a cannon next to my head. The world spun.

Ronan crouched down, studying it closer. "So, we've got a murder weapon, but no idea who it belongs to." Without touching the dagger itself, he picked it up with the cloth, holding it up in the fading sunlight. "Nice start, boys."

And as the sun glinted off the blackness of the obsidian, I remembered.

My heart sank like the wreckage before me.

"We know." I barely recognized my own voice as the words slipped out, as the world tilted yet again.

"What?" Ronan's voice cut through the numbness, awakening the anger.

My chest swirled, the storm roaring to life inside me.

I knew.

My stomach lurched as I fumbled with shaking fingers for the lifeline in my pocket, praying to any god listening that I was wrong. I'd never wanted to be more wrong in my life. I *had* to be wrong.

I knew I was not.

"Keira, what's going on?" Griffin's voice sounded a million leagues away as I finally unfolded the last crease of the picture.

Everything stopped, including my heart. With the last of my control, I pointed to the picture.

To where that same dagger sat prettily on young Aidan's hip.

26

Whispers and Wounds

My head spun, vomit burning my throat as my stomach emptied onto the sand. Limbs shaking, I went blind to the island around me, deaf to the indiscriminate curses of Griffin and Rhett, numb to Ronan's hand on my back.

I was nothing and no one. I'd been stripped of my senses and my identity, ignoring the truth that had stared me in the face for years.

I relished the emptiness. I knew what waited on the other end of it. Knew what I had to face.

Knew Aidan killed Papa.

My uncle killed my father.

And for what? The question burned through me, searing every exposed edge. What was my father's life worth? A captain's coat?

No, I could not dwell on the why, not now. I swallowed the sickness down before it could reach my lips a second time.

My husband's voice pulled me from the edge of oblivion. "You all right, Keira girl?"

"Are you?" My voice was as acerbic as the bile that stained the sand at my feet.

"No." His shoulders slumped, the admission stealing the last of his strength. "I'd feel much better if we weren't stuck here."

I tried not to let the panic seize me as I registered his words.

Stuck on the island of lost things. Of things that go bump in the night.

Stuck in this reality. In the truth of what Aidan did, the proof now strapped to Griffin's belt.

My breath came sharply, piercing my lungs with each inhale. "Then let's get back to the ship," I managed between painful breaths. I needed to escape, both the hellscape of *Hiraeth* and my head. "I never want to see this fucking island again."

A hand steadied me before I could take a stumbling step. "Not when it's getting dark. We are too deep in this jungle to make it back to the ship before nightfall." Ronan's gaze was steeped in pity, but his voice was firm. "As much as I hate this, it's the safer choice to hunker down here rather than wander blindly."

Panic threatened to surge again. I wrenched my arm from my husband's grasp. I needed to move, to run, to do something. Anything to stop feeling like the entire island was about to collapse around me and swallow me whole.

"You're in charge." I didn't—*couldn't*—look back to see the hurt I knew was blooming on his face as I fled toward the treeline. "I'll go get some firewood."

It was a petty excuse, but it was all I could manage as I wandered into the tangled greenery. Once I was out of sight, I collapsed onto the moss floor of the jungle, the colors and smells of the island a blanket over me.

Four years. Four years of blaming the only man I'd ever truly cared for, four years of killing his family off one by one in cold retaliation. Four years admiring my uncle, following his every footstep, begging for his praise. Four years of turning a blind eye to the truth, of ignoring the lies and avoiding the reality.

Four years *thanking* my father's killer for all the good he'd done for me.

I let the cool ground envelop me as the sobs came freely now, a waterfall breaking over the dam of my control. I fed the plants around me with my tears, sinking into the dirt floor as I lost myself to the isle of lost things. I let *Hiraeth* swallow my sorrow, my fear, my unending fury, until I was a shell, nothing more than the husk of a shipwreck washed upon her shores. Until I was empty.

It was hours later when my cousin's voice reminded me of myself, the sun long abandoning me to *Hiraeth's* darkness. "Ah, I was wondering where you'd run off to," he said as he spotted me in the small pool of his torchlight.

"Please, Griffin." My voice was hoarse and foreign. "Give me some space."

"I'm not here to talk, Keira." Griffin offered a smile, but it looked as shallow as I felt. He sank into the ground next to me, his heat comforting against the cold of night. "Just here to sit."

We stayed like that for hours or for minutes, I didn't know, just basking in the flickering torchlight, trying to hold ourselves together.

Eventually, Griffin cleared his throat, piercing the blanketing silence. "Why do you think he did it?"

My stomach threatened to empty itself again. "Griffin…"

He waved off my protest, face twisting in a discomfort that matched mine. "I know, it's impossible to answer. It just doesn't seem real. No matter how many times I go over it in my head, I can't grasp it. It's *Aidan*, for Lyr's sake. I might have believed Weylin capable, or even my Pa on a bad day. But *Aidan*? The dagger doesn't fit—"

The crack of twigs caught my attention, a welcome distraction, my senses crashing back into me. "Shut up, Griffin," I growled, hair prickling at the back of my neck.

"Keira, we have to talk about this eventually." Hurt colored his voice, but I held a hand to silence him.

"No, shut up," I commanded, my eyes straining in the dark. Another crack sounded, closer this time. "Did you hear that?"

Griffin nodded in response, muscles tense as he scanned the trees. I reached for the dagger at my hip, quietly readying myself for whatever lurked.

That's when I heard it.

Duweni….

The voice—no, voices, dozens of them in unison—not in my head for once, but *real*, hissing the strange name. I gripped my dagger tighter, jolting to standing, searching for any sign of life in the fading light.

"What the fu—?" Griffin's eyes went wide as the sound ricocheted off the looming trees, just as the voices echoed around us again, louder this time. Closer.

Ariannad.

A long, dark shadow burst through our meager light before we could react, black scales and ivory teeth latching onto Griffin's forearm.

His agonized bellow ripped the night as fangs sank into flesh, Griffin flailing to shake it off. I skewered the writhing, legless creature with my dagger, and yanked it off him, flinging it back into the darkness. "You all right?"

"Fine." Griffin grimaced, bracing the wound on his arm. Before I could tend to him, the hissing flared again, more and more voices adding to the nightmarish symphony.

Keeeeeirraaaaaaa.

I braced myself against my cousin's back, one hand clenched around my dagger, the other holding the torch out, every inch of me tensed and ready for the slimy beasts. They came in droves of five or six this time, slithering across the ground faster than anything I'd ever seen before, fangs exposed.

I inhaled sharply, swinging the torch before me. "Stay back, you little shits, or I'll set fire to you!"

The snake in the front of the rest hissed again, drawing back, ready to strike.

Until another, very *human* voice, cried out just beyond the trees.

The snake halted, then withdrew, the rest of the den retreating into the shadows once more.

Out of terror, or perhaps sheer curiosity, I took a step toward the voice, firelight casting long shadows in front of me. "Who—who's out there?" I called as I peered into the darkness.

I nearly jumped out of my skin when I locked eyes with a woman. She hid behind a nearby tree, peering from behind it with huge grey eyes and pale skin, stark against the blackness.

I blinked in shock, and then she was gone, not a trace of her presence left in the wavering light. I opened my mouth to call after her, if she was even real, but another voice broke the quiet.

"Keira, Griffin!" Ronan emerged through the trees, right where the woman had been a moment before. Had she been real, he would've seen her, would've bumped right into her...

I shook off the cold feeling that crept up my spine, and instead barreled toward my husband, sheathing my dagger and grabbing his outstretched hand.

"Are you hurt?" He held me closer, inspecting me for injury.

"I'm fine." I swallowed down the memory of the girl in the trees, returning to my corporeality. I swiveled towards my cousin, terror reaching down my throat again. "Griffin?"

Griffin winced slightly as I took his arm, but he covered it with a grin. "Little fucker got my arm, whatever it was, but I'm fine."

"A *neid*." Ronan cursed, shaking his head. The shadow of a memory crawled across his expression. "Talking snakes. Annoying little things. You're lucky it wasn't their larger, venomous cousin." He straightened, rolling back his shoulders and shedding whatever reminder had plagued him. Gingerly, he took the torch from me. "Let's get back to camp."

Griffin followed as Ronan led, but I hesitated, the phantom grey eyes still burning in my mind.

"I think I saw something..." I hedged, not wanting to sound absolutely insane. "Someone. A woman."

"The island plays tricks like that." Ronan rubbed a soothing hand over my back, but I didn't miss the concern flash through his eyes.

Lyr below, I *was* crazy. Ronan did not need my hysterical hallucinations to contend with as well tonight, not with the very real monsters that hid in the underbrush of this gods-forsaken place.

This time, I let him lead me, his hand on the small of my back relaxing away the tension there.

After a dozen paces or so, we made it back to the camp Ronan and Rhett had made for us, a small fire and some vegetation laid out to resemble a bedroll. Rhett was resting against one of them, but he shot to his feet at the sight of us. His eyes narrowed to the wound on Griffin's forearm, still trickling blood.

"You're hurt." His voice was stone as he rushed to my cousin's side.

"Just a scratch, I'll be fine." Griffin swatted him away, but softened, letting him inspect the bite marks.

"Let me see to it," Rhett insisted, his mask of indifference completely discarded. "You'll be useless in the morning if I don't, and I can't have you slowing us down. I want to get out of this nightmare." His words were sharp, but they lacked force, a flimsy facade.

Something warm stirred in me at the backward display of affection, at the two families made whole again, two unlikely friends a force against the history that plagued us.

The feeling sputtered out like a candle in the wind as I remembered the reason for their schism.

I'd forgotten. For just a moment, I'd been distracted enough by the voices and the snakes and the ghostly eyes to forget.

I would not forget ever again.

"I'll take first watch," I offered, plopping down on the outskirt of our encampment, bringing my knees to my chest. I'd let Rhett tend to Griffin, let Ronan tend the fire…I needed to tend to the rupture fracturing in my own chest, carving a cavernous hole inside me.

Ronan's footsteps followed a few moments later. "Keira, I know this place better than anyone, let me—"

"It's my watch." I cut him off before he could finish, staring absently into the dark. I hated shutting him out, but I wasn't ready for the alternative.

"Then let me at least keep you company." His weight shifted, uncertainty saturating his voice.

I looked to him, to the deep lines of worry creasing his forehead, to the hitch of his broad shoulders. He didn't deserve my walls, but I could not breach them tonight. I managed a smile, delicate as it was. "We'll need you to get us back to the ship in the morning. Get some rest."

Clever as ever, he heard the lie for what it was but didn't press further. "Goodnight, Mrs. Mathonwy," he mumbled, chest deflating, and fell back toward the encampment.

When his snores finally joined the chorus of the island, the hooting and howling and hissing, I let my sobs sing the harmony.

27

Hurricanes and Heartbreaks

I was barely conscious as we made our way back to the ship, the sleeplessness of the night before drooping my eyes, and the revelation of my uncle's betrayal weighing heavily on my heart.

The garish light of morning had roused the others, all eager to be rid of this nightmare. They had each stolen a few hours of sleep, but the eerie hisses and howls of the island's nighttime residents had kept them from deeper slumber.

I didn't so much as shut my eyes the whole night. I couldn't. Not when the nightmares were real. Not when there were beasts lurking in the shadows, their insidious voices calling to me.

Duweni. Ariannad. Same same same.

Not when the real monster shared my flesh and blood, wore my colors, and called himself my uncle.

When we finally crawled out of the vines and boarded the ship—*Papa's ship*—the dam holding back the ocean of my rage threatened to burst. Somehow it held as I bit my lip and squared my shoulders, and we set forth into the morning without a look back.

"They're back!" Reagan's cry of joy pierced the early morning air as she launched herself at Ronan, wrapping him in a hug.

"Aye, little dragon." Ronan smiled for the first time since we'd left the ship as he smoothed his cousin's curls.

"We were worried." Saeth's keen eyes scanned our disheveled forms for signs of struggle. "Everyone in one piece?"

She looked to me for an answer, but I had none.

I did not make it back in one piece. I'd left behind a part of myself on the pink sands of *Hiraeth*, one I'd never get back. The piece my uncle robbed from me, ripping it from my chest when he slit my father's throat.

When I didn't respond, Rhett cleared his throat. "A little snake took a bite out of Griffin, but otherwise, we're fine. You and Ellian?"

Relief washed over Saeth, softening the sharpness of her angles. "We made it back last night."

"Roland kept us calm and fed. Don't worry, Captain." Ellian grinned as he approached, looking healthy and well-rested.

Reassurance swept through me, but it was marred by a glimmer of envy. Envy that they did not know the crushing weight that saddled me now. But they would know. There was no putting it off any longer. We had come too far to look back.

When Griffin finally pulled the dagger and picture from his inside pocket to show them what we found, their laughter dissipated. They all hissed and howled and raged together, curses flying and tears streaming.

I wished I could join them, wished I could scream and cry and pound my chest. I couldn't.

My rage was quiet. It simmered inside me, swirling and boiling, begging for an escape. I gave it none.

I was saving every last drop of it for him.

The storms came as soon as *Hiraeth* was out of eyesight. Thunder clapped and streaks of white-hot lightning lit the sky. They sang the song of my fury, the pounding rain against the deck of the *Ceffyl* a war drum driving me forward. The ship creaked and rocked against the vicious dance of the waves, water toppling over the railing from every side. A sailor with any sense would've sent everyone belowdecks, but I would not let a single minute go to waste.

Not when this storm was mine, an answer to my bitterness. Not when I had a score to settle.

I needed to be back in Porthladd. I needed to see his face when we presented the dagger, needed the truth in front of me.

"Can we move any faster?" I called out to my rain-soaked crew. I had not left the helm in hours or days—whichever, I knew and cared not.

Griffin yelled back over the roaring wind, his red curls plastered to his forehead, "Keira, in this blasted weather? You know we shouldn't! Rhett is in the crow's nest and he can barely see fifty paces ahead. We can't make out a heading. We need to be battening down, not pushing forward."

"Fine," I spat against the rain, "but once the storm passes, I want us at full sail."

Ronan's voice tugged at my attention. "Keira, you should rest. Maybe eat something."

I turned to him reluctantly, his furrowed brow sending another pang of guilt through my core. The last thing I wanted was for him to worry. Not when he had been marked with so much pain already. He was another of Aidan's victims and he deserved so much better. He deserved nothing but sandy beaches and sunsets, surrounded by wealth and a family that didn't stab each other in the neck.

But if I let myself feel for him, feel anything at all, I would not be able to stop the tidal wave from washing me away.

"I'm not hungry." My voice was curt. If I let him too close, he'd be swept away, too.

Ronan persisted, grabbing the wheel with a firm grip. "It's been over a day since you've eaten or slept, Keira girl." He dared raise a hand and tuck a strand of sopping wet hair behind my ear. His sapphire eyes warmed me from within, the love in them too potent for me to handle. "A hunger strike isn't going to make anything better."

The feather-light touch of his fingers ripped a tear into the hold I had over my feelings. My throat bobbed, anger rising, searing hot. "How am I supposed to have an appetite when my uncle, when my own *kin*…"

I stopped myself, patching up the hole with another layer of ice and apathy.

He let go of the wheel, shoving his hands deep into his pockets, his expression pained. "We don't know for sure that's what happened. Someone could have stolen the knife…"

"We do know, Ronan," I growled, not at him but at the world. The storm around us quickened, the wind howling. My own head swam, all the ugly truths floating in front of my face. When I found the words, my voice was a deadly calm against the raging within. "Aidan was the one who woke me up that night. I never thought about it, never questioned him...but why would he have wasted time waking me up instead of trying to save Papa himself? I knew, I knew all along, but I was too much of a coward to admit it." I shook as I fought to hold back the tears. I would save every one of them for Aidan and Aidan alone. I inhaled sharply, letting the storm-scented air cool the burning core. When I met my husband's gaze, I was made of stone once more. "I was blind, Ronan. Blind and foolishly loyal. Not anymore."

"I hope for his sake, there is more to the story." Ronan offered a half-hearted smile, the action meant to soothe, but it only grated against my nerves like steel.

"He was his *brother!*" The tether broke as I slammed my fist against the wheel, slicing open the skin across my knuckles. I could not feel it, only the excruciating burning in my soul as the words found their way out of my throat like a dragon's breath. "There is no excuse. And all this time, he let me believe it was you and your family. Our pain, our loss, the blood on both sides, this entire war is *his fucking fault*. And he will pay for his treachery."

Ellian interrupted my tirade, darting up the stairs to the gallery two at a time, nearly slipping on the last one. Terror was clear in his eyes as he approached like a madman on a mission. "Captain, something is wrong."

"Aye, dreadfully wrong," I bit back, covering my bloodied hand.

He gripped my shoulders, nails digging into my flesh, the desperation shocking on a man so composed. "No, Keira, something *smells* wrong, I—"

He stopped mid-sentence, his head whipping toward a sound I did not hear. I followed his gaze, to where a Porthladdian war ship crested over a wave.

Before I could open my mouth, a cannonball tore through the starboard railing, splintered wood scattering across the deck.

Rhett's warning came not a moment later, the bell sounding in time with the thunderclaps above. "We're under attack!"

28

Warriors and Wolves

My sword was in my hand in a second, my legs barreling down from the main deck the next, Ellian and Ronan hot on my heels. Rhett was already descending from the mainmast, ropes burning through his hands as he continued his warning call. "Hostiles, starboard side!"

I sprinted across the rain-soaked deck to the spyglass, pressing the cold metal to my eye to survey our adversary. Raindrops clouded my sightline, but the outline of the ship was unmistakable. She was unnamed but Porthladdian for sure, her shape straight from the eastern docks. Black sails flew against the wind, a risk in this weather, but she held her heading.

Privateers. And she was going to ram us.

Griffin slid down from the rigging, reaching the dark conclusion at the same time I did. "We've got incoming."

A young voice pulled me back to my own ship. "What's going on?" Reagan leaned over the rail, squinting at the boat.

Ronan stormed toward her, pistol at his hip and fire in his eyes. "Reagan, get below deck, *now.*"

"I'm not leaving." Her eyes held not a trace of fear, but I could not say the same for my own.

I did not have time to argue. Grabbing her tiny wrist, I dragged her toward the cabin. She kicked at me, but I did not let go until I pushed her at a wide-eyed Saeth. "Take her to the brig and hide, both of you. If we start taking water, get to a lifeboat, but do not leave that hull under any other circumstances, clear?"

Saeth nodded once, biting her bottom lip, then grabbed Reagan's arm. "Aye, Captain. Be careful."

I pressed a quick kiss to her cheek and patted Reagan's head. It wasn't a goodbye, but a blessing that we'd see each other again. I'd never forgive myself if something happened to either of them. I pulled the second dagger from my boot, pressing the cold hilt into Saeth's palm. "If all else fails, go for the throat. Lyr keep you both."

Saeth ushered a pouting Reagan belowdecks, my chest tight. I was glad for the rain as tears slid down my cheeks.

I did not have time to contemplate my feelings as the second warning bell rang, Griffin's panicked bellow sounding with it. "Cannons! Everybody down, NOW!"

I fell to my stomach just as the second cannonball whizzed past my head, luckily missing the structure of the ship. In another second I was back on my feet, my limbs moving on their own, every instinct I'd been trained for singing through my veins. "Griffin, Rhett, get on those guns immediately!"

The fear had fled my voice. My only thoughts were the task: get everyone armed and prepare for impact.

I ran to the supply hatch, wrenching it open in a single pull, grabbing the extra weapons below. I did not feel the ache of my limbs or the cold rain plastering my hair to my forehead; only my heart pounding in my ears, the steady drum of war.

I surveyed the crew. Roland was at the helm, keeping her steady. He had his sword out, but he'd need something with more distance, like a pistol or crossbow. Griffin had both his swords still sheathed as he rolled the heavy balls toward the cannons, Rhett with a longsword at his side. They'd be all right, even better if they could start firing those damned contraptions.

Only Ronan and Ellian stood without purpose, a single pistol the only weapon between them. I'd need their help to run supplies, but they'd need heavier artillery. I grabbed what I could from the hatch and sprinted toward my husband, the steel in my arms anchoring me to my resolve. "You two, with me—"

Impact rocked the ship from the port side, knocking me off my feet. My knees skidded across the wooden planks, the weapons clattering out of my hands and across the deck. I winced at the sharp scrape and scrambled for a sword in front of me, shuffling to my feet again. I whipped around toward the disturbance that felled me, only to receive another rude awakening.

We'd been so preoccupied with the incoming warship on the starboard side, we hadn't noticed the cutter approaching the port, cannons ready and grappling hooks already hurtling toward us.

They were going to board.

"Eyes to port! We've got company!" The shout tore from my throat as I ran for the hooks, hoping to dislodge them before their masters could board—but I knew it was futile.

The first sailor jumped over the rail before I was halfway to it. My boots dug into wood as I skidded to a halt, wrenching my dagger from my belt.

No more running. My sword in my left hand and my dagger in my right, it was time to stand and fight.

The sailor was impossibly tall, her obsidian skin bleeding into the night around us, every inch of her sheathed in elegant, corded muscle. Despite the chill in the air and the rain soaking us all, she wore practically nothing, only a thin white band of fabric around her chest and a lion's pelt around her waist. Metal hooks accented her braided hair, enough to decorate a sail. A brilliant white smile carved her face as three equally imposing warriors hit the deck with thuds, then another six behind them.

Tannians. And from the look of the sharp, bronze-plated spears in their hands, mean ones.

Everyone on the ship went still, all focused on the doom in front of us.

I pushed back the fear that rose in my throat. "Get off my ship," I growled at the first woman, the obvious leader by the way the rest of them flanked her. My knuckles went white around my weapons. I was born of sea and steel, but even I was a second-class warrior when it came to the legendary Tannian assassins.

The woman cocked her head to the side. "Your ship? I heard you stole it." Her accent was thick, her voice as sandy as the desert she came from. She cracked her neck, gripping her spear with both hands. "Surrender, and we won't blow a hole in it. Our employer would prefer we keep it intact."

My heart stopped as I guessed at the only person who might have employed Tannians to fetch their precious ship. A ship they had killed for in the past.

I cursed my uncle's name to the Otherworld. He did not deserve the title of Captain, let alone the name of Branwen.

A lethal calm washed over me, my rage turning icy. I was both Branwen and Mathonwy, my father's daughter, and the true Captain of this vessel. In all the ways it mattered, this was my ship, my crew. Tannians or not, my uncle would not take it from me without a fight.

The mask slipped over me easily, the familiarity sending a wave of excitement through my core. I smirked at the leader, turning my dagger over in my hand once. "Sorry to disappoint your employer, but we aren't going down easy." Ronan stepped closer to me, his presence fortifying my nerves. I pointed my dagger at the woman, my voice low and lethal. "But you're not the only one with cannons, and you seem a far fetch from home."

"We have you surrounded and outmanned," a man directly to her left called with an accent thicker than blood, his voice deep and commanding. He looked at his leader, his eyes brimming with pride and predatory fondness. "And we were not paid to take prisoners."

I surveyed the man with disdain, my Mathonwy smirk unwavering. He was her second, then, and perhaps something more. I'd take his head first.

Ronan cleared his throat beside me, raising his sword and pointing it at the leader, danger dripping from every inch of him. "Aye, but we have a few tricks of our own."

The woman did not flinch, only tucked the spear under her arm, the sharp end pointed at my chest. Her smile widened into a snarl. "So be it, then. I did warn you."

Her spear was faster than lightning as she brought it down on me, so quick I barely had time to lift my sword to defend myself. I stumbled back to catch my balance, but she was on me again, a sharp kick to my abdomen sending me tumbling across the deck.

I tightened my grip on the hilt this time, ready for her as she lunged. I parried when she swung her spear, the steel of my sword clanging against her bronze. More metal sang around us as her crew engaged mine, but I didn't have time to gauge how they were faring before she lunged again. I swung my legs around, catching her feet, but she was agile as a mountain cat, her balance unshakeable as she sprang over me.

At least I had time to get back to my feet, dagger swinging. She dodged it easily, but while she was faster than me, she wasn't smarter. When she parried my attack, I dropped my dagger and grabbed her spear with one hand, ignoring the burning where the metal sliced open my palm. Shock spread across her features, and in the moment of her surprise, I yanked the spear, my knee connecting with her abdomen with a sickening thud. Hopefully, I bruised at least one of her ribs.

She keeled over in pain, the wind knocked from her sails, but I knew it wouldn't last long. I threw her spear across the deck, picking up my dagger. Spinning again, I brought my foot across her face in a sharp kick. Her head lolled to the side for a moment, giving me a crucial second to check on my crew.

Roland was at the mast, his sword slow as he battled two Tannians, each six inches over his height. Judging his wild expression, I knew the man would last, at least for another few minutes. Near the stern, Ellian had found himself a set of axes, which he was flinging with expert accuracy at a very surprised male warrior and his female companion. Ronan was five paces to my left, sparring with the brutish second, his pistol still at his hip. The self-righteous bastard would only shoot if there was no other way, which meant he still had the upper hand. My heart ached for him, wanting nothing more than to be at his side, but there were more pressing matters.

To the starboard side, chaos erupted. The warship was nearly upon us, and I knew if we didn't start firing, we'd be facing far more than eight.

The cannons were in place, but neither Rhett nor Griffin manned them, each swinging their swords, surrounded by four Tannian spears. I ran toward them, sliding on my knees despite the sting and coming up behind the Tannian assailants, slashing the backs of their legs as I moved. Two of them cried out in pain as they fell to the deck. I swung around, silencing the first one's cries with my blade against their throat. The second, realizing the source of his anguish, bared his teeth and lunged.

Strong hands clasped around my neck. I gasped for air but only for a moment as my cousin's sword severed the hands from their wrists, the second Tannian's screams piercing the night before his eyes rolled to the back of his head and he dropped, consumed by the agony. The hands fell into the pool of blood around me, and I kicked them as I stumbled to my feet again. I nodded to Griffin, wiping the blood from my sword on my sleeve, but we didn't have time to stop and catch our breath.

Rhett, who had been occupying the last two Tannians, a man and a woman, let out a snarl as a spear lodged itself in his thigh. But a Mathonwy grin spread across his face as he held the weapon in place, his stunned male opponent now unarmed. Griffin was at his side in less than a breath, his twin swords a whirlwind as he relieved the head from the defenseless Tannian's shoulders. Blood sprayed Rhett's coat, deepening the red. My sword clashed against the woman's spear simultaneously, but when her companion's head rolled into her foot, her disgust and distraction was all the advantage I needed to push her back and over the rail, down into the deep.

The familiar smack of her body against water was the only confirmation I needed. I whipped around to my cousins, not looking at the severed body parts at my feet. Griffin's eyes met mine, their usual amber now red with rage. He was the god of war embodied, Truth and Triumph his tools of death and destruction, and Lyr below, I was grateful for them both.

I did not have time to thank or fear him as another cannonball crashed into the foremast, shaking the entire ship. A crack ran down her frame, but she did not collapse.

Yet.

I could handle yet.

"Rhett, we have to load the cannons. If we don't sink that warship before they hit, they'll just keep coming." Terror boomed in my chest, but I tried to keep my commands calm and clear. It was my duty to see us through this, for those above deck and below. I sheathed my blades and moved to the first cannon, readying her for fire. "Griffin, put those swords to use and go give Roland some coverage so he can get this damned boat in position."

"Aye, Captain!" Rhett viciously yanked the spear from his thigh, then stumbled to shift the cannonball into its place.

The red in Griffin's eyes dissolved as he narrowed them at Rhett's leg, concern in the set of his lips. "Can you handle this?"

Rhett waved him off. "It looks worse than it is; go help my Pa."

I fired a stern look at Griffin as I heaved against the heavy cannon, pushing it back through the siding. "I'm here with him, Griff, now go."

He moved without another word, his purpose radiating through his strong back.

I looked to Rhett, to the blood dripping down his trousers. "Are you actually all right?"

He winked, the casual gesture so strange on his usually stony expression. "I will be when we sink that fucker."

I blinked twice. Perhaps the pain had made him delirious, but he held steady and grabbed the flint from its holder, ready to strike the wick.

Seizing the wick, I closed my eyes and focused in on my power, imagining the water droplets that soaked it evaporating into the air. I opened them again, the bone-dry wick ready. "Fire."

Rhett lit the wick with a smile and covered his ears. I followed suit, the resounding *boom* a victory cry.

Our eyes followed the cannonball, watching it make its mark straight in the wooden hull of the ship. An actual cry of hope escaped my lips at that. We'd need a few more to sink her, but perhaps we were not as hopeless as I had imagined.

Rhett's gasp of pain tore the hope from my chest.

I whirled around to see him prone on the deck, the Tannian leader digging her heel into his wound. Rhett thrashed to strike her, but she stomped on the wound again; this time his eyes fluttered into the back of his head and his body went limp, smacking against the deck as his consciousness faded.

"You'll regret that," I snarled, tearing my sword free again.

She held the sharp half of her spear in one hand and picked up Rhett's sword with the other. The cockiness was gone from her grin, replaced with pure malice. It was personal now. "I'll admit, at first I underestimated you. I won't make the same mistake twice. It would seem my employer wants me to earn my keep."

Our swords clashed together once more, each of her blows as heavy as they were fast. I gasped for breath under the anvil of her swings, barely blocking each one, my limbs protesting every time.

And she was only getting started. With a heavy downswing paired with a jab at my side I had to jump to avoid, she had me where she wanted me. Fast, far too fast, she brought an elbow across my face.

Stars swirled around my eyes, cheek stinging. I stumbled back, catching myself on the rail, but she brought her knee to my side, pain erupting where she struck.

She glared at me like a cat playing with its food. "You should've surrendered when you had the chance. Such a terrible waste of life." This time, she raised her sword, ready to end her game. But my limbs somehow found themselves, sidestepping as her blade lodged itself into the railing.

Lightning coursed through my veins. Pain still sang through me, but I would not die here. Not so close to the finish line. Not with so many depending on me.

I wiped the blood from my cheek as she struggled to free her blade. "You should talk less next time, you would've had me."

With a final tug, the steel sprang free. Determined to make me mark my words, the sword's tip grazed my arm in a bullet-fast swipe. I yelped in pain, and her responding chuckle was darker than the night around us. "You're already mine."

Another blow across my face with the pommel of the sword, so hard I was spitting blood. I tumbled to the deck, the wood splitting open the skin of my palms as I caught myself. Unyielding, she stepped on the hand still clutching my dagger, until a sick crack made my fingers go slack. I couldn't help the moan that escaped my lips as she kicked my dagger across the deck, disarming me before another kick connected with my ribs.

"Keira!" Ronan's voice was an arrow through the pain, somehow piercing the ringing in my ears. Instinctively, I reached for him, the outline of his body blurring as the pain set fire to my veins. I could feel the power rumbling in my chest, the small, healing part of it working to mend my broken parts, but it was too slow.

The woman grabbed me and turned me over, clutching my collar in her fists, her breath hot on me. "You think you're a warrior, but you are soft. Weak." I dug my nails into her wrists, wriggling to free myself, but she held firm and licked her lips, a predator about to devour its prey. "As is the rest of your crew. This was not personal, only business. But now? I will delight in tearing them all to shreds like you did mine."

My fury took over, the throbbing instantly numb. I would protect my crew until my last breath, even if they were numbered.

I let go of her wrist only to wrap my good hand around her throat, pulling myself closer to her. "You touch them, and I'll drag you to the Otherworld myself."

She blinked in surprise, a small choking noise escaping her lips, but she still had the advantage, her knee pressing into my bruised ribs. I bit back my screams as she spat in my face, drawing her knife to my throat. "I was going to make you watch, but I tire of your mouth."

Before she could slice open my throat, a deafening howl from the port side drew our attention.

To where Ellian's flesh was ripping from his body, bones cracking and fur spreading. Until a familiar green-eyed *blaidd* took his place, snarling in our direction.

29

Swordfights and Sea-dragons

The woman scrambled off me, midnight eyes wide with terror as she clasped her blade tightly. "Shifter," she hissed at the *blaidd*. "Betraying your own blood. You dishonor us."

No, not a *blaidd*. A *faoladh*—a shifter.

And not just any shifter. *Ellian.*

The whole ship went still, my crew and the Tannians, as they regarded the massive animal in front of them. My jaw dropped as realization dawned on me. The *blaidd* at the spring, Esme talking in the woods, Connor's office, Ellian's uncanny ability to know things he shouldn't…

Just like that day on the sand, the primal voice slid into my head, Ellian's green eyes meeting mine. *Explain later. Go check on Rhett and get those cannons going.*

I did not waste his gift as I crawled from my spot on the deck to where Rhett still lay unconscious. Every muscle screamed in agony as I moved, slow and sluggish, but I would not fail again. Ellian leaped into action at the same time I did, cornering the terrified woman with another ferocious roar.

As much as I wanted to watch him rip her to shreds, I focused my attention on Rhett. His eyes were shut, blood still seeping from his leg, the tan of his trousers now redder than his coat. I cursed under my breath. Patting the side of his face, I focused my power into my palm, like I had with Ronan at the spring. "Come on, Rhett, you're missing all the fun," I whispered as the warm tingles caressed my fingers, spreading from my core all the way to where my hand touched his cheek.

Rhett's eyes fluttered open, blinking back pain. He winced as he sat up.

I loosed a sigh of relief and moved my hands to his leg. "You all right there, big guy?" My power rippled through me again as his warm blood coated my palms. My own warmth answered, the flow slowing as the energy seeped from my fingertips into his leg. The work was shoddy, blood still trickling from a nasty cut, but it would hold.

Rhett's eyes went wide as he regarded my reddened hands. "Never better."

I wiped my hands on my trousers, their color now Mathonwy red to compliment my Branwen blue. I winked once, already moving toward the cannons. "Feel like sinking a ship with me?"

"I'd be honored," Rhett answered quickly, the dutiful soldier recognizing the need for speed. He did, however, glance over his shoulder once, his eyes searching for another Branwen-blue coat. "Griffin?"

I heaved against another lead cannonball, gritting my teeth against the pain that shot through my ribs. "Defending the helm."

Rhett grabbed the heavy ammunition from me, growling in frustration at my slowness, and swung around quickly to load the cannon. He nearly dropped it when he laid eyes on Ellian, who held the Tannian leader half pinned behind a crate. "What the—"

"I'll explain later. We need to move faster—"

"Agh, my rutting eye!"

My husband's cry of pain tore my focus to where he doubled up on the deck, clutching his head in agony, the Tannian second standing over him with a dark grin.

Standing over my Ronan. A sword pointed at his neck.

An anchor dropped in my gut. "Ronan!" My feet moved faster than my brain, pressing forward until an arm—Rhett's arm—caught my waist, yanking me backward.

I beat against him, screaming my husband's name again, but Rhett's sharp whisper steadied me. "Shh, he's fine, watch."

My eyes were fastened to my husband's form as the Tannian pulled back his sword, ready to strike. As Ronan's grimace of pain dissolved into a saccharine smile. As he pulled his pistol from its holster faster than the lightning illuminating the sky.

And fired it right into the Tannian's exposed heart.

It was the Tannian leader's turn to scream her fury into the sky as her second hit the deck and did not stir.

"He calls that one *live bait*," Rhett laughed as his arm released its hold.

I allowed myself another long look at the enigma that was my husband, who still smiled as he made his way toward me. Perhaps one day, I'd understand the dark corners of his cunning mind. Perhaps he really did have rotten parts. My returning grin was genuine.

Rotten and wicked, he was *mine*, and I was his.

I did not have long to think about it as another cannonball shook the ship, hitting the hull low, the entire structure groaning. I stumbled forward, smacking my knee on the metallic cannon with a sickening crack. I caught the rail as my leg gave out underneath me, the moan crawling out of my throat an answer to the agony throbbing in my knee.

I propped myself up, biting back pain as I swept over my crew, looking for other injuries. Everyone on the deck had remained upright...

A cannon blasted through my gut as I thought of the girls below. Those closest to the cannon's mark.

"Shit." My gaze met Ronan's, my terror mirrored in his expression. "Reagan and Saeth."

They had to be okay, the hull was sturdy.

But if something had gone wrong...

We won't lose anyone. It was a promise I intended to keep.

Ronan's face went as white as marble. "I'm on it." His hand grazed my cheek, a promise to return. "I love you, Keira girl."

"I—" I swallowed the curse before I could say it back. This night would not end that way. I would not damn him to the same fate as my father. "Be safe," I said instead, tearing myself from him. I waited to hear his footsteps retreat, then launched into my task once more. My leg shrieked as I moved to the cannons and crouched down, but the pain was an anchor, steadying me to my cause. I had already wasted too much time, the warship less than an arrow's breath away now. I clasped the cannon's wick without a look back. "Rhett, fire this rutting gun. Now!"

A cannon fired not a second later. It was not ours.

The warship had beat us to the quick, sending another cannonball directly our way.

Stillness swept the ship, all eyes focusing on the metallic death sentence whizzing past us, over the main deck to the gallery.

All eyes but Griffin's, whose back was turned. He still stood, defending the wheel, swinging his mighty swords at the Tannian brute in front of him. Taking his stand right in the line of fire. Fear bubbled up from the depths of my core as I reached for my cousin, but he was too far away.

Roland wasn't.

He didn't waste time as he leaped over the wheel and pushed Griffin out of the way of the cannon's blast. As he took his place instead.

Vomit surged up my throat as I watched the impact. Watched his entire chest cave as the armament, larger than his head, crushed it with a sickening smack.

"Papa! *No!*" Rhett was sliding across the deck within the next breath, abandoning the cannons next to us as he took the gallery steps two at a time to where his father lay dying.

We won't lose anyone.

My words rang through my ears, everything else around me falling silent.

I crossed the deck like a ghost, the pain in my leg somehow numb, past where Ellian still gnashed his canine teeth at the Tannian leader. Past where Griffin finally ran his sword through the remaining two assassins. Up the gallery steps, until I was knelt beside Rhett, staring into the cavern that was once Roland's midsection.

"No, no, no, hang on, come on." Rhett shook his father's shoulders, a bloody cough sputtering from the old man's disfigured core. His shoulders still rose and fell in weak, uneven breaths, but his eyes were closed. Rhett's tear-filled gaze found mine, terror brimming over the lashes. "Keira, help him! Do what you did for my leg, please!"

I looked again at the garish wound in front of me. The entire front part of Roland's chest curved inward, blood pouring out.

"Please." Rhett's voice broke over the single word.

Guilt rose to my throat like hot ash. I could knit together the flesh, but I could not reconstruct bones, or the organs crushed beneath. I swallowed back my own tears, unable to meet his pleading stare. "Rhett—"

"Gods above." Griffin finally met us, panic apparent in the slouch of his shoulders. He covered his mouth. "I'm sorry, I didn't see it—" He went to put a hand on Rhett's back.

"Get off me, no!" Rhett spat, tears carving jagged paths into the dirt and blood on his cheeks as he swatted my cousin away. "Come on, old man, you're going to be okay."

I placed a hand on Roland's shoulder, focusing the power in my palm to the spot where we connected. His energy answered back, but it wheezed in heavy breaths.

I could not save him. I had failed him as a Captain, had failed to keep my promise.

It was my fault, and I could not fix it. But I could try to ease his pain.

As I sent the thought down my arm, Roland's eyes fluttered open. His graveled voice was weak, barely a whisper through his labored breaths. "Take...take care of my boy."

Griffin knelt down, a smile on his tear-stained face. Realization was clear in his eyes, his fingers twitching at his side the proof of the truth. He was easing Roland's pain too, in his own way. In a way I could not. "You'll take care of him yourself."

Roland reached a shaky hand out, patting Griffin's forearm with bloody hands. "I guess we are even now. My debt is paid." The shadow of his once-contagious smile tugged at the corner of his bloodstained lips. "It was an honor, boy."

When his arm fell again, his chest went still, his last breath hanging in the air around us.

An inhuman cry ripped from Rhett's throat as he clasped his father's limp hand. "Papa, no, no, no, no. Shit!" He fell back onto the deck, his head in his hands as the sobs wracked through him.

Griffin brought him to his chest, wrapping his arms around his heaving shoulders. "Rhett, I'm sorry. I'm so sorry. This is my rutting fault."

I was still as I stared into Roland's empty eyes.

We won't lose anyone.

My fingers shook as I lowered his eyelids, the rain still falling like tears on his face. His energy did not answer back this time.

But mine did, a darkness stirring deep in my gut. It roared within me, churning from the very depths of my soul, from the depths of the ocean surrounding us.

I was a monster, a snake, and a liar. And I was angry, at myself and at the cruel world that had taken yet another piece of my family.

A sharp yelp pulled my attention from Roland's lifeless body. Ellian, still in his wolf form, toppled over, his fur matted with blood. His eyes met mine as he whimpered, the blow to his left flank not fatal but certainly painful. The Tannian woman snarled as she limped toward us, where we guarded our fallen friend.

She spat blood on the deck, her injuries noticeable but her smile victorious as she took in the scene. "You should've surrendered. This floating trash heap is not worth your lives." She raised an arm, covered in deep, claw-shaped gashes, toward the warship—only a spitting distance from impact now. "My friends are even meaner than I am."

In our grief and fear, we had abandoned the cannons. Ignored the larger, looming threat.

Griffin cursed under his breath. But I was no longer afraid, the monster deep within me exposing its fangs.

I was wicked and rotten, but I was born of this sea. I would not die in it. I would not sacrifice any more of my family to it. It was mine to command now.

And as I dove within myself, into those darkest, deepest parts, I felt it.

Felt *her*.

Like calling to like. My answering smile held no trace of humor. "So are mine."

The woman cocked an eyebrow, widening her stance as she prepared for another fight. I did not bother to even draw my blade as the rumbling in the deck answered the rumbling in my chest. The woman's eyes went wide, echoing my own crew's confusion as they braced for impact.

As a black-scaled, spiked head burst forth from the surface of the water, right on our starboard side, her roar louder than thunder.

Shrieks rang out from the warship as she rose from the depths, her full height taller than the masts. Lightning streaked through the clouds, outlining her gigantic silhouette, another roar shaking the night. The answering cries could be heard even from across the waves "The *Sarffymor*! Abandon ship!"

"Lyr's bollocks," Griffin cursed again, horror and awe fighting for purchase in his expression.

"We're screwed." Hysteria laced Rhett's dry laugh.

One of the dragon's yellow eyes found mine, a voice deeper than the sea itself filling my consciousness. *We are the same. Duweni.*

"End them," was all I answered back, my fury as ancient as hers.

I swear she smiled, scaly lips pulling back to show glistening white teeth, each one longer than I was tall. And then she dove, slamming into the warship, tearing a hole into its side with her massive jaws.

The Tannian leader bellowed with rage as my companion tore through the ship with ease and glee, her teeth destroying it before many of the sailors could jump over the side. Wood and metal screeched and groaned as the water consumed the scattered remains. The woman ran to the side of our ship, falling to her knees as she realized she was alone, her howl of agony piercing the night.

Now I drew my blade. My teeth were just as long and sharp as I approached her, leaving my friend to the larger task. "You should have surrendered."

Griffin grabbed my arm, a warning in his eyes. "Keira——"

I shook him off, stalking the woman like prey. She whipped around to face me, snarling as tears rolled down her ebony cheeks. She lunged to strike, but the swirling in my chest propelled me forward, dodging when she stumbled onto the deck again. A calmness washed over me as I regarded her, lifting my blade high above my head. "This is for Roland."

"The girls are safe, what——" Ronan burst through the door to the cabin, halting my downswing before I could strike. His relief quickly shifted to fear as he took in both monsters. "Gods above."

Shame washed over me as I saw my husband. He was good. He deserved so much more. He'd put his faith in me, and I'd let him down.

I was the real monster, rotten and wicked and broken. It was my fault Roland was dead, not this woman's. This woman, who was only fulfilling a contract, a pawn in my uncle's game. This woman, who had watched her crew die at the hands of mine.

My sword clattered to the deck.

I would not be like my uncle.

I would be better.

"Take the lifeboat and run," I spat, the *sarffymor's* roar emphasizing my point. "Fast."

"I do not fear death!" she bellowed, harsh and desperate. Pushing up to her feet again, she took a staggered step backward. Stillness coated her frame as she locked her dark eyes on Griffin. "But he should."

Grace was gone from her movements as she picked up my sword from the deck and, with a hysterical laugh, swung it down toward my cousin. He was faster, shifting to the left as she bore down, the blade only grazing the dagger from his hip. He winced but rolled out of reach from the second strike.

Without another word, she grabbed his discarded dagger and ran toward the starboard side. Perched on the railing, she held the dagger high, howling in victory.

And as the *sarffymor* closed its maw around her, I saw the sapphire-eye glint from the hilt—just as the Tannian woman and Aidan's dagger were swallowed whole.

As my scaled friend dove back to the depths she belonged to, I fell to my knees.

30

Forgiveness and Funeral Pyres

The ship's sickbay had been overcrowded with bodies before. Somehow, it felt fuller than ever, the presence of those who *should* have been there taking up more space than the actual bodies themselves.

Ronan and Griffin had helped me pile the Tannian bodies in the corner, shoving them hastily under a tarp to hide them from view. As much as we wanted them out of sight and mind, throwing them into the deep would've proven cruel; even assassins deserved a proper funeral pyre. We couldn't burn them until morning, or we'd be a blazing beacon for any other unfriendly ships sailing the deep.

Roland's body, laid gingerly on a table, was covered with more tact, the delicate white covering-cloth dotted with lavender sprigs. I couldn't bring myself to look at it. Or to face what I had done.

What I had failed to do.

Only Rhett and I were counted among the breathing in the room, and with how quiet we were, a passerby might think us dead, too. Maybe parts of us were, parts we preferred to bury within ourselves.

We did not speak, even while I applied one of Reina's creams to the gash in his leg. His wound was no longer deep, thanks to the shoddy work of my power, but it needed proper tending. Rhett did not even look at me, lying down so he faced the ceiling instead, the only sound the small sniffles escaping as tears streamed freely down his cheeks.

"I can take this from here, Captain." Griffin's voice through the door was enough to make us both jump as it shattered the uncomfortable silence. He leaned on the frame, his large arms crossed, looking between us. "Just get us home."

"I'm fine." I spread another thin coat of the harsh-smelling salve on Rhett's exposed wound, wishing I had something for the wounds we nursed within.

Griffin uncrossed his arms and came to rest a hand on my shoulder. "I need something to do, something good, Captain. Otherwise…"

I stopped my work to meet his gaze, to see the silver tears brimming in them. In our unspoken way, I knew he felt just as guilty as I did. Knew the wounds festering within him like they were my own. I nodded once in understanding.

Griffin cleared his throat, a forced smile on the corner of his mouth. "Let me take care of this idiot. Ronan needs you at the helm."

"All right." I put the salve down, wiped my hands on my apron, patted Griffin's shoulder once and moved toward the door. Before I could exit, the rope of guilt wrapped around my throat tugged hard. Swallowing against it, I turned to Rhett—looking at him, not through him, for the first time that night. "Rhett, I'm so sorry, I—"

"No, please don't say that, not like he's—" The words caught in his throat as he sat up, running a hand over his cropped blonde hair. He bit his lip, struggling for the next words, but when he met my gaze, there was none of the blame I deserved in his expression. "Thank you, Keira. For your help. And for your kinship."

I couldn't breathe as his words slammed into me, heavier than a cannonball. I turned on my heel to go, hiding the tears that sprang to my eyes. "Feel better."

I did not look back as I made my way through the bowels of the ship and up to the deck, barely breathing until the salt air hit my face and forced an inhale. My hands were on my knees as I tried to catch my breath, the guilt winding around my chest like a vise. Vicious sobs burst from my core, each wracking through me with an abandon I could not control.

"Shh, Keira girl, it's okay." Ronan pulled me into a tight hug before I could protest, his arms wrapping around me like twin blankets. The weight of them soothed my sobs until my breath was small and even once more. Wide hands stroked my hair as he whispered, his voice an anchor steadying me against the waves, "Gods below was I scared I wouldn't get to do this again."

I let my husband hold me for a while without speaking, my arms slipping around his slim waist in return. I felt so fragile, so weak, and I did not hide my vulnerability as I pressed into his chest, the citrus and sea-salt soothing the edges of my nerves.

There was so much I had to say to him. So many things to apologize for, so many things to tell him. I managed none of them, all buried deep within me. So, I asked an easy thing instead, the coward in me captaining this conversation: "Are the girls okay?"

Ronan let go, leaving a kiss on my forehead before he pulled back. I studied him, really drinking him in for the first time in what felt like forever: dark circles lined his eyes, his cheeks more sunken than I remembered them, his skin paler than it should be. He needed rest, but he was putting on a brave face, another mask. "They'll be fine. Shaken and sad about Roland..."

His name was an arrow through my heart, but I tried to school my expression so it wouldn't show. My eyes found the deck, unable to meet my husband's gaze. "Are *you* okay?"

"I will be when Aidan pays for his crimes."

I blinked back at him, surprised by the ferocity of his answer. Despite the lines of grief that creased the corners of his mouth, his expression was sturdy as he looked out to the horizon, the moonlight casting his skin the same shade as stone.

I folded my arms across my chest, my disappointment rising within me again, a reminder of another promise I couldn't keep. "Ronan, the knife..."

Hands tucked into the pockets of his leather trousers, he leaned back against the wood of the cabin. He hadn't changed yet, his coat discarded, wearing only a bloodstained white tunic with rolled sleeves to guard him against the chill. He didn't seem to care, his steadiness unwavering. "I know. But we have Tannian spears to show as evidence and eight people who will swear by Lyr, one of them a Councilman. It'll have to be enough."

Something similar to hope buzzed in my chest as I took his words in. Even against the odds, even with his kin dead and his prospects bleak, he'd still fight. He'd still hang on.

I laced my fingers through his. For him, I'd hang on, too. "And if that doesn't work, we also have a giant wolf."

At the mention of Ellian, Ronan's shoulders fell, but he squeezed my hand. "Have you talked to him yet?"

I'd been neglecting that conversation, too wrapped up in what had happened to process that particular truth. "What does one say, exactly?"

Ronan's eyes flicked to the foremast, where the outline of Ellian's human form was dark against the moonlight. Concern swelled in his expression. "I don't know, but I'm tired of him moping in the crow's nest."

"Since when do you care?" I nudged him with my elbow, cherishing the playful point of conflict.

He tucked an errant hair behind my ear again with his free hand, a sigh escaping his full lips. "Since he saved my wife's life. And my family. At the risk of exposing his darkest secret and at his own injury."

I looked toward my friend again, a new gratefulness reminding me not of what I had lost today but what I had gained on this journey. "Aye, I'll talk to him, Mr. Mathonwy."

Ronan's warm lips left another feather-light kiss on my cheek. "Then come right back, Mrs. Mathonwy. I think I need to hold you for another thirty years until I feel safe again."

The twinkle in his eye was a clue to exactly what kind of holding he had in mind, a light tap on my backside the confirmation as I walked away. As selfish as it was to want pleasure amidst so much pain, the thought of bedding him tonight sent an excited shiver down my spine. If anything, the scent of death, still thick in the air, reminded me just how little time we had in this world. I would not be wasting any more of it.

I threw a wink over my shoulder before heading for the rigging.

I was glad for the chill in the air as I climbed the rope ladder. Later tonight, there would be time for heat and passion. Now, I had to pretend I still deserved the title of Captain. The pain in my knee and hand was a dull groan as I launched myself up, rung after rung, until I hoisted myself through the scuttle door and onto the crow's nest.

Ellian's back was to me, his chestnut hair catching the wind his only movement. I announced myself with a cough. "Mind if I join you?"

He spun around quickly, but his mind was clearly still leagues away. He looked down, not meeting my gaze, as he shifted to leave. "Ah, I'll head down."

I blocked his way, sitting cross-legged in front of the hatch. "Ellian, I'm not up here for the view." I lowered my voice, painting a friendly smile on my face, hoping it hid the darkness that dwelled just below the surface. "I wanted to make sure you're all right."

He crossed his arms uncomfortably, the shyness so uncharacteristic for my usually boisterous friend. "The shift is controllable, don't worry."

A small spark of life lit in my chest once more, and I smacked his knee. "Will you stop being an idiot?" I laughed, the sound surprising me as it bubbled up from my chest. "You saved us all."

His pout remained steadfast. "No, your sea-dragon friend did."

I scoffed, relaxing back onto my forearms. "I wouldn't have been able to summon it if that Tannian bitch had succeeded in gutting me first." I channeled Griffin's ease as I continued, hoping to work the same sort of magic, "I owe you quite a bit, don't I, furball? You saved my life here, you warned me about Connor…"

"You don't owe me. That's my duty."

I cocked my head to the side. "Your duty?"

Ellian sighed, the tension in his shoulders finally uncoiling. He looked at me properly for the first time, wistfulness brimming in his voice. "Do you remember my mother?"

"No, I can't say that I do."

"She was one, too. A *faoladh*," he admitted, but I could tell the words felt foreign on his tongue, the set of his jaw still tense. "From Tan, actually."

Realization dawned on me, the Tannian woman's vile voice echoing in my mind again. "So that's what the woman meant about your own blood."

He leaned back onto the far side of the nest, his hands behind his head for support. As he spoke, I watched each word unravel another layer of the lighthearted exterior he had built so carefully. "Aye. The *faoladh* are sacred there, but they are also subjugated. My mother was kept as little better than a slave, nothing more than a weapon to her clan."

"How did she end up in Porthladd, then?" It was clear few had heard this story before, and I wanted to honor him by listening.

The knowing grin that filled his features surprised me almost as much as his words. "Your father."

"What?"

He shrugged, another truth unknotting itself from within him. "Aye. He rescued her on a trip to the Southern Isles after spotting her in a market. As the story goes, he nearly burned down half of the only port in Tan to save her. After that, he told her she was free to go wherever she wanted, but she decided on Porthladd. The land of good men."

"I had no idea." A small part of me ached that Papa had kept yet another secret from me.

"How would you know? She swore him to secrecy, said she'd eat him if he told anyone." Ellian's laugh was bright against the darkness. "But anyway, she met my Pa and fell in love, blah blah blah. But she also swore to your Pa she'd protect him and his kin at all costs, a gift in return for the one he gave her. When I was old enough to shift, the duty fell to me."

Talons of guilt lodged themselves in my chest. All this time, I'd taken advantage of his friendship, offering very little in return. I laid a hand on his knee. "It's a shame I didn't know her better, but I'm glad I see her loyalty in you."

His shoulders shrugged forward again, a rawness in his voice I couldn't name. "I owe you an apology."

The talons dug in deeper, drawing blood as the guilt consumed me. "What? Ellian, no, you've done so much—"

He held up a calloused hand to stop me. "Hear me out." I shut my mouth, and when he was satisfied with my silence, he continued, his voice softer, but no less genuine, "I'm sorry for coming between you and Ronan...and for trashing the house Esme built you. I thought he killed Cedric, but even then...I thought the best way to protect you was to have you by my side instead. I didn't realize how selfish my motives really were. You two deserve each other." His easy smile returned to his face, a glimmer of the confidence I knew and loved back in his smirk. "And Lyr below, you can protect yourself, darling."

His admission rattled through me, and while I knew it should shock me, I was instead filled with overwhelming gratitude. I had to pinch the inside of my hand to keep from crying. With all that had gone wrong in the last day, the reminder of all the things that had gone right in my life was an anchor, grounding me to myself again. "Thank you, Ellian." My voice quivered. "For your honesty, and for your friendship."

Ellian blinked, tears lining his own eyes before he wiped them with a forced cough. When he looked at me again, he raised an eyebrow, dripping with his usual pomp once more. "And if you know a friend who is interested in...hairier men...give them my name."

I barked a laugh, my shoulders shaking. "Well, Saeth looks at you like she either wants to kiss you or kill you, so you might ask her."

"Which is it?" His head tilted to the side, the action so unmistakably canine, another chuckle rippled through me.

"I can't tell." I leaned over to ruffle his dark curls before he could swat me away. "Just don't give her fleas, yeah?"

"Aye Captain." His voice was mocking, but there was a lightness in his eyes again. Still, he paused, one last cloud hiding the full brunt of his sunniness. "Sorry we lost your uncle's dagger."

Small victories, Keira girl.

This was enough. To know that through war and grief, there would still be moments where a friend could make me laugh and cry in the same breath. To know that even in loss, there was always something to gain...that was true victory.

My Captain's coat didn't feel too big as I nodded to my friend. "The dagger means nothing. What's important is that the rest of us get home safely."

I woke the next morning still entwined with Ronan, our naked skin warm wherever we touched. He slept, light snores marking the passing time as I watched him in awe. Careful not to wake him, I traced gentle lines across his chest as the memory of the night before filled me with a different warmth.

The promise to not make love until we were sure we were alone had disappeared the second I peeled my coat off, desperate in our need for some sort of comfort amidst all the agony.

Even in the graveness of our circumstances, our bruises and scars proof painted across our skin, it was one of the best nights of my life. So different than our first time, foreign to the passion and desire that drove us then. We had taken our time, quiet and careful as we made each other whole again. Each kiss was a bandage for an exposed wound, each gentle thrust a reminder of our oneness.

And as we reached the cusp, our bodies releasing the tension of the day, I almost said it. The words were right behind my teeth, and if I hadn't sunk them into the pillow, it would've spilled out as he spilled himself inside me.

There was no more avoiding it. I loved this man, every bump and scrape, every line and curve. Inside and out, I was madly, completely in love.

As if he could read my thoughts, even in his dreams, his eyes fluttered open. "Mmm, good morning, my love." He draped a lazy arm over my waist, his fingers brushing my exposed backside.

I swallowed back my words once more, the somber task ahead of us sobering the desire in my core. "Are you ready for today?"

Ronan stiffened as reality found its way back to him, too. He rolled off me with a sigh, tucking a hand behind his head. "As I'll ever be."

We dressed in a comfortable quiet, together, but still with enough space to gather our thoughts for what came next. I pulled on the best tunic I had with me, made of white cotton and lace. It needed to be pressed, but it would have to do. On top of it, the maroon coat I'd bought Ronan from Madame Neirida. It was far too big in the shoulders, too long, and I was not one for such extravagance. But it felt wrong to wear my colors today for Roland's funeral pyre.

"I lied. Red does suit you," Ronan commented as he pulled on his own scarlet long-coat.

I hugged the coat tighter around me, his scent still thick on it. "Let's go, you insufferable cad."

He held my hand as we made our way through the ship and onto the sunlit deck. Morning light started its stretch over the horizon, yawning as it reflected off the calm sea.

When my eyes adjusted, the outline of the pyres became clear. Three small, unadorned ones, each with two bodies piled upon them, on the port side of the ship. And on the starboard side, Roland's pyre stood tall. He was still wrapped in his shroud, now decorated with lavender for peace and delicate seashells for luck.

We were only a half a day's sail from Porthladd now, but the bodies couldn't wait any longer. It was bad luck to bring them ashore. So, we would say our goodbyes here, with the sunrise to greet them and carry them home.

Griffin and Ellian made quick work of the first three, a methodical silence falling over the task as Griffin pushed them into the deep and Ellian set them ablaze.

Ronan and I made our way to Roland's side instead. Reagan stood at the foot, tears streaming down her tiny face, Saeth a sentinel next to her. At the head, Rhett was hunched over, mumbling a prayer through his own gentle sobs.

Squeezing my husband's hand before releasing it, I let him go to his only remaining male cousin. He placed a hand on his broad back as he muttered his own prayers, his velvet voice steadying the quivering one beside him.

I flanked Saeth on her other side, grateful for her stalwart presence. She offered me a grave smile, nodding to my coat. "He would've liked it."

I linked my arm with hers, the only response I could manage. There was a strange comfort in her hardness, in the sheer, unadulterated honesty of her, and it fortified my nerves.

Griffin and Ellian joined us, wiping sweat off their brows as we all ignored the fires at our backs. Part of me felt sorry for the dead who would not be prayed for, their pyres burning west, but I had enough to mourn today.

Griffin took his place on Rhett's other side, Ellian bordering mine. He cleared his throat, his Councilman's authority washing over him as he addressed me formally. "Captain? Any words?"

I loosed a nervous breath, straightening my coat. "I'm not one for words, but neither was Roland." I gazed at the body in front of me, once belonging to my stone-voiced friend. My kin, even when

I didn't deserve the title. "He spoke through his actions. I regret more than anything that I did not see his goodness sooner."

"I'm going to miss him." Reagan's sputtering cry was unbearable, ripping through my heart.

Saeth kissed the top of her head, as if she'd been doing it her whole life. "Me too, little dragon."

Ronan cleared his throat this time, his hand still anchoring Rhett. "Roland wouldn't have wanted us to be sad." He winked at his littlest cousin, who wiped the tears from her eyes as his storyteller's voice slipped through. "He would want us to laugh and drink and cheat at cards. To put our backs into our work and our hearts into our play. To take care of each other. To live for another, just as he died for us."

My heart swelled, a strange mix of grief and adoration flooding my core. As always, my husband was right. I placed my hand across my chest, a salute regarded for the finest of sailors. "To Roland."

"To Roland," the crew echoed, voices laced with tears.

Rhett lifted his head, eyes red, but a smile perched gingerly on his mouth. "To Papa." Bent with a heavy heart, he stood, shrugging Ronan off of him. And with a final prayer on his lips, he pushed the pyre down the ramp and into the arms of Lyr.

Ellian hummed, lifting his bow. One by one, we joined in, our voices quivering with thick tears. And when the raft had floated thirty paces toward the horizon, Ronan lit Ellian's arrow right before he fired it. Striking true, flames licked the sides of the pyre, and our song rang out into the open ocean as our friend was released from his corporeal prison.

I don't know how long we stood there, holding each other as our throats went raw from sobbing, watching the pyre drift further and further from our hearts and into the sunrise. The sun had reached its noontide apex when we finally broke apart, Nef's yellow eye bearing down on us. There was no more time for mourning, and no more time for hiding, either.

Our chins high and our eyes dry, it was time to set sail. Porthladd was waiting.

The crew set to the task without much talk, the work a blessed distraction to us all. Even Rhett hobbled around, helping Ellian repair damaged planks and torn ropes. Saeth was in the sails, showing Reagan how to stitch them, each of us taking a part in healing the ship as we healed ourselves.

I let Griffin take the helm, trusting my cousin to keep her steady while I stood at the bow. I let the sea air kiss my skin, but even the sea couldn't soothe the waves in my core.

We were close enough to see Porthladd's outline, the Clogwynn Cliffs jutting out like teeth above the sea. We were so close. But so was Aidan. So was the Council, and all the other troubles we'd left behind when we set sail.

Ronan tucked an arm around my waist, his warmth behind me as we took in the horizon together. "Are you ready to be home?"

"Is it even home anymore?" The dry laugh sounded foreign as it bubbled up. I turned to face him, my back to the island I had no courage to face. My arms wrapped around his neck, fingers lacing in his golden curls, sapphire bluer than the sea itself staring back at me. "You're my home. This crew is my home."

His sigh held no judgment, only concern as he held me closer, whispering into my hair, "So are Reina and Vala and Tarran. Even Reese and Finna. Don't let Aidan ruin your happiness. If he does, he wins."

I smiled against my husband's chest, wrapped in warmth and love and safety in a way I'd never been before. He was right. Ronan would always be the port where I cast my anchor, but his embrace, while comforting, was not wide enough to hold all those I had to protect. The island was their home, and I would not forsake them out of fear.

As for Aidan, he had stolen my first home from me. From all of us. He'd painted himself as an oasis, feeding us sandy lies while he kept the water to himself. I would not let him starve us any longer.

"You're right. He doesn't own my happiness. But I'm about to ruin his."

Ronan let go, the cool wind licking my limbs in the absence of his warmth. But his voice was another blanket of protection, wrapping itself around me like the coat I still wore. "That's my Keira girl."

I held onto that fuzzy feeling until we made port, just as the evening sun was setting. This time, when I breathed in the Porthladdian air, I was not afraid.

This island had been my home all along. I was born at sea and had been wandering all my life in search of something else, but I was raised on the fish dinners of the Eastern Docks and swaddled in the soft cotton of the Southern Market. I scraped my knees on these cobblestone streets, and I learned to swim on the sands of these beaches.

My kin lived and died here. I would too, if that's what it took to defend it. Even from the threats that slumbered within its borders.

Small victories, Keira girl. What do you want, and how do you get it?

I wanted my crew to be healthy. I wanted my family to be whole.

And Lyr be damned, I wanted Aidan to pay for his crimes.

With the stars above me and the sea at my back, I knew my heading.

When I gave my crew their orders, even standing in Ronan's bloodred coat, I wasn't Mathonwy or Branwen. I was Porthladdian. I was ready.

"Griffin, Ellian, take Rhett and the girls to Mathonwy Manor and stay put until I come for you."

Ellian nodded once, his loyalty warming my heart. "Of course."

Griffin bristled, dropping the crate he'd been unloading. His eyes were daggers as he hurled words at me, knowing my next play as well as he knew every one of my strikes. "Keira, you are not seeing Aidan alone; you're not the only one with a score to settle."

"I'm not going to be alone. Ronan is coming with me." I kept my tone steady, as Papa had so many times when he held this title. He knew to get the crew seen to first, knew to put food in bellies and salves on wounds. Knew that a stiff drink and a hot meal made every problem a little easier to face. But I had other victories I needed to see through on my own. Ronan's resolute nod gave me the confirmation I needed to continue, "You'll get your moment to say your piece, I promise. After you all get some rest and Rhett gets that leg properly looked at."

Griffin opened his mouth to protest, but it was Reagan who uttered the next command, her voice just as steady as mine, "Come on, Griffin. Rhett is going to need you by his side when he tells Mama and Reese about Uncle Roland." She slipped a hand into his, softness in her gaze and her touch. My chest surged with pride as she continued, each word peeling back a layer of Griffin's outrage, "Sometimes, we are more helpful when we stay out of the way."

Saeth ruffled her hair as she passed. "When did you become the smart one?" She flashed a dagger-sharp smile as she led the way to the gangway, still in her trousers and tunic. "As much as I'd love to see my Pa's face when you tell him where I am, Keira, I'm not passing up a chance at Reina's famous cooking." She winked at Reagan, who giggled, bouncing to her spot on Saeth's left. "No looking back, Griffin. Keira can handle herself. We have new adventures to start."

Griffin still scowled but did not protest as he eyed our youngest cousin, the truth of her words singing to his favorite sword. Instead, he grabbed a pack of supplies and stood next to Rhett, offering a grunt as the others made to leave.

Pride flooded my chest with gratitude for the crew that had come to my aid. But this was a fight I had to face on my own. Emotion constricted my throat as I watched them turn to go. "Lyr keep you all."

A shadow of a smile filled Griffin's eyes as he fought to keep the obvious disappointment out of them. "Give him hell, Keira girl."

Ronan and I stood watch for a full minute as their forms dissolved into the hazy night of the docks. The tenor of his voice broke the moment and anchored me to the ship once more. "All right, Keira. Let me go grab my things from the cabin, and then we'll head out."

"Take your time." I offered my best attempt at a smile, my captain's courage faltering without my crew. "I'm happy to put this next part off a little longer."

"I'll only be a minute." He gave my hand a tight squeeze before peeling off toward the cabin.

Once he disappeared belowdecks, I exhaled, closing my eyes. The only sound that accompanied my breathing was the sea smacking the hull. The dock was empty, the usual hubbub already done for the day. It was just me and the sea, and the task ahead.

Talk to Aidan. Demand justice for Papa.

I inhaled again, treasuring this moment of peace as even the power in my chest held quiet.

Until the gunshot broke the silence.

31

Gunshots and Guilt

There was no time to brace for impact, but I didn't have to.

As the bullet fell to the ground *next* to me, halted by an unseen force, I felt Ronan's coat buzz. My eyes darted to the gold embroidery on the breast pocket, so similar to Ronan's tattoo, his words echoing through my mind.

Got it on the island. Keeps those who'd harm me from doing so when I'm not aware.

The *Hiraethean* protection charm. I owed Madame Neirida a life debt now, but I did not have time to contemplate her witchcraft as I whipped around, searching the black night for the shooter.

That's when I saw him, standing on the gangway like he owned it, his silver pistol still raised. Hazel eyes locked on mine, and no witchery could save me this time.

Protection charm. Keeps those who'd harm me from doing so when I'm not aware.

It did not hold as he faced me head-on and fired, the bullet piercing my shoulder.

White-hot pain shot through my right arm, my fingertips going numb as the rest of me burned, blinded by searing heat. A scream clawed from my throat as I crashed to my knees. I pressed my hand to the wound, hot blood lining my fingers, the world spinning in and out of focus.

Through the blur of pain I watched him approach, striding down the deck like he had so many times before.

"Thank ye, Keira girl, for sending the rest away." Aidan's voice was measured and calm, keeping tempo with the throbbing in my shoulder. He stopped two paces out of my reach, his leather boots close enough to spit on as he crouched down to meet my gaze. "It's better that it's just us two."

He wore my uncle's face, but gone was all the comfort I'd cherished. His eyes, once brimming with warmth and temperance, were colder than a shark's.

"You shot me," I spat through the shock, clutching my shoulder.

Aidan brushed the matted hair from my forehead. "Keira, why did ye have to go and make such a mess?"

My eyes finally focused on the pistol, on the triangles etched into the side, and my stomach dropped to my toes.

Weylin's gun. Enchanted by the god of death himself.

And my uncle, *my uncle*, shot me with it.

Anger bubbled beneath my skin, the searing in my shoulder yielding to the burning in my core. "Ronan is on the ship." I pushed to my feet, wincing in pain as I rose to my full height, but my voice was weaker than I'd hoped it would be as I watched the pistol. "He'll hear you."

"I plan on being gone before then." He stood, appraising me with squinted eyes—eyes that had once smiled at me. When he was satisfied, he sighed once, stuffed the gun back into its leather holster at his hip, and crossed his arms, sinking into a comfortable stance as if we were back in Branwen townhouse—as if this was a family meeting, not a gun duel. "Keira, I shot ye so ye couldn't fight before listening, but I swear I don't want to kill ye if I don't have to tonight. Despite what ye may think, I'm not a monster, and my war isn't with ye. So, let's cut the games and get to the point, shall we?"

The tether on my rage snapped, the soothing tone of his voice only fueling the venom in mine. "Papa trusted you. *I* trusted you. The Tannians? Griffin and Saeth were on that ship, too. We all almost died!"

His answering shrug sent another flare of volcanic rage through my veins. "Ye shouldn't have stolen the ship then! But if ye died, it would've been a necessary casualty to get what I need. What the *family* needs." His tone was unwavering, his expression unflinching.

My fingers twitched toward my dagger instinctively, but I hesitated, frozen in my place.

This was my uncle. The man who taught me to negotiate, the man who held me as I mourned Papa.

The man who killed him.

I would not be like him. I would not kill my kin.

But I did not know what to do with the man or the pistol in front of me.

"Was it worth being Captain?" I steadied my breath, mimicking his even tone. I wanted answers, not blood. Justice, not war. "I would have yielded to you. I always thought the world of you. You were the smartest and the best of us. So why, Aidan?" I took a brave step towards him, and he flinched back, his composure rattled for the flicker of a second.

"Aye, I am the smartest." His voice was once again devoid of familiarity; only an icy, ancient anger marked his words, and darkness enveloped his expression when his hand caressed the grip of the pistol. He circled me, a predator assessing his prey. "A fact your father always ignored. To him, I was just his scrawny little brother, even when I begged him not to split our profits with the Mathonwy leeches. His death was brought on by his own pride." His boots came to a halt and he looked at me with sorrow in his smile. "And ye know, I really thought ye were smarter than him. Craftier. Like me. Thought that ye'd marry the Mathonwy boy, see the loophole in your contract, and free us from both them and the tariffs. I wanted to share this with ye, Keira."

He paused, eyes searching mine, lips pursed as he waited for me to respond.

I didn't. I couldn't. My blood was ice, my stomach stone.

Aidan heaved a heavy sigh, gripping his pistol once more. "But yer just as blind as your father. Blind to what this family could be if we didn't have to split it all in half. How great we could have been. I had to take matters into my own hands again, and it seems I was the smart one. Like usual."

Heavy realization settled over me, almost dragging back to the deck. "Ronan's ship was you, too." I straightened, betrayal stinging worse than the bullet through my shoulder. "What, did you pay off the builder? Make it look like an accident so you can reap the benefits without the blame?"

The corner of his lips curled into a sinister grin. "Aye, clever girl. Now you're sounding like a Branwen again." His hand moved away from the pistol as he extended it toward me. His sunset eyes were bright, even in the dim moonlight.

For a moment, he was just my uncle. My Captain. The man that took me in, the man who was reaching out once more. His voice was soft, the same that had blanketed me in years of comfort and care. "We could still be partners. Ditch the boy, let the rest of their clan lick their wounds while we take advantage of the Council's ignorance."

Stone became molten lava within me, my rage reigniting with new vigor. This man was not my partner. My real partner was somewhere belowdecks, clad in red.

No, this man had killed my father. He'd cried his share of crocodile tears while it was his jaws clamped around our hearts.

Now he wanted to kill my husband. My Ronan.

I smacked his hand away with a snarl. "Sorry to ruin your plans yet again, but there's no more making it look like an accident. We found your dagger, we know you hired the Tannians. This time, you will pay for what you've done."

Hurt registered in his gaze, but it was quickly covered with rancid disdain. He folded his arms across his chest. "Do ye hear how silly ye sound? Tsk, I taught ye better than this, Keira! How ye gonna make me pay, girl?" He stepped closer, hot breath on my cheek as he grimaced. "Ye gonna kill me?"

My hand flickered to the dagger at my side.

It would be so easy. He was so close, his left side exposed. One fatal strike, right between the ribs, and it would all be over.

I was a monster in my own right, but I'd never be like him. I could never kill someone I'd once cherished, no matter what they had done to me. The Branwen crest had once been honor and perseverance. It had been sullied beyond recognition, but the man in front of me was still kin. Despite what he had done, I would still fight for my family's ideals. My *father's* ideals. No matter the profit to be had. No matter the cost.

I would rather die with honor than live as a liar and a cheat.

My voice was my father's when I spoke again. "No, I won't kill you. I'll leave sentencing to the Council."

A harsh laugh ripped from his lips as he narrowed his eyes, sending the power in my chest shrinking back. With his head cocked, he whipped the pistol out and raised it to my face. "I really didn't want to play it this way. But ye can't tell anyone if I kill ye."

The hair on the back of my neck stood on end, every muscle rigid with anticipation. But in my center, a strange calm coated my every nerve. I leaned forward, letting the cool metal of the barrel press against my forehead. I held my hands up in surrender, but my smirk covered the fear rising in my chest. It was a risk and a challenge, but I would not die a coward. "Don't forget, I'm a Mathonwy now. The contract still stands. You kill me, the whole family is banished, and what happens to your empire then?"

A slime-coated laugh bubbled from him. "Yer right. Both contracts. It's been over a month." With a click, he cocked the gun, an anchor dropping through my gullet as the bullet slid into its chamber. "Yer a divorced woman. One of us again. And I plan on lettin' yer husband take the blame... again."

Another pistol clicked, drawing our attention.

"Keira, get down." At the hatch, Ronan held his obsidian pistol high, the metal gleaming in the moonlight.

My heart fluttered at the sight of him, dark and dangerous and entirely mine.

Aidan's aim shifted to Ronan, his brows knitting. Relief washed through me sweeter than honey as I stepped back from the gun, my hands still raised, and crouched.

"Drop the gun, Aidan." Ronan was the picture of a calm, cloudless night as he eyed his mark with lethal precision. He knew he was the better shot, and so did Aidan.

But Aidan was more desperate. Lips peeled back over teeth, his crocodile grin held no ounce of pity. "You first, boy."

He pulled the trigger.

The shot vibrated across the deck, but I did not hear it. Nor did I hear the cry of pain that marked his face, or the scream that I felt rip my own lungs to shreds.

All I heard was the deafening thud as my husband hit the wood, doubled over himself. He clutched his midsection, blood already staining his white shirt, coating his hand.

Instinct took over as I ran, my only focus him.

Before I could get to him, he looked past me, fear bright in his eyes. "Keira, look out!"

A sharp smack to the back of my head sent me skidding across the deck. My shoulder hit first, a wave of dizzying pain spraying stars through my vision. I whipped around, searching for my husband through the blur.

When the world focused again, my uncle stood over me.

"Lyr's ass, I didn't want to shoot him." Genuine disappointment brimmed in his eyes. I tried to push myself up, but his boot pressed into my shoulder, sending another shot of fire down my arm. "Well, I'll just have to make it look like ye did it, Keira girl." He brushed my hair to the side with the barrel of his pistol. I spat in his face, but he wiped it off with little more than a frown. "Makes sense, really. Ye were so against this marriage from the start, but ye waited for the contract to clear and his family to leave before ye finally ended it."

Nausea rocked my center like a tidal wave. "No one will believe you," I snarled, my good hand slowly sliding to the dagger at my hip.

"Oh, but they will, Keira girl." He straightened, focusing his pistol on my forehead once more. I scurried out from under him, but he did not shift his aim. "Connor and Howell will, especially if I make a donation to their businesses. And Agatha came to see me just last week, concerned about ye after yer little stunt in her tavern. Thinks ye two are on the rocks as is."

I finally found my feet beneath me, tearing my eyes from the pistol to where Ronan was prostrate on the deck. His chest heaved, but blood pooled around him, his shirt redder than my coat.

I turned to my uncle, rage masking my pain once more, and drew my sword. "You bastard."

I did not give him another breath to attack. My shoulder shrieked as I brought my blade down, knocking the pistol from his hand, but I didn't care.

Aidan drew his own blade in the next breath, parrying my steel.

"Ye've always been quick, but yer tired," he simpered, pushing my blade and stepping out of my range. I lunged again for his right flank, but he flicked it away. "What, no storm, Keira girl? No lightnin' and thunder to hide behind?"

He lunged through a series of quick stabs. I dodged and swung underneath, but he did not relent, and my shoulder screamed in protest. I reached into my core to where my power slept, but nothing responded, only the burning pain in my limbs.

Aidan made another quick jab, slicing the side of my arm. I cried out, but my uncle only laughed again, the sound harsh and dark. "I bet yer feeling a bit sick as that bullet drains your powers. You're not the only one with a god on yer side tonight, and I guarantee mine is far more powerful." He walked over to Weylin's discarded gun and picked it up again, admiring it in the moonlight.

I took a protective step toward Ronan, putting his unconscious form behind me. Putting myself between him and the shining, silver death note. I felt like the *sarffymor* as I roared at my uncle, "I'm glad you already pray to the dark god because you'll join him soon if you lay another finger on my husband!"

And for the first time that night, lightning cracked across the sky.

I had not summoned the heat, but I let my best Mathonwy grin slide across my face. Let him think I had. I gripped my weapon tighter as if I held the upper hand, even though Aidan still held the gun.

Think tall, and you'll be tall.

Aidan's eyes flicked up to the sky, fear pulling at their edges. "A threat? See, yer no better than I am."

My sword felt heavy in my hand.

He had a point. Here we were, trapped yet again in the same cycle, our only resolution more fighting, more blood. My voice lost its edge. "I thought you were better than that, too."

Accusation flashed through his gaze, the pistol still trained to my face. "Yer hands are just as bloody as mine. How many Mathonwys did ye kill? How many of my Tannian friends?" He waved the pistol as he spoke, rage and disgust fighting for dominance in his expression. "If I'm a monster, so are ye."

His words stung just as sharply as the gruesome bullet in my arm. He was right. Part of me was a monster. A cheater and a killer.

An orphan and orphan-maker. An abomination and destruction incarnate.

But there was a part of me that loved. Part of me that was a daughter, a cousin, a *niece*. A part of me that wanted to hug my uncle as much as I wanted to hit him. A part of me that wanted to end the bloodshed, to try my hand at healing instead.

There had to be a part of him, too.

Inhaling a steadying breath, I dropped my sword.

Aidan's eyes went wider than cannonballs as he watched it clatter to the deck. I made no move to retrieve it, only taking a hesitant step forward. "You're right. I'm just as much to blame as you are. But I beg you, Aidan, make the better choice here. You clothed me and fed me and kept a roof over my head. You've fought for this family, for Vala and Tarran and everyone at home. I know there is good in you. You don't have to do this. We can start over, we can make things right."

His pistol lowered a fraction as he considered me. Considered my weapon on the ground. Considered my husband bleeding out behind me. Familiar hazel eyes—*Branwen* eyes—met mine. "You're right. I don't have to do this." He sighed, his shoulders relaxing as he exhaled.

"Thank you." I staggered forward.

I could forgive. Not forget, but forgive. I could put it all behind us, no matter how badly I missed Papa, if it meant ending the madness. If it meant saving the man behind me, and everyone else on this gods-forsaken island.

I opened my arms to embrace him, to embrace the change that had rooted itself in my monstrous core.

Hesitantly, he pulled me in, wrapping his arms around me. His embrace was cold, but I held him back, breathing in his familiar scent.

Forgiveness would not be easy, but it was possible. I closed my eyes and held him tighter.

But his nails dug into my back as he whispered into my hair, "It's over now, Keira girl. Ye lost."

My stomach turned into stone as I felt the metal of his gun press against my neck and the bullet click into place.

But the shot that rang out was not from the silver pistol.

My uncle went limp in my arms, the small hole in his forehead oozing dark red. I caught his deadweight, lowering his lifeless corpse to the deck, his eyes staring out into dark nothingness.

"I'm sorry, Keira." I turned to watch Ronan drop his pistol, clutching his gut once more. "He had you."

"The contract—"

"I know," my husband coughed, his face paler than Aidan's. "Let them banish me or hang me. It was worth it."

I stared back at my uncle, at the silver pistol still in his rigid hand. At the death spot on his forehead.

"I'm sorry, Aidan. I tried." I managed through the numbness that coated my veins. I unsheathed my dagger, driving it into the spot in one quick strike. The sapphire hilt, so similar to the one he'd used to kill my father, stuck out like a beacon. "Better a Branwen take the blame."

A thud behind me shook me from my numbness.

I spun to find Ronan laid back on the deck again, the full gore of his wound exposed to the night air save the bloody hand that covered it.

"Ronan, let me see." I dropped beside him, moving his hand out of the way.

Bile rose to my throat at the black, oozing wound. Blood gushed from it, the bullet wedged between so many vital pieces of the man I loved.

"It's just a scrape." He quickly covered it again, his mask slipping over his face as panic filled my heart. "I'm just miffed he ruined my coat."

"Shit, Ronan." I ripped a piece of my tunic off, putting pressure on the wound. He winced at the touch, but I had to stop the bleeding.

I closed my eyes, focusing on the place where my energy slept. I waited for the buzzing, waited for the tingling. Nothing responded, only a dizzying emptiness. My eyes flew open to meet my husband's, his knowing smile ripping a hole in my gut. Tears spilled over, my voice raw. "No, no, no. This isn't happening." I twisted on my knees to scream at the empty deck, the empty docks, "Someone help!"

"Shh, there is no one, it's all right." Ronan ran his bloodied hand through my hair, a brave grin painted on his features. He coughed again, blood coating his lips, accentuating the deathly pallor of his face. "I barely feel it."

"No!" I bellowed, shutting my eyes tight again. I begged for my power to manifest, begged for anything. Nothing came, not even a flicker. Instead, the pain in my own shoulder hissed and coughed, dark and cold where there was once heat and life. I smacked the deck, my knuckles splitting open. My breath wheezed through me, my fingers shaking as I pressed the now-soaked tunic over his wound. "No, *please*, why isn't it working?"

Ronan put his hand over mine, steadying the tremors as he struggled to sit upright. "Keira, listen to me. The pain is over now, Aidan is gone…" A cough silenced him for a moment, but his gaze was penetrating. "Our families need you to stay strong."

I placed a shaking hand on his jaw, feeling the softness of his cheek, desperate as I clutched his face. "Don't you talk like that. They need us, Ronan. *Us.*"

"I love you, Mrs. Mathonwy." A tear rolled down his cheek as he lowered himself to the deck, his still-warm hand grasping mine. "Loving you has been the most incredible adventure of my life, Keira. Thank you for letting me follow you around."

His eyes fluttered, threatening to close forever.

I patted the side of his face, my breath escaping me in gasps as tears wracked through me. I had to fix this. He had to be okay. "No, stop, please. Ronan." His eyes focused, and before he could slip into the darkness, I kissed him again. His mouth was so cold despite the warm blood that coated his tongue, but he pressed back. I willed every bit of myself into that kiss, praying for the tingles, for the buzzing that would be our saving grace.

When I pulled away, I did not let go of his face, my tears falling on his cheeks. "I love you, too. I love you more than anything in this world." The words were a battle song, not a curse. I had to save him. He had to live. "But I swear to Lyr, if you do not pull through this, I will kill you myself and then drag you back from the Otherworld by your stupid blond hair."

"Always a threat with you," he laughed, the sound almost whole despite the blood staining his moon-white smile. "Thank you, Keira girl."

Hope fluttered through my core and I gripped his hand tighter, staring into the brilliant blue of his eyes. He would survive.

Help was coming. He would pull through, even if he had to laugh until the pain disappeared.

I was not ready when his eyes closed.

And his heart stopped.

32

Springs and Sacrifices

My husband was dead.

Ronan was dead. His heart had stopped. His eyes had shut.

I stared at his face, so cold and serene. Like he was sleeping, far away in a distant dream. He was not asleep. His chest did not rise and fall with life. His eyes would not open.

My husband was dead.

A part of me died, too, as I clung to his lifeless body, sobbing into his chest.

Another part was furious.

A dark, primal wrath rippled through me, blacker than the night sky. This was not how it ended. My Ronan would not die here. I looked to the sky, to the blackness that matched my own. Even the stars hid from my rage. "If any of you good-for-nothing gods can hear me, heal him. Heal him, or I will hunt you all and end you instead."

For a moment, there was silence. But then a hesitant, familiar voice answered, as deep and sorrowful as my own.

I'm sorry. This is not how it was supposed to end.

A hoarse laugh burst from my lips. "Then *heal* him."

I cannot.

My chest buzzed with hysteria. "Fuck you," I hissed at the sky itself, my pain boundless. "You have done nothing but laugh and comment at my pain, and I'm sick of it." I gripped my husband's lifeless hand, raising it up as an offering. "Bring him back or fuck off."

Another aged voice answered. "Keira?"

I whirled to where Esme stood on the deck, wraithlike as the wind caught her silver curls. She strode to Aidan's body, a frown creasing her wrinkled face when she appraised the dagger in his skull. "I thought I heard shots." She froze as she saw Ronan, violet eyes brimming with tears. "Oh Lyr, Keira, I'm so sorry. I'm too late."

"It's not too late." I ran my hands over my husband's body again, searching for any sign of vitality. Nothing answered, but I would not give up. "It can't be too late."

A gentle hand rested on my shoulder. "He's gone, girl."

I swatted her away, darkness roaring in my chest. "No, don't say that!" I shook his shoulders, his head still lolling.

There had to be a way. If Lyr couldn't save him, I would. Somehow. "Ronan, come on, please."

Esme crouched in front of me, eyes fixed on his lifeless form for a moment. Then she grabbed my wrist to pull me to standing. "Let's go, we don't have time."

"I'm not leaving him." I tore my wrist from her grasp, panic rising in my throat. Tears carved down my cheeks once more, my breath ragged.

I would not abandon him. He was not dead. He had to be all right.

And if he wasn't, I would die here next to him.

Esme huffed, reaching for Ronan's limp arm instead. Effortlessly, she hoisted his body up, wrapping an arm around his midsection with a preternatural strength, lifting him to almost standing. "Good, because we are bringing him with us."

"Where?" I grabbed his other side, distributing his sagging weight between us. Wrapping his dead arm around my shoulder, I bit my lip against the pain, my own possessive hand snaking around his midsection.

He was so still. Another sob threatened to break me.

Esme scooped his left leg up. I mirrored her, careful not to let his head drop despite the pain singing through my shoulder. "The spring," she commanded, signaling me towards the gangway, "now. Before it's really too late."

I clutched my husband tightly, his body still slick with blood. The spring was nearly a mile away and up a hill. I looked down at his exposed wound, the blood already drying. "Esme, what if—?"

Lyr's voice returned to me, authority as deep as the sea rippling through my consciousness. *Do as she says.*

Hope flickered somewhere within me, and my nerves became steel. I'd carry him a thousand miles up a Pysgoddian mountain if it meant saving him.

Another, darker part knew we were running out of time.

"Let's move." The desperation was thick in my voice, but I didn't care as we began our trek.

Esme was faster, her gait unwavering, and I struggled to keep up with the pain slicing through my shoulder at every uneven step, but I would not slow.

We barely spoke as we journeyed, our focus on the task. We knew the way and we knew the cost.

"Keep up the pace, girlie," Esme reminded me whenever I slowed, violet eyes urging me on, her own strength never faltering. I gritted my teeth and pushed, ignoring every new shot of pain.

Through the streets of town, then into the *Dubryn* Forest, each step a new labor. My muscles ached, arms turning to lead under my husband's weight. Blood trickled down my arm, the only reminder of my own vitality the throbbing ache where the bullet still lived.

"Almost there, my love," I whispered to Ronan as trees turned from green to white. It was a promise to him and to myself. Each step was a step closer to getting him back. "We're almost there."

We climbed the rocky hill, our only light the waxing moon. Stumbling and straining, we pushed and panted on until we crested the rise. My breath caught in my throat as the turquoise water, smooth as glass, came into view, and my heart threatened to beat from my chest. "We're home, Ronan."

Esme's grunt knocked the wind from my sails again. "Get him in the water, now."

We were not done. There was still work to do.

We were not gentle as we lowered him into the spring, splashing and sloshing through the water until we were all waist-deep in the warm blue, Ronan propped up against the stony bank. I tried not to vomit as the water turned crimson, the blood from both mine and Ronan's clothes marring the clear ripples with gore.

With shaking fingers, I brushed the hair out of my husband's face, water washing the blood from his full lips.

He did not wake.

"What now?" My eyes begged answers from Esme, desperation rising and swirling within me.

Her voice was an arrow through the water as she tied back her silver hair, brow knit with determination. "Focus yer gifts...with the spring, ye should be able to, Lyr willing."

Hope hardened to dread within me. I gasped for air, the emptiness still boundless as the night sky.

My gifts were gone. Spent in the days before and stymied by the bullet in my arm. There was nothing left, even with the gentle water of the spring licking my limbs. "I can't, I—"

Wrinkled hands grasped the side of my face. "Focus. Try."

I nodded, sucking in a ragged breath. My eyes shut tightly as I focused within. My gift had always just been that—a gift. Something that had been given, but something that could be taken away. It was not mine.

But as I dove deep within myself, I knew I had to make it so. Command it, not coax it.

It was always yours. I'm only trying to help.

The water caressed my skin, cool and calming, like a gentle hand stroking my back, reminding me to breathe.

Yet nothing was there to command. Only emptiness. Only darkness.

My fists clenched at my sides as I looked to my silver-haired friend again, my voice hot iron. "Esme, nothing is happening."

Her brow furrowed. "It will. It has to." She placed a fortifying hand on my shoulder, but I winced in pain as her thumb brushed the festering wound. Eyes went wide, and she ripped back my coat to reveal the blemish. "Shit on Arawn's grave," Esme cursed through her teeth, hand recoiling faster than a viper. "What is that?"

"Aidan shot me first, but it's just a flesh wound."

Carefully, as if not to wake a sleeping beast, Esme touched the spot again. For the first time, I looked down at it, at the black veins spiraling out from the center, a spider's web of decay.

I cursed under my breath. Had the bullet been poisoned?

Esme swallowed hard, finger following the intricacy of the marred skin. "Arawn's mark." Her voice was grave as her eyes finally met mine, fear and awe brimming in their violet irises. "Yer his now."

My stomach lurched, the world spinning again in a dizzying frenzy.

Weylin's gun, enchanted by the dark god himself…

It was a curse, one none could run from.

"The gift." She looked down to Ronan, a tear finally freeing itself from her lashes. "It's keeping ye alive, but it can't save ye both."

Ice ran through my veins, the night air chill around me. I would not die, my gift the only thing swift enough to outrun the god of death. But not for both of us. Only one.

Ronan was dead. He was not coming back.

Unless…

"Then take it." Certainty steadied my voice for the first time that night. "Take it all, give it to him."

Esme shook her head, but I held a hand to stop her.

"Not you." I looked down to the water around me, to the spring that had saved my husband once before. It would again if I let it. If I commanded it. "Lyr, I know you hear me. You gave me this gift, right? Take it back. Take it and save him. Now."

I felt his anger flash through me at the defiance in my suggestion. *It is not my place.*

I laughed, the sound harsh and grating against the quiet of the night. "Then make it your place."

Esme gripped my good shoulder, desperation lined in every wrinkled crevice of her face. "Ye'll die, girl."

"I don't care!" I pushed her off, steel in my eyes and in my heart. My husband would live, even if I had to slit my own throat to make it so. "I don't care, just bring him back."

I cannot. Even if I wanted to.

This time, it was Esme who opened her mouth to argue before I could form a coherent thought. "Yes, ye could."

I gaped at her. "You hear him?"

She did not address me as she continued, her hands gliding through the water reverently, "It's been a long time, my love." Her voice echoed through the woods, carried by an invisible, ethereal wind. Each pass of her fingertips through the water, wrinkles dissolved from her form, the silver of her hair turning pale yellow, then golden blonde. "Longer than it should've been. It's my turn now."

My eyes struggled to drink in the transformation, blinking as Esme melted in front of me, the visage of a woman no older than thirty taking her place in the pool.

When Lyr spoke again, the harshness had also transformed, adoration kissing every word. But it was not me he spoke to. *So be it, my darling.*

The young woman—*Esme*—took my hands in hers, her skin smoother than the water's surface. I opened my mouth to speak, but no words came out, shock wrapping its fingers around my throat.

Esme smiled, not a wrinkle on her alabaster face, same violet eyes twinkling with new life. "I always knew it was my destiny to make ye two a home. I thought that meant I had to build ye a house, but this…" She looked around, to the sentinel white willows swaying softly in the breeze. When she met my gaze again, gentle tears kissed her cheeks, but there was no sorrow in her expression. Only love. She wrapped me in a tight hug, her gunpowder and storm scent unmistakable as she whispered into my hair. "This spring has been my home fer four centuries. Now, make it yers."

"What—"

The memory of Ronan's story fluttered through my mind.

Lyr fell in love with a Porthladdian woman…beautiful, with a temper as chaotic as a storm.

Esme. Esme was Lyr's mate. This was not his spring, but *hers*, a gift from the god who'd loved her as a man.

She let go, stepping back deeper into the water, where it came up to her neck. "I'm ready. Remember, don't let Ronan stray for too long, he won't look as peachy if he does. He has to keep coming back." Something wild brimmed in her expression. Something free. Her smile widened to reveal glistening white teeth unmarred by the world. "Thank ye, Keira dear. For lettin' an old woman see love again, and fer what ye one day will do fer this world."

Confusion melted into realization as her words hit me. As I recognized what she was about to do. "Esme—"

I was not quick enough.

Without a second of hesitation, she dove backward into the water, her arms spread wide with joy.

When she submerged, the water fizzed and whirled, chaos erupting from the deep. I grabbed onto Ronan, holding his corpse to me before it could be dragged under.

And Esme exploded. Her body gave way to thousands of tiny, iridescent bubbles, swirling and popping in the cool pool until they all dissolved into nothingness.

The water settled, bubbles turning to ripples, then to glass as the pool calmed again.

The only sound was my own breath when Lyr spoke again, his voice distant and faint, like a memory of a memory. *This is goodbye for now, Ariannad. Until the world stops turning.*

I struggled for words, for anything other than the deep sense of loneliness that enveloped me. Sobs sputtered up from my core again.

Esme was dead or gone, I didn't know, Lyr following her trail. Two more souls who had laid down their lives for mine.

And what had I done to help? What did I sacrifice?

Nothing. I was useless. My father was dead because I was naive. Roland was dead because I was foolish. My uncle was dead because I couldn't stop him. I'd done nothing but tear through this gods-forsaken island, piece by piece, ripping it all to shreds. I was a hurricane leaving nothing but destruction and death in my wake. Everything I loved turned rotten.

I was the curse. I was the murderer. And Ronan—the only home I ever had, the only person that I truly loved…Ronan was still—

Breathing.

My husband was *breathing.*

I looked again, watching his chest rise and fall. Looked at the touch of pink color that flushed his cheeks.

His sapphire eyes fluttered open.

☆ 33

Banishments and Betrothals

The sea was silent the day of my uncle's funeral. It licked the shoreline of the Traeth beaches, offering not even a whisper as the gatherers prayed for an answer.

The mourners, townsfolk and kin alike, were silent too. Vala, Donnall, Finna, and even Saeth and Griffin decorated the beach, standing in solidarity, watching the sun begin its ascent into the blue morning sky. Quiet tears kissed their cheeks, all of them standing tall, clad in brilliant Branwen blue as they cried for their fallen hero.

A space stood empty for Weylin, who had not been seen since the night Aidan died. He left no notice or explanation for his disappearance. We couldn't be sure, but Saeth had a theory it had something to do with Aidan stealing his guns. I could only imagine the price he had paid to obtain them. With his absence, I couldn't help but notice how threadbare my family seemed.

There were not many of us left to mourn.

Ronan and I stood back, hiding in the shadows as the people gathered next to the tall funeral pyre.

"Are you okay?" My husband mumbled into my hair as he kissed my forehead.

I squeezed his hand—I hadn't let it go in days—and raised an eyebrow. "You were dead two days ago, and you're asking me?"

It had been two days of feverish kisses and desperate hugs. Two days of holding my breath every time he closed his eyes, afraid they'd stay closed. Two days of telling the story to disbelieving loved ones. Of accusatory shouts from those who needed someone to blame.

"I'm right here, Keira girl." Ronan's voice anchored me back to my body. "You aren't alone."

I straightened my own blue coat as we took a step out of the shadows, resting on the outskirts of the mourners' circle.

Aidan's pyre was a testament to how well he was loved. Dozens of flowers in every shade of blue and purple covered his silken shroud, Vala's lavender sprigs chief among them. Seashells covered the edges, *ceffyl dwrs* painted delicately on their backs in the finest gold paint money could buy.

It was a pyre fit for a king.

It was also a lie.

I pressed further into my husband's side as Connor Yorath lit the torch. He stood tall, his slender outline stark against the sea behind him, his black robes out of place on the sandy shore. But his head was high, his voice dripping with false sincerity as he addressed the crowd. "Today, we say goodbye to a pillar of this community. A man who knew the meaning of family. A man who knew the meaning of Porthladd." With a flourish, he lowered the flaming torch to the pyre, the wood quickly catching. "Sail safely, Aiden Branwen. May Lyr keep you, and may the dark god show his mercy."

A few quiet sobs escaped the mouths of nearby mourners as the pyre was pushed into the water.

Finna was the first to spot us on the outskirts, her eyes red and puffy as she stared at us. "What is *she* doing here?" Each word was a knife in my heart.

"How dare ye?" Donnall stomped to where we stood, every inch of coiled muscle straining with anguish and rage. Accusation sang in his expression as he spat at me, "Ye didn't even bother to take yer knife from his skull!"

I felt a shift in the tide as curious eyes and ears focused in, desperate to catch every word of the family drama about to unfold. Gossip floated with the wind, hushed voices swirling with disdain and venom.

I heard she killed him...her dagger in his skull...bold of her to show up here. With her good-for-nothing husband...I heard they aren't even married anymore....

I swallowed back my retort, the cacophony of acidic words mixing with my living uncle's heartbroken stare enough to level me. Ronan bristled beside me, but I squeezed his hand, quieting him.

I deserved this. I deserved this hate.

But Griffin wedged himself between us, a calm hand on his father's chest. "Papa, watch yourself. She's your Captain."

Tarran flanked Griffin's side, his sunset hair combed back, its usual puffiness now schooled into order. "We don't know what happened, Uncle Donnall. If Keira says it was self-defense, it was self-defense."

Pride swelled in my chest, so rich I almost choked on it. I nodded to my cousins, tears welling in my eyes. I could never thank them enough for their loyalty. Griffin smirked, not an ounce of blame in his expression.

But I knew the truth. Knew how blameworthy I really was.

"Shut yer mouth, boy," Donnall growled at Tarran, smacking him upside the head.

"Don't touch him," I snapped, a protective, predatory rage boiling under my skin.

I knew Donnall was taking it hard. With Aidan dead and Weylin in hiding, he was the only one left behind to lead the family. But in the rage that contorted his features, I saw nothing of the jovial Second Mate I knew and loved.

"Repulsive Mathonwy bitch," he snarled in my face like a rabid dog. "Ye may be Captain, but we don't serve ye. Yer a murderer."

A stone dropped through my gut.

He was right. I was. I hadn't been the one to kill Aidan, but I should have been. And Weylin's disappearance was most likely my fault, too.

Another voice cut through the tension like a dagger through flesh. "Enough, you old fartbag, or you're next." Saeth folded her arms around her chest with a petulant scowl, the blue of what looked like my old tunic and trousers a sharp contrast to the ginger of her hair.

To my surprise, Donnall stepped back. "Go away." His voice was weak when he addressed me again. "Let those who loved him mourn."

He stalked off toward the shoreline without another word.

I exhaled, but it was shallow. Ronan's hand rubbed small circles on my back, soothing the rough edges of my guilt. "Don't let him bother you, Keira girl."

Tarran offered a sunny smile, but it didn't reach his eyes. "Aye, you know he's useless without my Pa. He'll come around once we find him."

I patted his arm gently, biting back the thick emotions swirling in my chest. "But he isn't wrong." I looked to where Donnall held a sobbing Vala in his arms, Finna at his side. To where he stared at the funeral pyre, his favorite brother burning to ash. "Go check on him, will you? He needs you now."

Saeth studied them narrowly, darkness simmering in her fox eyes. "When will you tell them Aidan killed Cedric?"

I watched the pyre drift towards the horizon, the flames reaching towards the heavens themselves. "There is no need now," I sighed, releasing the last of my resentment. I offered a prayer that my uncle would reach safe shores. "There is no honor in sullying a dead man's name."

"Aye, Captain." Griffin clapped the twins on their shoulders, breaking Saeth's trance as he ushered them onward. "Let's go, Tarran."

I watched them walk away, a lump forming in my throat. There would be time for reconciliation. For apologies and for truth. Today they needed to mourn with their families.

And I needed to celebrate with mine.

Reading my mind, Ronan tucked me to his side. "I love you, Keira girl."

"I love you, too, Ronan." I nuzzled even further into him, breathing in the citrus and sea. It was a scent I'd never take for granted again. "I love you, too."

"How touching." The chuckle behind us drove us apart, whipping around to where Connor Yorath stood with his hands tucked behind him further down the shore. He circled us, beady eyes zeroed in with shark-like precision. "Your uncle does have a point, you know. Your culpability is undeniable."

I straightened up as Ronan stiffened beside me. "I told Councilman Llewelyn what happened. He shot us both. It was self-defense." We'd reported Aidan's death to the Council the same night, with a frantic knock on Ellian's door and a rushed explanation of the truth. We were foolish to think there would be no official response.

Connor cocked his head. "Yet neither of you have a single mark. Only a black spot you claim to be a bullet wound."

My hand flinched instinctively toward my shoulder, to the death spot that still festered beneath my clothes. How he could've possibly known, I had no idea, but it was true. There was no longer a wound. My gift had made sure of that. Only the mark remained, a reminder of the debt I owed the dark god. "How did you—?"

"Back off, Connor." Ronan took a threatening step forward, his mass glaring next to Connor's frailty. "Now."

Connor recoiled, grimacing at my husband, but his voice was unshaken. "Mr. Mathonwy, I suggest you remove yourself from my face immediately, unless you wish the same fate as your ex-wife."

Ronan's eyes narrowed. "What fate?"

Connor's lips peeled back in a vicious smile. "Banishment, of course."

Fish flopped in my gut, a wave of nausea smacking into me with full force.

Ronan's mask cracked, his brow knotting. "For what?"

Connor steepled his spindly fingers in front of him, his victory apparent. "For the murder of Aidan Branwen and the disappearance of Esme Rhiamon." He stepped around my husband like he was no more than debris in the sand, until his hot breath was on my face, glee dripping from his tone. "I voted to see you hang, but your friends on the Council voted to banish you instead. Thought it was a more appropriate sentence since there was no reliable witness."

Something dark swirled in my chest, the world tilting on its axis. The word rang through me, rocking me from my center. *Banishment.*

"A sentence passed without a trial?" I bit back, but my voice was smaller than I intended it. I swallowed my fear, anger straightening my spine like a challenge. "Where is your sense of law, Councilman?"

Connor did not take the bait, his expression schooled into confident conquest. "You submitted a testimony directly. There was no need for a trial."

My head reeled, his logic a stab in the gut.

This had been his plan all along. I'd baited him and badgered him, challenging his power, circumventing his attempts at control. When I left for *Hiraeth*, I thought I had put him behind me. Thought I had won.

I was mistaken. Connor had played the long game, and my bastard of an uncle and I had played right into his hands.

"This is unfair, you can't do this!" Ronan protested, but I saw the realization in his eyes, his threat just as empty as mine.

We'd been bested.

Bested and banished.

Connor knew it, too, gloating in his triumph. "Yes, I absolutely can. You may appeal to the High Council, but I have a feeling their sentence would be even less kind." He brushed an invisible speck of dust from Ronan's coat before shifting his black eyes back to me. "You have twenty-four hours from this moment to be off this island. If you ever set foot on it again without the Council's express permission, you will be killed on sight."

Fury crashed through me, my knees weak with the sentence hanging over my head. "Why, Connor?" I blinked back treacherous tears that lined my eyes. "Why me? Why my family?"

"Isn't it obvious, Ms. Branwen?" My name was a curse on his odious lips as he stroked my cheek. I slapped him away, but for the first time in his life, he did not cower, his voice poisonous with his own sort of power. "Because I can. A good day to you both. I would say I'd see you soon, but I don't believe I will."

And with a twirl of his black cloak, he glided into the morning, his invisible dagger still in my heart.

Reina chopped the chicken with a ferocity unparalleled by any fighter I'd ever encountered. "Ye don't have to go." She waved her knife in my direction, a warrior-goddess in a kitchen apron. "We're going to fight this."

Warmth fluttered in my chest, her unwavering resolve cementing my own. I adjusted on the wooden stool so I was close enough to lean my head on her shoulder. Reina stopped her cutting, her citrus-spiced scent enveloping me as she rested her head on mine.

"I do have to go, Reina. I don't want any more trouble." I stood, shimmying out of the sweet embrace before my heart burst. It was already almost dawn. My time was up. "I'm already going to be late. Thank you for your hospitality."

The tears that welled in her eyes were almost enough to break me. She gripped my shoulders, bottom lip trembling. "Thank ye, Keira. Ye've done nothing but good for this family."

My own throat bobbed, but I would not cry. If I did, it might be enough to flood the entirety of the small kitchen and drown us all. I cleared my throat, breaking away before the kindness of her touch could send me under, looking instead to the open doorway. "Where is Reagan?"

Reese and Ronan filled the space a moment later, the former wearing an uncomfortable smile that creased the outline of his jagged scar. "She couldn't bring herself to see ya off. Cried all night about it. Sorry." He tucked his hands in his pockets. I withheld my chuckle, realizing where Ronan got his favorite tick from.

A part of my heart sank for Reagan, but relief washed over me simultaneously. That was a goodbye I didn't know if I could stomach.

I grinned back at my father-in-law, the peace between us new but steady. "It's fine. Please tell her to stay strong for me."

"For us." Ronan snuck past his father to stand at my side, his fingers lacing through mine.

I shot him a reproachful glare but squeezed his hand anyway. "You can tell her yourself, you're coming back."

And he would. Esme's warning was clear. Too much time away from the spring and my husband would be a corpse again. We had reached an agreement after hours of arguing: he'd spend a month at sea with me, then he'd come back.

I stared up at him, at the vibrant red in his cheeks, the crystal blue of his eyes. In truth, he looked healthier than ever, a new vitality behind his features. Lyr below, he even seemed taller, his spine straight and strong, like it had never seen a day's work at sea.

But the image of his cold, dead body still floated in my head, a nightmare waiting to resurface every time I shut my eyes. A shudder ran down my back at the thought. I gripped his hand tighter, afraid to let go.

Reina broke my trance as she stood next to her brother, linking her arm in his. "Goodbye for now, Keira," she hiccupped through a sob, sniffling. Reese handed her a handkerchief from his pocket, but I swore there was a glassiness to his eyes, too. After wiping her runny nose, Reina straightened, the queen in her kingdom once more. "I promise ye we'll do what we can to fight this."

"Thank you," I managed. I prayed to whatever god was listening that this was not a real goodbye, prayed to the stars that our paths would find a way to cross again.

As Ronan led me out of the house and down to the docks, I decided that if the stars wouldn't make it so, I would. I would be the master of my own fate.

Winding through the streets, I did my best to memorize every passing sight, every scent. I drank it all in, knowing it would be my last time doing so. All my life, I had denied this place as my home. But it was, every brick and smell and person a part of me that I would no longer forget. One day, I'd find a way to come home, no matter the cost.

By the time we reached the docks, the morning sun bright and ready, I didn't feel so lost.

The surprise waiting for me undid the very last of my resolve not to cry.

Griffin's tall frame was the first in view, his lengthy figure sprawled across a crate, the *Ceffyl* the only backdrop between him and the open sea. Next to him, Saeth sharpened a dagger while Rhett tied his bootlaces, all readying themselves for the day.

My crew had come to say goodbye.

Griffin spotted me first, his toothy grin bringing fresh moisture to my eyes. He stood, stretching like a housecat, then crossed his arms. "What took you so long?"

I pinched myself, steadying my voice. "Where is my ship?" I scanned the dock, looking for the tiny, single-masted sloop that we contracted to be my new home.

"You don't recognize the *Ceffyl* after all these years?" Griffin scoffed, gesturing to Papa's prize ship like an Ir'desian showman. He ruffled my hair before I could swat him away. "Wow, Shrimpy, Aidan must've hit you hard."

My nickname warranted an instinctive eye roll. "I can't sail her on my own, Griff," I sighed, taking in the *Ceffyl's* glory one last time. My heart ached, but I trusted my kin to take care of her. "And you all need her to keep up the trade."

Rhett finally stood, slipping his hand into Griffin's, an uncharacteristic grin on his face. "The *Ceffyl* needs a Captain, and last time I checked, that's still your job."

My eyes narrowed at the place where they touched, but I decided that was a conversation for someone else to have. My only task was goodbye. I pinched the bridge of my nose, holding back the tears. "Weylin will be back eventually. He and Donnall—"

"Have no legitimate claim to it and can frankly suck a toe," Saeth quipped, forcing me to bite back a laugh. Sheathing her dagger, she strode over to us with the confidence of a sailor twice her age. "Plus, they can't sail it alone either, and we are all coming with you."

"What? No." I folded my arms across my chest. "This is my sentence to bear, not—"

Three sets of boots down the gangway of the *Ceffyl* silenced me, my mouth gaping as they joined us on the dock.

Flanked by Ellian and Tarran, Reagan stuck her tiny hands to her hips, triumph in her stance. "We are staying, whether you like it or not." She winked, the tiny tyrant exercising her indisputable power over me. "And my mama said if you had an issue to tell you to pull your head out of your—"

"Reagan, enough." Ronan's laugh sparkled as he covered his cousin's mouth, tousling her hair. But he looked at me, nodding once, his involvement in this scheme clear as day on his face.

A whirlwind of emotions filled my core, battling within me for control.

My crew wasn't here to say goodbye. My crew was here to sail.

Tarran put my thoughts to words as he plopped down on a crate. "You didn't abandon any of us, Captain, and you both nearly gave everything for our sake. We know where our loyalties lie."

My heart threatened to stop, my cousin's acceptance unlocking a whole new wave of unadulterated love. "You, too?"

A single nod sent my heart soaring. "Aye, after Saeth called Donnall an old fartbag, I realized I'd look like a total pansy if I didn't come," he chuckled sheepishly. Saeth shrugged with pride at her handiwork. "Plus, I'm tired of missing out."

Ellian, still standing behind Reagan like her personal bodyguard, clapped my cousin on the shoulder, beaming. "That's the spirit, boy."

I looked to my friend, my savior in so many ways. "And you?"

The corners of his lips twitched downward, his shoulders falling. "No. I'm just here to say goodbye, and I'm sorry. I did what I could to reduce the sentence."

"I know." My voice caught in my throat. I still had one goodbye to bear, then. Perhaps the hardest one of all. "And I'm glad you're staying. I'll miss having my friend." I rested a gentle hand on his shoulder. "But Porthladd needs its greatest defender here."

Before I could protest, he pulled me in a bear hug, nearly crushing my spine, the ache in my shoulder throbbing under his cobra's grip. "Goodbye for now, Keira." He patted my back and released me, sweet air finding my lungs again. "I'll send word when I've worked this mess out. Saeth promised to write and let me know where you are."

Hope buzzed in my chest. If I could trust anyone to fix this, it was Ellian. I winked up at him, shooting a quick glance at Saeth. "Remember what I said about fleas."

I tried not to laugh at the blush that filled his cheeks.

"Can we get going?" Griffin whined, cracking his knuckles. "We'll lose the tide if we don't move now."

I looked to my husband, overwhelmed by the warm kinship that surrounded me. "Where are we going?"

"That's your choice, isn't it, Captain?" Tarran shrugged, grabbing one of the last crates to carry on board. "What's our heading?"

I scanned the faces of my crew, my *family*. They were abandoning the only home they ever knew to stand beside me without complaint. They were putting the past behind them, looking to me not with blame, but with acceptance. They were armed and ready, embracing the future with open arms, no matter what darkness it held.

I owed them more than I could ever say. More than anything, I owed them happiness. I owed them long, healthy lives filled with laughter and love and kinship. I owed them sunny skies and open waters.

It was not something I could promise them, but I would lay down my life trying.

And there were answers I still needed.

I rubbed the spot on my shoulder, the phantom ache deeper than muscle and bone. "South." The plan unfolded in my head, the horizon a beacon. It was time to put the sun at our backs. "We need to find Weylin, see what he can do about the mess his guns made. Knowing him, he's hiding in Ir'de. And who knows, maybe the land of a thousand scents and silks knows how to get spots out of skin."

Ronan met my command with an eager smile. "Aye, Captain, south it is."

Reagan bounced up and down, running up the gangway without hesitation, her voice carrying over the docks with uninhibited glee. "Let's go, let's go!"

The rest of the crew followed, our smiles bright and our weapons sharp. I did not need to look back toward the home I was abandoning. My home was coming with me, the sturdy wood of the *Ceffyl* carrying us all into the next adventure.

When the mooring was cut and the sails flying, I gave the order to set sail, my heart ready as I took the helm. Banishment was a sentence, but it did not rest heavy on my shoulders. The sun was shining on the glistening deck, and there was a promising westward wind that my sails ached to take hold of. Though Lyr had not spoken to me since the day at the spring and the sea no longer answered my call, I was not afraid of the deep blue before me. She still beckoned me, the vast, untamed expanse begging to be explored.

And as I stood next to my husband on the proudest cutter in the entire Deyrnas, I did not feel like I had lost anything at all.

Ronan cleared his throat loudly enough to catch the attention of everyone aboard. "There is one last thing before we set off."

The crew stopped their work, five sets of eyes trained on us with curiosity.

"What?" I demanded.

His hands slithered into his pockets, something wistful in his sea-glass eyes. "Our contracts...well, you heard both Aidan and Yorath. You're a Branwen again." He stepped closer, taking my hand in his, the wind dancing in his golden curls. When he spoke again, his voice was filled with intimacy, his sapphire gaze penetrating. "But this is your ship. And as Captain, you could declare us."

Recognition sang through me. I knew that legally, our union had ended, our silly contract coming to an end, but at no point had he stopped being my husband. I had promised him, before Lyr and in all the ways that mattered, to give my life to him. I knew all too well that he'd do the same for me.

But the opportunity to tease him was far too sweet a fruit to pass up. "Who said I want to be your wife?"

He blinked twice, his shoulders falling. "I—"

I held up a hand to stop him. Stepping closer, I laced my fingers more tightly through his, relishing in their perfect fit. I would never let go, not for anything in the world. And anyone who tried to come between us, man or woman or god, would meet my swift steel.

I lifted his hand to kiss the back of it. "Do you, Ronan Francis Mathonwy, want me to be your wife?"

"Pssh, Francis?" Saeth's snort sent a wave of laughter through the witnesses.

Ronan did not blink, his smile bright enough to rival the sun. "Aye. Until the end of time."

"Then as the Captain of this vessel," I let my voice carry, declaring my love before my crew and anyone else, monster or god, who happened to be listening, "I, Keira Laureli Branwen, with my wholehearted consent, give you my life, and whatever comes after, as your wife."

Rhett gave a dog whistle, Griffin echoing with a shout, "Kiss her already!"

"Aye." My husband's hand found the small of my back, lightning running down my spine as he pulled me to him. "Come here, Keira girl."

As he kissed me, soft and sweet, something rumbled in my chest, scratching at the surface, waiting to break free once more.

We broke apart, our cheeks flushed and our eyes hungry for more, the promise of forever tying us together. I turned, bolstered by my equal at my side, to the small gathering of bright, expectant faces below.

"What are the rest of you staring at?" I laughed, setting my sights on the horizon, ready for whatever the sea had in store. "Get moving. We have a wind to catch."

END BOOK ONE

Read on for an

EXCLUSIVE BONUS CHAPTER
from GRIFFIN's perspective,

and a

SNEAK PEEK
of book two,

Sister

of the

Stars

✧ 22.5

Betrayals and Bets

GRIFFIN

I had a bad habit of losing bets.

Fights were easy. Fights, I won. But wagers and bets were games for men far luckier and craftier than I.

My mama used to grumble that I was cursed by the fair-folk as a child. Said I never knew how to sit still or keep myself from walking straight into trouble.

The truth was, trouble followed me wherever I went. Like I was a magnet, it stuck to me closer than my freckles hugged my skin. I couldn't stay out of trouble because trouble was a part of me. And even with *Truth* and *Triumph* strapped to my back, I always managed to lose.

Today, trouble's name was Rhett Mathonwy. He scowled at me from the deck, mouth bleeding from where I hit him. Keira stood between us as lightning cracked overhead, the fight over.

And lost.

"Ellian, Roland, take them to the brig." She sheathed her daggers, tossing both of us dark looks before retreating to the rigging.

Ellian pointed to himself, as if he didn't hear her right. "Oh, me?"

Roland, Rhett's equally-troublesome father, crossed his arms. "Aye, Captain Keira, it would be my pleasure."

And to think I shook hands with the cheat on the docks earlier.

I shot to my feet, stepping right into a fresh load of trouble. "What, Keira, we just said—"

"I heard you both, and I'm glad you chose that way." My demon-bred cousin smirked, the glint in her eye sharp as steel as she waved over Ellian, her new guard dog. "But a few hours bonding belowdecks will serve you both well. The rest of us might actually get some work done in peace and quiet."

If I was trouble's whore, Keira was its master. Always evading it, making it submit to her will. Just as she imposed her judgement on me. Somehow, I missed the moment the little cretin became a Captain.

The burly blacksmith gripped my arm tighter than an Ir'desian whore held onto a councilman's cock. I tugged at my restraint, but the blacksmith held firm. *Lyr below, did this man mold steel, or eat it?* I shot my cousin a look that could boil a potato. "But what about the rowing?"

On cue, a gust of wind tangled my hair, the sails inflating like they were laughing with Keira at my expense. "Didn't you notice? Wind picked up."

"Let's go, lads." Roland grabbed his unruly son and motioned for Ellian and me to follow. "We'll be back up in a moment to help ye, Captain Keira."

It was not my first time being led to the brig of the *Ceffyl.* As the god of trouble's personal puppet—the trickster god's hand *firmly* up my ass at all times—the brig might as well have been labeled 'Griffin's room' instead. When I was sixteen, Uncle Cedric made me sleep there for a whole week after Keira and I tried to sail the ship on our own. Of course, it had been my Lyr-damned cousin's idea, yet I bore the greater consequence.

I'd take another week of Cedric's lectures if it meant space from Rhett Mathonwy and his blue-eyed, strong-jawed brand of headache. Ellian tossed me into the cell like I weighed no more than a feather. I stumbled onto the meager bed of hay, smacking an already sore bruise on my ass hard.

"Ye boys behave, now." Roland winked as he shoved his son in, the brawny boy falling into my lap. He scrambled off me as our two jailors retreated, laughing like a pair of Tannian hyenas.

As their laughter faded, all that was left was the silence between Rhett and me, thick and tangled with tension.

I leaned back onto the hay with a sigh, tucking my hands behind my head and shutting my eyes. If I knew Keira— and unfortunately, I did, as well as I knew my own name—we'd be stuck for at least a few hours, if not the whole night. So, I would make my shoddy attempt to get as comfortable as one could in a damp, dark cell with the man who killed his brother.

Owen. The man was a gentle giant, with my build but with none of the trouble I was drenched in. He never fought, only because he never needed to. It was hard to make enemies when the sunlight lived in your smile, when your words were as gentle as the summer breeze. If I hadn't envied him so much, I would've admired his sheer ability to let trouble glance off him like rain on a roof.

If I had listened to his quiet cautions, he might've been the one lecturing me today.

Use your head, brother. It's your strongest muscle when you let it be.

We never spoke of him anymore— it was too hard for Mama to bear—and his face was starting to blur in my mind from the lack of attention. Life was easier to live when the dead stayed buried or burned.

But the moment in Bachtref—the moment Rhett's sword pierced Owen's ribs, the moment his blood painted the earthen streets of Portwen—that stained my memory forever.

Trouble followed me wherever I went, and anyone close to me got caught in the current.

"I didn't mean it."

Opening one eye, I peered at Rhett in the dark, not sure I heard him right. Perhaps I had too much of Ronan's whiskey last night. "What?"

Rhett sat cross-legged, hands folded in his lap, head down, his substantial form somehow made small. His expression was unreadable in the shadows. "Your brother."

I shot up faster than a bullet from a gun, the god of war hot in my veins. "Don't you dare—"

Rhett silenced me as his slate-blue stare burned like fire in the water-logged cell. "I thought it was you."

The ugly, festering wound I hid beneath my armor winced at his words, ones that echoed in my sweat-drenched nightmares.

I *wished* it had been me.

My scoff was shallow, a flimsy patch in my armored facade. "That was supposed to make me feel better?"

"Yes." Rhett's smile held no trace of humor. "You deserved it. He didn't."

Rhett Mathonwy was my personally-potent brand of trouble, but at least he wasn't a liar. Still, the prideful creature in my gut reared its head, determined to defend the fool's sapphire I encrusted myself in.

"What did I do to deserve that?" I sat forward, head cocked to the side like a dog ready to prove my bite was just as bad as my bark. Rhett had muscle to him, but I wasn't called the Swordsinger because of my talent for braiding hair. If he wanted round two, I'd be happy to oblige. "I wear blue, so I deserve to die? That's your logic?"

Rhett stiffened, eyes narrowed, a bloodhound catching the scent of its prey. "Maddox told me what you did to him."

The name threw sand over the fire in my chest, extinguishing the fight completely. "What?"

I hadn't seen Maddox Pultain in two years. The burly blond was the prized stallion of Madame Jessa's brothel, and as the only man there interested in servicing her male clients, he was always in high demand, even in the stuffy town of Porthladd. Still, despite the price and potential embarrassment, like the Lyr-damned fool I was, I'd frequented his services for nearly a year after Uncle Cedric died, the chiseled man so good with his mouth, he could numb even the deepest of hurts.

That was, of course, until he robbed me blind and left me hogtied in his bed one night. I still never knew why. Perhaps he knew I had been losing interest—and coins—so he wanted to stick it to me one last time. Or perhaps, as all men do, he'd simply gotten greedy, for power or money or both.

Heat flooded my cheeks as I eyed Rhett. Had Maddox told him how much coin I'd spent? Or worse, had he been bragging about his petty victory to his other clientele? I ran a hand over my face to hide the blush. "Ugh, that prick. How much did he tell you?"

"Maddox is not the prick, you are. He said you sold him out to Madame Jessa after forcing him to—" Rhett started and stopped, anger straining his voice, stormy eyes hardening with fresh tears.

A stone sank to the bottom of my boots.

I was expecting his misguided perception of me, but his accusations—and his tears—sent a wave of something I couldn't quite name crashing through me. "Hold on, Blondie. I'm a lot of things, but I'm not a tell-tale, and I'm not a creep." My voice was lower than a sail on a breezy summer day, and just as tight. I laughed, a dry, crackling sound, but there was no humor in it. "And the last time I saw Maddox, he left me tied to his bed, extremely *unsatisfied*, with my entire coin purse in his pocket. The only reason Madame Jessa found out because she was the poor dolt that had to untie me."

Rhett stood, giving up his position like a rookie fighter as his fists clenched at his side. "He said that you—"

I silenced him with a smirk, realization cracking through me like a lightning strike. I quirked an eyebrow. "And you trust a professional whore on his word? He lies to people for a living, Rhett. Tells them what they want to hear, lets them believe that it's real...It's the point."

"That's—" He cut himself off, doubt creeping into the shadows of his face.

I studied him for a moment, the foolish hope still present in his ice-blue stare, the protective lift of his strong chin.

Rhett Mathonwy didn't try to kill me for his family. Not for Ronan, or Reid, or any of his good-for-nothing uncles. Rhett Mathonwy hadn't subscribed to his family's violence or greed, or their well-honed taste for violence.

Rhett Mathonwy accidentally killed my brother for a boy. One, by the looks of it, he was hopelessly attached to.

I expected my anger, red and riotous as it pulsed through me. I didn't expect it to taste like pity. I leaned back onto the damp bale of hay, hands behind my head. "Oh boy, do you have it bad. Tell me, when was the last time Maddox came to call? Hmm?"

His throat bobbed as he swallowed hard, mask slipping back over his face, the Red Fang instead of the lovesick boy once more. He leaned onto the bars of our mutual cage, tearing his gaze away. "It doesn't matter."

Poor, stupid thing. Maddox was a professional, one good enough that even I couldn't see through his games until it was too late. I remembered all too well how sweet his lies tasted on my tongue. At least in my case, Maddox had never been more than a drunken distraction, something to numb and soothe. But Rhett was only twenty, still a boy in so many ways despite his manly frame.

He never stood a chance.

And worse, I almost *admired* him for it. I'd never loved anyone enough to kill for them. Not even Owen, as was clear by Rhett's breathing form in front of me.

A small, abandoned part of me wondered what it would be like to have someone cherish me with such devotion. Not that I'd earned even a fraction of it, but there was something pure about it. Something beautiful. I was a half-drunk whore-hound, but even I could entertain beautiful dreams.

My pity melted into curiosity, a bad idea churning in my gut against Truth's protesting whine in my ear. I had a bad habit of baiting my prey. I cocked a grin as I stood, rapping my fingers against the cold iron bars. "Wow, Blondie. I didn't picture him as your type."

"Oh? And what is my type?" Rhett crossed his arms, as if trying to hide the soft underbelly he'd let slip before, an eyebrow twitching upward.

Trouble captained my tongue, the line cast perfectly. I gripped the bar nearest to me and rubbed it suggestively. "The five digits attached to your right arm?"

"No, that's not—"

"Lefty then?" My grin turned feral. "Talented *and* pretty, I see."

"Bastard," Rhett mumbled under his breath, amusement scattering like sand in the wind as he stared at the door, silently waiting for Ellian or Ronan to rescue him.

The fool obviously didn't know how long Keira could hold a grudge.

Still, I frowned, missing the heat of his rage. I knew how to play that game. Knew how to fight fire with fire. But like a cat with a canary, I didn't quite enjoy playing with my food if it was already dead. I needed the thrill of the hunt, especially if we were going to be stuck together in this hellhole for the foreseeable future.

Truth—or perhaps it was trouble in disguise again—muttered another intrusive thought into my ear.

If he didn't want to fight, there were other ways to get a rise out of him. I wasn't called the Swordsinger for my talent with blades alone.

I took a daring step closer, fingers brushing against his arm as I draped my hand purposefully over the bar. His eyes flicked to the place we touched immediately as he froze, every rigid muscle of him tensed for a fight. My voice dipped low, my song taking on new meaning. "Or perhaps your type should be someone that puts *your* pleasure first. Someone willing to get into that thick skull of yours and look at the boy willing to kill a man in Bachtref to defend his lover's honor." Trouble making me brave, I tucked a strand of his silken, straw-colored hair behind his ear. He shuddered, from disgust or arousal, I couldn't tell, but the lion in my chest roared with primal victory either way. "Is he the only man you've been with? Because if so, you poor thing. Maddox is handsome, but he's selfish."

Finally, fire heated his gaze again at the mention of his bedfellow's name. He smacked my hand away, staggering backward. "You don't know him like I do."

Fish in the net. I pursued, rising to my full height, meeting him eye to eye. "I'm telling you, don't waste your time."

This time, he didn't back away, face only an inch from mine as he growled, "What do you care if I do?"

His words halted me, suspended in the single breath that separated us.

What *did* I care?

This man killed my brother. This man broke my mother's heart and shattered my family to pieces. Why should I give a shit if some brothel worker toyed with him? Lyr's ass, I should've been writing Maddox a thank you letter.

We all killed Owen. Keira's words sang clearly through me like they came straight from one of my swords, an answer to a question I hadn't asked. Rhett didn't start this war. He was just a foolish boy leading with his heart. Foolish and *good*, as much as I was loath to admit it. Perhaps the feud wouldn't have started at all if we all shared the same selfless devotion to something larger than ourselves.

My grin lacked its usual fire as I finally exhaled, "I don't have any more brothers for you to mistakenly stab."

Rhett blinked, mask slipping off as something unlocked in the pretty grey center of his eyes. He didn't step back as he cleared his throat, but his tone was softer this time, still stony, but a smooth rock that had been eroded by a gentle wind. "His name was Owen, right? Auntie Reina said he was in school with her when they were kids. Said he was kind. He didn't deserve what I did, and it haunts me. I'm—"

"Don't say sorry." I placed a hand on his chest to quiet him, a door closing in my heart as another opened. It was me who took the first step back. "Don't know if I'm ready for that level of bonding, Blondie."

I could play and taunt and tease. I could let go and move on, a ship without a mooring drifting off into the blue.

But I could not reminisce—couldn't *forgive*. Rhett or myself.

He nodded as if he understood, thick arms crossing in front of him as he locked away that part of himself again. For the first time in my life, I was grateful for the silence that enveloped us. I didn't have words for the strange cocktail of conflicting feelings stirring in my center.

Rhett broke the silence first, ice cracking to reveal a roaring river underneath. His shoulders slumped as he sagged into the bale of hay, long limbs stretched out. Gone was the stone sentinel, polished and hard, revealing the untamed, unbuffed boy of twenty underneath. Frustration rolled off him like thunder clouds over a stormy sea. "How is any of this going to work?" A shallow laugh rumbled in his chest. "This trip...this...truce."

Another knot untangled as the boy unraveled before me, a palm running over his face.

"You're asking me?" I titled my head, curiosity swimming to the surface once more and banishing the last of the shadows back to the Otherworld. "You hate me."

Rhett shrugged, sinking further into the hay. "I hate a lot of things. If I didn't talk to any of them, I'd be very lonely."

Lonely.

The word clanked around in my gut like the swords strapped to my back, heavy and metallic.

Uncle Cedric used to tell us Branwens were never lonely because we always had each other. Where there was one of us, there were always two more, ready and waiting with a word of encouragement or a warm smile or a mug of ale.

But I didn't have to be alone to be lonely. Uncle Cedric never knew what it felt like to be the dark horse. Cedric was a Captain. A leader. He never knew the deep, bone-crushing loneliness of a second-born son with trouble in his veins. Never knew the eternal, empty loneliness of a forgotten brother, cursed to survive with the guilt while his sibling lived on as a martyr. No smile or sip of whiskey or sweet whispers ever filled those holes. I'd tried hard enough to know.

Trouble did, though. Trouble gave a broken man something to fight against. Trouble gave the betting man something to root for. To live for.

If Rhett Mathonwy wanted the remedy for loneliness, I had trouble to spare.

I plopped onto the hay bale beside him as I cast my favorite mischievous grin his way. "Are you a betting man, Rhett?"

He snorted, unfazed by my proximity. "I like to keep my coins, so no."

"Well, I am. I'll admit, I've lost as much as I've won, if not more. I can't seem to stay out of trouble." I winked at him, enjoying the way the blush colored his fair cheeks. "But the good thing about losing a lot is that you learn to not get disappointed. You're right. This truce might be another loss. It probably won't work out."

"Great." A sarcastic smile twisted his handsome features, and I almost laughed for real. Whatever strange peace we'd come to would probably dissolve too, but I would relish in it while I could.

I rolled to my side, bracing my head on my hand as I stared at him. We were only a few measly inches apart again, but Rhett didn't shy away. Had anyone seen us, they might think we were lovers, or even more intimately, *friends.* Not two war dogs biding our time until our leashes were cut and we could devour each other once more. "But then again, our families are all so fucked anyway, where is the harm in trying?" I mused aloud, fool's hope and trouble steering my course right into shallow waters. "We only stand to gain."

Rhett's gaze pierced through my armor like a well-sharpened blade, his broad chest rising with a heavy breath. "You assume that everyone plays fair. Cheaters will still find a way to take the cards you didn't think to protect."

I didn't know if his words were a warning or a threat. I didn't care.

Use your head, brother. It's your strongest muscle when you let it be.

I should've told him to fuck off. Should've used my head for once and run in the other direction.

"How about a side wager, then?" I said instead, thinking instead with my most troublesome parts.

Rhett rolled his eyes. "I said I don't bet—"

I cut him off before he could finish. "If you're right, and this all goes bottom up, I will walk up to Maddox, hand him one of my swords, and let him run me though himself."

Rhett sat up, searching my face for a bluff. "And if I'm wrong?"

The beast in my chest purred with victory. The truth was it didn't matter which of us was right. I trusted Keira and Ronan. I knew that they wouldn't lead us astray, even if trouble was intent on rearing its ugly head now and again. But even if they failed, if we all failed, I would win either way.

If Maddox wanted to fight, I'd give him the first blow, then tear him to shreds. If not for what he did to me, for what he did to this sad sack.

But if I was right...

"If I win, you let me show you what a good time really looks like," I said as I reached out and grazed my hand over his stubbled cheek.

To my surprise—and delight—Rhett didn't lean away from my touch, but *into* it, lips brushing the inside of my palm as he spoke. "You have yourself a deal, Red."

Sister of the Stars

I

Curses and Cures

Death had a *smell*.

Not the smell of decomposition and rotting flesh, as I'd expected. Instead, it smelled of fear and regret. Of opportunities missed and moments lost. Of the hateful words I couldn't take back and the ones I left unsaid.

In the sweat-soaked nightmares that pulled me from rest every night, death smelled like citrus and metal as my husband bled out before me again and again. It smelled like cedar wood and burnt lavender, the memory of Aidan's funeral pyre.

Death smelled like the wretched, festering black spot on my shoulder, a reminder of not only the souls I'd sent to the dark god, but the promise that if I did not find an answer, I would soon be his, too.

I was drenched in the scent from dawn to dusk, its haunting odor inescapable no matter how I tried to rid myself of it.

It had been two months since my uncle died. Two months of banishment from the only home I'd ever known. Two months at sea, my only respite the warm taverns of whatever island we were haunting. Two months of restless nights in dusty inns, of nightmares that had me screaming loud enough to wake up everyone on my floor. Two months of scouring half the *Deymas* for Weylin, or for any hint of something that could clear the spot on my shoulder and the darkness that made a home in my soul.

"I have a good feeling about this one, Keira." Ronan pressed a kiss into my hair, the setting sun haloing his in gold as we walked side-by-side through the stone-laid streets of Hud. Wafts of poultices and potions assaulted my nostrils from the open windows of several sand-stone shops, each busy with customers.

I doubted the one we sought would be so inviting.

"Ronan, we can't get our hopes up," I mumbled, but the knot in my stomach betrayed me. I *had* gotten my hopes up, despite the many times they were dashed.

Even though it was near night, the air was still uncomfortably warm, sticking to my sweat-licked skin. Two months in the heat of the South, and I still wasn't adapting. We'd spent the last month turning Ir'de upside down. There was nothing that money couldn't buy in the land of a thousand scents and silks, and our hearts were full of hope as the island blanketed us in her extravagance. But the scent of death followed me through the winding streets despite the pungent spices in the air, each day growing stronger. And despite the island's abundant namesake, there were no answers in the marketplace, only dark glares and unfriendly responses.

They all said the same thing as they gazed on the growing black spot on my shoulder, fear spreading across their features like wildfire. "Go home and take your filthy curse with you, *melthith.*"

Melthith. Cursed one. The title weighed like shackles as my crew and I were turned away again and again, until Ir'de sent us back to the sea once more.

Ronan was quiet as we found the clinic we were looking for, the last building in this particular row. The outside needed upkeep even more than the shack at the spring. Long arms of ivy clung to its side, masking the tan of the sandstone in deep greens.

I supposed my face turned a similar color as we approached, the nerves in my gut rising to my throat. "This is it?"

"Aye, Keira girl." Ronan's voice was tighter than a sail in a windstorm. "Griffin's source was right. It's a dump, but perhaps that's exactly what we need."

I raised my hand to knock, swallowing down the lump of fear. I was Keira Mathonwy, Captain of the *Ceffyl Dwr*. I did not falter or yield.

A phantom pang in my shoulder reminded me otherwise.

Before I could bring my fist to kiss the wood door, it swung open. A woman who could've been Esme's age stood in front of it, beady green eyes staring up at me from wrinkled sockets. A knife twisted in my gut as I remembered my fallen friend, another death that followed me wherever I went.

I shook off the memory, focusing on all the ways this old woman was different. She wore a simple grey smock, painted with stains in every color, but the way her mouth quirked up made me shudder in my boots. The magick of the island armored this woman's very bones, ancient and angry as the sea itself.

"Can I help you?" Her voice sounded like ash and smoke, her Huddian accent thick with age.

Ronan laced his fingers through mine, his confidence seeping into my skin and awakening mine. "We were sent by a man named Jesper Vicaries." His other hand shook, so he stuffed it in his pocket. We didn't know how secure a source Griffin's newest gambling buddy was, but we'd prayed to Lyr all the same. The woman did not answer, but her brow furrowed in recognition, and I let go of the breath I was holding.

"He said you were the finest healer in Hud once... and the one most willing to take a risk," Ronan added.

The woman's emerald gaze narrowed, fixating on me as if she could smell the death scent, too. "Come in, then, and be quick about it." She ushered us through the cedar door, her stare never leaving me.

Another wave slammed through my gut as I crossed the threshold. The inside, much unlike the exterior, teemed with life. Plants of every variety dangled from baskets while sprigs of herbs dried from the rafters, the collection second only to the foliage of *Hiraeth* itself. On the shelves and counters were vials and pots filled with tinctures and mixtures like nothing I'd ever seen before, the entire room a testament to the work and dedication of the old crow before me.

I inhaled deeply, the cacophony of smells almost enough to overpower the death scent. A part of me spared a thought for those at home, for Vala and Reina who waited there. I imagined their eyes growing wide as they drank in the greenery.

The waves in my stomach ceased. For them, I could take whatever this woman had in store for me. For them, and for the rest of my family back on the ship, I could look death in the mouth and smile at it.

The old woman coughed, drawing me from my trance. "What risk are we talking about tonight, travelers?"

Ronan opened his mouth to answer, but I held up a hand to stop him. There were no words for this, other than the odious title I'd been given.

Melthith.

Instead of speaking it aloud, I unfasted my laces and lowered the collar of my deep blue tunic, allowing the full gore of my shoulder to blacken the room. The mark had spread. Once a single spot just beneath my collarbone, now a splotch the size of a grown man's hand with spidery fingers reaching down my veins toward my bicep. I kept my expression tame, but even I was loath to look at it. "What do you have that can treat this?"

The woman's answering hiss knocked the wind from my sails again. When she looked away from the mark and back to me, her eyes were almost as black as the spot itself. "I take it you know what it is you are asking?"

I nodded once, my stomach turning to stone. Another dead end.

"Can you do anything for it?" Ronan's voice laced with worry as he gazed at the spot, the color blanching from his cheeks in perfect contrast.

"You know as well as I do, boy, that this is not something one can heal." The woman chewed on her wrinkled lip. "You need someone who knows the ancient ways...or a miracle."

Ronan scoffed, denial scrunching his nose. "Doesn't half of Hud practice the old ways?"

The woman crossed her arms, unfazed by his curtness. "There is old, and then there is ancient." She pointed to my spot again, her frame rigid with fear. "This is a *god's* spot. And no matter what any of the crackpots on this island might say to make a coin, only a handful of people in this world know the ways of the gods."

The shred of hope tore from my chest, but Ronan was not dissuaded so easily, his Mathonwy mask slipping into place. "Mr. Vicaries said you might be that person exactly."

She shrugged and busied herself with watering a nearby fern, but I didn't miss the lie in the corner of her eye. "Jesper is an old barfly with loose lips and a wild imagination. You know how people talk. I am only a simple healer, nothing more."

Papa always said nothing worth having came free. Our coffers were limited, our shredded trade agreements with Porthladd devastating most of our savings. But with some smuggling and Griffin's occasional gambling win, we'd saved a small purse for moments like this. And I could smell the woman's power—and her greed—as clearly as the death scent.

Emboldened, I plopped myself into the only chair in the room and exhaled. "He said you would say that." Placing my boots on the worktable, I nearly knocked over half a dozen of her precious plants as I pulled the delicate coin purse from my pocket. I dangled it in front of her like a carrot in front of a horse, and her dark eyes sparkled. "He also said you might need something *extra* to remind you."

She swallowed hard, her eyes darting back and forth between the coin purse and my rancid shoulder. After a moment of deciding, she pinched the bridge of her nose. "I may have a vague idea of what you are talking about."

Ronan exhaled a breath of relief. The last morsel of hope rooted itself once more as I scowled at the woman. "So, what can I do about this?"

"There is nothing that can get rid of a *melthith*, not anymore. I knew a healer a long time ago who might have had the power, but she's been gone for half a century." The woman shoved my boots off the table and shot me a dark glare, but she came closer, studying the spot with needle-point scrutiny. "The only way to *clear* that spot is to pay the dark god the soul he is owed."

I tried not to let the anchor that slammed through my gut show on my face as I tucked the coin purse back into my pocket. "This is a waste of our time, Ronan, let's go."

"Wait..." The woman grabbed my unaffected shoulder with surprising strength, anchoring me to the old chair. "I can't get rid of it, but I know of ways to stop it from spreading."

Something unknotted within me. We needed answers, and yet again, there were none. But if there was anything to slow this process, to buy me time, I'd take it, if only to smooth the permanent wrinkles in my husband's worried brow. And I'd pay prettily for it, too.

Ronan ran a frustrated hand through his hair, but I could feel how his shoulders relaxed ever-so-slightly. "You should've led with that, woman. Whatever it is, tell us. We'll do it."

Evergreen eyes rolled with disdain. "You may call me Madame Hedd, not *woman*. And don't be so eager. You will not like what I have to say."

Rage bubbled beneath my skin, the woman's games sparking a fire in my core. I came here for answers, not for tricks and riddles. I was already short on time and coin. My hand flew instinctively to the dagger on my hip. "Spit it out, then, *Madame Hedd*."

She didn't flinch at my dagger, her gaze flitting instead to the pocket that held the purse. "Hand over the crowns, this information is not free, travelers."

I tossed her the bag, imagining Griffin's wince when he found out I wasted his precious winnings. She caught it with ease, snatching it from the air with more excitement than I thought possible from a woman of her age. The action reminded me again of Esme, sending a wave of regret through my middle. The memory of her gunpowder-and-thunderstorm scent was enough to bring tears to my eyes, but I would not open that basket of fish, not here. I focused instead on the sheen of greed in the woman's gaze as she weighed the bag in her hand.

After it satisfied her, she tucked it into her apron and looked back to me, appraising me with the same scrutiny as she had the bag. "The curse drains life force. You seem strong, it's surprising you've lasted this long. But it will consume you too, eventually. Unless…"

"Unless…" Ronan prompted, his agitation palpable. I glanced up at my husband, at the dark circles that were now permanent residents under his eyes. His patience had been wearing thin the last few days, and his skin paled in echo of it. We didn't have much time left until he'd need the spring again.

"Unless you give the curse another life force to drain." The woman carried on, grabbing a handful of leaves from what looked to be a peppermint plant and stuffing them into a vile of blue liquid. But before her next words, she stopped her fussing, eyeing my midsection with a sharp glint of mischief in her expression. "As a woman, you are lucky. There's a straightforward method for that."

A stone dropped through me at the insinuation, at the repugnant words said without weight. The echo of a cool voice brushed the back of my neck as if Connor himself was there to whisper in my ear.

A child, Ms. Mathonwy.

"No." I fought to suppress the taste of bile on my tongue. I grabbed Ronan's blue coat sleeve and dragged him toward the door, not waiting for his protest. "We are leaving."

"The man who owned the silver pistol." The woman's misty voice halted me before I could reach the threshold. I shot her a glare darker than my spot at the mention of the very pistol that put it there.

Weylin's pistol.

My uncle had been in the wind since Aidan's death, not even showing his face for the funeral. My family assumed he was on one of his drunken benders, or that he had finally pissed off the wrong person at the wrong bar and gotten himself killed. But I had a hunch it had something to do with why Aidan wielded his most prized weapon that night at the docks. We'd been searching for him for two months.

Madame Hedd studied me, catching how the hairs on my neck stood straight. A crooked smile crossed her features as she reeled me further in. "Your friend is still missing, yes? I could help you track him."

A strange tingle travelled down my arm as the thought crossed my mind. Would Weylin have answers for us as the true master of the pistol? Or would finding him only bring on the troubles he was so intent on hiding from?

My words were bullets. "He is not our friend, and I don't want anything from you."

Madame Hedd patted the pocket of her apron where my precious coin rested. "Fine. Don't let me help you, I still got paid." She shrugged and tossed the vial of peppermint and blue liquid to Ronan. "But at least take this. For the fatigue and nausea."

"I'm not nauseous," I hissed at her, snatching the vial from Ronan.

She tore it right back from me, plopping it firmly in Ronan's hand again. "Not for you," she sneered at me, then cast a knowing glance in Ronan's direction. "For the walking corpse here."

Fire coated my veins as rage shot through me. "Go rot." I stormed out of the greenhouse without a glance back and into the equally-warm night, the thick air closing around me as I struggled to breathe.

My hands found my knees as the world spun. The death scent was thick in my nose, burning me from the inside out. Everything was hot, my clothes sticking to my skin suddenly a burial shroud.

There was no way out of this curse. Either I died, or something…no, *someone* else did. And my husband was running out of time while I chased this fairytale. Had he been nauseous? Had I missed the signs? The pale skin, the bags under his eyes…

No, I hadn't missed them. I had ignored them. Pretended it didn't mean anything, that it was just stress and exhaustion haunting his gaze.

For the walking corpse.

"Keira, wait." Ronan's hand on my back anchored me back to my body. I turned to him, to the greying skin spread thinly across his high cheekbones, to the eyes that lacked their usual sparkle. This was my fault, and still Ronan was concerned for me, when it should've been the other way around. His voice was tight, worry thick in his tone. "She was the last on the list, Keira girl. If she can help, we have to consider the option."

A wave of nausea rolled through me. Perhaps I needed the blue vial after all. "Did you not hear what she was suggesting?" My voice quivered, just as weak and useless as I felt. "Ronan, a life force…"

A child, Mrs. Mathonwy.

Connor's words were as clear in my head as Lyr's once were. But I hadn't had the sea god's sage advice or sarcastic comments in months. He had abandoned me to the dark god and whatever fate waited for me.

I would not let an innocent creature bear the burden instead.

Ronan must have read my thoughts on my face, and he paled further. "I would never suggest that, Keira. But Lyr below, there has to be *something*. Maybe you can drain a different kind of life force, like an animal or plant."

I held up a hand to stop him. I knew in my soul there was no hope.

But no matter what happened to me, I had to make sure my husband and my crew were safe. That this mark did not sink them when it took me. "There will be something." The smile I painted on my face was a lie, but my words felt true. "But not this. I'm not going to blacken my soul to save it."

The muscles in his jaw flickered as he saw right through my brave face. "Aye, Captain."

I wiped the sweat from the back of my neck, straightening my spine. "Don't you 'Aye, Captain' me, you know I'm right." There was a flicker of my former authority in my voice, enough to almost convince myself. I grabbed my husband's hand, the coolness of his palm a respite against the southern heat. "I love you, Ronan."

A faint blush rose to his cheeks, fighting the edges of the shadows that rested there. "I love you too, Mrs. Mathonwy." He tucked me into his side, leading me down the road toward the northern docks. "Come on, we left Griffin in charge. If we don't get back soon, there won't be a ship left."

"Well look what the dark god dragged in." Griffin greeted us from his hammock on the main deck as we boarded the Ceffyl. He rolled from it, his ginger hair pointing in every direction, and stretched his limbs like he'd been sleeping most of the afternoon. So much for leaving him in charge. I scowled at him, but it only made him smile. "Still cursed?"

"Still a prick?" I folded my arms. My eldest living male cousin was more like my brother or my best friend, but with a word and a wink, he knew exactly how to rile me. "Lyr below, I left you in charge."

I didn't see Rhett until he rolled from the hammock a moment later, blush coloring his cheeks. The two had grown inseparable during our time away, so I was less surprised than I was annoyed that they'd both been slacking. Rhett offered an apologetic smile and nudged Griffin's side. "Sorry, Keira, Griffin's affliction is incurable. If he doesn't cause some sort of mischief every ten minutes, he will drop dead."

Forgetting his audience, Griffin smacked Rhett's ass with a gut-churning *thwack*, a low growl escaping his throat. "Watch it, Blondie, or I'll afflict you."

"Lyr below, get a room, you two make me sick." Saeth voiced my thoughts exactly as she climbed down from the crow's nest. I said a silent prayer of gratitude for my youngest cousin. At least *one* of them was working.

She dropped down to the deck with ease, a budding sailor now. She'd recently chopped her copper hair to her chin, the sharp cut following the even-sharper line of her jaw. In the last months, she'd become one of the crew's most valuable assets, and it struck me how well she *looked* the part now. The memory of a silk-wrapped little girl running down a dock in her corset and heels filled my chest with pride. She had chosen this fate that day, and a part of me knew she'd never look back.

Another part of me knew she'd be the one to keep it all together if I failed to find an answer.

"Any luck, Captain?" She watched me with her hawk eyes, expectant and hopeful.

Shame washed over me, the air too hot again, even with the sea breeze playing with my long braid.

"We are still exploring options." Ronan squeezed my hand, the simple gesture threatening to break me.

"That's a no." Saeth voiced my thoughts again, and to her credit, she did not let her shoulders slump like mine did.

"Aye, that's a no." I lifted my chin, my only defense against the growing pool of worry in my core.

"We'll find something, Keira." Stony resolve replaced the mischief in Griffin's expression. He folded his arms and jerked his chin to where his twin swords rested against the mizzenmast. "Truth knows. You'll be just fine."

I wished that alone was enough to soothe the rawness in my nerves.

"Where is Reagan?" I scanned the deck for her, not ready to tell the little dragon the bad news.

Rhett winced. "Terrorizing Tarran, trying to get him to teach her to shoot."

"Unacceptable." Ronan ran a hand through his hair. "That little girl will turn me gray before I'm thirty, Lyr willing I live that rutting long."

On cue, Reagan sauntered up the steps from below deck, nearly as graceful as her mother now. The two months at sea had done her well. Her deep purple tunic and tightly-cinched sword belt hugged the faint outline of muscle along her form, her newfound womanliness only accentuating it further. But behind her eyes, the familiar dragon's fire still burned, fierce as ever. She directed the blast toward Ronan.

"Stop calling me a little girl, I'm thirteen now." She narrowed her chestnut eyes and flipped her braid over her shoulder to emphasize her point. "I'm old enough to learn."

Tarran shuffled up the steps behind her, his usually-sunny disposition darkened as if he'd just been punched in the gut. Knowing Reagan, she probably did just that.

"Do you prefer little demon, then?" I raised an eyebrow at my kindred spirit, my expression some mix between admonishment and approval I was sure. She winked back at me, and I couldn't help the shadow of a laugh that warmed my chest. "Tarran, you look worse for wear."

"I didn't teach her, I promise," my cousin sighed, plopping down on a crate, his entire frame sinking. A glimmer of hope breathed life back into his deflated chest as he eyed the blue vial strapped to Ronan's belt. "Any news?"

Another knife twisted in my chest, but Griffin saved me from answering again. "She found a cure, but she's going to need your liver, Tarran." He clasped the freckled boy's shoulders with put-on gentleness. "Sorry, buddy."

"What?" Tarran's eyes widened as he turned to me, panic clear on his sun-kissed face. "That's—"

Saeth's shrill laughter interrupted her twin before he could perjure himself any further. "Don't tease him, Griffin, you'll break the last three of his working brain cells."

Tarran shot her a surly look. "Shut up, Saeth, go write another letter to your fleabag Ellian."

"You know what? I will."

Their banter and the responding laughter from the rest of my crew, *my family*, was almost enough to make me whole again. Maybe there would be a way. Maybe this wasn't the last option.

Lyr below, stranger miracles had happened. If someone told me a year before that I'd be banished on a ship full of Mathonwys and Branwens after sailing to a mythical lost island and then fighting my uncle to the death, I'd have slapped them.

No, this wasn't the end. I would find a way, no matter what it took. And in the meantime, my family was looking at me to lead them.

I was a Captain. It was about damned time I started acting like one. I straightened the sleeves of my tunic. "Saeth, any news from Ellian?"

Saeth snapped her attention back to me at the mention of her favorite topic, abandoning her brutal assault on Tarran like an old sock. "Aye, I just picked up the letter in town. Seems Connor has appointed the new councilman." She produced said letter from her tunic, and I didn't miss the twitch of her lip as she reread the contents. "Greyson Leary is his name."

I scoured my memory for any details of the man. "Leary. I know the name. Son of a smaller shipping family...I think he sails the *Madyn*."

"Aye, that's the one. She's a pretty ship," Ronan offered, settling onto the crate next to Tarran.

"He cheats at cards, too." Griffin sank back into his hammock with a pout.

I didn't know enough about the man to make a decision on him one way or another, but one thing was clear: if Connor was appointing him, then he was not on our side.

Saeth folded the letter with care before tucking it back into its place, throat bobbing with emotion. When her eyes met mine, there was something dark and dangerous in them. "Keira, Porthladd is getting restless. Connor is still pulling strings, passing tariffs and sanctions left and right. Ellian's getting worried. And frankly, so am I."

I sighed, pinching the bridge of my nose. My banishment had cost me more dearly than I expected, but I hadn't thought about what it cost the people I left behind. I couldn't set foot on

Porthladdian soil, but my crew could. The people there needed them more than I did right now.

And if Connor Yorath tried to sink me for it, I'd drag him down with me.

"I think it's time to go back anyway." I squared my shoulders. "It's been a month, and Ronan is starting to look sickly."

My husband rolled his eyes, his brave mask perfectly in place. "I'm fine, Keira, I'm more worried about you."

My tone was gentle. Now was not the time to hurt his pride. "I know, but you should check in with the aunts, see how all of Connor's shit is affecting them. And at least we know how to make *you* feel better." I stroked his cheek, admiring the fine blond stubble. "I won't risk us both."

Ronan tucked an errant strand of hair behind my ear, letting his mask slip just for me. Fear rested there, but so did hope—and love, brighter than ever, despite the darkness that hunted us. "To Porthladd, then?"

I smiled at my husband, hope stirring in my core for the first time in a long time. "Aye, my love. To Porthladd."

Porthladd's form stretched across the horizon was enough to bring me to my knees.

The sun was high, noontide lapping her edges with gentle kisses, the late fall air giving me a proper use for my coat for the first time in two months. We were anchored half a league from the shore, as per the terms of my banishment, but I could still make out little details from my perch on the bow. The green and white of *Dubryn* Hill. The yellow sand of the *Traeth* beaches. Smoke and steam rising from chimneys in the town square.

I missed it all terribly.

Ronan stood behind me, tentative. This was not our first trip back. We had made a stop after our first month at sea to bring what limited supplies we were allowed to carry to Reina while Ronan took a soak in the spring. Last time, I stowed myself below deck for the duration of the visit. I hadn't wanted to see it, to be tempted by the quaint charm and the easy waters. Like a coward, I hid from it, unable to face the reality.

Today, I needed whatever little morsel of my past I could get.

Ronan wrapped his arms around me, nuzzling his face into the crook of my neck. "How does it feel to be home?"

I tore my eyes off the shoreline, shifting in his grasp so I faced him instead. "You're my home."

"It'll be a short bath, I promise." He kissed my cheek, lips cold. I hoped it was the weather, not his affliction, that chilled him.

I slid my arms around his broad back so he couldn't see the worry that clouded my expression. "No, take your time. You need it."

"I love you, Keira girl," he whispered into my hair, the only words that could truly make me feel at home.

I'd never miss an opportunity to say them back. Never again. "I love you more, Ronan."

Boots on wood and a chuckle broke us apart. "And I love you both the most." Griffin was already dressed and armed. His Branwen blue coat, sleeves still missing, covered a deep red tunic I could only assume was Rhett's, intended to give his poor father a heart attack. His swords, Truth and Triumph, sat at their proper place on his back, completing the look. "Let's go, pretty boy, my Ma's berry bread is waiting."

A wistful wind tugged at my heartstrings, but I covered it with a scowl as I smacked my cousin's arm. "Save some for me, you cad."

"Keira, which sword do you think will make Vala cry harder?" Saeth said by way of hello, admiring two of my favorite blades, balancing them in her delicate hands.

I rubbed my temples. I was happy to miss whatever trouble she was planning. "Leave the swords, Saeth."

She quirked her head to the side, just as she did whenever the details of a bad idea were falling into place. "You're right, I'll spend the night at Ellian's and avoid home altogether."

Ronan laughed brightly, and I nudged his side. Poor Ellian was in for a rough night.

The rest of the crew said their goodbyes with little fanfare, Reagan especially excited to see her mama. I kept a brave face as I waved off the longboat, until they were nothing more than a tiny dot against Porthladd's mass.

Until I was truly alone.

It was almost noon already, and they'd all be back by sundown, but time seemed to crawl by as I counted the seconds. The sea slapped against the boat in time with my counting, a siren song calling for me. For a moment, it was as if I could feel it again. The tingle in my fingertips, the purring in my core. I closed my eyes, reaching into that hidden part of myself, the part that could command seas and call forth storms.

As it had been since the day my uncle shot me, it was empty. There was nothing left to answer my call, nothing to conjure or conquer or control. Nothing of Lyr's gift left, only the vacant shadow of what once was.

I was alone, and I was powerless.

After ten minutes in my solitude, I decided to stop feeling sorry for myself and do something with my time. I grabbed the swords Saeth left behind and started my routine, the dance as familiar as my own name. Jab, swipe, parry, dodge. Again. Over and over until sweat streaked down my back, even amidst the cool breeze. Jab, dodge, swing. Until my shoulder ached, deep within my bones. I gritted my teeth against it.

The dark god would not have me. This body was mine to command, now and for the end of time. Strike, swing, jab.

After an hour or two of swinging blindly at my invisible opponent, I threw my swords to the ground. It was too quiet. I missed my crew's laughter, Ronan's working hum, Griffin sharpening his weapons. Lyr below, I even missed Saeth and Tarran's bickering.

I hated this. The waiting. The *wanting*. I imagined Reagan, tucked into Reina's kitchen, swapping stories while her delicious chicken roasted over the fire. Or Griffin and Rhett, sitting uncomfortably at Vala's table while she roasted *them* about their relationship, Tarran watching and laughing at them for once.

A glutton for punishment, I let myself imagine Ronan lowering himself into the spring, the closest place to a home I'd ever had, wishing desperately that I was there too, soaking and swimming and whatever else came next.

I needed to stop thinking about this. Lyr's ass, I needed to stop thinking, period.

I did so the only way I knew how.

I dragged the hammock from its hold and pitched it in record time, grateful for something to do with my hands. The sun was still high, so I had to squint at the sky when I finally laid back. But I pulled my coat around me, breathing in the familiar salt air. The sun in the south was my enemy. Harsh, incessant, burning. But here, it was my dearest friend, caressing my cheeks with gentle warmth as I let my body sink further into the hammock.

This was home, too. This ship. This sunshine. I could miss a few meals and laughs if it meant I could keep this.

As I laid there, alone and finally content to wait, the whispers started.

Keiraaa.

I jolted upright, searching for the source of the voice.

No, not voice. *Voices.*

Hundreds or thousands of them, whispering my name from the shadows.

Keeeiraaaa. Ariannad. Duweeeeeni.

Same.

Same.

I drew my sword instinctively, whipping around for the source of the mysterious chorus. But I knew in my core that there was no one there. The voices were inside me, in the deepest parts of my soul, much like Lyr's once was.

But this was not my sunken friend. These voices held no warmth or familiarity. They were cold, a dissonant symphony of ghosts calling from a dark beyond I could not see and could not run from.

One voice, a man's, darker than midnight and colder than ice, cut through the noise.

We're all the same when we're dead, Keira girl.

Deyrnasian Pronunciation Guide

Annwyn ⤳ (ahn-wEEn)

Arawn ⤳ (ah-RAH-wihn).

Bachtref ⤳ (bAHk-trehf)

Blaidd ⤳ (blAY-iht)

Ceffyl Dwr ⤳ (kEHf-eel dweer)

Clogwynn ⤳ (klAWg-ween)

Ddraig ⤳ (trAY-ihg)

Deyrnas ⤳ (dAY-er- nahs)

Dubryn ⤳ (dOOH-breen)

Duweni ⤳ (dOOH-wehn-ee)

Faoladh ⤳ (fohl-AHd-uh)

Hiraeth ⤳ (hih-RAYth)

Hud ⤳ (hOOHd)

Ir'de ⤳ (EEr-uh-day).

Lechyd Da ⤳ (lEHtch-ee-dAH)

Lyr ⤳ (lEEr)

Neid ⤳ (nEE-ihd).

Orwellin ⤳ (awr-wEHl-ihn)

Porthladd ⤳ (pAWrth-laht)

Pysgodd ⤳ (pEEs-gawt)

Sarffymor ⤳ (sahr-FEE-mawr)

Tan ⤳ (tAHn)

Traeth ⤳ (trAYth)

ACKNOWLEDGMENTS

If it wasn't obvious after 33 chapters of Keira's story, I'm a firm believer that a captain is nothing without a crew. This book is merely a product of the love of the many, *many* people who stood behind me through this process. *I am* a product of your love. Here is my (very long) list of thanks I owe.

To Renee, my editor, my very first critique partner, and most importantly, my friend: This book would not exist without you. Thank you for navigating me through the trenches of self-publishing, for keeping my course steady when I was tempted to drift, and for being a beacon of light and love.

To my partners in crime, Danielle and Sydney: How can I begin to describe the impact you two have had on my writing and my life? Thank you for the late-night messages that soothed the rough waves of my anxiety, for the fathoms of free advice, and endless wells of unconditional support. I am honored to be walking this road with you, and I know our friendship will be lifelong.

To the rest of my critique partners: Katie, Maxi, and Rowan: thank you for loving this book at its roughest and for lifting it to its best. You each deserve an entire page of acknowledgment for both the constructive criticism and unyielding encouragement you've offered.

To my sister and alpha reader, Jenn, thank you for being the first set of eyes on this story, for being the first person I go to with my passions and my problems, and for simply being my built-in best friend. Our sisterhood is biological, but it runs so much deeper than that.

To my proofreaders, Savanna and Lisa: thank you for being the last set of eyes, for catching my many mistakes, and polishing this book into something beautiful and shelf-ready.

To my beta readers, Jenni, Sara, Ashley, Lauren, Camilla, Julia, and Christina: thank you for your essential feedback, your kindness, your dedication, and most importantly, your criticism. You all helped me refine this story, turning a half-decent book into something I am proud to publish.

To my amazing cover artist, Fran: I'm obsessed with your work, and I'm so glad the universe led me to your page! Working with you was a pleasure. Thank you for putting up with my pickiness and turning it into something beautiful. I could not have imagined a better face for Keira's story.

To my fabulous map designer, Tom: thank you for taking the picture in my head and making it a reality. Your flexibility and intuition made this process so easy. Your patience is unparalleled.

To my street team, Cass, Cassidy, Jenni, Z, Ashley, Elsa, Stephanie, Stephanie H., Meaghan, and AD: For lack of a more poetic way of saying it, you guys ROCK. The biggest fear I had entering the self-publishing world was the daunting task of marketing, but having you all at my back made it easier. Thank you for getting the word out into the void, and for being such wonderful people.

To my insta tribe: there are too many of you to name, but I am so grateful for the connections we've made and the family we've built! It is so essential for writers to lift each other up instead of tear each other down, and I'm forever humbled to have found a home with all of you.

To my real-life family: thank you for instilling the love of stories in me in utero and for encouraging me to tell my own story in every way I can. Thank you for the lifetime of advice, much of which turned into the foundations of this book. And thank you for being my greatest champions, through every talent show, graduation, and now, book release. I love you all!

To my fiance, Armand. I love you with every rotten part of me, and I am so lucky to have found someone I'd sail to the Otherworld for. Thank you for holding me through the tears of this process and for being my cheerleader through the good. Thank you for the well-timed snacks, for the head rubs, and for seeing all of me and still staying by my side. I can't wait to be your wife.

And finally, to you, dear reader: thank you for reading until the end, for not throwing this across your room and quitting. This book is a piece of my soul, and I hope you carry some part of it with you. You are the reason I write, and I am honored that you've indulged me this far. Thank you for joining me on this journey, and I hope you'll be back for book two.

ABOUT THE AUTHOR

Growing up on the east coast in small-town New Jersey, Lina spent her early days playing pretend and making up stories for her friends and family. Little did they know, that pastime would soon turn into a lifelong passion for storytelling in all of its forms. While she's a grad student and therapist by profession, she's a writer at heart. When she's not scribbling ideas about fictional worlds into the margins of her notebooks, Lina spends her time reading anything she can get her hands on, driving her fiancé crazy with her wild daydreams, and snuggling her adorable pups.

CPSIA information can be obtained
at www.ICGtesting.com
Printed in the USA
BVHW030855151120
592768BV00021B/180/J